H. M. PULHAM, ESQUIRE

H. M. PULHAM, ESQUIRE

BY JOHN P. MARQUAND

LITTLE, BROWN AND COMPANY · BOSTON

A serial version of this story appeared in McCall's
under the title of GONE TOMORROW

387

TO A. H. M.

FOR HER SCRAPBOOK

To the Gentle (or Otherwise) Reader

If this novel, which deals with the imaginary problems of
the imaginary Henry Pulham and his imaginary friends, is
well enough written to hold a reader's attention, it will be
because my characters have assumed a transient reality in the
reader's mind, and on the strength of that illusion rests this
book's sole prospect of artistic success. If my characters can
stand up by themselves in their inky world, the reader cannot
help associating them with certain types of living persons,
familiar to him in the realm of his own experience; for
characters worth their salt in any novel from Richardson's
works down inevitably fall into some familiar life group.
From this association, the reader may conceivably go further
and state that one of these fictitious individuals is exactly like
So-and-so of his own acquaintance. If he has ever known the
writer, or has even known anybody who has known of him, he
can speculate from whom in the author's experience this
character was drawn. This sort of thing forms the basis of a
great deal of literary gossip among persons who have never
written fiction.

Of course any writer in any field whatever, every time he
sets down a sentence, is translating his observation of life as
he has known it. But when it comes to drawing a character
from life and setting his personality upon the printed page,

nearly every writer whom I have ever met will tell you that no actual human being is convincing in this highly artificial environment. Living men and women are too limited, too far from being typical, too greatly lacking in any universal appeal, to serve in a properly planned piece of fiction. A successful character in a novel is a conglomerate, a combination of dozens of traits, drawn from experience with hundreds of individuals, many of them half known and half forgotten; and all these traits have been transformed by passing through the writer's mind. From a writer's standpoint it takes a vast number of disconnected memories and impressions to create a satisfactory illusion of reality.

Take Bo-jo Brown in this book for instance — he is intended to be recognized at once as a familiar type formed by college athletics. If he assumes any shape in these pages there should be something in him that strikes a responsive note in any reader who knows or has ever heard of his kind. I have seen a good many college athletes in various parts of the country, but Bo-jo Brown does not resemble any one of them. He is intended for a book. If he were to step out of the pages into a room he would be pathetically distorted. The same is true with Henry Pulham, Kay Motford, Bill King and all the rest of them. The same is true with the setting, and even the element of time must not be taken seriously. Only for the purpose of a dramatic frame and to illustrate changes in attitude and manners, the action begins and finally ends in 1939. Thus Henry and his classmates fall arbitrarily into the Class of 1915 at Harvard University, of which I am a member — but I never knew Henry or any of the others there, and neither did anybody else. They are intended to represent the ideas and thoughts of a certain social group, not limited to Boston or Cambridge, since this group exists in every other large community.

When it comes to names, Sinclair Lewis has remarked that you must call characters something. In christening the characters in this book I have endeavored to give them simple names suitable to an everyday environment. If there are any real Bill Kings or Henry Pulhams or any others I assure them that their names appear by coincidence and with my apologies and that their namesakes are not patterned after them.

This is not an essay on the art of fiction. It is only intended to explain the meaning and the purpose of the statement appearing so frequently in novels and repeated here — that all incidents and characters herein are entirely fictitious, and no reference is intended to any actual person, whether living or dead.

JOHN P. MARQUAND

Kent's Island
Newbury, Massachusetts
1940

Contents

I PLAY UP — AND PLAY THE GAME ... 3

II MR. HILLIARD TELLS ALL ... 15

III THE THOUGHTS OF YOUTH ARE LONG, LONG THOUGHTS ... 29

IV WE WERE GOING OUT TO DINNER ... 36

V THE GOLDEN AGE ... 48

VI I CONSIDER MR. CHIPS ... 62

VII IT NEVER HELPS TO TALK ABOUT IT ... 72

VIII MAY I HAVE THIS DANCE? ... 79

IX ADVENTURES IN COMPANIONSHIP ... 85

X BOYS AND GIRLS TOGETHER ... 98

XI YOU'D BETTER ASK FRANK WILDING ... 109

XII A GREAT EXPERIENCE, THE WAR ... 115

XIII SOMETHING BASIC ... 123

XIV LET ME DRAW A DIAGRAM ... 136

XV I MAKE MY LETTER ... 142

XVI I MUST GO DOWN TO THE SEAS AGAIN ... 161

XVII WHEN THE GIRL YOU LOVE LOVES YOU ... 181

XVIII I REMEMBER MARVIN MYLES ... 192

XIX IT HAD TO HAPPEN SOMETIME ... 206

XX FOR I'LL COME BACK TO YOU ... 216

XXI GOOD-BY TO ALL THAT ... 224

XXII KISS AND DON'T TELL ... 243

XXIII FRANKLY, ONLY A SYMBOL ... 259

XXIV	I Break the News	271
XXV	It's a Long, Long Walk	279
XXVI	The Music Goes Round and Round	291
XXVII	We Westerners Like Our Fish	302
XXVIII	It All Adds Up to Something	317
XXIX	What Did I Do Wrong?	328
XXX	They Possibly Might Start Talking	338
XXXI	Yoicks — and Away	346
XXXII	Pale Hands I Love	362
XXXIII	Rhinelander Four —	375
XXXIV	With Pleasure Rife	386
XXXV	He Was Certainly Low in His Mind	397
XXXVI	Two in the Bowl	406
XXXVII	Home from the Hill	415

H. M. PULHAM, ESQUIRE

I

Play Up — and Play the Game

Ever since Bo-jo Brown and I had gone to one of those country day schools for little boys, Bo-jo had possessed what are known as "qualities of leadership"; that is to say, he had what it takes to be the Head Boy of the School. Thus when we went on to St. Swithin's it was almost inevitable that Bo-jo should end up in his last year as Head Warden, whose duty it was to administer the rough-and-ready justice of that period. They say that they don't paddle recalcitrant boys as hard as they used to in our day, but then perhaps the younger generation doesn't turn out such strong boys as Bo-jo.

I heard him make some such remark himself on one of those numerous occasions when our college football team was not doing as well as one might have hoped.

"The trouble with kids now is," Bo-jo said, "they suffer from moral and mental hebetude."

Of course he knew perfectly well that none of us knew what "hebetude" meant — Bo-jo always had some trick like that up his sleeve.

"My God," Bo-jo said, "don't you know what 'hebetude' means? You took English, didn't you? If you don't know, look it up in the dictionary."

It was safe to assume that Bo-jo hadn't known what "hebetude" meant either, until he had read it somewhere a night or two before; but Bo-jo always had a way of using everything, because he had the qualities of leadership. That was why he became one of the marshals of the Class at Harvard and why he married one of the Paisley girls

3

— and of course he didn't have to worry much after that. He naturally became the president of the Paisley Mills in time.

Some of the boys used to say Bo-jo was conceited, but Bo-jo was always able to do everything he said he could. He could walk up and down stairs on his hands, for instance, and he could memorize whole pages out of the telephone directory. It was only natural that he should have had his name on the Humphrey I. Walker silver cup for THE BOY WHO MOST NEARLY TYPIFIES THE IDEALS OF ST. SWITHIN'S — and he could have had his name on other cups in later life, if they had given cups like that.

I wondered occasionally why it was, as time went on, that there seemed to be quite a clique that did not like him. It certainly is a fact that when Bo-jo used to come around, five or six of us would always get into a corner and say things about him. Bill King, for instance, always used to say that Bo-jo was a bastard, a big bastard. Perhaps he meant that Bo-jo sometimes threw his weight around.

"Some day," Bill said, "someone is going to stop that bastard." But then Bill never did like Bo-jo and Bo-jo never liked him either.

I remember when Bill discussed him once at a big dinner party where everybody got swept together from odd corners and all the men were in the library and didn't seem anxious to join the ladies. Bo-jo was telling what was the matter with the football team and what was going to happen to Electric Bond and Share, so you can guess the date, and I was sitting next to Bill, listening to Bo-jo's voice.

"My God," said Bill, "I don't see how you stand him."

"Bo-jo is all right," I said.

"Well," Bill said, "it's my personal opinion he's a bastard."

"You said that before," I said. "As a matter of fact, there're lots of nice things about Bo-jo."

"The trouble with you is," Bill said, "you always play the game."

"Well, what's wrong with playing the game?" I asked.

"Because you're old enough not to be playing it," Bill said.

4

I knew what he meant in a way, because Bill came from New York and he had a different point of view.

"Now, here's one instance," Bill said, "that brings out my point. What does everybody keep calling him Bo-jo for?"

"Everybody's always called him that," I said.

"That's it," Bill said. "As a matter of fact, his name is Lester — Lester Brown — and as you say, everybody has always called him Bo-jo. And I can imagine who called him Bo-jo first. His mother did. Probably the first thing he ever said was Bo-jo. Now, don't you frankly think that's perverted? If he had ever had a good kick in the pants — "

"You never did like him," I said.

"He's a bastard," Bill said, "and he's never had a kick in the pants."

"Well, if you only tried to know him — " I said. "If you only tried to like him, there are lots of nice things about Bo-jo. After all, he does a lot for the Class."

"My God," said Bill, "what's that got to do with it? Just because I was thrown by accident with six hundred people into an institution of learning why do I have to be loyal to the Class?"

"You don't really mean that, Bill," I said.

"Are you being serious?" Bill asked.

"Well, more or less," I said. "Of course it all was an accident, but the Class means something to a lot of people. A lot of people have got a lot out of it."

"What have they got?" Bill asked.

"Well, I don't know exactly," I answered, "but we shared a common experience."

"And what sort of an experience?" said Bill. "And why should anyone be any better for sharing an experience with Bo-jo?"

"Well," I said, "you're different. I've known Bo-jo almost all my life. He can be awfully nice when he wants to. I think a good deal of what you don't like in his manner is because he's shy."

"That's the excuse they always make about snotty people," Bill said. "They're always shy. He ought to get a kick in the pants."

5

"You said that before," I said.

"And I'll say it again," said Bill, "because I like to say it. It gives me solid satisfaction. Someday he's going — "

"No," I said, "I don't believe he will, and if it ever happened, he would be too tough to feel it."

Bill began to laugh. It always pleased me when I made him laugh. He laughed so that his shirt bulged out in front and several people stopped talking.

"Hey," Bo-jo called across the room, "what's the joke?"

"Harry said your behind's so tough you wouldn't feel a kick in the pants," Bill answered.

Bo-jo thought it over for a second and then he began to laugh too.

"You have to get on with people if you've known them all your life," I told Bill, "and if you're living in the same town and if their wives went to school with your wife, and besides we both belong to the same Lunch Club."

Bo-jo and I never ate at the same table at the Lunch Club, because he usually sat with old Mr. Blevins, who ran the Lowe Street Associates. Sometimes, however, we would find ourselves side by side at the row of washbasins downstairs.

I don't exactly know why I keep bothering so much about Bo-jo Brown. The reason must be that he signifies something which in some way explains a good deal about Bill and me. I was certainly surprised and pleased when he called me up and asked me to the Downtown Club for lunch, because nothing like that had happened for a long while and there was no reason why it should.

We had called him Bo-jo so long that I did not know who he was when Miss Rollo told me that there was a Mr. Brown on the Number 3 extension.

"I think he wants to speak to you personally," Miss Rollo said.

This sounded a good deal like Miss Rollo. She had been in the office for fifteen years, came from East Chelsea and lived with her mother, but sometimes she still got confused by the telephone.

"Did he give any other name," I asked, "besides Brown? There are lots of Browns."

6

Miss Rollo put her finger up to balance her pince-nez, which always had a way of slipping down the bridge of her nose.

"I'll ask him what his name is," she answered.

A minute later Miss Rollo was back. I had almost forgotten about the telephone call when she returned, because I was busy going over Mrs. Gordon Shrewsbury's investment list, and I was wondering whether it would be better to sell out her Atchison. Rodney Graham only yesterday had said that they were selling out all their clients' Atchison—not that there was anything bad about it, but that it was obvious that railroads no longer had any future.

"The name is Lester," Miss Rollo said.

"I don't know him," I said. "What does he want?"

"He wants to speak to you personally," Miss Rollo said. "He seems to know you, Mr. Pulham. Perhaps he's someone you play squash with."

"What?" I said.

"Someone you play squash with," Miss Rollo said. "Someone in the bumping tournament."

"Never mind," I said. "All right. I'll speak to him."

I walked across the room to the desk which had the Number 3 extension.

"Hello," I said. "Who is it?" And then I heard Bo-jo's voice.

"Is that you, Harry?" he called. "What's the matter with you? It's Bo-jo, Bo-jo Brown."

"Why, yes," I said. "Hello, how are you, Bo-jo?"

"What the hell's the matter with you?" Bo-jo asked. "Are you so busy you can't talk?"

"No," I said. "There was just a little mix-up here. They didn't give your name right. How are you, Bo-jo?"

"Fine. How are you?"

"Well, I'm fine too," I said.

"Everything going all right?" Bo-jo asked.

"Yes," I told him, "everything is swell."

"Well, I haven't seen you for quite a while. Why don't you *ever* call me up, Harry?"

7

"Well, you know the way it is," I said.

"Yes," Bo-jo said, "that's the way it is with me too. I'm so pushed around I never see the people I want to see. We ought to get together more often, shouldn't we?"

"Yes," I said, "that's right, Bo-jo."

"You and Kay must come out to dinner sometime."

"Yes," I said, "that would be swell, Bo-jo."

"Well," Bo-jo said, "we'll have to fix it up. We don't see enough of each other, do we?"

"No," I said, "not nearly enough."

"Well, that's the way it is," Bo-jo said. "Now, we've got to stop it, Harry."

"That's right," I said. "We've got to stop it, Bo-jo."

The corners of my lips hurt and I discovered that they were twisted into a mechanical, cordial smile. I was rather touched by his just thinking of me and picking up the telephone, and I wondered why I never did things like that.

"Well," Bo-jo said, "I've been meaning to get hold of you for a hell of a long time. What are you doing for lunch today, Harry?"

"For lunch?" I said. "Why, nothing, Bo-jo."

"Well," Bo-jo said, "that's swell. How about coming up to the Downtown Club where we can talk? Let's see — it's twelve now. Twelve-thirty, how about it?"

"Why, thanks, Bo-jo," I said. "I'd love to."

"Twelve-thirty," Bo-jo said, "sharp."

I hung up the telephone and looked out of the window at the parking space opposite, where the office building had been torn down on account of taxes, and at the policeman in his white pulpit directing traffic. The sky was blue and cloudless, a clear April day. I was pleased that Bo-jo had called me up, but the idea of talking to him for an hour at lunch struck me as a little difficult.

"Miss Rollo," I said, "I'm having lunch with Mr. Brown at the Downtown Club. That was Bo-jo Brown, All-America tackle. We went to college together."

8

"Oh," Miss Rollo said. "When will you be back, Mr. Pulham? Mr. Waterbury is coming to see you at two."

"Well, if I'm late tell him to wait," I told her. "Or if he can't wait, all the names for the bumping tournament are in the right-hand drawer of my desk. And if Mrs. Pulham calls up tell her I won't be able to take Gladys home from dancing school this afternoon. Is there anything else, Miss Rollo?"

Outside in the hallway the rear elevator came down very slowly. Once it had made me impatient to wait for it and once we had even complained about the service, but now its deliberation was not annoying. It was better to take things easily. The elevator was like a London lift. It was somewhere up above me, moving down in its iron-grilled cage with the marble staircase twisting about it. First there came a network of steel cables, looped beneath the car, and when they disappeared the car was there. The woman who ran it was in soiled gray with an overseas cap and she looked something like a hostess in the old American Expeditionary Force. Her name was Tilly and that was all I knew about her. Except for Tilly the elevator was empty.

"Hello, Tilly," I said.

"Good morning, Mr. Pulham," Tilly said. "It's a nice morning, or afternoon — rather."

"That's so," I said. "It is afternoon."

"I see you and Mrs. Pulham was in Cohasset for the week end," Tilly said.

"How did you see that?" I asked.

"In the paper," Tilly said. "I always follow all the tenants in the building in the paper. It's like a game, kind of."

Outside on State Street it was warm and the traffic was thick. Washington Street was the way I had always remembered it, except for the jam of automobiles. There were a great many newsboys calling out headlines about Czechoslovakia and the crowd moved very slowly, as it always did when I was in a hurry. Out by the Common an old lady was feeding bread crumbs to the pigeons out of a paper bag and some sailors were standing by the subway en-

9

trance. As long as I could remember there had always been someone standing watching someone feed the pigeons.

I was not a member of the Downtown Club, but the doorman seemed to be expecting me.

"Mr. Brown is in the back room," he said, "he and his party."

This was a little surprising, because I had understood that Bo-jo and I were going to have lunch alone. I walked past the cigar counter and past the billiard room, which had been redecorated since the days of Prohibition, and down at the end of the back room I saw Bo-jo Brown, sitting at a table with four other people. At first I thought he must have met them there accidentally, and then their faces took on a sort of pattern. They were all members of our Class at Harvard, but not the ones whom Bo-jo Brown would ordinarily have asked to lunch. They were Curtis Cole, who was in his father's law office down on State Street, and Bob Ridge, who sold life insurance, and Chris Evans, who I had heard was on the *Boston Globe,* and Charley Roberts, who had something to do with the Eye and Ear Hospital. Bo-jo saw me right away and got up.

"Harry," he said, "it's swell to see you."

"It's swell to see you, Bo-jo," I said.

"You know all these boys, don't you?" Bo-jo asked me.

"Yes," I answered, "I've known them for quite a while."

"For damned near twenty-five years," Bo-jo said.

"How do you mean?" I asked. Bo-jo began to laugh.

"Now, listen!" he said. "Did you boys hear that one? Harry doesn't know what's going to happen a year from June."

Then everyone else began to laugh.

"Oh," I said, "you mean it's our Twenty-fifth Reunion."

"What you need is a drink," Bo-jo said. "What do you want — an old-fashioned or a Martini?"

"I've got to get back to the office after this," I said, "but you boys go right ahead."

"Oh, hell," said Bo-jo. "Forget the office. This is an occasion — an important occasion. We don't see much of each other, do we —

not nearly as much as we ought to. William, get Mr. Pulham an old-fashioned. I remember how you used to drink them at the Westminster, Harry. Do you remember downstairs in the Westminster freshman year?"

"Oh yes," I said, "the Westminster."

"William," Bo-jo said to the club attendant, "get two old-fashioneds for Mr. Pulham, and then a round of the same for everybody else. Harry had better start catching up with us."

"That's right," said Curtis Cole. Bo-jo sat down again and I drew up a chair between Curtis Cole and Chris Evans, and no one spoke for a moment.

"Have a cigarette?" Chris asked me, and he glanced at me sideways. The sleeve of his coat was frayed and his forehead was lined with wrinkles, and I tried to think of something to say to him. I tried to pick up some thread of the past, but I could not remember much about him.

"I haven't seen you for quite a while," I said.

"No," Chris said, "not for quite a while. How's it been going, Hugh?"

"Harry," I said.

"Oh, yes," Chris said, "Harry. God, I must be losing my mind! How's it been going, Harry?"

"Fine," I said.

"Well, that's great," said Chris, and I turned to Curtis Cole.

"Curtis," I asked, "do you still play golf at Myopia?"

"Myopia?" said Curtis.

"Yes," I said. "I always associate you with golf at Myopia."

"It must be someone else," said Curtis. "I don't play golf."

"Oh, yes," I said. "I don't know what's the matter with me."

"I sail," said Curtis, "whenever I have any time. In the S Class. I wish you'd come out in the boat someday."

"That'd be swell," I said. "What do you suppose we're here for?"

"Damned if I know," said Curtis.

"Well, it's swell to see you," I said. "I haven't seen you for quite a while."

"Hurry up there, Harry," Bo-jo called. "You're one behind us."

I turned back to Chris again, trying to think what it was I remembered about him.

"Chris," I said, "what's the latest news from Europe?"

"It looks bad," said Chris, "but you can't tell."

"Do you think there's going to be a war?" I asked.

"What's that?" called Bo-jo. "What are you saying, Harry?"

"I was asking Chris if he thought they were going to fight," I said.

"Now, listen," said Bo-jo, and he moved his hands quickly. "I can tell you something about that. I had New York on the private wire just before we came up here. We're nearer peace this moment than we have been for the past five years. Sorry that's all I can tell you, fellows, but you remember what I said. Peace nearer than it's been in the last five years."

"I suppose you mean that Chamberlain's going to welsh again," Charley Roberts said.

Bob Ridge looked across the table at me. There was one thing about Bob Ridge: being in the life insurance business, he knew who everybody was.

"Harry," Bob said, "did you get that little thing I sent you on your birthday?"

"My birthday?" I said. "I don't remember."

"Well, of course it wasn't anything much," Bob said. "Just a letter-opener."

"Oh, yes," I said. "I remember now."

"Of course it wasn't anything much," Bob said, "but I thought you'd like it on your desk, just to remind you you're a year older."

"Now, wait a minute," Bo-jo called. "Nobody here is going to sell anything to anybody, and nobody's going to talk about bonds or the European situation. That isn't what we're here for. We're just here to get together, because we ought to see more of each other. And now that we're here, I want to propose a toast." Bo-jo slapped his hand on the table and stood up.

"Do we all have to stand up, Bo-jo?" I asked.

"Everybody who hasn't got the guts to stand up," said Bo-jo, "can just roll under the table. I'm proposing a toast to the Class — the best damned Class there ever was — and to the Class that's going to have the best damned Twenty-fifth Reunion there ever will be, because you and I and all of us are going to make it that way. And that's what we're here for, because we want ideas about it. Now, toss the drinks off, fellows, and let's go up to lunch."

Bo-jo walked upstairs ahead of us in quick springy steps, head up, shoulders back. Chris Evans, who walked beside me, slouched as though he were still bending over a desk. His eyes behind his glasses had a pinched, tired look. I was quite certain that I did not look as old as Chris or any of those others, and neither did Bo-jo. Bo-jo and I had kept ourselves more fit.

"I don't see what Bo-jo wants me for," I said to Chris, "if he is looking for ideas. I have never had ideas."

The lenses of his glasses glinted as he turned toward me. Chris had that sour look worn by most newspapermen and writers.

"We'll find out," Chris said. "I can't recall that he ever spoke to me in college."

"Oh, well," I said, "you know the way things are, Chris. You make friends later."

"You're damned well right you do," Chris said.

"This way, boys," Bo-jo called. "The first door on the right — unless anybody wants to get washed first. Does anyone want to wash?"

No one wanted to wash.

"It looks as though we're in a private dining room," I said to Chris.

"Come on, boys," Bo-jo called. "Come on. First door on the right."

"The voice of a schoolboy rallies the ranks," Chris said.

"What?" I asked.

"The voice of a schoolboy rallies the ranks," Chris repeated. "Play up! Play up — and play the game! By Sir Henry Newbolt. God's gift to the British Empire."

"Newbolt?" I said. "I never heard of him."

"Well, you hear him now," Chris said.

In front of us Bob Ridge was speaking to Curtis Cole.

"Curtis," he was saying, "that specimen —"

"What specimen?" Curtis asked.

"The one you gave us at the office," Bob Ridge said.

"Well, what the hell about it?" Curtis asked.

"You must have been drinking water beforehand, weren't you?" Bob Ridge asked. "You were, weren't you?"

"God almighty," Curtis said, "what's the matter with drinking water?"

"The doc said we'll have to do it again, Curtis."

"We?" said Curtis. "Where the hell do you come in?"

"Well, I know it's silly," Bob began, "but some representative of the company must be present. It's just a regulation."

"Come on, boys," Bo-jo called. "Come on."

II

Mr. Hilliard Tells All

The private dining room contained an oval table. There was a picture of the Grand Canyon on one wall and a yellowed photograph of Boston after the fire of 1872 on the other.

"All right, boys," Bo-jo said. "Sit down anywhere. And get the soup on. We're all hungry."

First there was oxtail soup, and then came breaded veal cutlets, and then came a choice of blueberry pie or ice cream — a heavy lunch, more than I was used to eating, more than any of us wanted to eat — except Chris Evans, who looked hungry. The conversation was scattered as though we had come to realize that we were not there to talk. Curtis was telling me about his boat. Bo-jo was talking to Charley Roberts at the end of the table.

"Charley," he said, "what do you do for exercise these days?"

"I think about it mostly," Charley said.

"That's the way it is," said Bo-jo. "Doctors never take care of themselves."

"There isn't any time," Charley answered.

"Now, don't pull that on me," Bo-jo said. "Every doctor I know is always on a cruise or amusing himself whenever someone is having a baby. You doctors always consider yourselves as a class apart."

"We don't," Charley said.

"You doctors," Bo-jo told him, "always pretend you know everything. Now, actually, there are just as many boneheads in the medical profession as there are in business. Why, I damned near went to the medical school myself."

15

"That ought to bear your statement out," said Charley.

"I'm just saying," Bo-jo said, "that doctors don't know everything."

"Well, they don't," Charley said.

"They either assume they know everything," said Bo-jo, "or else they take the other tack. They say they just don't know."

"Well, what do you want us to do?" Charley asked.

"Now, that's begging the question," Bo-jo said. "And you've got plenty of time to exercise if you want to. Look at me. Sometimes I don't get home till ten o'clock, but I always have time for exercise. If I can't do anything else I get on the rowing machine."

"Whose rowing machine?" Charley asked.

"My rowing machine," Bo-jo said. "I have one in my dressing room in town and one out in the country. If all you boys had rowing machines you'd be better off. Every morning of my life I get on it for half an hour before breakfast, and when I get home I get on it and get up a good sweat before I change, and frankly I'm just as fit as I ever was. Do you know what I did last night?"

Faces turned toward him. No one knew what he had done.

"I was up at Joe Royce's for dinner, and I don't know how it came up, but somehow he bet me that I couldn't walk downstairs on my hands. I walked down two flights of stairs on my hands."

"Did you get corns on them?" Charley asked. Bo-jo began to laugh, and he beckoned to the waiter.

"You can pass around the Scotch-and-soda now," he said. "We'll have brandy with the coffee."

Curtis Cole had stopped talking about the boats, and Bob Ridge leaned across the table.

"Curtis, before we forget it we might make an appointment."

"What for?" Curtis asked.

"What we were talking about, Curtis. It's just a formality. What time do you get up in the morning?"

Curtis Cole's eyes opened wider.

"Now, look here, Bob," he said. "I know you've got to make a living — "

"It's my personal opinion," Bo-jo said, "that Bill King's a bastard. I wouldn't be surprised if he were a Communist, and we don't want any smart, unconstructive cracks. What we want is something full of pep and good nature. Who else is there?"

Bo-jo looked around the table.

"Well," he said, "can't anybody think of anybody else? All right. I'll tell you what we'll do. We'll let Chris think about it for us. Chris, you think up the names of five people who can write a show and let me know the first of the week."

"All right," said Chris.

"And now we've got to keep our minds open," said Bo-jo. "Are there any other suggestions?"

"How about getting one of those professionals," Curtis Cole asked, "who organize song and dance shows?"

"All right," said Bo-jo. "Now we're talking. You make it a business to look it up, Curt. Send me in a memorandum of five of those professionals the first of the week. And now I've got an idea."

"Go ahead," said Charley. "It must be good."

Bo-jo glanced at the ceiling and flicked his cigar ash into his coffee cup.

"The main problem as I see it," he said, "is to get everyone in the proper spirit. Now, I don't know anything that makes people more happy than a good fight."

"A fight?" Bob Ridge asked. "What sort of a fight?"

"Boxing," said Bo-jo. "Two good game, fast lightweights, to fight ten exhibition rounds. We ought to get them cheap just for the publicity."

Charley Roberts looked at Bo-jo with interest. "Are you serious about that?" he asked.

"It surprises you, doesn't it?" Bo-jo inquired. "Well, it did me too when I thought of it first, but the more you think of it the better you'll like it. Two good game boys, right on a platform in the Harvard Yard, pasting each other. Why, it'll drive everybody crazy! It'll take them out of themselves. They won't remember where they are."

"You just tell me what time you get up in the morning," Bob said, "and I'll be right there."

"What the deuce are you boys talking about?" Bo-jo asked.

"Nothing," said Bob. "It's just a business matter, Bo-jo."

"Well, what are you going to do to Curtis in the morning?" Curtis Cole pushed back his chair.

"He isn't going to do one damned thing to me in the morning."

"It's just a matter of business, Bo-jo," Bob said.

"Now, we're not here to talk business," Bo-jo said.

"I'm glad to hear you say it," Curtis said.

"What are you so sore about?" Bo-jo asked. "What's the matter with you, Curtis?"

"We'd better skip it," Curtis said. "But I'm just tired of having my classmates try to sell me things."

"Now, listen, boys," said Bo-jo, "let's not talk about business."

After the dessert was taken away we had coffee and brandy and cigars. I looked at my watch. It was two o'clock.

"Bo-jo," I said, "this has been perfectly swell, but I ought to be getting back."

"Now, listen," said Bo-jo, "no one has to go back for a while, anywhere. If you boys just relax and lean back and listen, I've got something to say that's important. We've got to put aside personal matters. We've all got to do something for the Class."

Bo-jo leaned his elbow on the table. He passed one of his hands over his close-cropped head and his eyebrows drew together.

"I don't know how it is," Bo-jo said, and he gave a quick short laugh, "that I always get things put over on me. I'm always the one who has to do all the work. Now when we have to get ready for the Twenty-fifth here I am and everybody comes around to me and says, Well, go ahead, get it started, you're elected. Well, all right. I'm going to get it started. There'll be a lot of committees before we get through — entertainment committees and God knows what; but in the end it's going to come down to the graduates who live around here. It's up to us whether or not our Twenty-fifth is going to be something to remember, and when I thought it over I wondered how it would be if we started with just a small, informal committee, made up of people who didn't want to blow their own horns, but who are loyal to the Class, and who aren't afraid to work. That's why I picked you men. We're just our own little committee and by God we're going to take our coats off and pitch in." No one said anything.

"Now, don't look so blank," Bo-jo said. "It isn't going to be tough when we get started. We're all going to get right behind this and push it through, and we're all going to have a damned good time. Of course the whole system is pretty well worked out. The classmates and their wives and kids arrive and we put them into dormitories. But then the wives have to be entertained, and the kids have to be entertained, and we have to be entertained. Someone's got to see that the kids don't all get mixed up. Well, the wives can do that. But the thing that's bothering me is the big final entertainment, the one the whole class takes part in, the wives and kids and everybody. Now, last year they had a band playing popular tunes and the kids sang the old songs. Everybody had a good time except some of the kids got lost. Now, has anybody got suggestions about an entertainment?"

There was another silence.

"Come on — come on," Bo-jo said. "Naturally there'll be a ball game and a men's dinner and an outing at some country club or else at someone's place at Brookline, if anyone at Brookline has a place big enough. But what worries me is what about the entertainment. How about it, boys?"

"Someone might write a show," Curtis said. "I hear they did that once."

"All right," said Bo-jo. "Who can write a show? Can anyone here write one?"

No one seemed able to write one. Bo-jo's glance, level and confident, turned diagonally across the table toward Chris Evans.

"How about it, Chris?" he asked. "Can't you write a show?"

Chris put both his elbows on the table.

"I don't know how, and besides I haven't got the time."

"Well, go ahead and try," Bo-jo said. "That's the ⁇⁇ ⁇an do."

"I haven't got the inclination," Chris said, and ⁇⁇ grew edgy. "And I haven't got the time because I wor⁇ living."

"Well, we've all got to take a little time out and work ⁇ said Bo-jo, "and it's going to be like a vacation. We're all g⁇ recapture something of the old days. Frankly, now, doesn't ⁇ one agree that the happiest time he ever spent was those four ⁇ back at Harvard?"

No one replied, and it was hard to tell whether the silence m⁇ agreement or not.

"And there's one thing more," Bo-jo said, "that I know yo⁇ agree with. Our Class is the best damned class that ever came o⁇ of Harvard, and the reason is that we've always pulled togethe⁇ Now, it's been suggested that someone in the class write a show⁇ Well, that's a good suggestion, and that's what we're here for⁇ Well, who can write it — someone who was in the Lampoon or the Pudding or something? We had one of the best damned Pudding shows I ever saw. Do you remember Spotty Graves doing the tightrope act? We've got to have Spotty in the show."

"Spotty Graves has passed on," Bob Ridge said.

"Passed on where?" said Bo-jo.

"He passed on the year before last," Bob Ridge said. "He left a wife and four children, and only five thousand dollars in insurance. Not enough to clean up with."

"Oh, yes," said Bo-jo. "That's right. I remember now, but that's beside the point. Now, we certainly have a lot of literary birds in the Class if we try to think of them, a lot of quiet birds who didn't distinguish themselves much. That's one of the things that gripes me about Yale. The Elis are always wheeling out the Yale poets and the Yale literary group. Why, hell, we have a lot of the same thing in the Class, except we don't shout about them. Now, who is there who can write a show?"

"There's Bill King," I said. "Bill always has a lot of ideas."

"But I thought the whole object of this thing was for everyone to remember where he was," Chris Evans said.

"That's beside the point," said Bo-jo.

"If you're going to get them," Charley Roberts said, "why not pick heavyweights?"

"Now you've got the spirit," said Bo-jo. "I've thought of that. They're too expensive, Charley."

"Well, why not get ten niggers in a battle royal?" Charley asked. "That ought to take the boys and girls out of themselves."

Bo-jo Brown wrinkled up his forehead.

"Now, look here, boys," he said, "we didn't come here to throw water on good ideas. There's nothing easier than knocking. Bob, I want you to go down to Mike's Gymnasium on Scollay Square. Just go and see Mike personally and ask Mike for the names of some good boys who want publicity, and let me know what you find first thing next week. Got it, Bob?"

"All right," Bob said, "if you really want me to, Bo-jo."

"Now we're getting somewhere," Bo-jo said. "Now, suppose we don't have boxing. That gets us back to song and dance stuff, doesn't it? Charley, you haven't got a job yet. Suppose you get busy and ask around about talent in the class — boys, girls, everybody — tap dancers, saxophones, stunts — We've got to have a lot of stunts — people who can do card tricks or impersonations."

"I haven't got much time," said Charley.

"You told us that before," Bo-jo said. "Just get off your fanny and get busy."

Bo-jo pushed back his chair and rose.

"Well," he said, "I've got to be getting back to the office now. We're all started — set to go. There's nothing like a talk around a table to get ideas. I've had a swell time and I hope you all have, and we'll get together sometime soon. Oh, Harry — "

"Yes," I said.

Bo-jo slapped me on the back and took a firm hold on my arm.

"Harry, here, thought he was going to get off easy. Well, I

haven't forgotten Harry. You're coming right down to the office with me now."

"Now, listen, Bo-jo," I said. "It's three o'clock."

"Don't I know it's three o'clock?" Bo-jo asked me. "I'm not crabbing about the time, am I? Besides, it won't take long — your job hasn't really started yet. All right, boys, is everything all straight? All right. Let's go."

The club was nearly deserted when Bo-jo and I got our hats from the checkroom. The only members left in the newspaper room were four old gentlemen who would have been my father's age if my father had been living. They sat in black leather armchairs rustling the papers, and I heard one of them speaking querulously.

"You can blame it all on Wilson," he said, "and the League of Nations."

Outside on the sidewalk Bo-jo took me by the arm again.

"Well," Bo-jo said, "it's a great life, isn't it?"

"How do you mean it's a great life?" I asked.

"Exactly what I say," Bo-jo answered, "a great life. What's the matter? Are you sore about something?"

"I was just thinking," I said. "I never realized that I'd been alive so long."

"What the hell's the matter with you?" Bo-jo asked. "What got that idea into your head?"

"Up there at lunch," I said. "I'd never realized that we were all so old."

"Now, that's a hell of a way to talk," Bo-jo said. "We're not old."

"We're in our middle forties," I said.

"That isn't old," Bo-jo said. "You're just as old as you feel. I'm just as good as I ever was, and so are you, but I see what you mean. Those other people up there looked terrible. It's because they don't take care of themselves. Not enough exercise. Too much worry."

"Maybe they have to worry," I said.

"No one has to worry. Look at me. I never worry."

His grip on my arm tightened. He began walking faster with the swift, elastic step of youth, drawing deep breaths of the humid spring air. There was still a crowd in front of the subway station, sailors talking to girls in tight silk dresses, two or three newsboys, a blindman and the old lady feeding the pigeons bread crumbs out of a brown paper bag.

"There's one thing I can always do," Bo-jo said. "I can always get people to work."

"I know you can," I said. "It's a gift, Bo-jo."

"It's just knowing how to handle them," Bo-jo went on. "Now, those boys are going to wear their fingers off. There's nothing like class spirit. It gets you out of yourself. If you want to be happy, get out of yourself."

On Washington Street in front of the news bulletins the paper boys were shouting. Their voices rose above the scuffling of shoe leather on the pavements.

"London Cabinet in session," they were shouting. "All about it. Braintree woman burned to death. All about it."

"It would be funny," I said, "wouldn't it, if it started all over again? It's about the same time of year."

"Forget it," Bo-jo said. "Get it out of your mind."

Bo-jo's offices were large and newly decorated. There was a rail with a boy sitting behind a table. Bo-jo pushed me in front of him.

"Come on," he said. "Come on."

"All right," I said, "but I can't stay long, really."

"Come on," said Bo-jo. "It won't take a minute. It's about the lives."

"You mean about the lives of the Class," I asked, "the biographies?"

"What's the matter with you?" Bo-jo asked. "Do you think I'm talking French? Come inside here and look."

Bo-jo opened the door of a long room. There were two large tables against the walls heaped with papers and form letters and two girls were seated at desks typing.

"Look here," I said. "This anniversary of ours is more than a year off, isn't it?"

Bo-jo slapped me on the shoulder.

"Now you're talking," he answered. "But we're not going to get caught out. It's time we began organizing."

I still could not understand him.

"All these papers," I said, "all these pictures — they haven't got anything to do with our Class, have they?"

"Now you're getting it," Bo-jo answered. "Of course it isn't *our* Class. This is the year ahead of us, this year's Twenty-fifth. Their Class Secretary works right in this office — you know him, Jake Meek — this is his staff and we're using the same girls for our book. This is Miss Ferncroft, Mr. Pulham. This is Miss Josephs, Mr. Pulham."

The girls turned around in their swivel chairs and smiled.

"Where do I come in?" I asked.

Bo-jo slapped me on the shoulder again and nearly threw me off balance.

"Why," he answered, "you're the one who's going to chase everybody and get their lives. You're going to have general oversight of the book — all the paper work, all the editing — someone's got to do it."

"Why doesn't our Class Secretary do it?" I asked. "That's what he's meant for."

Bo-jo frowned.

"Now, that isn't the right way to look at it, Harry," he said. "You know Sam Green. Sam's the best damned secretary any class has ever had, but he's got to have help, hasn't he? Now, let's get this straight. Are you going to let the Class down, or aren't you?"

"But look here, Bo-jo," I said. "I'm not accustomed to doing anything like this, and besides I haven't got the time."

Bo-jo gave my chest a playful push, causing me to take two steps backward.

"Now you're talking," he said. "I knew you'd get into the spirit of it. Time — why, the job doesn't really begin until next autumn. All you have to do now is to go over the general organization with Miss Ferncroft."

"But look here," I said. "This will take hours and hours."

"And when you take off your coat and start pitching in," Bo-jo went on as though he had not heard me, "you're going to be fascinated by it, and we're all going to have a swell time working together. I'm busy now and I've got to duck out. It's great to have seen you, Harry. I haven't had such a good time in years."

"Wait a minute, Bo-jo," I said.

Bo-jo pulled the door open and waved his other hand.

"It's a big meeting down the street," he said. "I'll see you later, boy" — and then the door closed, and I was on one side of it and Bo-jo was on the other.

I looked at the papers for a moment and then I looked at Miss Ferncroft. It was only right that someone should do this for the Class, but I did not see why it was up to me particularly; and yet I did not want to be disagreeable.

I picked up some of the typewritten sheets which were clipped together. They began with a printed form, dealing with the life of someone in college just about my time.

"And then there are the photographs," Miss Ferncroft said. "We're having a great deal of trouble collecting the photographs of before and after."

They would be the pictures of young men in high collars taken from the first Class Report, and then there would be the pictures of the way we were today, bald-headed, gray-headed, weary — and what had it all been about?

"So you can see," Miss Ferncroft said, "why Mr. Brown needs help."

"Yes, I can see," I said.

Then I began to read the manuscript which I was holding. It was written by someone whom I had never known. The name was Charles Mason Hilliard.

Born: Ridgely, Illinois, March 23rd, 1893; son of Joseph, Gertrude (Jessup) Hilliard.

Prepared at: Ridgely High School and Brock Academy.

COLLEGE DEGREES: A.B., LL.B.
MARRIED: Martha Gooding, New York City.
CHILDREN: Mary Gooding, Roger, Thomas.
OCCUPATION: Lawyer.
ADDRESS: (*Business*) Mortgage Building, New York.
(*Home*) Mamaroneck, New York.

"He doesn't give any dates," I said.

"That's the trouble," said Miss Ferncroft. "No one ever follows instructions."

I continued reading Charles Mason Hilliard's personal history.

After leaving Law School I joined the firm of Jessup and Goodrich in New York. Five years later I was employed by the firm of Jones and Jones. I am now a partner in the firm of Watkins, Lord, Watkins, Bondage, Green, Smith and Hilliard. I have been very busy all this time practising corporation law and trying to raise a family. My work at Law School was interrupted by the war in which I served as a First Lieutenant, Engineer Corps. This seems to me a strange interlude, unrelated to my other activities. I still like to go to the football games and cheer for Harvard. My chief avocation is watching my children grow up. I am an Episcopalian, and I bowl occasionally and sometimes play golf. In politics I am a Republican, hoping that the day will come when Mr. Roosevelt leaves the White House. Ten years ago it was my good fortune to be sent on business to the Pacific Coast. I made the most of this opportunity for travel and still hope sometime, if I ever have a long enough vacation, to take the family to see the Grand Canyon. Harvard has always seemed to me the best educational institution in the world, and I can hope for nothing better than that my sons will follow my footsteps (which I trust they will do, if we can get Mr. Roosevelt out of the White House) and gain from our old Alma Mater what I have gained, both in experience and peace of mind. I have not had the time which I have wished for reading good books. On leaving college I started Gibbon's *Decline and Fall of the Roman Empire* and Nicolay and Hay's *Lincoln*. I am still working on them in my spare time and hope to report to those who are interested at the reunion that I have finished this self-imposed stint.

"Is this characteristic?" I asked Miss Ferncroft.

"Well, they all seem to be pretty much like that," Miss Ferncroft answered. "It's funny. Most of them have been so busy working that they haven't had time to do anything."

"Would you give me a sheet of note paper, please, Miss Ferncroft," I asked her, "and have you a fountain pen?" She handed me a sheet of note paper, and I sat down in front of it. I did not like what I was going to do, because in a sense it was disloyal to the Class. Nevertheless, I had been making up my mind. It was an imposition.

Dear Bo-jo [I wrote],

It was perfectly swell seeing you at lunch, and as you say, the idea of working on our Class Book is fascinating. I can't tell you how much I wish I could go ahead the way you ask me, but, as a matter of fact, I am going to be very busy, especially toward autumn, and I do not feel I am quite the person to undertake the responsibility. I can't tell you how flattered I am that you feel I am up to it.

What I had written sounded weak. I tore the paper up and put it in the wastebasket and started out again.

Dear Bo-jo,

You shoved this job off on me, because you thought I'd be flattered and because you think I am easily imposed upon. Though I accept you and eat your lunch, I can see that you are a fathead. What do I care what happens to the Class Report?

This was more what I wanted to say, but somehow you can't say things like that. I tore the paper up and tried another sheet.

Dear Bo-jo,

I forgot to tell you that it looks as though I shall have to take a long business trip to New York and Kay and I have been talking about going out to the Pacific Coast next autumn and next winter. Fascinating as all this work will be, I am sure you can see how I can't readily undertake it, but thanks ever so much for asking me.

I was aware that none of this was true. It might be possible that I could suggest to Kay that we go away somewhere, but if I did so it was doubtful whether she would do it, with bills coming in the way they were. I tore the letter up and threw it in the wastebasket.

Dear Bo-jo [I wrote again],

Before I really start out on this perhaps we'd better talk about it a little more.

Yours,

HARRY

I folded the letter and placed it in an envelope and handed it to Miss Ferncroft.

"Will you please give this to Mr. Brown?" I said. "Sometime when he isn't too busy. And I'm afraid I'll have to be going now."

"But you'll be back, won't you?" Miss Ferncroft asked.

III

The Thoughts of Youth Are Long, Long Thought.

I was preoccupied and not particularly pleased with myself when I was out on the street again. I had not faced Bo-jo Brown and told him what I thought — not because of any personal timidity, but rather because it was just as well not to have the reputation for being a sorehead, and besides there were certain traditions about friendship.

Nevertheless, it all gave me a strange sense of frustration and failure. That table full of papers made me think of my own life, which would appear in our Class Book. As I thought of what I should write, the effort of Charles Mason Hilliard returned to me. His words seemed to keep time with my footsteps along the sunny street.

Nothing much had changed in the office when I got back, but in some way I had changed. I was recalling all sorts of things which must have lain dormant in my mind, odd details of childhood, of New York and of the war, of faces and names which I had almost forgotten. For some reason, I remembered the fence which used to be behind the stable at Westwood. I could remember exactly the way the sun looked on the white paint, and the game my sister Mary and I used to play of walking on the top of that fence and of pausing at each corner, pretending that we were stopping in a foreign country on our way around the world. I could remember the horse stalls in the stable, trimmed with neatly braided straw, and the harness room with its glass cases and the smell of oil. It was so clear that if I had wished, I could have sprung off that forgotten fence; I could have run through the vegetable garden and the cutting garden, over the terraces and across the lawn to the house, remembering every detail.

"I was detained at a meeting," I said to Miss Rollo. "I hope everything is all right."

"Yes," Miss Rollo said. "Mr. Maxwell has gone home."

"Did he say why?" I asked. "He isn't sick, is he?"

"He said he wanted to stop at the vaults on the way."

"Oh," I said. "Get me the broker's on the telephone. Get me Mr. Eldridge."

Sitting at my desk I could still remember. I could remember the flags on Fifth Avenue in New York after the war and the plaster arch near Twenty-third Street.

"Mr. Eldridge is ready," Miss Rollo said.

"Hello, Nat," I called. "How are you?"

"Just the same as I was this morning."

"How's the market?"

"Closed strong," Nat said.

"What's Atchison?" I asked.

"Up a quarter. No, wait a minute. Up three-eighths."

"We've been talking it over here, Nat," I said. "You can sell seventeen hundred and fifty shares at the opening tomorrow."

"Thanks," said Nat. "Anything else, Harry?"

"Have you got your name down for the bumping tournament?"

"Why, no," said Nat. "I haven't got time."

"What the hell do you mean, you haven't got time?" I said. "I've got to get names down for the bumping tournament."

"All right," said Nat. "Put my name down if you want to. Good-by."

"Miss Rollo," I said, "put Mr. Eldridge down for the bumping tournament and send him out a bill for his entrance fee."

"Yes," Miss Rollo said. "And Mr. Pulham, Mrs. Pulham called up fifteen minutes ago. She wants you to call her back."

"All right," I said. "See if you can get her."

It was curious, if you were in the right state of mind, the things that came back without any effort and without any reason. There was the billiard room at Westwood after dinner. My father was chalking his cue. I remembered how the blue chalk powdered his slightly bent, arthritic fingers. I could not have been more than sixteen, but I remembered the exact position of the balls, and my father was asking me to get him the bridge.

"Here's Mrs. Pulham," Miss Rollo said.

"Hello, Kay," I said.

"Harry," Kay said, "don't forget we're going out to dinner."

"Where?" I asked.

"The Rodneys'," Kay said.

"The Rodneys'?" I said. "Do we have to go out there again?"

"You remember very well how it happened," Kay said. "When Beatrice asked us you said yourself there wasn't any way of getting out of it. Be sure to get home early."

"Mr. Pulham," Miss Rollo said, "there's something else. A Mrs. Ransome called you up. She wants you to call her at the Hadley."

The name came out of nowhere and meant nothing. It seemed to jump off a springboard and to plunge into a sea of other names. I tried to recall anyone I had ever known named Ransome. There was a Ransome once who had tried to sell me an oil-burning furnace. There was also a Ransome who had been a golf professional, and another whom I had met once on the way to Europe, and one who had once given me figures for laying a tiled drainage bed around a septic tank.

"Ransome?" I said to Miss Rollo. "I don't think I know any Mrs. Ransome."

"Mrs. John Ransome," Miss Rollo said. "She's staying at the Hadley."

"Well, what did she want?" I asked. "She must have wanted something."

Miss Rollo adjusted her pince-nez.

"She just wanted you to call her up as soon as you came in."

"Then get the Hadley and see if she's there," I told her, "and after that get me the page of the *Herald* with the cross-word puzzle on it."

I walked to the window and looked out at the vacant lot and at the antiquated brick buildings beyond it. The shadows of the chimneys were growing longer and the blue of the sky was softer. It was late afternoon, after four o'clock.

"I have Mrs. John Ransome, Mr. Pulham," Miss Rollo said, and I sat down again at the desk, and cleared my throat.

"Is this Mrs. Ransome?" I asked. "This is Mr. Henry Pulham. Did you want to speak to me?"

"I'm not really speaking, am I," I heard her voice ask, "to H. M. Pulham, Esquire?"

"Yes," I said, "this is Henry Pulham."

"Don't you know who I am?" she asked.

"No," I said. "It's probably the telephone. Perhaps it's a bad connection."

"It isn't bad," she said. "It's Marvin — Marvin Myles."

"Marvin?" I repeated, and my voice must have had a queer sound. I had never heard that she was married.

"My God, Harry," she said, "are you trying to pretend you don't remember?"

"What are you doing here?" I asked.

"I'm up for overnight," she said. "I'm up from New York. John is attending a directors' meeting. You didn't know me, did you?"

"It's just that you came out of nowhere," I said. And I wondered what directors' meeting it could be, but I did not ask her. I sat listening for what she would say next and she waited so long that I thought she was off the wire. Then she said:

"Harry, I want to see you. Don't you want to see what I look like?"

I could not believe that I would want to see her so much.

"Why, yes," I said, "I'd like to, Marvin."

"Come on," she said. "Come right away. I'm in a place called the Pharaoh Room. I wish you'd hurry, Harry."

"I've got to go out to dinner," I said.

"Well," she answered, "there's lots of time. I know what you're thinking."

32

"What?" I asked.

"You're thinking someone may see you," she answered. "That's what you would be thinking."

"When did you get married?" I asked. "I didn't know."

And of course it was none of my business at all. It was a good thing that she was married.

"Didn't Bill King tell you?" she asked. "A year ago. He was in your class at college."

"Ransome?" I said, but the name didn't mean anything. "Ransome?"

"Don't sound like that," she said. "He didn't know you either."

"Oh," I said. "Well, I think it's fine."

"Remember," she said. "The Pharaoh Room. Harry, are you happy?"

"Why, yes," I said, "I'm fine. I'll be right over."

Then I hung up the telephone and I saw Miss Rollo standing near the desk. I certainly did not want anyone in the office to start talking, and I wondered if anything about me looked queer.

"Here's the afternoon mail," Miss Rollo said, "and here's the cross-word puzzle."

I stood up and straightened my coat and straightened my tie and put on my hat. I hoped Miss Rollo did not think anything out-of-the-way had happened, and I spoke perfectly naturally.

"We'll go over the mail in the morning," I told Miss Rollo. "I'm leaving for the day."

The more I thought about it the more convinced I was that I had no business meeting Marvin Myles again, although of course it had all been over years ago, but it wouldn't do any possible good, and you never could tell whom you might see in a place like the Pharaoh Room. There might be a daughter of someone I knew, for instance, going there to dance.

I had not been in the Hadley Hotel since my great-aunt Frederica Knowles had died there fifteen years before. Upstairs the Hadley was just what it had been, a place where you went to live if you were an old lady, because the Hadley was just like home. But

33

downstairs in the basement it was all different and not meant for old ladies. Over the basement door, under the brownstone steps, was a neon sign "The Pharaoh Room," and an awning, and a young black boy in buttons. The Hadley, I knew, was managed by the Coffin Real Estate Associates and I could not imagine how old Mr. Jacob Coffin could have thought of a place like the Pharaoh Room in a family hotel, but there it was. There was a checkroom and a carpeted hall with a frieze representing an Egyptian bas-relief, and down at the end of the hall were strains of jazz music and the sound of a great many voices.

"Check your hat, sir?" the girl in the cloakroom was saying.

And then I was sure it wasn't right. Suppose I walked down the hall into the bar where Marvin would be waiting. It would not do any good, because it was all over. Suppose Kay ever heard about it. After all I was married and Marvin Myles was married. It was all over years ago.

"Check your hat, sir?" the girl asked again. And then another girl, quite pretty, with a tray full of gardenias and cigarettes, walked by and looked at me.

"No thanks," I told the hatroom girl, "not now," and then I was out on the street again, with all the brick buildings of the early development of Back Bay around me.

There was a drugstore half a block away. I found the telephone booth and called up the Pharaoh Room. After all it was a good deal better, much more sensible than seeing her.

"Will you please give a message to Mrs. John Ransome?" I said. "Tell her that Mr. Henry Pulham's office called. Mr. Pulham has been unexpectedly detained. He is sorry he can not meet Mrs. Ransome."

I was all right when I was out on the street. I had come near to making a fool of myself, but I hadn't. There was nothing that I had to conceal from Kay, and besides it was better to get home early, better to walk home, because we were going out to dinner. She shouldn't have called me up. I never had, not for years, in all the times I had been in New York; and she shouldn't have asked me if I were happy.

The best thing for me to do was to go to the Club for a game of squash with Gus, the professional, even if I had to wait for a chance to play with him. A good game with Gus would put everything back in its place, even if it made me late.

IV

We Were Going Out to Dinner

When I got home and closed the door behind me there was a faint odor of gas in the front hall, not enough to make it necessary to open things, but enough to show that the new cook Kay had found still did not understand the leak in the pilot light. At the end of the front hall the dining room door was open, and I saw the silver on the Empire sideboard. Ellen was setting two places on the bare mahogany table, so I gathered that Gladys would probably be having her best friend, little Gertrude Counter with buck teeth, in for supper because we were going out. Bitsey, Gladys' black cocker spaniel, ran down the stairs and barked at me. He was a fool with all the brains bred out of him, but then everyone always said that a cocker was the best dog for children. I was tired of having Bitsey bark, since Bitsey and I made our tour of the block together every morning before I went to the office, rain or shine, and again the last thing at night.

"Shut up," I said.

Bitsey shut up and waddled into the dining room, and I walked upstairs.

Kay was in the parlor, sitting in the corner near her writing desk talking into the telephone.

"Harry," she said, "you'd better hurry — hurry! You're awfully late."

"There's plenty of time," I said, "if my shirts are back from the laundry."

"Ellen has been looking for your studs," Kay said, "and we can't find them anywhere."

"Aren't they in the little round box on the bureau?" I asked. "Not the square box, the round box."

"No," Kay said. "Hello, is that you, Gracie? My dear, I wish I hadn't run away so early. How did it go?"

"Kay," I said, "if that girl has sent my studs to the wash again —"

"You don't mean she had those same crackers with fish on them?" Kay said.

"Kay," I said, "did she put my studs in the wash or didn't she?"

"Harry," Kay whispered, "do be quiet! It's just Harry, Gracie — the age-old hunt for studs. Well, if she's so intelligent why do you suppose it is that she never says anything? She just moves around and rattles that Navajo jewelry. She moves around quietly, because she's the Friend of the Indian."

"Kay," I said, "can't you talk to Gracie some other time?"

"Harry," Kay said, "do be quiet! If she goes back next year she'll sit in a corner and beat a drum." Kay began to giggle. I sat down and lighted a cigarette and looked at the Inness painting above the mantelpiece, and then at the hole that Bitsey had chewed in the corner of the rug, and then at the books on the table by the window. There had always been something wrong about the parlor. There were plenty of chairs, plenty of sofas, but we had never been able to get them grouped so that more than three people could sit in any one place. Now the room had an untidy, weary look, because we were going out to dinner.

"Why," Kay was saying, "I never said any such thing. I couldn't have said it, because I don't know anything about them."

"Kay," I said, "won't you please stop talking?"

"Harry," Kay said, "do be quiet! They literally haven't got a cent. The children are all on scholarships."

I got up and walked to the library and opened the door. Kay's voice still followed me. Gladys and Gertrude were in the library, listening to the radio.

"And now," the voice was saying, "don't forget that you can join the Magic Circle, too, and sit with the other lucky boys and girls on the Magic Robe of Big Chief Buffalo. You can join the

Magic Band and learn the Magic Sign and the Password. Where is he going to take Billy and Lizzie next? We leave them now lost in the midst of a Central American jungle. But how can you get a snake's eye ring — just like the one that Big Chief Buffalo gave to Lizzie just a minute ago? Why, you can get it before you say Jack Robinson. Just go right now and speak to Mummie. Tell her tomorrow when she goes to the Grocery Man to buy you a box of Tuffies. I'll spell it for you. Write it down, so you won't forget. All ready with the pencil and papers, kiddies? T-u-f-f-i-e-s spells Tuffies."

Gladys and Gertrude looked up when they saw me, resentfully, I thought. I tried to remember what it was you thought about when you were twelve years old.

"Why, hello," I said.

Gladys and Gertrude began to giggle.

"Who's Big Chief Buffalo?" I asked.

"He's a man," said Gladys, and they both giggled.

"What's the Magic Robe?" I asked.

"Buffalo skins," said Gladys, and they giggled.

"What are Tuffies?" I asked.

"You eat them for breakfast," Gertrude said. "They're nasty," and they giggled.

I thought when I was in the bathroom shaving that there was something wrong somewhere. There were French lessons and skating lessons and riding lessons and a school where everyone was supposed to be happy, and yet when Gladys got home she listened to Chief Buffalo. Then I remembered that when I got home from school I used to read about Nick Brady and the opium ring behind the barn.

"Harry," Kay was calling, "hurry."

Kay and I were going out to dinner. Now that I was in a hurry I did not have to think about Marvin Myles.

Kay was sitting in front of her mirror, upping her hair.

"We're going to be late," I said. "Has the garage sent the car over?"

"No," Kay answered. "You'd better call them up. You're the one who's late."

"I'm all ready," I said.

"You haven't got your trousers on."

'It takes about ten seconds to get my trousers on," I said. "Where are my pumps?"

"Where you put them."

"I don't see why Ellen can't lay my things out on the bed," I said.

"Because Ellen's hip's been hurting her," Kay said.

"Well, why don't we get somebody whose hip doesn't hurt?" I asked.

"I would, if we could pay the servants enough, dear," Kay answered.

We were saying the same things, just as we had said them a thousand times before we went out to dinner.

"What kept you so long?" Kay asked. "Were you working on the bumping tournament?"

The car was outside the door. I stood in the front hall smoking.

"Kay," I called, "aren't you nearly ready?"

"Yes," Kay called. "I'm coming. Don't keep shouting."

I heard her running down the stairs. She had on her gray chiffon dress.

"Have you got the keys?" she asked.

"Yes," I said. "I always have the keys."

"Did you tell Ellen to take Bitsey out?" she asked.

"Yes," I said, "and I told her to keep him out of the parlor."

The front door slammed behind us. My collar chafed against my neck. I started the motor. We were going out to dinner.

"Wait a minute," Kay said. "My bag — I forgot my bag."

"Oh," I said, "all right. I'll go up and get it."

"The gray bag," she said, "in my upper drawer — and a handkerchief — and, Harry, wait a minute. My compact — it's on the dressing table."

"Anything else?" I asked.

"No," said Kay, "that's all. I wouldn't have forgotten if you hadn't kept calling to me. Why do you always keep pacing around and calling?"

"All right," I said. "I'll get them."

We were going out to dinner.

I sat at Beatrice Rodney's left at dinner. Mrs. Thomas East was on my left, the wife of Dr. East, the child psychiatrist. Then there were the Patterns. He had some sort of a tenuous connection with the Harvard Business School — not on the faculty, but in round table discussions on how voluntarily to decrease production. Walter Pattern had asked me to one of them once, but he had never asked me again. His wife usually discussed what she had read in the last Consumers' Research bulletin about electric refrigerators or razor blades, and she always explained that she couldn't say much about it, as the information was confidential, intended only for members of the Consumers' Research. It was awfully nice of the Rodneys to have asked us, for the dinner was obviously carefully planned for interesting talk by interesting people.

Kay and I must have been included because Beatrice considered that I was utterly characteristic, completely true to type; once she called me a norm, but I am not entirely sure what she meant, and perhaps she did not know either. I do know that, if I had wanted, I could have told all those people a good many things about themselves which might have surprised them. Beatrice thought that I was a norm, and I thought that she was a norm. It may have been that both of us were right.

I don't know why it was always an effort for me to go to the Rodneys'. Although I had always known Phil Rodney — we had been to St. Swithin's and to Harvard together — we never had enough in common with each other to be comfortable, and another difficulty was that they and their friends were always so gaily sure that they had the right answer to everything. They were always doing interesting and unusual things, such as experimenting with raw vegetables or studying glacial striae. They always had difficult views, and once they had had dinner with Mr. Hopkins in Washington, and they knew all about the Tennessee Valley Authority.

40

"Everything's so interesting now, isn't it?" Beatrice Rodney said.

"If you mean everything's in a mess, you're certainly right," I said.

Beatrice laughed musically, and I knew that I had said something characteristic.

"It isn't really a mess, Harry dear," she said. "It's only the confusion attendant upon change. It simply means that your class is not wanted any more."

We were eating fried chicken and candied sweet potato with marshmallow on top. I had eaten the same thing several times before at the Rodneys'.

"I don't know what you mean by 'my class,'" I said. "If stocks don't pay dividends you and Phil won't have any chicken."

"Not this kind of chicken," Beatrice said, "but of course we'll all get along. We'll be able to sell little things. We'll all take part in small industries. Phil and I are working on an industry now."

"What sort of an industry?" I asked.

"Well, it's sort of a project," Beatrice said, "for the whole community. Phil has bought a loom. He has it in the garage."

"What does he do with it?" I asked.

"We're learning how to weave," Beatrice said. "Everyone in the neighborhood comes out on Sunday for lunch and we have doughnuts and coffee and we weave. You must try it sometime. You must come out and bring Gladys, or George at Christmas vacation."

Upstairs after dinner all the men were talking about collective bargaining and about farm allotments. I could think of a great many obvious answers to nearly all their arguments, but my answers sounded hollow, like something in a textbook which was out of date. In the parlor later Phil Rodney asked us if he could get us Scotch-and-soda or beer or ginger ale, and I sat listening to myself and listening to the rest of them. Of course most of it was beyond my depth, because I never seemed to have time to read much, but we were all simply paraphrasing what we had read somewhere, and the one who had read the most books was the best talker. I heard Kay quoting what I had supplied her from the headlines of the paper that morning, as though it were all original and new.

Beatrice had leaned back her head and was talking with her eyes shut. It was a habit of hers which had always made me nervous.

"If I could only write," she said. "If I could just set down everything that came into my mind."

"Anyone can write," said Dr. East. "Harry here can write."

"He could only write about the furnace," Kay said, "or to the gas company when the stove leaks."

"What?" I said.

"Harry's been asleep," said Dr. East.

"Harry," Kay said, "what *is* the matter with you?"

"I was just thinking with my eyes closed," I answered.

"Kay says you could only write about the furnace," said Dr. East.

"Well," I said, "there was a girl in New York once who used to think that I could write."

"What girl?" Kay asked.

I found myself the center of attention. They were all looking at me. They were all amused, but Kay must have known whom I meant.

"Come to think of it," I said, "I have to write my Class life pretty soon."

"I'd like to read it," said Dr. East, "it would be a human document." And everybody laughed.

"I'm afraid we'd better be going home," Kay said. "Harry's always cross in the morning if we don't go home early."

We stood in the front hall with the front door open. Kay had on her rabbit fur wrap and I had found my scarf, and Kay had rescued her bag from where it had fallen behind the parlor sofa.

"Good night, Beatrice," I said. "I had a swell time. I had a swell time, Phil."

When the doors of the car were shut and the lights were on, Kay and I were shadows in the dusk. Sometimes I have wondered if driving home from dinner would not be easier if the interior of all cars could be lighted. Then perhaps even though you were tired you would not say exactly what you thought. Even before Kay spoke I could tell from her silence that I had not behaved.

"Perhaps I'd better drive, Harry," she said.

"Oh, no," I said. "I like to drive."

"Well," Kay said, "most wives seem to drive their husbands home. There's usually a reason."

"I only had one cocktail," I said, "and a little weak whisky and water after dinner."

"You were the only man who took a highball after dinner," Kay said. "All the other men just had water or ginger ale."

"Well, never mind all the other men," I said. "If I hadn't had that whisky I'd have gone to sleep."

"I don't know why you can't get out of the habit of drinking after dinner," Kay went on. "I've told you again and again, Harry, again and again and again, that it makes you stupid. Your eyes were glazed. You almost went to sleep when Mrs. East was talking to you."

"If I hadn't had that drink," I said, "I'd have gone to sleep. Why didn't they play bridge?"

"Because just for a change," Kay said, "we happened to be talking with interesting people."

"All right," I said. "Can't we talk about something else?"

Kay did not answer. I was thinking about the day and the day moved uncomfortably in my memory. I had been sleepy after dinner, but if you work hard perhaps it is natural to be sleepy. Now Kay and all the women were different. They did not have to get up at eight in the morning and they could take naps in the afternoon.

"Harry," Kay said.

"What?" I asked.

"Didn't you think Beatrice was attractive?"

"Yes," I said, "of course."

"She made that dress herself. What did you and Beatrice talk about? I heard her laughing at you."

"About weaving things," I said.

"What did you and Mrs. East talk about?"

"About sex," I said. "I don't see why we have to talk about it at the dinner table."

"Her husband's a psychiatrist," Kay said.

"What difference does that make?" I asked.

"You never like women," Kay said. "Harry, you've always been afraid of women. I believe you've always had a secret guilty feeling of inadequacy."

"Who were you talking to after dinner?" I asked.

"I was talking to Dr. East," Kay said. "He was saying that very few women are really satisfied, particularly the women in our generation."

"Sometime," I said, "I'm going to tell him what I think of him."

"Oh, Harry," Kay said, "don't be so silly."

I did not answer.

"Harry," Kay said. I did not answer.

"Don't be so stuffy, Harry."

I was thinking of Bo-jo Brown and the Class Reports. I was try-ing to remember whether I had ever heard of the Charles Mason Hilliard whose life I had read: Occupation, lawyer; Address, Mortgage Building, New York; Home, Mamaroneck, New York. The words went by me in little flashes, like the lights on the street outside, and like the lights of the cars that whirled past us. "After leaving Law School I joined the firm of Jessup and Good-rich in New York. Five years later I was employed by the firm of Jones and Jones. I am now a partner in the firm of Watkins, Lord, Watkins, Bondage, Green, Smith and Hilliard."

"Harry," Kay said, "what are you thinking about?"

"About my life," I said. It wasn't entirely true. I was wondering what Marvin would have looked like, if I had seen her.

"Oh, all right," Kay said, "if you're going to be cross."

Now if I were to write my own life it would sound a good deal like Charles Mason Hilliard's. "I am an Episcopalian and I bowl occasionally and sometimes play golf. In politics I am a Republican, hoping that the day will come when Mr. Roosevelt leaves the White House." There was nothing wrong in that. Charles Mason

44

Hilliard was marching with all the rest of us through a term of years, marching with Marvin Myles, and Bo-jo Brown, and Kay and me, with all our friends and enemies, out into nowhere.

"Harry," Kay said, "you haven't answered my question."

"What question?" I asked.

"Are you happy?"

"Yes," I said, "of course."

I had never allowed my mind to wander in exactly that way. I was just considering how amazingly easy it would have been not to have married Kay. Of course I had realized that it was the sensible thing to do and the sort of thing of which my family would approve, but there were a dozen other girls that it would have been equally sensible to marry. If I had not been feeling the way I had, if I had not gone to a house party at Northeast Harbor, if I had not been asked to take Kay sailing, I might just as well have become engaged to May Barrister, or to Ruth Quiller, or to one of my sister Mary's friends.

"Harry," Kay said, "is there anything bothering you?"

"No," I said, "of course not, Kay. What makes you ask?"

"Because you're so peculiar," Kay said. "I speak to you and you don't answer."

"Isn't it all right," I asked, "if I sometimes just sit and think?"

"You must be annoyed about something," Kay said. "What was it I said to make you this way?"

"What makes you say that?" I asked.

"Because I know you, Harry," Kay said.

There was every reason why she should have known me, but I was not sure that she did. I was not sure that I knew her either. We had simply experimented and finally arrived by hit or miss at a method of getting on together. We walked up the steps and I found my keys. There were a lot of keys on my ring which should have been thrown away, but I could always find the house key in the dark.

"Will you call the garage and have them send for the car?" Kay asked.

"Yes," I said.

"And don't forget to take Bitsey out. Ellen may have forgotten."

"No, I won't forget," I said.

"And if I'm asleep when you come up will you undress in the bathroom and try not to stumble over things?"

"All right," I said. "Good night, Kay."

"Good night, dear," Kay said, and she held out her arms to me, and we kissed in the front hall. There was still that slight smell of gas. It might have been that one of the pilot lights on the kitchen stove had started leaking.

I switched on the lamp above the desk where I sat sometimes to pay bills or to work on the income tax. The library was gloomily quiet and comfortable. Bitsey was asleep on a corner of the sofa, and Gladys had left a pile of cut-out papers before the fireplace. The radio was on a corner of the desk, and I turned it on.

"And so it remains to be seen," the commentator was saying, "what steps England and France will take to curb this pressure. What small nation of Central Europe will be next? How far can this continue before the democracies take a stand? Is war inevitable? I wish that I might tell you, but instead I must say good night."

I switched the radio off, and I opened the upper drawer and took out a sheet of paper.

"Name," I wrote: "Henry Moulton Pulham."

BORN: Brookline, Mass., December 15th, 1892.
PARENTS: John Grove Pulham, Mary Knowles Pulham.
MARRIED: June 15th, 1921, Cornelia Motford.
CHILDREN: George, May 29th, 1924; Gladys, January 16th, 1927.
DEGREES: A.B.
OCCUPATION: Investment counsel.

It looked, as I wrote it, like something on a tombstone. Once Bill King, when he had had a good deal to drink, had told me that anyone might have an arresting gift of self-expression. He said just write about your life, that anyone's life is a good story. If I were just to put down everything that had happened to me that day . . .

"Harry," Kay said.

I had forgotten that I had left the library door open until she spoke. She was standing there in her green dressing gown.

"I went to sleep and then I woke up," Kay said. "What *are* you doing? Take Bitsey out and come to bed."

"All right," I said.

"You never do sleep well if you drink after dinner," Kay said. I put the paper in my desk drawer and closed it. There was no use arguing that my sleeplessness had nothing to do with drinking. When Kay went upstairs I took the paper out again and looked at it. It stared back at me blankly. Once I had won·a prize for an essay at the school and later I had written advertising copy and commercial reports, but I never possessed the literary gift that came naturally to a man like Bill King. Instead all my phrases were too formalized and too flowery and the thoughts that moved me most deeply remained a secret in my mind — impossible to transform into sentences and paragraphs. My name on the top of the paper still looked like something on a tombstone.

V

The Golden Age

I was born on our old country place, called Westwood, near the west boundary of Brookline; and most of my childhood summers were spent there, except for a month between the middle of July and the middle of August, when my sister Mary and I and a nurse or governess were all packed up and sent to Maine. Westwood consisted of sixty acres of woods and fields, purchased by my grandfather. Across the road opposite the front drive my great-aunt Frederica Knowles lived on a place nearly as large. I can remember when we looked from the window of the little room, where Mary and I customarily ate our supper with Fräulein, that we would often see the pheasants come out of the woods at the far end of the lawn, and twice we even saw a deer.

Only a few days ago, when it was necessary to take Gladys to a birthday party, I found myself driving past the old front entrance, and I turned up the drive just to look at it. It gave me a very odd feeling, a feeling that I had been drawn, as they say ghosts are, to familiar places, but very little I saw was familiar. The high granite gateposts were still there and some of the great elm trees. A good many of the silver and copper beeches and some of the great white pines had been blown over by the hurricane, but others had been cut down to make room for the houses of a real estate development. These buildings, set in their own little gardens, in what was called Westwood Park, were all replicas of brick and wood colonial architecture and closely resembled magazine advertisements for asbestos roofs or southern cypress or white lead paint. Our house, built out of brownish stone, with a mansard slate roof and a Gothic

"Who said it?" I asked. I did not know what it meant, but I liked the way it sounded.

"Patrick said it," Mary answered, and then Fräulein called in German, telling us to come to dinner.

There was a new white cloth on the table and an arrangement of roses in the silver bowl in the center. My mother was at one end, straight and beautiful.

"Come," she called. "Hurry, children." Hugh pulled out Mary's chair and helped her with the napkin. I sat down and tucked my own napkin inside my Eton collar.

"Well, well," my father said, "and what have you two been doing? Did you go to Sunday School?"

He knew very well that we had gone to Sunday School, just as we knew that he and Mother had gone to church, for he had on his long-tailed coat and his pearl cravat.

"John," my mother said, "haven't we forgotten something?"

"Now, what the deuce?" my father asked.

"John," my mother said, "you've forgotten grace."

"Oh, yes," my father said. "Oh, Lord, bless these Thy gifts for our use, for Jesus' sake. Amen."

"I wonder if you children saw the dew on the lawn this morning," Mother said. "It shone on the grass like diamonds, but it is prettier than any diamond. Do either of you know what makes the dew?"

My father took no part in the conversation about the dew.

"I'll have a glass of sherry, Hugh," Father said. "Hugh, is the carving knife sharp?"

"Yes, sir," Hugh said softly. "It was sent out yesterday."

"That's good," Father said. "It was very dull last week."

"I'll cut Miss Mary's meat, Hugh," Mother said, "and I think you've forgotten her pusher."

"Yes, madam," Hugh said.

"Harry can cut his own meat," Mother went on. "Harry, you're a big boy now, dear, but try to keep your elbows down and don't lean too far over the plate."

52

porch, had entirely disappeared — it must have been a job to take it down — and so had the stable and so had the gardens and the terraces. The only building left was the superintendent's cottage near the gate, and a boy and girl played in its yard who might have been Mary and I.

"Daddy," Gladys said, "weren't there any other people living here when you did?"

"No," I said.

"Well, why don't we still live here?"

"Because we didn't have the money to keep it up," I said.

"But what happened to the money," Gladys asked, "if your father kept it up?"

"There isn't as much money as there used to be," I told her.

"But where did it go to?" Gladys asked.

"I don't know," I said.

I had stopped the car and I was staring at another world, and I could never explain that world to Gladys.

"Some day," I could hear my mother saying, "you will be very rich, Harry." I recalled the talk I had heard of "the lost generation," and I realized that I and my contemporaries were part of it, and the life we had learned to live was gone, like Westwood. Then I wondered if we had not given our children very much the same sort of life. It might be the fate of children always, to be brought up in an idealistic, antiseptic world. The only difference was that the schools now took our children away from us and taught them some inaccurate facts about the home life of the Eskimo. Perhaps the result was just the same.

When my father used to start for town in the morning Mary and I would look through the banisters of the second floor down on the wide front hall. Patrick and the dappled grays would be waiting beneath the copper beech on the drive and my father would come out of the room which was known as his "den."

"Mary," he would call, "Mary." He was not calling to my sister but to Mother — in those days we used to call my sister "May" and sometimes "Pussy."

49

"Mary," he would call, and my mother would come out of the morning room, beautiful with the sunlight on her soft brown hair.

"Yes, John," my mother would say, "what is it?"

My father would be looking through his pockets, slapping himself.

"That woman has taken my key ring again," he would call. He would be referring to Katreen, the parlormaid.

Then Katreen and Hugh, our butler, and Nancy, the upstairs maid, would all move about the hall, looking under things.

"Katreen hasn't taken it, dear," my mother would say. "What would Katreen want with your keys? Where did you put them last?"

"Everything gets moved around," my father would say. I could not understand him then, but I can now. My own keys always seem to be in some other trouser pocket in the morning, or in the suit which has just been sent out to be pressed.

"Nothing has been moved, John," my mother would say.

"Then, damn it all, Mary," my father would ask her, "what's happened to my key ring?"

"Perhaps the children have taken it, sir," Hugh would suggest. "Master Harry has been playing in the den."

"Hugh," my mother would say, "Master Harry never touches Mr. Pulham's things. Have you looked through your pockets, dear?"

"Through my pockets?" my father would ask. "Where do I usually look except through my pockets? Wait a minute. Oh, my God, here they are!"

I don't know why that scene should come back to me so vividly, except that such moments in childhood always seem important. Childhood, as I recalled it, was a time when you always were trying to adjust yourself to something new. There were certain shadowy individuals who fell into a relationship that became increasingly clear as time went on, and there were a few brilliant moments — the memory of a butterfly, of flowers in the garden and of the singing

50

of crickets, the first fall of snow, the stars in a black sky — b of it lay behind a sort of haze. I have read a good many bo childhood, such as *The Golden Glow, The Believing Year* none of them convinces me, for they are an adult's effort to p a child's mind. I can still remember my feeling of aloof horr the sight of my father in the playroom when he tried to be or us and tried to pretend, as he did nearly once a week, that he a bear. Of course we were polite and we laughed at him; although we knew he was making an effort, we also knew that was making a spectacle of himself. And when he tried to be bear once, when the Dodd children came to supper, Mary and were humiliated.

Once a long while later I spoke to him about it. It was one o the last conversations we ever had, but there was still a sort of constraint between us when I mentioned it.

"Do you remember when you used to play bear?" I asked him.

"Yes," he said. "That was a lot of fun."

"Well, you were an awfully bad bear," I said, and the curious thing was that he was sensitive about it.

"I made a very genuine effort," he said. "I gave it a lot of thought and study, and I don't agree with you. I was a damned good bear."

He paused and looked almost wistful.

"You never knew," he went on, "the effort your mother and I used to make to take part in your lives. All those damned games, all those paper caps and snappers, and that woman in the nursery — that was your mother's idea. I never did like Germans."

I really never thought of Father as a human being until I was nine years old. Mary and I had been dressed in clean clothes and had been turned out on the terrace behind the house just before Sunday dinner. In the distance by the stable I could see Patrick sitting by the open door and the sun made the wheels of the carriages shine and there was a smell of roast beef from the kitchen.

"Harry," Mary said, "what does son of a bitch mean?"

51

I held my knife and fork very carefully and began to cut the slab of roast beef. There was a piece of Yorkshire pudding beside it and a browned potato.

"Mummie," Mary said, "may I mash my own potato, please?"

My knife slipped and my meat slipped from under it and my potato rolled upon the white tablecloth.

"Son of a bitch," I said.

I glanced around the table inquiringly. The tall clock in the hall outside was striking the half hour and I could hear a squirrel chattering in the oak tree on the lawn. Hugh stood behind Father's chair. Father stood with his knife poised above the roast. My mother had lifted her napkin to her lips, and I could see her eyes staring at me over the napkin, wide and incredulous.

"Harry," she said, "oh, Harry!" and then she sobbed.

My father set down the carving knife and I still remember the smell of golden beef-fat and Yorkshire pudding.

"Go upstairs to your room," he said.

"What?" I said.

"Go upstairs to your room," Father said, "and stay there until I send for you."

"Oh, Harry," Mother sobbed, "Harry!" And then I began to cry. I began to cry because I was frightened.

"John," Mother said, "I've told you — I've told you."

"Be quiet, please, Mary," Father said. "I hope I'm gentleman enough never to have used such an expression, and I'm sure I don't know where he heard it. Harry, did you hear me? Go upstairs."

I ran up the stairs as fast as I could and down the hall to my room and slammed the door. There was still that smell of cooking. It was a pretty room with a little four-post bed and with white curtains and a little shelf of books and a small golden-oak writing desk. There was a picture over it of a young knight, kneeling in front of an altar and looking at the hilt of his sword, praying, my mother had explained, that he might be a good knight. She had hung the picture so that I might see it the first thing when I awoke

53

in the morning, and the last thing when I fell asleep. I walked over to the door and kicked it.

When I hear certain persons speaking of the happiness of childhood I wonder if they have not forgotten a good deal about it. Childhood has seemed to me like a great many other periods in life. When you are in them you don't have much of a time. It is only when you are out of them and probably in something worse that you remember the more genial aspects. I could think of them sitting downstairs finishing their dinner. I have never cared much for Sunday dinner since, and I have never cared much for Sunday. It has always seemed to me that there is something unnatural about the day which makes for family quarrels.

There was a knock on the door a long while later and it was Hugh in his green-striped vest with brass buttons. Although he moved silently and quickly, Hugh was a heavy man, with white hands and a pale, rather handsome face. Hugh was smiling the way he smiled when the pantry door was closed and no one could see him but the maids.

"You nip off downstairs," said Hugh. "Your papa wants to see you. He's waiting in his den. Oh, my, my, such language! Come now, your papa is waiting."

Hugh walked with me down the front stairs and across the lonely hall to the door of my father's room.

"Here's Master Harry, sir," he said. The room was not beautiful, but it was interesting. At one end in a case were my father's shotguns which I must never touch. Hanging on the mahogany paneling above the mantelpiece were some birds and fish mounted in bas-relief and covered with glass. Then there were a good many books which my father very seldom read. His name in white letters was on a black strip of cloth above the door and on the wall were some hunting prints and some framed notices and letters, known as "shingles," which had been given him in college, and near them was a shelf of pewter and silver cups. Jack, his Gordon setter, was sprawled on the rug near the fireplace. My father was sitting in a morris chair, smoking a cigar. He had taken off his morning coat

54

and was wearing a velvet smoking jacket and before he spoke he cleared his throat.

"Sit down, Harry," he said, "over there, where I can see you," and he pointed to a heavy leather chair opposite him. I sat down and he flicked the ash of his cigar into the empty fireplace and blew a cloud of smoke into the air above him and looked at it.

"Well," he said, "don't look so frightened, Harry," and he cleared his throat. "We're just going to have a talk about those words you used. Did you know what they meant?"

"No," I said.

"Well," Father said, "I didn't think you did. Now, I'm going to tell you exactly what they mean. Now, Jack there, what do you call him, Harry?"

"A dog," I said.

"And Tessie, out in the stable, what do you call her, Harry?"

"A dog," I said.

My father rubbed his hand over his heavy black mustache. I suppose he must have given a good deal of thought to what he had to say.

"You're right," he said, "but only partly, because Tessie is a lady dog. She's a very good lady dog, as a matter of fact. She has a pedigree as long as her tail. Now, a lady dog has another name. It's a name that is not used in the house, but one which you may hear men using sometimes when they are talking about dogs. A lady dog sometimes," my father cleared his throat again, "is called a bitch. Now, remember, that is not a nice word, and you must not use it in mixed company."

"What is mixed company?" I asked.

"When boys and girls and ladies and gentlemen are together, that is mixed company; and people do not use such words in mixed company. Little boys who use them get sent upstairs. Now do you understand me, Harry?"

"Yes," I answered.

"Well," Father went on, "sometimes Tessie and Jack have puppies."

55

"I thought only Tessie had puppies," I said. "Does Jack nave puppies too?"

My father looked at me and pulled at his mustache.

"Jack is the father," he said. "There has to be a father, just the way you have to have a father and have to have a mother, but let's not mind about that, Harry. You'll find out about that later, and if I were you I wouldn't ask your mother about it either. I was simply saying that Tessie is a bitch." Father paused and sighed and threw his cigar into the fireplace. "Now, when Tessie has puppies, some of them are girl puppies and some of them are boy puppies. The men at the kennel call the little boy puppies dogs and the girl puppies bitches. Now, that's where the expression comes from, Harry."

"What's an expression?" I asked.

Father sighed again.

"The words you used in the dining room; somehow those are wrong words."

"Why are they wrong words?" I asked.

Father got up and opened his mahogany humidor.

"Get me the cigar cutter," he said, "over on the table. Those words are never to be used in front of ladies."

"Why," I asked, "if a lady dog is a bitch?"

Father lighted his cigar.

"Because I say so," he answered. "Now, have we got that clear?"

"Yes," I said, "but I don't see why."

"Never mind why," my father said. "As you grow older, Harry, you will find there will be a great many things you have to do without asking why. There was a great poem written about it once by the greatest poet who ever lived — Alfred Lord Tennyson. It was about the Charge of the Light Brigade. Well, the British were fighting the Russians. Now, don't ask me why they were fighting the Russians, because I don't remember. Well, someone ordered six hundred men in the British cavalry known as the Light Brigade to charge right into thousands of Russian soldiers and into hundreds of Russian guns. Now, those men in the Light Brigade knew they weren't enough to beat the whole Russian Army. They knew they were nearly all going to be killed, but when the order was given they charged."

"Why did they have to?" I asked.

"That's just what I'm trying to explain," Father said. "It doesn't do any good to ask why.

> "Theirs not to reason why,
> Theirs but to do and die . . .
> Bravely they rode and well . . .
> Into the jaws of death,
> Into the mouth of hell."

Jack got up quickly from his rug, wagging his tail.

"Down, Jack," my father said. "Charge. Now, that's curious when you come to think of it. You tell the Light Brigade to charge, but when you tell a dog to charge he lies down. And you needn't ask me why. That's the way things are."

"Were they all killed?" I asked.

"Charge, Jack," my father said. "Now, don't bother about that. I only mentioned it to show that people must do what they are told, whether they have a reason for it or not. Now where was I? Oh, yes . . . It's the same way about words. Now, hell is a bad word and so is damn. Sometimes I use them, but it is even bad for me to use them. You'll get to recognize those words by the way they sound."

"What are some of them?" I asked.

"Never mind them now," Father said. "Perhaps we've talked long enough. Someday you'll be grown up, and I want you to be a gentleman."

My father stood up and squared his shoulders.

"Well, that's about all. It's puzzling to know what to do sometimes, but you will know if you're a gentleman."

There was a tap on the door. It was Katreen, the downstairs maid.

"Mrs. Pulham sent me, sir," Katreen said. "She's upstairs with a headache. She would like to see Master Harry."

The shades were drawn in Mother's room so that it was cool and dusky. There was a smell of cologne and Mother was reclining on her chaise longue with a thin blue blanket drawn over her.

"Come in, dear," she said. "I have a little headache."

I sat down on a low chair beside her and she held my hand.

"You're getting to be such a big strong boy," she said, "and you've been seeing Father — the men of the family talking in the den."

"I didn't know it was a bad word," I said.

"Of course you didn't, dear," she answered, "but Father told you, didn't he? You must see bad things, but never do them, darling."

"All right," I said. "I won't, Mother."

"Because I want you to be my knight," she went on, "my strong little knight, like the picture in your room. It reminds me of a poem by the greatest poet in the world — Alfred Lord Tennyson."

"About the Light Brigade?" I asked.

"No, dear," my mother said. "I have always thought that was a horrid poem. About Sir Galahad, the knight who found the Holy Grail. It was a cup and no one could touch it who wasn't pure. Sir Lancelot couldn't touch it."

"Why couldn't he?" I asked.

"Because he was in love with Queen Guinevere," Mother answered.

"But why couldn't he touch it, Mother?" I asked her.

"Because Queen Guinevere was King Arthur's wife, darling," Mother said, "and men mustn't be in love with other men's wives, least of all a knight."

"Is a knight a gentleman, Mother?" I asked.

"Yes, dear," my mother said, "a knight is always a gentleman, but Sir Galahad was more than that — he could touch the Holy Grail. Do you know what he said in the poem? 'My strength is as the strength of ten because my heart is pure.' And you must be my little knight."

"Mother," I asked.

"Yes, dear," she said.

58

"Could Father touch the Holy Grail?"

"Darling," my mother said, "your father is kind and gentle and brave, but there is only one knight who could ever touch the Holy Grail. I am going to take a little nap now. Good-by, my little knight."

It took me quite a while to get over the idea that my father was the ablest man in the world and that my mother was the most beautiful woman, and I only learned a good deal later that we weren't distinguished people. The first inkling of it came when my mother was getting over another of her headaches and we were alone in her room again. I was struggling, as I have a good deal since, to get my relationship straight with the world around me.

"Mother," I asked her, "do you love me better than Mary?"

"Why, darling," she said, "I love both my dear little children equally. No matter how many children I might have I would love them all equally."

"Mother," I asked her, "were you and Daddy surprised when I was born?"

"No, dear," she said, "because we knew that you were coming."

"How did you know?"

"There are ways of telling, dear," Mother said.

"Were you glad when I came?" I asked. "What was the first thing that you and Daddy did when I came?"

"The first thing?" Mother said. "Let me think. I believe that the first thing that Daddy and I did was to send Hugh down to the telegraph office with a message to enter you at St. Swithin's School."

"Why?" I asked.

"So that they would surely have room for you, dear. It's hard for some boys to get into St. Swithin's."

"Did Father go there?" I asked.

"No, dear," Mother said. "You see, your father came from Methuen and I came from Hingham."

"But why didn't Grandpapa send him?" I asked.

Mother sighed and put a few drops of cologne on her handkerchief.

"I don't think your grandpapa knew how important it was, dear. You see, Methuen is a long way from Boston, and Father did not come to Boston until he was all grown up and in Harvard, and Father and I want you to have a happier time than he did, although a great many people at Harvard liked him because he was very strong."

"Why did Grandpapa live in Methuen?" I asked.

"Why, he worked there, dear," Mother said. "He made things in Methuen."

"What sort of things?"

Mother put some more cologne on her handkerchief.

"Grandpapa Pulham made hooks and eyes in Methuen for ladies' dresses, darling," Mother said, "and you must never be ashamed that he made such useful things. That's why Grandmama gave the big stained glass window to the Unitarian Church in memory of him."

I stood beside the chaise longue and she threw her arms around me and held me very tight for a minute. Her cheek, very white and soft, was against my cheek. Even when she was old Mother's skin was clear and beautiful.

"Harry, dear, we want you to be happy," she said, "a happy little boy and then a happy man, and you must always tell Mother if you aren't happy and tell Mother just what you think about everything, because mothers want to know. You are happy, aren't you, dear?"

I like to think that my own generation is more sensible and that we do not bring our children up to be snobs and that we are pretty well over worrying about such things. For my part, I always like fresh points of view. Bill King, for instance, came from New Jersey and went to some unknown preparatory school and did not know anyone when he went to Harvard, and yet I still maintain that he is the most brilliant member of our Class. Sometimes I think that I shall not mind if my son George does not make a Club at Harvard.

A conversation comes back to me which I carried on at about this time with Jack Purcell, but which would never take place at present. The family used to be very pleased when we were asked to play with Jack and Joy Purcell. Jack and I used to make spiders out of pieces of cork with legs made from his mother's hairpins. We had learned how to do it out of the *American Boy's Handybook*. We also learned a good many other things from that volume, such as the capture, care and feeding of field mice.

We were making spiders when the subject of our parents came up.

"Your father isn't much," Jack said.

"Oh, twenty-three," I said, "twenty-three, skidoo."

"He's a mere adventurer."

"Who said he was?" I asked.

"My mother said so," Jack said, "last night. She said your mother and father are nouveau and mere adventurers."

"Twenty-three, skidoo," I said again, but I have always liked Jack Purcell. He is one of my oldest friends, and two years ago the Purcells asked Kay and me to dinner at Magnolia.

VI

I Consider Mr. Chips

Three years ago I started to read *The Education of Henry Adams.* In fact, I have worked on it ever since I purchased a special reading light which would not keep Kay awake. It was my idea to read a worth-while book fifteen minutes every night before I went to sleep, since reading in the daytime hardly ever seems to be possible. But there were difficulties, for Kay developed a habit of calling across from her bed to mine, usually when I was in the middle of a very hard sentence, and if she did not, I would find myself growing sleepy. My mind would suddenly grow blank and I would discover that I had read a great many pages without absorbing their meaning, and then I would be obliged to go all over them again.

The last thing which I propose is to compare myself to Henry Adams, or indeed to any other member of the Adams family, who still continue to be the most brilliant family in America. Mr. Adams has given me a great deal of food for thought, although I do not like his cynicism. With all due respect to him, I think it is best to take life with a smile and to look up, not down, and to look forward, not back, although that is just what I am doing now, but I am looking backward with the idea of looking forward. However, what impressed me most about that book was how little Mr. Adams' surroundings changed from the beginning to the end of his life, for he ended just where he started — in the horse-and-buggy age, without the addition of very much plumbing. Yet here in my own life, which is not entirely over, I am already in an entirely different world. I was thinking of it the other evening, after I had put Henry Adams down and switched off the light.

"Harry," Kay called to me, "are you awake?"

"Get a horse," I said. I was thinking of our first automobile, a Rochet Schneider, which had a canopy top with tassels on it.

"Get a horse," the boys were shouting, as Father drove through Brookline village. "Get a horse!"

"Harry," Kay asked me, "are you talking in your sleep?"

"No," I answered. "What is it, Kay?"

"Did you remember to fix the thermostat?"

"Yes, I fixed it," I said.

"I should think it would be worth while to get a thermostat with an electric clock, so that we wouldn't need ever to bother about it, and I don't see why we need a choreman any more. There aren't any ashes."

"There's the garbage," I said.

"Oh, yes," Kay said. "I forgot about the garbage."

"Get a horse," the boys were shouting, and the Rochet Schneider snorted and palpitated beneath us, so that the single brass lamp on its dashboard scintillated in the sunlight.

The strange thing was that we all knew the boys were right. There was no way of telling that we as human beings were entering another epoch, as definitely different as the glacial period was from the age of the dinosaurs. All at once everything happened. Everything changed, before we knew it had changed.

There are certain things, however, in human contacts which have not changed. A good deal of life as I know it really began when I went to boarding school. When I left Westwood one September afternoon, home grew smaller and faded into the clouds, like the land when you leave for Europe. After that I was always going away and always coming back, but whenever I came back part of me did not belong there.

"Father's going to take you in the Winton," Mary said.

My trunk was on the floor of my room with all the things I needed, such as a blue suit and stiff white collars and two laundry bags and a shoe bag and blankets and a comforter and sheets and pillow slips and a Bible and stockings and corduroy knickerbockers.

"Father told Patrick this afternoon," Mary said, "and Patrick has been working on the engine all day."

Then Hugh came in. He opened the door without knocking.

"Now, now, now," Hugh said. "What would Madam say if she knew you were in here, Miss Mary?"

"Oh, go bunch," Mary said.

"Such a way for a little lady to talk," said Hugh, and he smiled at me. "They will beat the living daylights out of you, Master Harry. I know what they did to Master Alfred Frothingham, who was a much nicer-spoken young gentleman than you. Master Alfred walked lame when he came back for the Christmas holidays."

Hugh liked to talk of the Frothinghams, a much better place than his present one.

"Oh, go chase yourself," I said.

"Now, now," said Hugh, "such a way to talk, such language. The young gentlemen tied Master Alfred up by his thumbs. Master Alfred told me so himself. And then they put weights on his feet, and they stuck red-hot needles in Master Alfred, so that his flesh all burned and smoked and sizzled like a steak over coals, and then they beat Master Alfred with cricket bats."

"Oh, go soak your head," I said. "They don't have cricket bats in America."

"That's right, Harry," Mary said. "Hugh is nothing but a great big nasty liar. They don't have cricket bats in America."

"Excuse me, miss," Hugh said. "Baseball bats, I should have said. Master Alfred still had lumps on him when I left the place, horrible big welts all over him, and holes where they inserted the needles. Master Alfred was covered with running sores."

"*Ach,*" I heard Fräulein say to her, "Mrs. Pulham, you are so brave!"

'Fräulein, dear," my mother answered, "I'm only doing what anyone ought to do."

I know only too well that there is nothing like a mother, and a man, I think, understands this better than a woman. That is why the best tributes to motherhood come from men. I recall particularly

Whistler's portrait of his mother, which always gives me a burning feeling in my throat when I see it, and that poem of Kipling's about "Mother o' Mine." I have been told that it is sentimental, but I think that it is very true.

Those nervous headaches of hers, which grew worse as she grew older, were particularly severe that September. I remember being struck by my father's expression when he thought she did not see him. He looked puzzled and not entirely sympathetic, and once when I was walking down the hall, their door was open and I heard Father say:

"Now, Mary, he's only going to school."

The morning before I left I was sent to say good-by to everyone on the place, to Patrick and then to Charley and Joe in the garden, and to the two Italians who came in by the day to help, and then to Mr. and Mrs. Roland, who lived in the cottage by the gate. I had been aware for some time that my status with all of them was altering, and I was embarrassed when the men wiped their hands before they shook hands with me. I even felt constrained with Bob Roland. Bob was the superintendent's son and just about my age.

"Well," I said, "so long."

I saw Bob looking at my new clothes. We stood there, eying each other like strangers, although we were very good friends.

"So long," Bob said.

"I'll see you at Christmas," I told him.

It was a fine September day. The sunlight was soft, and a breeze was blowing through the elm trees.

"We'll all miss Master Harry, madam," Hugh was saying.

Patrick was cranking the Winton. It would cough and then it would stop, and he would run over to the steering wheel and move the spark and the gas, and then he would crank it again and run back to the steering wheel. Finally the engine responded, and he crawled into the tonneau in back. Father pulled his cap over his eyes and pulled on his leather gauntlets.

"All right," he called. We had to speak very loudly, and Mother waved. I had a queer feeling in the pit of my stomach — but there is no use describing what everyone has felt.

"Don't fall out," Mother called. "Hold on tight, darling."

I can remember the sun and the colors of the trees and all the country roads. There were no roadside stands or gasoline pumps and no advertising signs. I remember the yellow trees in Weston and how a horse in front of the general store reared and broke his bridle. I remember the piles of pumpkins and squashes outside the barns near Sudbury and the carts full of apple barrels. I was tired when we got to Worcester, where we stopped for the night.

"Well," said Father in the hotel dining room, "you'll be there tomorrow."

I had never been with him for such a long time in my life, but we did not say much.

"I wish I were going with you," he said. "You see, I never went to boarding school. They were newfangled things in my day. Now everybody goes."

We did not reach school until about four the next afternoon. We were delayed by two blowouts and a puncture on the Springfield Road. All that road is paved and unfamiliar now, but when I was there last the school had not changed much. There were some new buildings, but that was all. There was the same smell of oil on the floor and the same impersonal and cleanly, but human, smell coming from the cubicles of the small boys' dormitory.

Parents were helping put things in bureau drawers and everyone was very cheerful. Father had taken me downstairs to shake hands with Mr. Ewing, and one of the Third Form boys had shown us where I was to live.

"Well," Father said, "I guess that's about all. You'll write me if you want anything, won't you?"

"Yes, sir."

"Well, all right," Father said. "Is there anything we've forgotten?"

"The coat hangers," I said.

"I'll send them by express," Father said, and he blew his nose. "That's all, isn't it?"

"Yes, sir."

"Don't bother to go down with me," Father said. "You'd better go to the lavatory and wash your face and hands — in good cold water. Use a lot of good cold water. There isn't anything else, is there?"

"No, I guess that's all," I answered.

"Well, behave yourself." My father looked around the dormitory and blew his nose again. "And have a good time. You're going to have a fine time."

"Yes, sir."

"And if you don't," Father said, "don't let anyone know it. Well, good-by, Harry."

If you have not prepared for college at one of the older and larger schools, with traditions and a recognized headmaster, you have missed a great experience. You have missed something fine in intimate companionship. You have missed that indefinable thing known as school spirit, which is more important than books or teaching, because it lasts when physics and algebra and Latin are forgotten. The other day I tried to read a page of Cicero and I could not get through a single line, although I got a B on my Latin entrance examination, but I can still remember the school hymn word for word. I am quite sure even today that I can tell, after a five minutes' talk with anyone, whether he attended a public or private school thirty years before. I believe that I can go even further than that. I can tell whether he went to a really good boarding school or to a second-rate one. The answer is always written in his voice and manner. That is why school is so enormously important.

I owe a debt of gratitude to my school, and I believe it was the best school then and it is the best school now. No matter what else has happened to me in the way of failure and disappointment I am glad that I went to St. Swithin's. More than once the particular thing I learned there, which you can call manners or attitude, for want of better words, has helped me in my darkest moments, and I have Mr. Ewing to thank for it, my old headmaster.

"In order to be a leader," Mr. Ewing used to say in chapel, "and to take the place which is made for you, you must learn first to obey and serve."

This sort of thing is hard to express to anyone who has never been there. I have tried to explain it to Bill King more than once. I told him on one occasion that I was sorry that he had not gone to St. Swithin's, that he would have been quite a different person if he had gone there.

"You're damned well right I would have," Bill said, "but I like to think I couldn't have stood it."

"You could have, Bill," I told him, "if you had started in the First Form. The way to get the most out of school is to start at the beginning. Very few boys are taken in after that, because they don't get the most out of it."

"You mean, they have minds of their own," Bill said.

"That isn't what I mean at all," I told him. "The Skipper can't do a proper job on a boy unless he has him all the way through."

"Skipper!" Bill said. "Can't you stop calling him the Skipper?"

"That's all right," I told him. "The graduates of any good school have a nickname for the headmaster. I wish you really knew the Skipper, Bill. If you really knew him you wouldn't indulge in so many half-truths."

"I do know him," Bill said. "I crossed the ocean with him once."

"That isn't really knowing him," I said. "You can only know the Skipper when he's up at school doing his job. He's different anywhere else."

"Wherever that old jellyfish is," Bill said, "he's a conceited, pandering poop."

"My God, Bill," I said, and I had to laugh. "You just don't know the Skipper. He hadn't been more than a few years out of Harvard when he came there. You should have seen him on the football field! The Skipper's sixty now and he still plays games."

"Mr. Chips," Bill said. "*Good-bye, Mr. Chips.*"

"And what's wrong with Mr. Chips?" I asked.

"What's wrong with Mr. Chips?" Bill said. "Frankly, everything was wrong with Mr. Chips."

"You aren't talking sense," I said. "I can think of nothing finer than Mr. Chips's last remark. 'Children? . . . I've had hundreds of them, and all of them are boys.'"

"Don't," Bill said. "You'll have to go away if you make me want to cry. Could anything be more unnatural than herding a lot of adolescent males together who ought to be with their parents and their sisters and their friends' sisters, learning the usual amenities of life?"

"The school wasn't unnatural," I said. "We were all able to see family life there, Bill, a good deal happier and more successful than what lots of us saw at home."

"How much did you see of it?" Bill asked.

"We used to see a lot of it," I said. "We were all brought up with the Skipper's children. Why, Mrs. Ewing always saw that every boy came in once a week to tea, and the Sixth Form always came in on Sundays for a pick-up supper."

"It sounds like a biological laboratory," Bill said. "It's like the neurologists at all those nervous-breakdown places. They have to have a happy married life or else they'll be fired. Well, go ahead. What did the Skipper teach you?"

"You can sneer at it all you like, Bill," I told him. "It doesn't affect me, because you don't understand. The Skipper had the guts to stand for what he stood for. That's more than either you or I have."

"We don't get a house and a salary for it," Bill said. "We don't get paid for having guts. Don't get mad, Harry. You couldn't help it. Most of us were sent away from home somewhere and made to adjust ourselves to some arbitrary, artificial world that was built up by some positive and not intelligent individual. The only thing you can do is to try to snap out of it. Say good-by to it fast. Good-by, Mr. Chips."

"There are a lot of things you never say good-by to," I said, "if you go to a first-rate school."

"Yes," Bill said, "that's true. Not when they catch you young."

"You have to have standards to live," I said.

69

"Did you ever meet a poor boy there?" Bill asked. "Did you ever learn that people are abused and hungry, or what a minimum wage is? Did you ever get outside and go downtown? Did anybody ever teach you what the other ninety-nine per cent of people think about?"

"You learn that later," I said. "I spent the happiest time of my life there, the most worth-while time. I wish I were back there now."

"The old subconscious desire," Bill said, "to crawl back into your mother's womb."

Now, I can be amused by people when they talk that way. I am even broad-minded enough to see their point of view, but there is nothing easier than to make fun of something that you do not understand.

I wish I might go back there again, because I did well at school. I was never one of the leaders. I never stood high in my form. I was too light for football, but of course I played it, because everyone had to play. I never did like baseball, but I wrote things for *The Crier,* the school paper. None of this meant very much, but I was an integral part of something — a part of a group.

I wish I could go back. Whenever autumn comes, even now, if I am in the country, I seem to be close to school. I still have all the indefinable sensations which mark the beginnings of a new year. I think of the fresh pages of new books and of the Upper Field and of the Lower Field, with their goalposts, and of the tennis courts and of the red and yellow of the maples. And I can see the Skipper, younger then.

"That was well played, Pulham," I can hear him saying. "Show fight, always show fight."

Every autumn I can see the faces of my form. Their names run through my mind, and their nicknames, and their physical peculiarities. It was a good form. Out of it came a banker and a state senator, two doctors and a scientist, a drunkard, and a good many brokers and lawyers. One was killed along the Meuse in the Argonne drive, and one was killed in a motor accident, and one has

70

died of heart failure — five of them have been divorced, two of them are dead-broke — on the whole not a bad record. I wish that I were back. I have often said that to myself before I have gone to sleep. I wish that I were back where there was someone like the Skipper to tell me what to do, someone who knew absolutely what was right and what was wrong, someone who had an answer to everything. There was always an answer at school, and a good answer. No matter what the world was like you could still play the game. I wish to God that I were back.

VII

It Never Helps to Talk About It

I was very much surprised once when my sister Mary told me that she used to hate my guts whenever I came back from School. It happened when I stopped in one afternoon perhaps a year ago with a paper for her to sign. It was a Saturday afternoon and Mary was just back from riding, still in her tweed coat and boots and breeches. Jim, her husband, was out somewhere and Mary asked if I wanted a cocktail. We each had several cocktails, a good deal more than we should have had, perhaps. I took them, because they seemed to be about all that Mary and I had in common that afternoon. Our lives had drifted a long way apart, but we each wanted to be agreeable.

"Take another one," Mary said. "It will put hair on your chest."

That speech of hers made me wonder what Mother would have said if she had been alive to hear her. Mary put her arm through mine and pulled me down on the sofa.

"You're not so bad when you loosen up," Mary said. "Have another drink. Put it down the hatch." And then for no reason that I can think of, unless it was the gin and vermouth, we were talking about the old days, just as though we still saw a lot of each other. That was how she happened to say that she always hated me when I came back from school.

"I was definitely maladjusted," Mary said. "That was why I had those screaming fits."

"You're still maladjusted," I told her.

"Father was all right," Mary said, "but I never could hit it off with Mother. I don't blame the Governor —"

"Now, look here, Mary — " I began.

"Is there any harm, sweetheart," Mary asked me, "in being frank every now and then? She actually told me once that sex was a cross you had to bear, one of women's burdens."

"Now, look here, Mary," I said.

"You were in love with her," Mary said, "it was all Œdipus."

"There was no one in the world sweeter than Mother," I told her, "and I'm not going to sit here — "

"Darling," Mary said, "why can't we talk about things frankly and naturally? It's fun."

"It isn't fun to throw mud at your parents," I said.

"They couldn't help it, Harry," Mary said. "It was all just subconscious, just like our mutual antipathy. Subconsciously we both hate each other, because we both started competing for our mother's love."

"My God," I said, "I don't hate you, Mary. I've always liked you very much."

"Those emotions are all mixed in together," Mary said. "I transferred my love to you even when I hated you."

"What are you talking about, Mary?" I asked her.

"I've been going to Doctor Stanwick," Mary said. "He gives me a lot of ideas about how to handle Jimmy."

"What's the matter with Jim?" I asked. "Aren't you getting on?"

"Never mind about Jim," Mary answered. "I was in love with Father and you were in love with Mother, and then I was in love with you and I hated you."

I could see even then that we had been drinking more than was good for either of us, and Mary began to laugh again. I put my glass down on the coffee table. I hoped that Jim would not come in.

"Mary," I said, "you're drunk."

"Oh, boo to you," Mary said. "Do you remember when I threw a rock at you at North Harbor? I did it because I was in love with you — just the way Mary Shelley was in love with Percy Bysshe." I

73

did not answer and Mary looked down at the toes of her riding boots. "And the funny thing about it was that we were all emotionally and sexually involved and none of us ever knew it."

That conversation was of course completely fantastic, but no more peculiar than others I have heard, now that everyone can talk frankly about everything.

"Now, Mary," I said, "we were a perfectly normal family."

"But I didn't say we weren't normal," Mary answered. "It's part of natural evolution to fall in love with your parents, but I'm frank to say I resent a good deal that they did. They were a total flop as child-rearers."

"Now, wait a minute, Mary," I said.

"Why wait?" Mary answered. "I'm not criticizing our parents any more than other parents. Most of them were silly, lazy and uncultivated. I only blame them because they never taught us anything. Whoever wrote the commandment about honoring them couldn't manage his own children, and besides, that generation completely ignored sex."

"Well," I told her, "I don't see that we get much further by recognizing it."

Mary turned her head toward me.

"Let's be frank," she said. "When did you first have a sexual experience?"

This startled me. I certainly did not want to tell her, and yet I did not want my sister to think I was afraid to face facts. I was not afraid. I simply did not want to face them.

"Well, I can make a pretty good guess," Mary said. "You learned a lot from Sylvia."

I sat up and then sank back. I did not look at her, but I knew that she was smiling in a way that I never liked. She was referring to our first cousin, Sylvia Knowles, who used to visit us in the summer at North Harbor.

"There was nothing about Sylvia," I said, "absolutely nothing." Mary began to laugh.

"That's right," she said. "A gentleman never tells, even if the little girl had pigtails. You used to go out in the bushes with Sylvia. You know you did."

"Look here," I said. "Suppose you get this straight. There was nothing about Sylvia, absolutely nothing."

"You never got to first base with her," Mary said. "I never implied that you did, darling. I know Sylvia. If it had been that little Mitchell girl who got fired from Miss Lacey's, she might have been a real help to you, but instead of that you picked out Sylvia, because all nice boys were afraid of the Mitchell girl. You used to go out in the bushes behind the rocks after supper, and I was madly jealous. That's why I threw a rock at you at North Harbor."

"My God, Mary," I said, "why shouldn't Sylvia and I have walked over by the rocks after supper?"

"Don't be so naïve," Mary said. "I always knew you did, and Hugh knew it, and all the maids knew it, and what's more Mother knew it too."

I felt my face growing red.

"There you are," Mary said. "Instead of treating the thing naturally as any sensible human being would, you're blushing. What did you and Sylvia use to do out there in the bushes?"

"You won't believe me," I said. "We just played a sort of game."

"Go on," said Mary softly. "What did you and Sylvia play?"

"All right," I said. "I'll tell you, just to show how wrong you are. We played a game called a chewing game. Sylvia thought of it."

"She did, did she?" Mary said.

"It wasn't anything," I told her. "We would take a piece of grass — the grass grew pretty long there — and we would tie a knot in the middle of the grass and then Sylvia would chew one end of the grass and I would chew the other. The game was to see who came up to the knot first. As a matter of fact, we were quite aware that it wasn't right, and then Mother caught us doing it — "

"That was because I told," Mary said.

"Oh," I said, "you did, did you? If you want to call that a 'sex experience' there it was. Sylvia and I never spoke to each other after that, not for years and years."

"Oh, God," said Mary, "what a life! Did you ever talk to Sylvia about it?"

"Why, no," I said. "Why should I?"

"Oh, Lord," said Mary. "Don't you see the awful things it did to you — being given a sense of guilt over chewing a blade of grass?"

"It didn't do anything," I said, and then I asked a question which I should not have asked except for the Martinis. "What about your own sex life?" I asked. "When did you have the initial sexual experience, Mary?"

Mary threw her arm around my neck and buried her head against my shoulder. I was startled, because she was very seldom demonstrative. The shoulders of her tweed riding coat were shaking, and at first I thought she was laughing.

"Mary, you're drunk," I said.

"I know I am," said Mary, "and I don't care. I never knew anything about anything until the war. When I was eighteen I used to think that babies came by rubbing the wedding ring."

"You're exaggerating," I said.

"I'm not," said Mary. "Before God I'm not, because you and I were nice and everyone was nice. They left us little babes in the woods. To hell with them — to hell with them!"

I should have known that Mary could not hold her liquor.

"Just forget about it, Mary," I said. "Sex isn't important if you take it naturally."

"Naturally!" Mary said, and she choked. "Did anyone ever let us?"

The front door downstairs slammed and Mary straightened up and shook her hair back.

"There's Jim," she said. "Where's that God-damned paper, Harry, and what's the date?"

"What was Jim's first sexual experience?" I asked.

"Oh, shut up," said Mary. "Anything about sex always makes Jim angry. Harry, please shut up."

My brother-in-law came in, walking heavily. Jim was somewhat overweight, and the small dinosaur which he wore on his watch chain shone brightly.

76

"Where have you been keeping yourself?" Jim asked. "How is Kay?"

"Kay's fine," I said.

"We've all got to get together sometime," Jim said, "and talk about the old days at North Harbor."

"Yes," I said, "we ought to get together."

I can remember it all very clearly, although I must have tried for years to forget it. Sylvia was much nicer than Mary — gentler, prettier, and she had no fits of temper. The white dress that she always put on after supper was very much neater and fluffier than Mary's, and she had very soft gold hair in two braids and mild blue eyes. I liked her first when I found that she was not afraid to catch crabs off the pier and she never screamed the way Mary did. We became friends one day when Mary was angry about something and stayed in her room and later we used to walk around together a good deal and I tried to show her how to skip stones on the water.

"I know a game," Sylvia said. "I saw some people playing it at a picnic. I'll show you if you come behind the rocks. It's a secret."

"Why do we have to go behind the rocks?" I asked.

"Because it's a secret," Sylvia said, "and there's a good deal of spit in it."

We looked at each other shyly. We were entirely alone, nothing but the tall grass and the singing of the crickets.

"It's just a game," Sylvia said. "You see, you take a piece of grass and tie a knot — " We knelt down behind the rock and Sylvia looked at me.

"I wouldn't do this with anyone but you," she said.

I remember the singing of the crickets. I never realized how pretty she was. I could understand why it was a thing not to be done in public.

"Let's do it again," I said.

"All right," said Sylvia. "We'll do it three times — and we'll do it three times every day after supper, but you mustn't tell anyone."

"No," I said, "I won't."

"Children," I can hear Mother calling to me still, "whatever are you doing behind the rocks? You'd better come in now."

I can never understand why I felt deeply humiliated. It was not anything she said.

"It's cold behind the rocks after supper," Mother said. "Sylvia, Mary's been looking for you. Harry, you can come with me and help me pick nasturtiums. Isn't it beautiful when the sun's going down?"

"Yes," I said.

"You're getting to be such a big boy," Mother said.

I did not answer. I looked at Sylvia running toward the house.

"Harry," Mother said, "you're always gentle with girls, aren't you? Girls aren't very strong. Girls are different from boys, and Sylvia is your cousin. You must always be gentle with Sylvia."

"Yes," I said.

I looked down at the ground. I could feel her watching me. I could not have looked at her if I had tried. I actually wished that I were dead.

"It's better," Mother said, "not to be alone with girls. Harry, will you promise me — don't be alone with Sylvia again?"

"All right," I said.

"Harry," she said, "what makes you speak so crossly?"

"Leave me alone," I said. "Just leave me alone."

"Harry," Mother answered, "I'll have to speak to Father."

"Leave me alone," I shouted. "Leave me alone!" And I turned and ran away.

I do not know whether she ever spoke to Father, but it was as close as I ever came with either of them to a discussion of sex.

VIII

May I Have This Dance?

"Well, Harry," Father used to say when I was about sixteen, "what do you read at school?"

And I would tell him that we were reading *Macbeth* or *The Mill on the Floss.*

"We don't have much time to get together," he told me once. "I used to see a good deal more of my father when I was your age, because I came home every night. There are a lot of things I ought to tell you."

Father himself was like required reading, something which you faced with a sense of duty and were rather surprised if it interested you. He was like *Ivanhoe* and *Silas Marner* and Goldsmith's *Vicar of Wakefield* with footnotes in the back, and the *Roger de Coverley Papers* and Southey's *Life of Nelson* and Milton's *L'Allegro* and Tennyson's *Princess.* In vacation time he was like the lists of suggested summer reading, something to be gone through with, but something, I knew, that was not connected with my real interests. He was not like Dumas or like Winston Churchill's *Crossing,* or like the romances of Robert W. Chambers where girls sometimes appeared in the hero's bedroom in negligee. He was not contemporary or sprightly. At any rate, there was not much time for Father and not much time for reading either.

All my activities were too carefully planned to allow for an interruption such as Father. My friends and I were on a schedule at school and on vacation. Even when we were at home we were being caught up in a manner of living which was beyond our parents' control. There were sailing lessons with a man who was known as "the Captain." There was a tennis lesson twice a week at the country club and a golf lesson. In the winter vacations there were dances. It seems to me whenever I was at home that I was always going somewhere or getting ready to go somewhere.

But I never guessed that I was following a line from which I could not turn. If anybody had told me when I met Cornelia Motford first that I was going to marry her I should have been very much surprised. I met Cornelia at the Junior Bradbury Dances, the second series that started close to the cradle and ended in the vicinity of the grave. In fact, only two years ago Cornelia and I were asked to subscribe to the Senior Bradbury Supper Dances. If we had accepted we would have seen the same faces that we had seen at the Baby Bradburys almost thirty years before.

"Don't you remember," Kay asked me, "what a good time we had at the Junior Bradburys?"

"I never had a good time," I said.

"You always looked awfully cross," Kay said, "and you had two pimples on your forehead and one on your chin."

Then I laughed, although it was not entirely courteous.

"I was cross," I said, "because I had to dance with you. When Mrs. Pringle caught me, I couldn't do anything else, could I? 'Isn't some nice boy going to dance with the little Motford girl? Where's a nice boy? There's a nice boy,' and then Mrs. Pringle caught me."

"I always had everyone I wanted to dance with," Kay said.

"Mrs. Pringle fixed that up," I told her. "You were sweet, but no one wanted to dance with you."

Mrs. Pringle was large and heavy, in a black dress with spangles, and she had a black ostrich fan and diamond earrings and a prehensile sort of nose. Mrs. Pringle headed the committee for the Junior Bradburys and you could not get in if Mrs. Pringle did not want you.

I suppose that hall must still be the same with the boys' coatroom on one side of the entrance and the girls' coatroom on the other and the supper room beneath in the cellar. You were not allowed to stay in the coatroom long, because Mr. Pringle was sent every fifteen minutes or so to clear out the boys and Mrs. Pringle did the same for the girls.

The hall was a great rectangle of polished oak on which they sprinkled granulated wax just before the evening started. Its ceiling was decorated with paper ribbons and paper bells. There was a piano in one corner and some small chairs and racks for the musicians and down at another corner was a group of gold chairs, technically known as the dump, where you left your partner after the number was ended. Along one wall, placed upon a strip of carpet, were several more comfortable seats where Mrs. Pringle sat when she was not busy with other arrangements, as did also Mrs. Halstead and Mrs. Jennings and two or three other members of the committee. Above the entrance door there was a balcony the front rows of which were occupied by the girls' mothers and behind were paid chaperones and behind these were governesses. The boys stood under the balcony, some in blue suits and some of the more sophisticated in tuxedos. There was a certain amount of camaraderie and small talk among us and we used to discuss in undertones the various advantages of the girls and to classify them vulgarly as Peaches or Lemons or Pills. It was fashionable to assume an air of boredom, as too much interest made you conspicuous.

I remember the evening very well, because it was the first time that I fell in love, and I remember all the tunes that were played from "The Red Mill" and "The Dollar Princess." I was standing under the balcony with Joe Bingham and some of the other members of my form at school.

"Hello, there, Harry," Joe said. "Been having a nice vacation?"

"Yes, fine."

"How many times have you been to the theater?"

"Four times."

"I've been five times."

"Well, I'm going tomorrow afternoon," I said.

"Who's taking you?" Joe asked.

"The Abbotts."

"Oh," Joe said. "I bet they don't give you anything to eat afterwards, except an ice cream hen in spun sugar. Have you been to Fox's Joke Shop?"

"No," I said.

"You can buy tin bedbugs there, and look what I bought."

"What?" I asked.

Joe pulled a miniature chamberpot from his pocket on which was written in gold letters "Go 'way back and sit down."

"Put that away," I said, "or you'll get fired out of here, Joe." Joe put it away.

"We'll show it later to some of them in the coatroom," he said.

"You can. I won't," I said. Joe glanced knowingly about the room and buttoned his white gloves.

"Quite a bunch of pills tonight," he said, "quite a bunch of pills."

The girls sitting across the room were dressed in pink or blue or white. They wore long white gloves and black silk stockings and low-heeled patent leather slippers and their hair was not quite up and not quite down.

With the first strains of the music we started across the room, walking fast, but not running. Someone pushed me and I slid into Joe and I saw Mrs. Pringle frowning at me, and then I was standing in front of a girl whom I had never seen before. She was sitting there with her hands folded and the orchestra was playing "My Hero." She wore high heels and her hair was entirely up, faintly reddish, all done in little coils. Her eyes were deep violet and her lips and cheeks were much redder than the other girls', which makes me wonder if she used lipstick and rouge, but on the whole I do not believe that this could have been possible.

"I don't think we ought to dance," she said, "because I haven't met you," and then she added something that was charming, "but we might pretend we've met each other."

She stood up and I put my arm around her, gingerly, supporting the small of her back with my gloved hand. Her left hand rested on my shoulder in the approved defensive attitude and our other hands met beneath our gloves. She smelled of perfume. No other girl I had ever danced with had smelled of perfume.

"What's your name?" she asked. "Mine is Betty Wayne. I come from New York."

"I didn't think you came from here," I said.

"No," she said. "Do you come from here?"

"Yes," I answered. "I go to St. Swithin's School."

"That's a nice school. Do you know a boy there named Joe Bingham?"

"Yes," I said.

It was shocking that his name should have been brought up when I considered the object in his pocket. We bumped into another couple hard. It was Joe Bingham.

"Joe is a very bad dancer," I said.

"Do you like to talk when you dance?" she asked. "I always talk, or else I sing. Would you like to hear me sing?"

"All right," I said.

"My hero," she sang, "my heart is true."

It was not like the Junior Bradburys. It could not be the Junior Bradburys.

"I knew you didn't come from around here," I said.

She did not answer, but hummed mysteriously beneath her breath.

"New York is a fine place," I said.

"Yes," she answered.

"I've been there, of course," I said.

"Yes," she answered, "of course."

And then the music stopped and she dropped my hand and I took my glove away from the small of her back.

"Well," I said, "thank you very much."

"Thank you," she said, "Harry," and then it was too late to ask her where she was staying. I never spoke to her again nor have I ever seen her. I walked away from the dump and was standing dazedly thinking of her, when the music began again, and that was how Mrs. Pringle caught me

"Here's a nice boy," Mrs. Pringle said and seized my arm. "No one's dancing with Cornelia Motford and no one's having supper with her."

"May I have this dance?" I asked.

"Yes," Cornelia said. Her hair was straight and black and tied up behind with a blue bow. She was in a white starched dress and her hands were too large. Her nose was turned up, her eyes were brown and her face was white.

"Where do you go to school?" she asked. The orchestra was playing, "Old New York where the peach crop is always fine."

"St. Swithin's," I said.

"Do you like dogs?"

"Yes," I said.

"I've got a dog," Cornelia said, "a cocker. His name is Floppsy. Don't try to slide so much and keep time to the music — one, two, three; one, two, three."

After that we said almost nothing, and yet there I was, dancing with the girl I was going to marry. I might have married any girl in that room except Betty Wayne.

Kay spoke to me about it once a long while afterwards.

"Do you remember when I first met you," she asked, "at the Junior Bradburys? We didn't say much, did we?"

"No," I said, "not much."

"It's funny we ever got married. Don't you think it was romantic that we met at the Junior Bradburys?"

IX

Adventures in Companionship

I always say that Harvard is the most democratic institution in the world, but secretly I do not believe it, because all my friends, with the exception of Bill King, were the friends I made at school. For instance, even today when I see a man who is too carefully groomed my emotions move in an old instinctive groove. Again, if I meet a man who is too anxious to please I feel that he is trying to "suck up." There was nothing more undesirable back at Harvard than to be someone who "sucked up." You did not have to do it if you were the right sort of person.

Joe Bingham and I roomed together all through Harvard. We were in Randolph during our freshman year and other members of our form at St. Swithin's lived in the same entry. Bo-jo Brown and Sam Green were right across the hall and they used to pass a football to each other every morning. Sam, even when he studied, used to balance a football in his hand. That was why his forward passing came to be phenomenal in his last two years at college. Steve Rawley was in that entry too, and was the sort of person the book agents were always after. He bought Balzac's *Droll Stories* and *The Human Comedy* bound in silk and sets of Fielding and Smollett and Edgar Allan Poe. He used to hide in our room when the book agents came to collect their installments. Then there were Bob Carroll and Pink Stevens. Bob had been the funny boy of our crowd. He used to wrap himself in bath towels and recite "Horatius at the Bridge" and how the Highwayman came riding up to the old inn door and how Gunga Din hoped you liked your drink. He could also play all the songs from "The Pink Lady" and "The Quaker Girl."

It is rather startling to go to Harvard now and see what has happened to Mt. Auburn Street. I wonder if the street Arabs scramble for pennies any more. The old eating places are gone and most of the shops are changed. Harvard's bright color has faded in my memory. It has been washed out like my childhood, very flat.

What I remember best about it is Bill King, and Bill too is entirely different now. It has always amazed me that I ever got to know him, that is, very well. I was alone in my room one autumn afternoon our freshman year, finishing my daily theme for English A, when he knocked. The door was opened by a thin boy in a gray suit who was a complete stranger. It was unusual for strangers to appear in our entry. His clothes were perfectly all right and so were his soft shirt and tie. It must have been his manner that told me he had not gone to one of the larger schools.

"Is your name Pulham?" he asked.

"Yes," I said.

"Oh, well, to hell with it," he said. "Do you mind if I sit down?"

I did not mind if he sat down, exactly. Yet at the same time I did not know what good it would do. He was not my type of person.

"Did you want to see me?" I asked.

He kept looking at me as if he could not find an answer. We were both half grown up then and correspondingly inadequate.

"No," he said. "I've been looking for people whose names begin with P for two hours, and to hell with it."

"Oh," I said, "you mean you're out for something."

"That's what they call it, isn't it," he answered, " 'out for something'? They say the way to get to know people here is to go out for something. I'm asking everybody whose name begins with P if he'd like to act in the Dramatic Club."

"Oh, I couldn't do that," I said. It seemed to end the conversation, but he still sat there.

"You don't mind if I sit here, do you?" he asked. "I just want to talk to someone. I've been around here for two months and no one's spoken to me."

"Where did you go to school?" I asked.

86

"In New Jersey," he said.

"Oh," I said, "New Jersey."

"Well, what the hell's wrong with that?" he asked.

"Aren't there any other people from your school?" I asked him.

"No," he said, "not anybody. And I've always heard what a good time you had at college."

"What's your name?" I asked.

"King," he said, "Bill King."

"It's just that you don't know anybody," I said.

"Well, what I'm asking you," he answered, "is how I get to know anybody in this place? Will you come in town with me and go to dinner?"

Before I could answer he continued speaking, quickly.

"I know a lot of places in town. I spend a lot of time down in the North End. There's an old hotel where they have a parrot and a dog in the dining room. Listen, is there anything wrong in my asking you to go down there to dinner? Well, never mind. I just asked you."

Then something in the way he said it made me ashamed of myself.

"Thanks," I said. "I'd like to go."

He stood up.

"That's nice of you," he said. He paused and swallowed. "You're the first person I've seen here who isn't a nickel-plated son of a bitch."

I had an uneasy feeling that I was doing something out of the ordinary, that I was associating with someone dubious, but still I was pleased.

Joe Bingham came in a moment later and looked at Bill King distrustfully, just as I had looked at him.

"This is a friend of mine, Mr. King," I said.

"Oh," Joe said, "hello."

Then Bo-jo Brown came in.

"Hello, you bastards," he began, but of course he stopped when he saw Bill King.

"This is a friend of mine, Mr. King," I said.

87

"Oh," said Bo-jo, "I thought it was the book salesman. Are you any relation to Kinkey King?"

Bill King shook his head.

"All right," Bo-jo said. "I didn't think you were. Who the hell are you anyway? I've never seen you anywhere."

Then Steve Rawley came in, and Bob Carroll. They both looked at Bill King too, but I don't think they ever knew that I did not really know him, for now it was too late to tell them.

I had never known anything exactly like that evening with Bill King. We went to a part of Boston that was entirely new to me, off Scollay Square and through the crowded streets of the North End. Once he was there Bill seemed entirely at home. The New England House, which has disappeared long ago, was downtown beyond the dimly lighted market district. Downstairs where they had sawdust on the floor men were drinking ale in soiled butchers' aprons, and upstairs in the dining room an old lady sat in a corner behind a desk with a gray parrot hanging above her, and a fat, mangy dog sniffed at you. There were long tables with bread and butter and jars of pickles in the center, and big waitresses who shrieked orders down the dumbwaiters into the kitchen. I had never seen anything like it, but Bill King seemed to know it very well. Afterwards we went to a place where we drank ale out of pewter mugs, and after that we went to a moving picture and vaudeville show, where there was a man who did tricks on roller skates and where the audience joined in singing popular songs.

Bill could get on perfectly well anywhere, even when I took him home to Sunday dinner. The anxiety of my parents to meet my friends often caused me a profound embarrassment, for I knew how I felt about most of my friends' parents when I saw them. They were almost invariably peculiar, presenting a display of uncouth mannerisms and inanities of thought. I did not want anyone to feel that way about my family, but Father and Mother kept insisting that I bring some friend home for Sunday lunch. My main reason for bringing Bill King must have been that he did not know anyone and that his opinion would be harmless.

88

I took him to the house on Marlborough Street, after the family had moved in from Westwood for the winter. Hugh opened the door and smiled at me and said, "Good morning, Master Harry," and then he added in a tone that had certain implications, "You look tired. You must have been studying hard all week."

I knew that I looked tired, because I had been on what was known as a "party" with Pink Stevens the night before. I had not been able to eat my breakfast and I had no appetite for lunch.

"I'm not tired," I said.

"You'd better have some spirits of ammonia before your father sees you, Master Harry. You have no idea how you look, a horrible sight," Hugh said.

I took Bill into the downstairs parlor, where the Inness landscape hung over the mantelpiece and where the French chairs always stood in uncomfortable rows.

"Hugh is always that way," I said to Bill. "I don't look badly, do I?"

I often wished that the family did not have a butler. It was too ostentatious, too much like the parlor. Bill and I stood there, looking at the little tables and the pictures, and then I heard steps on the stairs. Mother came in first in a billowy purple dress with a very high neck.

"Kiss me, dear," she said. "Harry darling, you look so tired. Sometimes we really think that Harry tries to conceal us from his friends, Mr. King. Do you try to conceal your mother from your friends?"

"My mother's dead," Bill said.

"Oh," Mother said, "oh," and she sat down on the settle beside the fireplace where the cannel coal was burning. "Sit beside me, Harry, and do sit down, Mr. King. Do you think Harry works too hard?"

"He's been studying a good deal," Bill said.

"Harry, dear," she said, and she took my hand. "I'm sorry you lost your mother, Mr. King. Mothers mean so much. Harry and I have always been such friends."

I think she really meant it. I knew it was what she had always

89

wanted. Bill King sat down carefully on one of the French chairs.

"You don't have to tell me what you've been doing all the week," Mother said to me, "because I know. Mrs. Motford said you danced with Kay twice on Thursday night — and now I have a surprise for you. Kay's coming to lunch."

"Coming to lunch?" I repeated. "Coming to lunch here?"

"Why, you act as though you weren't pleased, darling," Mother said. "I don't see what gets into boys. Do you know Kay Motford, Mr. King?"

"No," Bill said, "I'm afraid I don't."

"She's such a dear," Mother said, "a dear, sensible girl. She's one of those girls who doesn't think about herself, or think about her looks. She thinks of other people."

"She must be very nice," Bill said. "That's a beautiful Inness, Mrs. Pulham."

"Oh," Mother said, "do you know about pictures, Mr. King? I've always loved that picture, I've always loved the sky." And then she was talking to Bill King about Inness. It seemed incredible to me that Bill King should wish to talk about Inness, but from Inness he went on to Mr. Sargent, and then Father came downstairs.

"What are we waiting for?" Father asked. "Where's lunch? Where's Mary?" and he walked out into the hall.

"Mary," he shouted. I winced slightly. I had hoped that he would not shout.

"John," Mother said, "this is Mr. King. We're waiting lunch because Cornelia Motford's coming."

"Oh," said Father, "hello, King. Who in blazes is Cornelia Motford?"

"She's a friend of Harry's, dear," Mother said. "You remember Cornelia, the Cecil Motfords' girl."

Father began to blow his nose loudly. I wished that he would not blow his nose.

"She isn't a friend of mine," I said. "I just happen to know her, that's all."

Father began to laugh knowingly.

"She isn't a friend of yours," he said, "but you asked her to lunch?"

"I didn't know she was coming to lunch," I said. "Kay Motford is a lemon, if you want to know."

"Then why is she coming to lunch?" he asked.

"I don't know why," I said, "except Mother asked her."

"Well, I don't see what all the fuss is about," Father said, and he blew his nose. "Where's Hugh? Where's the sherry?"

"John —" Mother began.

"I guess Harry and Mr. King are old enough to have a glass of sherry," my father said. "All the boys at Harvard drink, don't they, Mr. King?"

Then Mary came downstairs. She had pigtails and a white dress halfway below her knees and her complexion was bad. She curtsied when she was introduced to Bill, and then she looked at me and grinned.

"Harry's girl is coming to lunch," she said.

"Mary," my mother said, "Mary!"

"Look here," I began, "if you want to know —" I stopped because the doorbell rang, and I felt like the victim of a hideous conspiracy.

Kay looked like an illustration of "The Little Colonel When Her Knight Came Riding." Her hair was pulled back tight in a bun, her shirt waist was as stiffly starched as a nurse's uniform. She was thin, too thin, but her face was pudgy, and her brown eyes were bright and her nose was shining.

"Hello, Mrs. Pulham," she said. "I've been out walking with the dogs."

Then Hugh came in with some glasses on his silver tray, and five minutes later we were in the dining room.

"Well," Father called when we sat down, "what are we waiting for?"

"Grace, dear," Mother said. "You forgot it."

"Oh, yes," Father said. "For what we are about to receive may the Lord make us truly thankful. For Christ's sake. Amen."

It has always seemed to me that family luncheons have nothing to do with anything else in existence. We were all acting, speaking set lines all the time we were at table, and it was the same in the library upstairs. I know the way Father felt now. First he tried to talk about football and then about how different Harvard was when he was there; and then he hit upon the subject of President Taft and Theodore Roosevelt. Father was saying that Theodore Roosevelt was a social menace and that his attack upon self-respecting men, who had made the nation what it was, broke down confidence. Bill agreed, but I do not think he meant it. Bill was always looking at people and listening.

"Now, that's a sensible boy," my father told me afterward, "the first sensible friend you've ever brought around."

I could not see why, because Bill had not said anything.

"He's such a gentleman," Mother said. "He's the nicest boy I've seen."

I don't know why she thought he was nice, except that he spoke about Inness in the parlor.

It was my definite conviction that the family had never behaved worse, that they had never been more obtuse and dull. I explained to Bill that Sunday lunch was always awful.

"It's like home," Bill said, "it's like home anywhere."

"Is it that way where you live?" I asked.

"It's that way anywhere. God Almighty, it's sad."

"Why is it sad?" I asked.

"It's sad," Bill said, "because they try so hard. It's sad because we don't like anything they do. We're thinking about one sort of thing, and they're thinking about something else."

It was the first time I realized that Bill was clever.

"Your mother thought she could make you happy by asking that little what's-her-name to lunch," he went on.

That is the way Bill referred to Kay, as a little what's-her-name.

"It's sad," Bill King said, "because your father is so fond of you that he's shy. It's sad because it's all the way that everything goes."

Bill would actually have got on very well at Harvard, I think, if he had cared about trying. It was true that he did not have any connections, but if he had gone out for something besides the Dramatic Club, such as the *Lampoon* or even the *Crimson,* and if he had bothered with the people to whom I introduced him and who usually liked him, he would very possibly have made a Club. The trouble was that he did not seem to care to make the effort. When Kay Motford asked him to her coming-out party at the Somerset, for instance, he refused the invitation, and it was the same when he was asked to the Bradburys. At the time when everyone was worrying about Clubs he never bothered to be seen with the right people; he never bothered to do the right thing.

That attitude of his made me very angry once shortly after Bo-jo Brown had thrown out his hip in the game with Dartmouth our junior year. Bo-jo would hobble down on his crutch to watch the football practice, but he knew that he would not be well enough to play against Yale. Everyone in our entry felt very badly for him. Bo-jo would sit in his room with his crutch beside him and watch Sam Green balancing a football in his hand while he studied for his hour examinations, and if anybody came in Bo-jo would tell exactly how it happened.

"Listen, boys," he would say, "I want you to get this straight. There isn't anyone in the world, not anyone, who could wrench the ligaments in my hip if I was ready for them. That Dartmouth bastard didn't like me. He was out to get me. He said he was. No one living can hurt me when I'm ready."

"That's right, Bo-jo," everybody said. "That's the boy, Bo-jo."

"Now, listen," Bo-jo said. "Here's the way it happened, and if you don't believe it, Sam Green will tell you. You saw it, Sam."

"That's right," said Sam. "I saw it, Bo-jo. We were right on the ten-yard line."

We were all on the ten-yard line as soon as Bo-jo and Sam began talking.

93

"And Max called the play through me. He always calls it through me if he wants first down, and I got that slob off his feet and we made five yards. We'd have made ten yards, Sam, if you'd been carrying the ball."

"Oh, no," said Sam. "I don't think so, Bo-jo."

"You would have. There was a hole a mile wide. Well, the whistle blew. The play was over. I was just standing up, relaxed, perfectly relaxed, and he pulled my leg and I went down on top of him."

"How do you mean, he pulled your leg?" I asked.

"My God," said Bo-jo, "don't you understand English? I was standing up, perfectly relaxed, and I started to step over him, and he said I stamped on him. You know damn well I didn't stamp on him, did I, Sam? I was just stepping over him to get out of his way."

"That's right, Bo-jo," said Sam. "He was laid out flat. Why should you want to stamp on him?"

"Listen, boys," Bo-jo said. "I was just walking over him, relaxed, and he grabbed my leg. He got me off my balance, and then the ligaments went, and I sat down on his head. I could feel the whole hip go, just because I wasn't ready for him. And then do you know what he did?"

"What?" I asked. Bo-jo always wanted somebody to ask him.

"He bit me," he said. "That's what they do at Dartmouth."

"Bit you?" someone repeated, and that was what Bo-jo wanted.

"You don't believe it, do you? Well, his teeth marks are still there. Take my pants down if you don't believe it. Somebody help me take down my pants." It was an interesting exhibit. There was no doubt that someone had bitten him.

"Well, that's the way it is, boys," Bo-jo said. "And I don't know what's going to happen now with Yale."

Those were the days when it was important to beat Yale, and the night before the game an unusual thing happened. Bo-jo shouted through the entry at seven in the evening.

"Hey," Bo-jo shouted, "everyone come in here."

Bill King was in my room at the time and he came too. Bo-jo was sitting in his morris chair and Sam Green was standing beside him.

"Hello, boys," Bo-jo said. "Hello, King. You don't have to go away. The team is coming up. Sammy Lee's bringing them, and I'd sort of like my friends around."

We all stood against the wall, looking at Bo-jo Brown. We all knew that it was an unusual honor. It was a privilege to be standing there, a privilege to be asked to witness such a scene.

"It's a lot of bunk, of course," Bo-jo said, "but I'd sort of like you boys around."

"Maybe I'd better go," Bill King suggested. "There'll be a lot of people."

"Hell, no," said Bo-jo. "Stay around as long as you're here."

"They're coming now," said Sam.

We could hear the footsteps in the entry, and the hall and Bo-jo's room were filled with people. The assistant coach, Sammy Lee, came first, an older man who had a beefy square face and blue eyes and very short hair.

"How's it going, Bo-jo?" he said. "I brought the boys around to see you." He put his hand on Bo-jo's shoulder and turned and addressed the group.

"Well, men," he said, "here's Bo-jo Brown, and I guess we all know how we feel about Bo-jo Brown. We all know that Bo-jo won't be in there with us tomorrow, and we all know what that means. But there's one thing that all of you men can do. I want you all to go up and shake hands with Bo-jo Brown and tell him that we're going to beat the living hell out of Yale tomorrow, even if he isn't there. All right, men. Shake hands."

I felt my breath catch and I felt a lump in my throat. It was hard not to be moved by the simple solemnity of the scene. As the team filed past him, mumbling a few broken words, Bo-jo's face grew red.

"Do you want to say something to them, Bo-jo?" Sam Lee asked.

Bo-jo seized his crutch and stood up and leaned against it. It seemed hardly decent to be present, because his eyes were bright with tears.

"All I can say is," Bo-jo said, "give 'em hell. To hell with Yale." And then his voice broke in a sob, and he sat down and covered his face.

"Men," Sam Lee said, "I guess we know how we all feel. How about it? Three times three for Brown!"

I do not know if they have such scenes now, but I know that I was weeping and that I was not ashamed of it any more than Bo-jo. We tiptoed away, softly and reverently, and I found myself in my own room with Joe Bingham and Bill King.

"God," Joe Bingham said, "that's something I'll never forget."

Bill King lighted a cigarette.

"I won't forget it either," he said. "It makes me want to puke."

"What?" I said. "What do you mean, Bill?"

"It makes me want to puke," Bill said.

I was looking at Joe Bingham; his face was blank and shocked. Bill King puffed at his cigarette.

"Now, wait a minute before you speak," he said. "Wait and try to think what there is to cry about. Bo-jo Brown isn't going to die, is he? What is there to cry about? Suppose we don't beat Yale, what difference does it make? It's only a football game."

Joe Bingham found his voice first.

"I never thought," Joe said, "that you were such a son of a bitch. And if you don't like what I say, we can finish it off right now."

Bill King flicked the ash from his cigarette.

"He doesn't really mean that, Joe," I said. "You're just trying to get a rise out of us, aren't you, Bill?"

"You know damn well I'm right," Bill said. "What difference does it make?"

"It makes a lot of difference if anyone goes around talking like that," I said. "People won't like you, Bill. You'll get in wrong. You'll make a fool of yourself."

"You know I'm right," Bill King said. "Both of you really know it."

"It isn't the right spirit," I said.

"To hell with it," Bill King said. "Good night, boys."

Joe Bingham and I must have been glad of each other's company after Bill King had left.

"Harry," Joe said.

"What?" I asked.

"Why don't you say something?"

"I'm thinking," I said.

"Do you know what I think?" Joe Bingham said. "I think he's a sorehead."

"Maybe he is," I said.

"My God," Joe Bingham said. "I wish we'd had him at school. I wish the Skipper could have heard him. We'd have paddled his tail off and put him under the pump."

"Yes," I said, "I guess we would have."

"But I suppose there are a lot of radical bastards all over the place who aren't getting anything out of college," he added, "who just don't know what it means. Harry, do you know I'm kind of sorry for him? He'd have been all right if he'd had hell beaten out of him in some good school."

X

Boys and Girls Together

Bill asked me to come down with him to New Jersey during the Christmas holidays, and I do not remember much about it, except that Bill lived very simply with his father and a maiden aunt. Bill's father was an architect, a thin, gray-headed man with rheumatism, who spoke in a querulous voice. They lived in a shabby, brown-shingled house on a small suburban plot, and they had only one maid. I imagine now, though I did not notice then, that Bill's Aunt Ellie helped with a good deal of the work, when she was not reading or playing bridge or mending. We used to play bridge every night and Aunt Ellie and Bill's father would quarrel over the hands, and the quarrel usually was resumed at breakfast lasting until Mr. King took the 8:15 for town. Bill once told Aunt Ellie that she looked like the queen of spades, and she did have that same expression, particularly when she was dressed in black, and she never forgot a card. We seldom played cards at home, and almost never bridge, because Mother always said that bridge was a waste of time, that it was much better to have interesting conversation.

I thought the first night I stayed there that I should hate the visit, but instead I got to like it very much. I liked the things that both Miss King and Mr. King said, and I liked the way they treated us as though we were grown up. When he was not playing bridge, Bill's father was usually reading and at table he talked rapidly. He explained that he did so because he would rather hear himself talk than listen to us. When the soup came on at dinner he would say that the Arabs were an interesting race and would continue about Arabia until dessert.

"Bill doesn't know anything," he used to say. "He never reads."
"The old man's hip hurts him," Bill explained.

I do remember particularly one thing Bill's father said.

"Bill's clever. He inherits that from me. I'm almost the cleverest man I know. I can learn without working, just like Bill. I'm so facile that I know that all my associates are idiots. That's why I'm where I am now — nowhere; because I've always been too clever and too contemptuous. You can wait and see, if you don't quarrel with him, what it will do to Bill."

Bill and I spent several evenings in New York and there was a spirit in the city which I think was more American than it is now. It was a city undisturbed by war and income taxes — a city that ran without traffic lights. There were big private houses on Fifth Avenue, and Murray Hill was still a residential district, and there were all sorts of places where you could go to dinner, and barrooms where there were only men. "Peg o' My Heart" was playing, and "The Firefly." When I think of it I always think of music, and now the popular tunes, which still run through my thoughts, are about all that are left of it — "You Great Big Beautiful Doll," "Alexander's Ragtime Band," "That Haunting Melody," "Doing That Society Bear." That last song was all about cuddling up close to your Vanderbilt and wrapping me up in a beautiful diamond quilt, and about Hetty Green and Rockefeller, and about how Mr. Gould began to holler "Let him spend another dollar." There were still horses on Fifth Avenue when we sang those tunes. There was still a feeling of permanence, a serene belief that Mr. Gould would always have another dollar.

Yet in all that time events were moving which we did not notice much: the Middle West was going dry; the amendment for the income tax was passed; there were rumors of labor trouble and rumors of war, and the Marines landed in Veracruz. But it must be that such things do not matter when you are young. Everything was simple then, and I often wish I were back in that time, because it was the time for which I was trained to live.

Bill spent a week with us in North Harbor the summer the World

99

War started. But the beginning of the war was not as important to me as Mother's not being well. It was her heart the doctor said, and she was to be quiet and she could only go up and down stairs once a day. I saw more of her that summer than I had ever seen, because she was always asking for me. I used to sit in her room for two hours every afternoon and read her Jane Austen and Trollope. And sometimes when I stopped reading I would find her looking at me, strangely, as though she did not know me.

"What are you thinking about, Mother?" I asked her once.

"About you," she said, "and how they took you away. I was thinking about that day you went to school. That was when they took you away. Do you remember what good times we used to have?"

I remembered them and I told her so.

"You won't forget them, will you?" she asked me.

"No," I said, "I won't."

"Tell me about your friends," she said. "You have so many friends."

I told her about Joe Bingham and Bo-jo Brown and all the rest of them, but I did not tell her everything and probably she knew it.

"Harry," she asked, "do you ever see Kay Motford?"

"Mother," I said, "please don't worry about Kay Motford."

"I'm not worried, darling," Mother said, "but don't you think it would be nicer if you saw more of a sensible girl like Kay and less of that Louise Mitchell?"

"Where did you hear of Louise Mitchell?" I asked.

"Mothers have ways of knowing things, darling," she said.

"Now, listen, Mother," I said. "I can't help it if I see Louise Mitchell and if I'm decently polite."

"Darling," Mother said, "it isn't what I mean at all. I only mean that everyone knows that Louise is silly about boys."

"Now, listen, Mother," I said. "Just because a girl's a little different— What have you heard about Louise? Has Mary been telling you anything?"

"So, it's true," Mother said. "You're interested in Louise."

"Mother," I said, "I have to be polite to her, don't I? I'm not interested in Louise, but I have to speak to her."

"Kay Motford never chases after boys," Mother said. "Kay is a dear, sweet girl."

I wanted to ask her what Mary had told her, but I thought it was better not. I wished that Mary were not old enough to go to the Country Club.

Mother also was always talking about "someday." Someday I would marry a nice girl and someday they would build us a house on part of Westwood. Someday I would be a partner in Smith and Wilding, after starting in the bond department. I might go abroad first for a year if I wanted, but the main thing was to get settled first. It was all so taken for granted that no one ever spoke about it much, but I knew that they were all beginning to think about the time when I would marry that nice girl.

Father himself brought the matter up one Sunday evening by saying that he believed in marrying young.

"Now, I married your mother when I was young," he said, "and I have never regretted it. The main thing is to find the same sort of person that you are."

"But I haven't been thinking about getting married," I said.

"That's all right," Father answered. "All of a sudden you will see that life isn't right without it. I remember when I first thought of getting married."

Father cut the end off a cigar and lighted it.

"Something's happened to the cigars. The box was almost full last week. Have you been smoking them, Harry?"

"No," I said.

"Well, someone's been into the box," Father said. "I suppose it's Hugh. What was I talking about?"

"How you thought about getting married."

"Oh, yes," Father said. "I thought about it when I was sitting in a barrel in the marshes, shooting ducks. I was just sitting, looking over the pond, and I realized that I was all alone, that I ought to be doing something for someone. Then I thought about your mother. You'll get the same idea sometime — it will come over you all of a sudden."

"I haven't got it yet," I said.

"But you will," Father answered. "It's a good thing to be prepared for it, Harry — a good thing to be thinking of the right sort of girl. Now, I've always liked the Motfords."

"Look here," I said. "Honestly, Father, I'm not interested in Kay Motford. I don't want to marry her."

"Well," Father said, "someone like her, that's all."

"Well, it doesn't do any good to throw her at me," I said.

I was certainly right about that. I began to dislike anyone who was a nice sensible girl. I began to be suspicious whenever Kay asked me to the house, and when I sat next to her at dinner before a dance I felt it had all been arranged beforehand. Kay told me later that she felt a good deal the same way.

The younger generation at North Harbor were always one big crowd. We would meet at the beach in the morning and race eighteen-footers twice a week or play tennis at the club, and in the evenings we would all go to the moving pictures or dance.

Kay was always sunburned and her nose kept peeling and she generally wore sneakers. Louise Mitchell was quite different. Louise was not good at games. She wore high heels and she did not like to walk. She always liked to be alone with someone and everyone always wanted to be alone with Louise, and so at the Country Club dances she seemed to be away somewhere most of the evening. But even in her absence you were aware of her presence, because you always wondered whom she was away with. Yet she always made you feel better about it when she got back.

"Why," she would say, when you cut in on her, "where have you been? Is there something I've done? You aren't angry with me, are you? Why did you just abandon me and let me get stuck with that nasty Albert Oliver?"

No matter what might happen, you always knew when she came back that she had been waiting for you all the time.

"Why didn't you see me?" she would say. "I was right there in the corner, signaling to you. I was just there trying to get away from Joe Bingham."

When I took Bill to the Country Club dance I warned him about the girls he might get stuck with.

"There's Alice Oliver," I said. "You want to look out for her, but you want to be particularly careful of Kay Motford. She's a nice sensible girl."

"All right," said Bill. "Isn't she the one who came to lunch freshman year—the one in the blue dress?"

"And there's Louise Mitchell," I said, "in green. You don't have to worry about her at all."

Then as we stood near the piazza doorway I explained about the Bingham girls and about Eleanor Frear and all the rest of them. The orchestra was playing "You Great Big Beautiful Doll," and the air from the sea was soft and damp.

"There's quite a crowd," Bill said.

"Yes," I said. "Just remember the main thing is not to get stuck with Kay. She's dancing with that bird who's staying at the Frears'. She's probably been with him for half an hour."

"All right," said Bill. "Don't worry. I'm all right."

I did not worry about him, because Bill was always all right anywhere. Louise Mitchell saw me and waved to me. Her hair was yellow and her dress was yellowish-green, something like the color of sea water near the shore. She was dancing with an older man who must have been down for the week end. I hurried toward her and cut in at once.

"Harry, where have you been?" she said. "I've been looking for you everywhere, looking and looking."

"I just came," I said. "Let's go out and sit somewhere. Aren't you feeling tired?"

"I think I'd better dance for a while. I don't know why it is that everyone talks if you just go out and rest for a few minutes. You don't mind, do you, Harry? Because you know I'd rather talk to you than anyone in the world. Oh, dear, here comes Albert Oliver."

"Tell him you're tired," I said.

103

Louise squeezed my hand.

"I can't," she said. "I hate it, don't you, not being able to do what you want? You know there's no one I hate more than Albert Oliver. You'll come back, won't you, Harry?"

The trouble was that everyone else was always coming back.

"Awfully sorry, Harry," Albert said. "There's something I have to tell Louise. Louise, I found out what Mrs. Frear said about you. It's a scream. You'll just die laughing."

I watched Louise pirouetting in Albert's arms, listening to what Albert said Mrs. Frear had said, but she did not die laughing.

It was always said that North Harbor was just one big family and that everyone of every age did things together. Thus there were couples on the dance floor making awkward motions in their attempts to do the one-step, unaware that they were too old to be dancing. There were the married set, who never had much to do with us, and callow youths and stringy girls of my sister Mary's age, who got in everybody's way. As far as social intercourse went, these groups might have been in separate rooms, for each was absorbed in its own particular problems. I could see Louise Mitchell, listening to the poisoned tongue of Albert Oliver. I must wait until someone else cut in before I could cut back. I could see Mary dancing with one of the little Frears — the beach at North Harbor and the tennis courts and the golf course were always overrun with Frears — and I saw Bill King's blond head. He was dancing with another of the Frears. Bo-jo Brown once said that Bill danced as though his pants were full of tacks, but this was only jealousy because Bill moved skillfully, contemptuously, in and out between the other couples. I only saw him vaguely, for someone else was cutting in on Louise. I could be back with her in a moment, but then I heard a voice beside me. It was Guy Motford, Kay's older brother. Guy was older than I and bigger, out of college and working in Boston with Leeds and Stratton.

"Hello," he said, "I've been looking for you. Someone's got to dance with Kay."

"I'm awfully sorry, Guy," I said. "I'm pretty busy now."

104

Guy put his arm affectionately around my shoulders as though he were just my age.

"She's been dancing with that Eli for half an hour," he said. "I'll get somebody else in five minutes. I'll promise you, word of honor."

"I'd love to, Guy," I said, "just as soon as I've had one more dance."

"Now, listen, Harry," Guy said. "Just do it for me. I'll be watching. I won't let you down."

I knew that there was nothing to do about it. I saw Kay's blue dress moving nearer.

"Go ahead," said Guy. "Please, Harry."

After all I would have to dance with Kay once sometime. The music stopped and Kay and her partner stopped near me. Her partner looked hot and tired, but he applauded violently.

"Hello, Harry," Kay called. "I want you to meet Mr. —— I don't know why I forgot your name. I'm never good at names."

"Siegfried," her partner said.

"Oh, yes," said Kay. "I don't know why I forgot it." Then the music started again. I was standing facing Kay. Mr. Siegfried was gone.

"Why," Kay said. "What happened to him?"

"I don't know," I said. "He's gone."

"But where's he gone to?" Kay said, and then she bit her lower lip.

"Never mind," I said. "Let's dance."

"You don't have to," Kay said. "I can go out and fix my hair."

"Why, there's nothing the matter with your hair," I said.

"I saw you talking to Guy," Kay said. "He asked you to dance with me, didn't he?" I didn't answer.

"Didn't he?" Kay said.

"No," I answered, "he didn't."

Kay looked at me; her eyes were hard and bright.

"You're a rotten liar," she said.

It occurred to me that there was no reason for her to be disagreeable about it.

"And you're a rotten dancer too," Kay said. "You never can keep time to the music."

"I'd do better," I said, "if you didn't always try to lead."

"I like to keep time to the music," Kay said. "Don't dance with me if you don't like it. I can go up and do my hair."

The music stopped again and did not continue, even when everybody clapped. I saw Louise Mitchell disappearing, and Albert Oliver was with her again.

"Go out and chase Louise Mitchell if you want to," Kay said. "It's all right for you to leave me now."

"Why, Kay," I said, "I'm having a fine time."

"I wish you wouldn't be so polite," Kay said. "Why don't you ever say what you think?"

"I saw you yesterday," I said, "walking with your dogs."

"Yes," Kay said. "I saw you too. We don't have to talk if you don't want to. Let's go and find Guy."

"He's probably in the bar," I said. "Let's dance."

The music had started again and Kay shrugged her shoulders.

"All right," she said. "You've got that friend of yours, Bill King, staying with you, haven't you? He's awfully good-looking."

"Yes," I said.

"Harry," Kay said, "will you *please* keep time to the music."

"I'm sorry, Kay," I said.

"Can't you ever say anything?"

"What do you want me to say?" I asked.

"Anything, anything at all. Have you been reading the newspapers? Do you know that France has declared war on Germany?"

"Yes, I know," I said. "I think the French will lick them."

The orchestra was playing "Waiting for the *Robert E. Lee*." I looked around the room over Kay's shoulder. Louise Mitchell was not there.

"Harry," Kay said, "do you hear what I'm saying?"

"No," I said. "I'm sorry, Kay."

"Let's get out of here," Kay said, and she walked toward the door and I followed her.

"You don't have to stay with me," Kay said.

Of course I had to stay until someone asked her to dance. Kay walked down the steps, across the putting green, over toward the first tee that overlooked the ocean, and I followed her.

"It's cloudy tonight," I said.

Kay did not answer.

I took a box of cigarettes from my pocket and lighted one. Smoking was still new to me.

"England will have to fight," I said, "if Germany's in Belgium."

Kay did not answer; she stood looking at the sea.

"Have you got a handkerchief?" she asked suddenly.

"Yes," I said, "of course."

"Then give it to me," Kay said, "and please go away."

I handed her my handkerchief and she snatched it out of my hand and blew her nose. It was too dark to see her face.

"Why, Kay," I asked her, "what's the matter? I haven't said anything rude, have I?"

"No," said Kay. "*Please go away*."

"But I can't leave you out here alone," I said. "If there's anything I said, Kay —"

"Don't talk," Kay said. "I'm all right. We'll go back now. I'm going home. I'm going to walk."

"Then I'll walk back with you," I said. "You can't walk home alone."

We walked very fast back into the circle of light by the club veranda, and as we walked up the steps we came face to face with Bill King.

"I've been looking for you," Bill said to Kay. "I want to find someone who can dance."

"All right," said Kay, and she turned toward me and stared at me for a second. "Here's your handkerchief, Harry."

I have often thought of that scene. Bill did not need to ask Kay to dance, and yet he did, and I was left standing there, wondering why he asked her. I stood staring after them; Bill's arm was around her and Kay was smiling. I walked down to the bar off the locker room, a big room with heavy mission furniture, and I stood by the doorway, looking in. There were some men my father's age sitting around a table.

"It will be over," I heard someone say, "inside of three months. They can't lick the French Army. If you say they can, you don't know the French."

I stood there, listening to the clash of voices and to the music coming through the open door. There was no way of telling then that a world was ended or that a page was turning. Words and thoughts were rising like a storm, and Kay and Bill and I and all the rest of us were going to go right through it. We would all go through it like a train going through a dark tunnel, and we would emerge into the daylight at the other end to face an entirely different country.

XI

You'd Better Ask Frank Wilding

When I started in to work with Smith and Wilding, the summer
I finished college, Father and I stayed at Westwood, after Mother
and Mary moved to North Harbor. In the evenings after dinner
Father would frequently talk about old Mr. Wilding, the head of
the firm. In Father's eyes he was a hero, and an infallible prophet
of world events.

"Frank Wilding is never wrong," he said once. "I don't believe it,
but Frank says we will be in the war by next spring."

I never knew where Mr. Wilding got his information. He had
some system of forming judgments of his own, some way of sort-
ing facts and putting them together which was nearly always right.
I have often wondered whether it was instinct more than brains.
If I could write I should like to do a pen portrait of him, for he
was a superlative product in his way, an ideal of a sort of business
success which has vanished. Yet I wonder if he were alive right now
and in possession of a certain amount of vigor, whether Mr. Wilding
would not do rather well. At any rate, he was right, for we were
in the war eventually.

In the winter when Mr. Wilding reached the office, always at
exactly half-past eight, he would hang his black overcoat and his
derby hat carefully on a hat tree in the corner and would place his
overshoes squarely underneath the coat. In the summer he would
hang his straw hat in the same place — a hat which was something
like a modern leghorn, soft and yellow, with a frayed band around
it. As soon as he arrived Miss Joslin, who still wore leg-of-mutton
sleeves, would come in with a few letters. She would always be out

again in half an hour. Then he would call for Mr. Withers, the head of the bond department. Then he would lean back in his swivel chair, watching the customers file into the board room before the market opened, and at exactly half-past ten Mr. Riley, the head clerk, would hand him a paper with the opening prices, written in a steady, copperplate hand. At half-past twelve exactly he would walk to his club for lunch and he would be back at his desk promptly at two o'clock to read the bulletins from the news bureau, still with his door half-open. He very seldom received a caller. He very seldom spoke to his partners, and precisely at five o'clock he would be driven home to Brookline, where they say he went to bed at nine. He seldom did anything positive, but nothing ever escaped him. He never raised his voice, but somehow he always seemed more integrated than anyone else there, more completely in touch with life.

It was one of my duties for the first two weeks that I worked there to bring Mr. Wilding a pint of milk and two crackers at exactly eleven o'clock. Mr. Wilding would fold his paper across his knees and would ask gently about the market. Then he would say, "Thank you, Harry," and pick up his paper again. Though our conversation hardly ever went further, by the time two weeks were over I had a feeling that Mr. Wilding knew me very well.

"Mr. Wilding wants . . ." they used to say, or "Mr. Wilding thinks . . ." But I never could tell how anyone knew what he wanted or thought.

When I started in with Smith and Wilding it was customary to pay new candidates in the office a flat sum of three hundred dollars a year. Although the whole atmosphere was money — and we were right in the beginning of the boom of the War Babies then — we apprentices were working under great pressure without a thought of money. There were six of us starting in the office that year, all from Harvard and all with good connections. Every morning we were given a list of prospects, all the bad ones to whom the regular staff had not been able to sell anything, and we set off to peddle the bonds that Smith and Wilding carried, each of us equipped with a description of the securities, which we were supposed to have carefully digested. We went in and out of offices all day long up and down the financial district, but it was not like business.

If I ever sold any Smith and Wilding bonds to a stranger that summer I cannot seem to remember it. It was surprising, though, how many family connections there were and how many people knew my father.

"Hello," they used to say. "So you're John Pulham's boy."

I should have felt better if I could ever have made a stranger buy a bond. I took the matter up once with Mr. Withers, who told me it would come in time. Mr. Withers had been fullback on the Harvard team about ten years before and he still had the old fighting spirit. When he called the salesmen into his office his voice had a spellbinding quality and he used to refer to Mr. Wilding as "Uncle Frank."

"Now," he used to say, "these four-and-halfs are going to be hard to move, but Uncle Frank wants us to move them quick. Now, get into it, on your toes, and out on the street."

He said a lot more which made a good deal of sense, but most of it was lost on me, as I would listen dazedly, trying to follow his phrases. The established salesmen always had the banks and insurance companies and all the leads that ever amounted to anything. The neophytes were simply being run ragged for the good of their souls. It was all part of a Spartan system.

"You can't sell bonds to people unless you know them," Mr. Withers said. "Just keep calling on them and sweeten up your connections. You're not complaining, are you, Pulham?"

"No, sir," I said, "of course not."

"A bond salesman never complains," Mr. Withers said. "I'd hate to think that you were yellow, Pulham. A bond salesman always has guts."

When I think of Smith and Wilding I always think of leather upholstery and cigar smoke and the staccato sound of the tickers, and of the boy on the tall stool calling out quotations to the other boys up at the blackboard. I can never forget the unwearied activity behind the cashier's cage where the clerks in their sleeve protectors sat on stools in front of the ledgers. They belonged to a different society which I did not know well, since they did not have much to do with the front office, but Mr. Wilding knew them all. It was an honor to work for Smith and Wilding in those days. Everyone in the office said it was an honor, and nearly everyone outside was respectful and envious. Smith and Wilding was a good banking firm and they were kind to me. I have never forgotten how kind, at the time when I went to war.

Bill King found a job the summer we graduated as a reporter on the *New York World*. We exchanged letters occasionally and he came up to visit us when he had a week's vacation. He was anxious to see the office and I took him in for a few minutes one day after lunch. Bill knew the inside of everything, all about the war and what was the matter with the Administration; he put his hands in his pockets and looked around the board room.

"It looks like the Union League Club," he said. "They might as well be gambling on the races. If you want to make a little money buy steel. Steel's going up."

"If I were to buy stocks I'd be fired," I said.

Bill began to whistle.

"All the necktie boys certainly do sell bonds," he said.

Mr. Wilding's door was open and Mr. Wilding was having his shoes shined, sitting with one foot on the bootblack's box, his hands clasped over his stomach.

"Oh, my," Bill said, "who's that? He looks like Ralph Waldo Emerson."

"Bill," I said, "don't talk so loud. That's Mr. Wilding, the senior partner."

Mr. Wilding unclasped his hands from his stomach.

"Harry," he called, "come in here."

You always jumped when Mr. Wilding spoke. I hurried through the gate that separated the partners from the customers' room and stood beside his desk.

"I think you'd better do that shoe over again, Tony," Mr. Wilding said. "I want a higher polish. Harry, who is that young man out there?"

"He's a classmate of mine, sir," I said. "His name is William King."

"King," said Mr. Wilding, "King. He doesn't come from here, does he?"

"No, sir," I said.

"What does he do?"

I told him Bill worked on the *New York World*.

"Bring him in," Mr. Wilding said. "I want to see him." Mr. Wilding folded his hands across his stomach and looked up at Bill King.

"So you work on a newspaper, young man?" Mr. Wilding said. "I heard you say that I looked like Ralph Waldo Emerson. It flatters me, but I'm not a minister."

"No, sir," Bill said. "I don't suppose so."

"Would you care to work here?" Mr. Wilding asked.

"No, thank you, sir," Bill answered.

"If you ever should," said Mr. Wilding, "let me know. That shoe is all right. You may start on the other one now, Tony. Harry, get me the last quotation on steel."

I never knew what Mr. Wilding saw in Bill King and Mr. Wilding never explained.

"What's the matter with the old man?" Bill asked later. "Does he think he's a hero in a Horatio Alger book — the kind old man gives the boy a chance? He knew damned well I wouldn't work in that doghouse, and you'd better get out of it, Harry."

"Why?" I asked.

"Because you'll never be like him," Bill said, "not in a million years. Did you ever look at his eyes? I might be like him, but I wouldn't want to be."

"Boy," we heard Mr. Wilding call.

The office boy near the rail leaped as though he had been stung and ran to Mr. Wilding. A moment later the boy hurried across the board room with a white slip of paper which he gave to Mr. Jones, the customers' man. Bill stood watching with his hands in his pockets.

"Harry," he asked me, "do you think he could have heard me when I said something about steel?"

XII

A Great Experience, the War

Ellen, the one maid who could always get on with Kay, is forever breaking things. Nearly every day there is a crash in the pantry and her excuse is always the same.

"A part of it just came off in my hand."

Just yesterday Ellen smashed one of our Canton china plates in the dining room. She explained that it must have been cracked already, because a part of it came off in her hand. The noise made me start, and when I saw all the pieces on the floor by the pantry door, somehow that broken plate reminded me of the way the war smashed everything. I do not mean that I was shell-shocked or anything like that, but I was always picking up pieces of things after the war, pieces of human relationships, pieces of thoughts, and when I tried to put them together again they never seemed to fit.

If you had been to a school like St. Swithin's you were able to understand army discipline. I do not think that I was a bad soldier, as I look back on it after twenty years. Yet in other ways I was not fitted for the war at all. I never realized how little I knew about anything or how desirable life was, until I got to France and was reasonably sure that I would be dead or wounded within a certain time.

I still have a photograph of myself taken for the family just after I had been commissioned as second lieutenant in the officers' reserve. A week or two later I was transferred to Camp Upton, and assigned to a regular army division, waiting for the transports. It is hard for me to recognize the rather thin, frail-looking boy in a garrison cap which was lost when I got to St. Nazaire. The fore-head is good, the eyes are steady, the mouth is a little large — not a bad-looking boy — but I wish there were a photograph of me taken when I got home in the spring of 1919, because I should like to compare the two. I am sure a good deal was rubbed off my face when I got back. I am looking at a picture, not of myself, but of someone who was killed. I have always kept it in an envelope with a few of the letters I sent home and with one Kay gave me, which I wrote her, and with my second lieutenant's commission and my discharge and with the order giving me a medal. The medal is upstairs in the box under my collar studs and I have never cared to take it out, because old General Rolfax only had it given me to save his own face. He should have been court-martialed for incompetence in ordering my company out into an untenable and useless position and then forgetting to recall it or to send out ade-quate support. As a matter of fact, he would have court-martialed me to make things look better, if it had not happened that I had a copy of his order in my pocket. That was the way war was, I sup-pose.

Henry Pulham, Second Lieutenant — Infantry: The only surviving officer of his company, after a reconnaissance in the town of M——. Lieutenant Pulham consolidated and held his position, although sur-rounded by the enemy, from dawn until dark of July 27th; refusing to surrender, Lieutenant Pulham continued his defense under heavy fire and, repulsing three assaults of a superior force, withdrew with his command under cover of darkness; recrossed the Vesle River and re-joined his regiment.

The funny part of it is that a good deal of it is true, although now I cannot imagine doing such a thing. We had two machine guns and a lot of hand grenades and some automatic rifles and the morale of the German infantry in front of us was pretty low, or else they thought they had us anyway. They would have had us too, if it had not been for a Jewish corporal named Reinitz who found a way down to the river after dark. I recommended Reinitz for the medal, but to no avail because he went to prison for attacking a French girl two weeks later—but that was the way the war was. Of course I like to think that I behaved myself properly, but I cannot help remembering that at least fifty lives would have been saved if we had given up when they asked us. The offer was made after a handkerchief was waved on the end of a rifle and an officer in dirty gray climbed out of the cellar hole of a house about fifty yards from where we were dug into what was left of a barnyard. When the man stood up, I stood up too and crawled out over the rubbish to meet him. I had just enough German to speak to him from what I remembered from Fräulein and the nursery, which made our conversation a strange intellectual effort. He was a captain and he was as grimy as I was and as lousy as I was and just about my age. He said we were surrounded and that he thought we had better give up. I told him that if any of my men wanted to, I would send them over.

"If they will kindly hold up their hands," the Captain said.

I felt in my pocket and drew out a package of cigarettes. We each took one and lighted them and I offered him the rest. It was a hot, dry day and the perspiration was streaming down our faces. We stood there smoking for a minute, for he seemed in no hurry to go away.

"Beautiful thanks for the cigarettes," he said. "I shall give you five minutes. If you or any of your men desire to come we shall be pleased to see you."

He smiled and saluted.

"If Americans are like you," he added, "I shall come to America."

He never came to America and he never used the cigarettes, because he was dead fifteen minutes later. I crawled back over what was left of the wall, aware that I had to make a speech and that I had never been good at talking to enlisted men. I tried to think what Bo-jo Brown would have said, but it was not much help. When I got back over the wall I called Sergeant Brooks.

"Sergeant," I said, "if any of the men would like to go over, they can do so in the next five minutes, but I think the right thing for me to do is to stay here with anyone else who wants to. You can pass the word around, Sergeant."

Sergeant Brooks cleared his throat.

"Listen, you bastards," he called, "if any of you are yellow you can go on over. The Lieutenant says he's going to sit down here. He don't want to live forever."

I wished that I could have spoken the way Sergeant Brooks did. He was a good man and he was busted for drunkenness a month later.

"Attaboy, Lieutenant," someone called. "Who said Lieutenant Pulham wears lace drawers?"

"That will do, men," I said.

"Jesus Christ!" someone called. "Here they come, Lieutenant!"

The whole thing has always been a blur to me of physical weariness and physical fear, and, anyway, I have always been skeptical of the word of anyone who has been able to give a clear account of an infantry combat. At one place they got as near as twenty feet and we stood up throwing grenades at each other, like boys in a snowball fight. Then they crawled back and tried it again half an hour later, but they never pushed in seriously, because they must have thought they could get us eventually without undue loss and because the Germans were tired and pretty well broken by then. After that they simply sat down and waited and telephoned back to the seventy-seven's to take us under fire. The fire was not very accurate — a good many of the shells were duds — and the lines were so near that the artillery was as damaging to them as it was to us. Artillery was always firing into its own infantry. Then the fire stopped and I saw them drawing back their line. They were probably cursing their artillery the way we cursed ours, and then it began to get dark. The whole thing was a mess, because they could have finished us with one good rush, but I suppose they did not want to die any more than we did. Whoever it was who ran the show must have decided to wait until morning.

I have often thought of Captain Rowle, who was in command of the company when we crossed the river. He was a red-faced, dumpy man in his thirties, who had done two hitches, as he called them, with the Regulars before he had been commissioned. I experienced little feeling of personal grief for Captain Rowle, when he lay in a cellar hole dying from an abdominal wound, because he had always ridden me, and in his lighter moments had made fun of the way I talked. He may have had excellent reasons for feeling that I did not amount to much, but it struck me as strange that none of those officers seemed to like me and that I did not like them, especially since I always got on well enough with my own crowd. I never could seem to get it out of my head that most of them had not gone to St. Swithin's or Harvard; instead they had been educated at colleges which they called "schools" and had lived in environments which I could not picture. They were most of them foul-mouthed and noisy boys, who discussed their sexual prowess and who were always after cognac. It was only later that I began to understand that they were just as good as I was and often a great deal better, but I could not seem to be deeply moved when Frank Murphy, the first lieutenant, was killed, or when Eddy Boyle, who was a senior to me, was shot in two. I did not want to see Rowle much when Sergeant Brooks crawled over and said the Captain wanted to speak to me.

"There's something he wants to say to you," said Sergeant Brooks. "He's damned near through."

We had been able to drag some of the wounded into a cellar hole and Captain Rowle was half sitting up, leaning against the wall. His face was a greenish white and the first-aid bandages over his hairy abdomen were covered with blood and the only first-aid man who was left was squatting near him.

"That son of a bitch won't give me any water," Captain Rowle said.

"You ought not to drink water, sir," I told him.

"For Christ's sakes," said Captain Rowle, "don't I know when I'm through? Give me some water."

I gave him some water from the first-aid man's canteen.

"Thanks," Captain Rowle said, and he asked some questions about the men and gave me a letter to send to his wife. "You've got to get out of here," he said, "and I don't want anybody to say we came out here without orders. Someone's going to catch hell for this. I told the Colonel before I started that I wanted it in writing. Put this in your pocket. Don't let them say I used bad judgment. It's there in writing."

He gave me a sheet of paper and I put it in my pocket.

He seemed to be relieved that I had it and told me to go back where I belonged, but just when I was leaving he called me back.

"I've been thinking," he said, "what it was made you into such a little twerp. I guess it was how you were brought up. You'll be all right when you loosen up, Pulham. Shake hands."

"I guess I know what you mean," I said. "I'm sorry."

"Just remember this isn't a God-damned university club," said Captain Rowle.

I got on better after that — I seemed to know more about people. I got to know Major Groves and a lot of the others in the battalion mess in Coblentz pretty well that winter and I found myself thinking once, as I looked around the table at them, that I would have had a hard time coping with most of them a few months before. Major Groves had a hardware business somewhere near Austin, Texas, and he used to talk to me about it when we drank Rhine wine in the evening. He had a quiet, plaintive Southwestern voice.

"Why don't you ever talk about home, Pulham?" he asked me once.

"I guess I'm not so good at talking," I told him, "but I think about it a lot." I was thinking about how I had kissed Louise Mitchell good-by, and now it did not seem possible. I wanted to keep everything at home away from the Major and all the rest of them, not because I was ashamed of it, but because they would not understand. Some of the letters from home had reached me that evening, one from Mother telling about the Red Cross and asking me when I would get back, and one from Father asking the same question. There was also a letter from the Skipper.

I have been writing all the old boys [he wrote], and you are on the list. The worst of it here is the lack of news. I suppose you know that

Stephens and Trimble were killed in the Argonne. Their names are now on a temporary plaque in the chapel. I heard from Joe Bingham yesterday. He tells me that Bo-jo Brown is a physical director. Please write soon and tell me about yourself with some details about the war. I try to read the letters at chapel as soon as they come in.

Then there was a letter from Kay Motford answering one I wrote her, thanking her for a sweater which she sent me.

"Dear Harry," she wrote, "everyone is very busy here. There is a great influenza epidemic, but everything is a good deal the same." Then she went on, telling how much the same it was and about what everyone was doing. It was strange that none of those letters made me feel homesick. I did not seem to give a particular damn what anyone was doing. "I don't know whether you heard," she wrote, "that Louise Mitchell is married." I had not heard and I did not seem to care about that either.

"I don't know what it is about home," I said to the Major. "All they ever taught me was to behave like a damned fool."

"Well," the Major said, "the home folks wouldn't know you now."

The idea troubled me, because I was afraid that I would not know them either. I was wondering what I was going to do when I got back.

"Now," the Major said, "they must be right pleased about that medal."

"I never told them," I said.

"Now, Harry," the Major said, "that ain't fair."

Once it had not seemed possible that a major could be a good officer if he allowed himself to lapse into bad grammar, but now the war had altered my point of view without my knowing exactly when or why. Actually it was not so much the war itself as those almost forgotten human contacts. I hated nearly every minute of it, and still hate it. I have never been able to understand all the sentimental talk about a week's leave in Paris, where you used to be chivied by the military police and cheated by fatherly cab drivers and pursued by prostitutes, except when I think of it in terms of human contact. Those shadowy friends, those acquaintances of an evening, taught me more than I ever learned in school. There were farm boys from the Middle-west, Italians from the New York slums, factory workers, ranchers, sons of small town shopkeepers — but we all had a common point of view then, difficult to analyze, which was expressed in bawdy songs and jokes, and incredible as it may seem when I consider certain individuals, a common something which you might call decency. The members of A Company even when they were drunk and disorderly were all nice boys, once you got to know them. It surprised me to realize that most of them were considerably more admirable people than the Y.M.C.A. secretaries, who tried to teach them to be nice. It surprised me that most of them were braver and more generous than I was.

"When they get to shooting at you," the Major said once, "the boys find out right quick what you are."

It still made me lonely when I realized that no one else in the officers' mess was exactly like me. I remember how the Major reacted when I told him once that my family lived largely on their income.

"Listen, boy," the Major said, "you wouldn't kid me, would you?"

I have often wondered what happened to the Major. We exchanged a few letters in the beginning and he came to my wedding, but I have not heard from him for years or from any of the others. There was a process after the war of trying to get back to what you had been before, of trying to combine what you had learned with what you had been taught to ignore. I cannot blame myself or a good many of my friends for having made a mess of it, for the two things could not fit together. When you got back it was like the broken plate.

"If I had had the guts — " I sometimes find myself thinking, and a part of the old restlessness comes back.

XIII

Something Basic

After my discharge, which was handed me the day I landed at Hoboken, I went to the old Waldorf on Thirty-fourth Street with four hundred dollars of back pay and with what was left of my belongings tied up in a bedding roll. My two locker trunks and my cot and folding chair, and all those other things which we had been told were a part of every officer's equipment, had been lost six months before, leaving me with two dirty blankets and a soiled uniform which I was wearing, one clean shirt, some woolen socks and a change of underwear. The clerk at the marble desk looked at me and glanced at my bedding roll.

"I'll have to ask you to pay in advance," he said, and I handed him a hundred dollar bill.

"I've been thinking for quite a while," I said, "that I wanted to sleep at the Waldorf."

The people around me looked sleek and fat and beautiful. There was music in the dining room and no sign of the war.

"Don't worry," I told the clerk. "I'll get some other clothes tomorrow."

"I suppose you've just come in, Lieutenant," the clerk said. "Well, it was quite a war."

"Yes, it was quite a war," I said.

Up on the eighth floor the bellboy put my bedding roll on a stand and opened the window. I could hear all the noises on Fifth Avenue and I could look out and see the lights.

"Is there anything else you want, sir?" he asked.

There was a good deal that I wanted. I was trying to pick up the pieces.

"You can run me a hot bath," I said. All the appointments in the room seemed inordinately elaborate. I looked at my wrist watch. It was only half past six. "And you can get me a Scotch-and-soda and an order of oatmeal and cream."

"Oatmeal?" he repeated.

"Go ahead and get it," I said. "Oatmeal, and half a dozen oysters."

I do not know why my mind had been dwelling so long on this combination. There had been a good deal of discussion about what we would do when we got out of the Army and I was only doing what I wanted. I kept thinking that I had better make the most of it, that this might be my last chance. The telephone was on the table beside the bed, and I was near enough to my family to reach them. I loved them and it was the right thing to call them at once to tell them that I was finally back, but I did not know where to begin. Then I thought of Bill King. I thought of him when I drank my whisky and ate my oatmeal. I began wondering if he might be back, but the only proper thing to do was to call the family.

Hugh's voice was on the wire. I heard it with a blank sort of amazement that Hugh could still be alive.

"Is Father in, Hugh?" I asked. "It's Mister Harry." Then I heard Hugh calling at the top of his voice and then Father was speaking.

"Where are you, Harry?" he called. "Are you all right?"

It seemed incredible to me that he could not have understood that I was all right if I was at the Waldorf. I tried to imagine him by the telephone in the library.

"How's Mother?" I said. "How's Mary?"

"Now, listen," Father called. "Are you listening? Get the midnight train."

"I can't," I said. "I've got to get some clothes. I'll be up tomorrow."

"Never mind the clothes," Father shouted. "Get the train."

"I can't," I said. "There're some things I have to do."

He would not have understood it if I had told him that I wanted a short time by myself. Until I thought again of Bill King, I did not want anyone to talk to me about the war or anything. I wondered exactly how I should ask for Bill in case anything had happened to him, but he answered the telephone himself; his voice was sharp and impatient.

"Bill," I said, "it's Harry."

"Well, it's about time you got back," Bill said. "Where are you?"

I told him that I was just off the boat and just discharged.

"Well, come on out here," Bill said.

I asked him if he would not come here instead and spend the night in the other bed. I told him there were a lot of things I wanted to talk about, and he came.

It must have been nine o'clock when he arrived. I was curious to see whether he would look as I remembered him. I was worried about our being able to pick up something where we had left it off, because he looked like the people I had seen out on the street, very clean and very prosperous. There was just a moment of constraint. Then I was sure he was glad to see me.

"Well, what are you sitting up here for?" Bill asked. "On your first night back? Let's go out and see the town."

"It's funny," I said. "I don't want to see anything just yet."

He seemed to know the way I felt. He sat down and lighted a cigarette and in a minute everything was simple. First he told me the news of everyone and then we ordered up some drinks.

"To hell with the Army," Bill said, "and to hell with West Point."

He made me laugh as he went on. Bill had a lot of stories about generals and about Paris and about the Y.M.C.A.

"And at that point," he kept saying, "I wished to God you were there. You'd have done the right thing."

"Oh, shut up, Bill," I said, just the way I used to.

"So they put you into the Half Moon, did they?"

"It was a good division," I said.

"Don't tell me that all the officers and men were fine fellows," Bill said.

"They were, Bill, really, when you got to know them."

Bill began to laugh.

"I bet you learned a lot of bad habits," he said. "Go ahead and tell me how you won the war."

"Let's not talk about it."

"All right," Bill said. "It's funny how some people act when they get back. You'll get over it in a week or two."

I had asked him there to talk to him, but when it came to the point I felt reluctant.

"I suppose so," I said. "I don't know how it is, Bill. I don't seem to want to go home."

A good many people have said harsh things about Bill King, among them that he was hard-boiled and cynical and always looking out for himself. I can only say that Bill was very kind to me that night.

"I suppose you won't understand it," I said. "It's just that I'm just not used to it any more."

"You must have had quite a shaking up," Bill said; "but if you don't want to go back, why should you?"

"What else can I do?" I asked.

"Now, don't make me cry," Bill answered. "You can get a job. Go back home and tell them you've got a job. I'll get you one, I'll get you one tomorrow."

I sat for a while considering. It must have seemed simple to him, but it was not simple to me.

"Where can you get me one?" I asked.

"Where I'm working," Bill said. "The advertising business. I'll call you up tomorrow after I've seen Bullard. I'm in strong with Bullard."

"But I don't know anything about it," I said.

"Harry," Bill told me, "nobody there knows anything about it either. Look at this." He pulled a newspaper clipping out of his inside pocket and handed it to me. "It was in the *Times* this morning."

"The man for whom we are seeking," I read, "will preferably not have written advertising copy, but will have had a college education and a background of business experience and will possess besides a serious and pleasing personality, combined with a sense of taste and form. For such a man there is a definite opportunity in a large and growing organization which will take every care of his advancement."

"Don't read any more," said Bill. "Bullard had me write it. You'll do as well as anybody else."

"But what does it mean?" I asked.

"It doesn't mean anything," Bill said. "Just remember that nothing much means anything these days. Do you want it or don't you?"

A year ago it would not have seemed possible.

"All right," I said. "I'll try it," but I could not understand myself.

"Bill," I asked, "do you think that anything's the matter with me?"

"Hell, no," Bill said. "Just get yourself off your mind."

"I can't," I said. "There must be something the matter with me not to want to go home."

"Try to act your age," said Bill. "This war has taught a lot of people that it isn't worth while living if you can't do what you want. How you gonna keep 'em down on the farm, after they've seen Paree?"

"But I wasn't down on the farm," I said. "I had everything."

Bill waved his hand toward the window.

"You listen to me," he said. "You don't know what's going on outside there — labor trouble, Communism, economic upset, the League of Nations. No one knows what's going to happen, but you can be damned well sure of just one thing."

"What?" I asked.

Bill pointed his finger at me.

"You were brought up in a certain tiny, superfluous segment," he said, "that is going to be nonexistent. You say you were given everything, and what does it amount to? Not to a bucket of slops."

He made me angry, but he continued speaking before I could stop him.

"Put it this way. Take the insect world."

"What's the insect world got to do with it?" I asked.

"Don't interrupt me," Bill said. "Take the insect world. Insects possess instincts rather than brains. When their environment changes so that their instincts play them false their species disappear. Now, you're an insect with thwarted instincts."

"What about you?" I asked.

"Me?" Bill said. "I'm changing my instincts as quick as I can. It's easier for me, because I've never had the intensive instinct course that you've had. I've not been in your hive of bees."

"You used to like our beehive," I said.

"Of course I liked it," Bill answered. "It was a nice comfortable beehive, but they're going to smoke it out. I like your father and mother and all the other bees, but you've got to get out of there, Harry."

"Let's talk about something else," I said.

When I was halfway over to the office building near Forty-second Street next morning I should certainly have turned back, except that I could not let Bill down after he had made all the arrangements. I was still in the uniform of the old Half Moon Division, because the two suits I had ordered from Brooks would not be ready for another day. The elevator let me out in a large reception room which was not like any other office that I had ever seen. I saw a handsome Persian carpet and some red leather chairs. Behind a girl seated at a Jacobean table was a wall of richly bound books and an artificial fireplace with artificial coals. On top of the bookcase was a bronze plaque which read "REFERENCE LIBRARY, J. T. BULLARD, INC." Until I saw the girl at the table I had almost forgotten how very pretty American girls were. She looked up at me and smiled. Perhaps I was not so bad-looking myself, even though my uniform was shabby, but then she must have been taught to smile at everyone.

"Oh, yes," she said, "Mr. King said you were coming. I'll call him," and she reached for the telephone.

"Won't you sit down?" she said, and smiled again, but just at that moment a side door opened and there was Bill.

"Hello, Harry," Bill said. "Looking at the books?" As a matter
of fact, I had been looking at the girl at the table, thinking of
something to say to her that was casual, yet merry. I was wishing
that I could be like Bill, always with a ready remark.

"What are the books for?" I said.

Bill looked at the girl and back at me.

"It says on top," he explained. "It's our reference library — part
of the J. T. Bullard service, isn't it, Miss Ayling?"

"Yes, Mr. King," the girl said.

"Come on," said Bill, and he opened the door through which he
had entered and took me by the arm. We walked through a large
room, full of desks and typewriters, to a partition in back.

"Don't ever try to be funny in front of that little bitch," Bill said.
I frowned at Bill, but he did not appear to notice. The country had
certainly changed since I had left it. "She repeats everything," Bill
went on. "Just an industrial spy. Now for God's sake be natural.
Bullard's waiting for you."

At the end of the main office a girl at a typewriter got up when
she saw Bill and opened a door a crack.

"You can go right in," she said softly.

I thought of Mr. Wilding's cubicle when I saw Mr. Bullard's
office. You could have put ten of Mr. Wilding's offices in that room.
The wall was decorated with tapestry. The floor was covered with
a noiseless carpet, and it was quite a walk to where Mr. Bullard sat
behind an antique Italian table. When he saw us he pushed his
chair back and stood up. The light from the window on his left
struck his horn-rimmed glasses, so that it was difficult to see his eyes.
He looked like a professor about to deliver a lecture, except that
he looked more prosperous. His double-breasted gray suit was
beautifully cut. His gray hair was carefully trimmed and brushed
back from his forehead. His voice was vibrant and sonorous.

"Draw up a chair for Mr. Pulham, William," Mr. Bullard said.
"Will you have a cigarette, Mr. Pulham?"

"No, thank you, sir," I said.

"He doesn't mean that," Bill said. "He'd like a cigarette."

Mr. Bullard opened a silver box on the table.

"Now, William tells me," Mr. Bullard said, "that you would like to work with us. I hope you noticed the preposition — with us, not for us. We all work together here, a great big team — a family, aren't we, William?"

"That's exactly what I was telling him last night," Bill said. "A great big team."

Mr. Bullard stabbed into the air with his forefinger.

"In any form of work," he said, "that team spirit comes into play. I am just playing with words, you understand. You can comprehend my next simile, having been in the Service. We all go over the top for an idea."

"That's right," said Bill. "Exactly the way to put it."

"First we sell ourselves on the idea," Mr. Bullard said, "and then we go over the top for it. No one hangs back. Each contributes what little he can. Sometimes I consider myself merely a sieve that sifts and sorts ideas. I'm just playing with words when I say this, but at the same time I'm trying to paint a picture of the challenge which this type of work presents. Now would this sort of thing appeal to you, Mr. Pulham?"

"I don't know," I said. "I don't know anything about it, sir."

Mr. Bullard looked out of the window and no one spoke for a while.

"It's something in your favor," he said. "It is better to write on a fresh page. It is better to know nothing than to be possessed of a lot of undigested facts."

"He's willing to give up a good job just to try this," Bill said.

"Yes," said Mr. Bullard, "I know, I know. Has he seen Walter Kaufman yet? What is Walter's reaction?"

"I'll go out and get him," Bill said.

"I do want Walter's reaction," Mr. Bullard said. "Now, Mr. Pulham, let me ask you a question. What do you hope you'll be doing ten years from now?"

The door opened. A red-faced, solid-looking man entered with Bill following just behind him.

"Oh, Walter," Mr. Bullard said, "this is Mr. Pulham."

Mr. Kaufman pivoted on his heel and faced me. His head was bald, but his eyebrows were yellow and bushy. His eyes were a pale blue, and his mouth was grim.

"How are you, Pulham?" he said.

"Walter," Mr. Bullard asked, "just playing with words, what is your first immediate reaction toward Mr. Pulham?"

"You mean without any thought?" Mr. Kaufman asked.

"Just a snap judgment," Mr. Bullard said.

"Mr. Bullard," said Mr. Kaufman, "there is something basic there."

"There is nothing," said Mr. Bullard, "like an immediate reaction. Let me see — today is Wednesday. You might talk to Mr. Pulham, Walter, and have him come on Monday."

"You'd better come out with me, Pulham," Mr. Kaufman said.

Mr. Kaufman led us into another smaller office where he sat down at a flat-topped desk.

"All right," he said. "Monday morning at nine. That's all."

"Don't you want to ask me anything more?" I asked.

"No," said Mr. Kaufman. "Take him away, King. Show him the Copy Department."

Bill took me by the arm and steered me down an aisle through the main office.

"He just wanted to look at you," he said.

"But they can't hire people that way," I said.

"Oh," Bill answered, "can't they?"

I was confused, but in my confusion my admiration for Bill was growing. He had a confident, almost benign manner that seemed to hint that he knew a great many important facts, that he was beyond all ordinary office routine. I had forgotten that adaptability of his. I was like a new boy at St. Swithin's being shown the school by a Six-Former. It was the way it was when the Colonel's adjutant first showed me my quarters.

"Over in those offices," Bill said, waving his hand, "are the representatives who handle the clients."

131

I learned later that they led the dangerous life of palace favorites, as the possibility that one of them might leave at any moment, taking the account with him, made each of them a potential menace.

"That's where J. T. keeps his eye peeled," Bill said, "here today and gone tomorrow. The iron ball starts rolling any time."

I did not know what he meant, but I did not ask him.

"Over there is the Media Department," Bill said; "college boys, trying to make good."

I did not know what he meant by media either.

"The Art Department is over there," Bill said, "and the layout men are over there. J. T. pays those boys."

"What are layout men?" I asked.

"Idea artists," Bill said. "Never mind about it now. And over here is the Copy Department. That's where we work, and don't you stick your nose out of the Copy Department without me. No one better see much of you for a while."

"But what am I going to do?" I asked.

Bill smiled pontifically.

"Didn't I tell you?" he asked. "That's so. I didn't. You're my assistant. You're going to follow me around and carry my tools. You don't object to that, do you?"

"No," I said, "of course not."

"It's just a way to start, my boy," Bill said. "Now, the Copy Department is divided into small rooms to promote thought. That's one of J. T.'s ideas. We used to be in a big room and then he divided it into cells. We're responsible to Bullard and Kaufman. Don't take any backwash from anybody else. Be genial and co-operative, but no backwash. Here's our cell."

Bill opened a door with ground glass on it, which let us into a smallish room, lighted by a single window. There were two desks, the flat tops of which could fold back and expose a typewriter, like the stenographers' desk at Smith and Wilding. The one near the window must have been Bill's because it was vacant. The second desk was in a corner near the door. A girl was bending over it, writing on a yellow sheet of paper with a soft lead pencil. She turned around and looked at us for a second, and then began to write again, arching her back over the desk, displaying a row of pearl buttons that ran down the nape of her neck between her shoulder blades. I had an impression, I do not know why, of arms and legs. Her ankles were locked tightly together under her swivel chair, and one of her high-heeled slippers was half off, displaying the heel of a golden-brown stocking. I do not know why I remember such a little thing as the heel half out of the slipper.

"Well," Bill said, "here we are. They'll move in something for you to sit at. Thank God, there won't be room for anybody else."

The girl straightened up her back and pushed a stray wisp of hair under the half-invisible net that girls wore then.

"Is that marine going to come in here too?" she asked.

"Yes," said Bill. "The whole U. S. Army is camping here. This is Harry Pulham, Marvin Myles."

"Is he a friend of yours?" she asked. "He doesn't look it."

"Is that a compliment," Bill said, "or a cold rebuff?"

"Work it out on the slide rule," she answered.

"Aren't you going to shake hands with him?" Bill said.

She held out her hand. Her mouth was large and the corners of her eyes wrinkled when she smiled.

"Well, hello," she said.

There was a silence and I felt it was up to me to say something.

There was a pencil drawing on her desk, pasted on a piece of cardboard, a quick sketch of a girl in negligee, looking at her legs. Underneath the girl was printed: "You too can have stockings of sheer beauty."

"Is that picture an advertisement?" I asked.

She swung her chair farther around. "It's a layout," she said.

Bill sat down on the edge of his desk and put his hands in his pockets.

"This is all new to Harry," he told her.

"My God," said Miss Myles, "is he another of J. T.'s ideas? Have you seen what's just been sent in?"

She pointed to a printed sign on the wall, and we both turned to read it.

"*Let each word,*" I read, "*however humble, be an arrow pointed by the barb of thought and feathered with the wings of beauty.*"

"That Yale boy with the squint is going around tacking them up," she said.

Bill nodded.

"It doesn't look bad, does it?" Bill said. "I turned in that thought."

Marvin Myles pushed back her chair, stood up, walked to a green tin cupboard, put on a coat with fur on the collar and pulled a bell-shaped hat half over her eyes.

"Well, I can't stand any more on an empty stomach," she said.

She opened her handbag, pulled out a box with a mirror in it, stared at herself and dabbed some powder on her nose. Then she took out a lipstick and passed it over her lips.

"Well, I'll see you later, I suppose," she said.

She walked out with a long, swinging stride and the door, equipped with an automatic device, closed silently behind her. Bill sat on the edge of his desk with his hands in his pockets and he seemed to have forgotten me entirely.

"What does she do?" I asked.

"Who?" Bill asked.

"Miss Myles," I said.

"Women's copy," Bill said. "She went to the University of Chicago."

I had always considered that college was a handicap for girls, and the girls I had known who went to college went there as a last resort. It made me nervous, like everything else in the office.

"I never saw a girl do that before," I said, "that is, a nice girl."

"Do what?" Bill asked.

"Powder herself like that," I answered.

"Wait a minute," Bill said. "I've got to dictate a memorandum." He hurried out of the room, leaving me standing there, trying to put things together. I looked at the drawing of the girl and her stockings on Marvin Myles's desk. Then I found myself reading what she had written in a round, legible hand upon the yellow paper.

A swish and then a rinse. That's the Coza way. Try this two-minute test yourself tonight. Wash one pair of stockings with ordinary soap flakes; then into clean, warm water drop a pinch of Coza. Watch the snowy whiteness dissolve to lathery foam.

It all sounded cheap and unimportant. I was unable to read any further because Bill came back with a slip of paper in his hand.

"Mercury Clock Account," he read. "The clock is a factory which handles the most precious of all commodities — Time. Suggest this thought can be enlarged with layout of factory and Mercury line in the foreground. Headline — One Tiny Jeweled Pivoted Wheel Turns Eight Million Dollars' Worth of Machinery."

Bill opened the green steel cupboard and took out his hat.

"Would you stop to read that or wouldn't you?" he asked.

"I wouldn't," I said.

"All right," Bill said. "Let's go out now. I'll see you to your train."

Out on Fifth Avenue Bill linked his arm through mine.

"Bill," I said, "I don't think I'm going to be any good at it."

"Don't worry," Bill said. "You stick to me. It'll take you out of yourself."

Then all at once I felt very grateful to him.

"I don't know how to thank you, Bill," I said. "You're sure it won't be too much for you, having me in there?"

"Hell, no," Bill said. "Now, listen, Harry. You're coming back, remember. Don't let them change your mind."

"Bill," I asked, "what's Coza?"

"It's soap," Bill said.

XIV

Let Me Draw a Diagram

The first conviction I really had that I was coming home was when I was in my chair on the one o'clock. The faces of the passengers had a familiar look as though they and I were part of a family. Most of them were my parents' age and wore their same set, serene expression, and their voices were like my parents'.

The faces in the club car were younger. The talk up there was about the textile business and a railroad strike and the fight that was starting over the League of Nations. The voices sounded like echoes of my own voice as I sat down and lighted a cigarette. They pulled me home like the engine. There was something especially familiar in the way a man was sitting reading a newspaper across the aisle. His feet were under him as though he were about to spring and I knew the hands that held the paper before I saw his face.

"Bo-jo," I called to him, "Bo-jo Brown!"

Bo-jo crumpled his paper noisily and sprang up.

"Where did you come from?" he called, and he sat down beside me.

His voice was so loud that everyone turned to look at us, but I did not mind.

"I just got back," I said, "just coming home."

'Porter," Bo-jo called, "fetch out two Scotch-and-sodas. Do you know what's happening? The whole damned country is going dry. So you got to France, did you?"

"Yes," I said.

"Well, it was a great war, wasn't it?" Bo-jo said. "If you amounted to anything they never let you get to the front. Did you notice how that was? Did you get to the front?"

"Yes," I answered.

"Well, I guess they didn't think much of you," Bo-jo said. "Now, take me. I was in the best damned outfit and just when we were getting on the train, what happened? I got orders to be physical director in a new division. My God, what I said to them! But it didn't do any good. The whole lot of us went to a physical directors' school. There was Siegel from Brown — you remember Siegel from Brown. And there was Dunbar from Yale — the one who fumbled first down on the six-yard line. What happened to you?"

"Well," I began, "I was in the Half Moon Division — infantry," but Bo-jo did not listen.

"Did I tell you that Dunbar was down in that physical directors' school? It was a great experience — the war."

"Yes," I said. "It sort of changed me somehow. There's something about seeing people getting killed — " but Bo-jo did not listen.

"You remember Dunbar, don't you? Each one of us had turns drilling, you understand? And we were exhaling and inhaling, and there was Dunbar telling me to exhale, and do you know what I said?"

"No," I answered.

"Well, I said, 'Hold it, Dunbar,' and then Dunbar saw me. You remember that play, don't you?"

"What play?" I asked.

Bo-jo looked at me and scowled.

"The play when Dunbar dropped the ball and when I recovered. Have you got a pencil? Wait. I've got a pencil."

Bo-jo pulled a pencil and envelope out of his pocket.

"Now, listen. Here we were on our six-yard line. Yale's ball. First down. Just when Perkins snapped back the ball I came in through a hole like this. I was there and Dunbar was there. He saw me coming through that hole and he started moving before he got the pass. He didn't get his fingers around it and it slipped and there I was. You remember now, don't you?"

"Not exactly, Bo-jo," I said.

"My God," said Bo-jo, "are you shell-shocked? I fell on that ball and rolled over and there I was running. I was there and Simmons was over there. You know that Eli in the backfield, Simmons? Just between you and me, Simmons was a yellow bastard. He could show off, but he didn't have the guts. When I start going I get going. You remember now, don't you?"

"Yes," I said, "right down the field."

Bo-jo picked up his glass of whisky.

"To hell with Yale," he said.

"That's right," I said. "To hell with Yale."

"And it's certainly time you got back and got in touch with things."

All sorts of matters which I had put aside grew important as Bo-jo talked. I began asking him how the Skipper was and what had happened at school and about our form and about our crowd at college and about the girls who had come out. Quite a lot of them were married, Bo-jo said — the war had that effect. Ten from the School, Bo-jo said, some of them before our time, had been killed or had died in the service from the flu, and the Skipper was getting the School architect to design a permanent plaque in the chapel to hold their names. Most of the crowd were working in bond houses. The whole business, Bo-jo said, was like football; the play was over and everyone was picking himself up, rubbing the mud off his face and getting back in position.

"The Class is going to get together in June," Bo-jo said. "All the old crowd is just getting into formation and going ahead again."

Bo-jo slapped me on the knee so hard that I jumped.

"We had the best damned class that ever came out of Harvard. I don't know what's the matter with the new kids. They haven't got the guts we had."

"What new kids?" I asked.

"The younger generation," Bo-jo said, "the ones who didn't get to war. They can't hold their liquor. They're spoiled and all they seem to think about is sex and they talk about it. You wouldn't believe it. They talk about it in mixed company."

The best thing to do with Bo-jo was not to say much, but to let him talk. He was pointing out that things were upset, that all the

138

working classes, even the mill hands and the day laborers, were making too much money, and instead of being contented it gave them bad ideas. It made them lazy. Now he was as democratic as anyone, Bo-jo said, but it wasn't right to see day laborers and working people, who should save their money, spending it on silk shirts and automobiles and giving their women silk stockings and fur coats. If they only knew it, they were biting off their noses to spite their faces. If women had to have silk underwear and silk stockings what was going to happen to the cotton business? As I listened to Bo-jo's monologue my mind began to wander.

"What's that you said, Bo-jo?" I asked.

"Are you shell-shocked?" Bo-jo inquired again. "I said I'd see a lot of you now you're back."

It was the first time I had had to face it, and I cleared my throat. The train was coming near to New London. I could see the white houses and stone walls and old apple trees and glimpses of the Sound.

"As a matter of fact," I said, "I'll be working in New York. I'm going into the advertising business."

"The advertising business!" From the way Bo-jo Brown looked at me I could tell what he was thinking.

"Suppose you start advertising a cake of soap or a diaper pin!" Bo-jo laughed so that everyone in the car stopped talking. "My God," he said, "wait till I tell the boys! You can't do that." I was not at all sure that I could either.

I had an idea that something tremendous was about to happen to me when I left the train, although everything was just the same, the smell of everything and the way the lights shone through the dusk, and the shape of the houses and the faces on the street. It all caught me by the throat and left me shattered. There is not much use in going over it. There was a time when I used to think that all my mental struggles and emotions were unique, that such problems had never been faced by any other person. Now that I am older I know there is nothing that is new.

"Darling," Mother said, "how thin you look and what a dirty uniform!"

Father, I remember, was almost shy. He kept looking at me curiously and half respectfully, as though I were a stranger. He seemed very anxious to know if I had been in any fighting. I could not see why it was important to him whether I had been at the front or not, until I found that other fathers were telling anecdotes about their sons. Father and Mother looked older and smaller, but Mary was entirely grown up — tall, dark and quite pretty.

"Harry," she asked me, "did you kill any Germans?"

"Yes," I said, and I think it was the first and almost the only time that Mary was really proud of me. "As a matter of fact, I got the D.S.C."

I was rather ashamed of myself when I alluded to it, and I only did so because I wanted them to be pleased. I went upstairs and found the medal and the citation in my bedding roll, wrapped up in a pair of dirty socks, and I gave the medal and the paper to Mother.

"I want you to understand," I said, "that it doesn't really mean anything. I thought I ought to tell you about it in case you found out some other way." I had to go on now that I had started. "It wasn't anything," I said. "If you get me a pencil and paper I'll show you. We were just out there." It made me feel sick inside to tell about it and it reminded me of Bo-jo on the train. "We were in here, across the river, like this, and they were over there and over there."

There was one thing that I did not want — to be thinking about it always, building it up in my mind, repeating it. I did not want my life to stop with just that moment. I only spoke of it so that the family might have some satisfaction, since it seemed to me that it was about all that I could do for them. If it had not been for that medal I do not believe that I should have got back to New York, or that I should ever have seen Marvin Myles again.

The thing to do was to tell them and get it over with. It would have been easier if I had not understood exactly the way they would feel, particularly Father. I remember exactly where I was standing and where he was standing. If you were to give me a pencil and a paper I could show you. It was upstairs in the library, and he was standing there and I was standing there. He had just poured me out a pony of Napoleon brandy.

"I guess you're old enough to drink brandy now," he said.

"Father," I said, "I think I ought to tell you something. I'm going to New York on Monday. I have a job there in the advertising business."

XV

I Make My Letter

Once Marvin Myles asked me when I first loved her, which I imagine is a question that a good many people have asked each other, and I told her that I had loved her from the first minute that I had seen her. I was in a state that makes you believe such things. As a matter of fact, it must have been quite a while before I even noticed Marvin Myles. When I worked down there at J. T. Bullard's, probably I was in exactly the right condition to get myself emotionally involved with almost anyone. Certainly she was not my type, for when I was twenty-four I had no liking for girls who were aggressive or for girls who knew too much. Marvin was not my type, but there was something in her character which I grew to depend on. I do not think this means that I was a weakling. Certainly I have never admired men who are too dependent on women. The truth was that I was in a mental fog during my first few weeks in the J. T. Bullard agency — even more maladjusted than I had been in the Army.

For two weeks I could not seem to get anything through my mind in any proper proportion and Bill did not have much time to help me, because he was generally in conference over the Coza account. That was the term they used when they referred to the advertising business of the soap company — a contract which Mr. Bullard had just landed. There were Coza Flakes and also several grades of toilet soap. Bill and Mr. Kaufman were working on one of these, trying to make it into a soap which would appeal to men.

"There's no reason for you to understand it," Bill said. "It will come over you in time in a great flash of light." Bill shrugged his shoulders. "Now, here's what you are going to do," he went on. "Here's a field report of the washrooms in the hotels and men's clubs of five key cities. It tells whether they use liquid soap or soap powder or soap cakes, and the brands. You're to tabulate the survey on this big sheet. Just sit here and keep tabulating."

It was more or less a clerical job, one at which I was conscientious and industrious, and I found myself at lunch hour and in the evening becoming interested in hotel lavatories and in the types of soap-containers tacked near the washbowls. After two weeks the thing became such an obsession with me that my mind was loaded with interesting facts about the soap they used in the Elks' Club in Davenport, Iowa, and the soap they used at the Commercial Hotel at Baton Rouge.

I used to start in with the soap tabulation every morning, right there next to Marvin Myles. I used to say good morning to her and that was about all. Bill was usually away, so that we sat for hours alone in that office, hardly ever speaking. I did not have much time to be curious about her, with more and more sheets of the soap survey coming in.

It must have been sometime in May, after I had been in New York about three weeks, that I was sent out for a day with Marvin Myles. I had just hung up my hat and started on the soap chart when Bill called me.

"Kaufman wants to see you," Bill said. Since the day I had met him I had hardly laid eyes on Mr. Kaufman, or on Mr. Bullard either.

"Is he going to fire me, Bill?" I asked.

"He just wants to see you," Bill said. "Act as though you were in a hurry."

Mr. Kaufman was sitting behind his neat, bare desk. Marvin Myles was sitting near the wall, listening while Mr. Kaufman interviewed an artist and a man from the Art Department. They had propped up a pen-and-ink drawing on the table in front of Mr. Kaufman, a full-length figure of a young man in a heavy ulster, who must have been watching some sporting event, since he carried a pair of field glasses and a Yale banner. Mr. Kaufman had set his elbows on his desk and his chin into the palms of his pudgy hands. The artist was a bald-headed, prosperous, middle-aged man. When I came in Mr. Kaufman was scowling at the picture and the artist was scowling at Mr. Kaufman.

"I can't tell you what's the matter with it, Mr. Elsmere," Mr. Kaufman was saying. "It simply doesn't convey the idea. For one thing you don't see the buttons and the stitching."

Mr. Elsmere looked annoyed.

"May I ask you," he inquired, "if you can ever see the details of buttons on a coat at such a distance?"

"What do I care about distance?" Mr. Kaufman said. "I'm not paying you for distance."

Then he saw me and scowled at me too.

"What do you want?" he said.

"I was told you'd sent for me, Mr. Kaufman," I said.

"Oh," said Mr. Kaufman, "yes. You're Pulham, aren't you? Well, sit over there by Miss Myles. No, don't sit there. Come over here beside me and look at that picture. Here's a completely new reaction, Mr. Elsmere. What do you think of when you see that picture, Pulham?"

"I don't know, sir," I said. "I don't know what you mean."

Mr. Kaufman thumped his fist down on the desk.

"There, you have it," he said, "that answers it, doesn't it? He sees your picture, that you're charging us a thousand dollars for, and he doesn't know what it means."

Mr. Elsmere looked at me and the top of his bald head grew red.

"Perhaps he hasn't any brains," he said.

Mr. Kaufman pointed his finger at Mr. Elsmere.

"Do you think for one moment that the average person who sees this is going to have any brains? My God, Mr. Elsmere, we're not trying to be intellectual. Now, look at that picture again, Pulham. Which is more important in it, the man or the coat?"

They both seemed to be hanging on my reply.

"The man is more important," I said.

"There you are," said Mr. Kaufman. "That settles it. The coat is showing off the man. Don't you agree with me, Mr. Jack, that there is no thought behind that picture?"

The Art Department man cleared his throat.

"It's very beautiful work," he said. "There's nothing like Mr. Elsmere's pen-and-ink, but thought — no, perhaps there isn't thought."

"All right," said Mr. Kaufman. "Then we'll have to put thought in it. Put a girl beside him. Have her looking at that coat. Have the breeze blowing back the bottom of it, showing the inner lining. Take that flag out of his hand and put his hand in the big roomy pocket. Have the extra-size collar turned up around his ears. Have it snowing. It's the coat, not the man. The girl wishes to God she had the coat. She can see him luxuriate in the warm fleecy lining. If you want to do business with us, Mr. Elsmere, you'll have to think. Get it back as soon as you can and don't try too hard with the girl. It isn't the girl — it's the coat. All right. You can take it away now."

Mr. Kaufman turned toward me unsmilingly.

"Now, draw up a chair. Miss Myles, draw up a chair. You understand, don't you, Miss Myles — a quick cross-section of reaction, something warm, something human, something I can read aloud? Just explain it to Mr. Pulham. Then I'll know if you have my idea."

Marvin Myles turned in her chair to look at me and Mr. Kaufman folded his hands. "It's on the survey for Coza Flakes," she said. "Mr. Kaufman said you could come with me."

"It will be more apt to make them talk," Mr. Kaufman said. "Now, what are you going to do, Miss Myles?"

"I'm going to knock on the door or ring the bell," Marvin said.

"And when the door is opened Mr. Pulham is going to put down the suitcase so it will be hard to close the door," Mr. Kaufman said. "Now, explain your approach, Miss Myles."

"Well," Marvin Myles answered, "I'm simply going to say, 'Good morning. We haven't come here to sell anything. We wonder if you would mind giving us a few moments to talk about your cleaning problem. We have a remarkable new soap. We want to give you some, to try.'"

"And when she says that," Mr. Kaufman said, "you pull a sample box out of your pocket, Pulham, and hand it to the lady. Go ahead, Miss Myles."

"Then I say," Marvin continued, "'I wonder, if you have a moment, if you could give me something soiled to wash?' Do I have to do that, Mr. Kaufman?"

"It will be a great experience for you," Mr. Kaufman said. "You have the question form there with you?"

"Yes," said Marvin.

"Well, try to make it informal, a great big party, a lot of fun," Mr. Kaufman said. "But keep your mind on the consumer reaction. First the suds, then the quickness, and while she's talking you ask her, Pulham, what sort of soap her husband uses; but it's the home atmosphere I want. You follow me, don't you, Pulham?"

"You mean we're going to knock on somebody's door and ask if we can wash something?" I said. Marvin Myles glanced at me.

"I'll tell him all about it," she said. "If the suitcase and the packages are ready we'll start right away."

"Try to get twenty-five reactions," Mr. Kaufman said, "and make up the report tonight. The office will be open. I'll be here working on footwear."

"All right," Marvin told me. "Get your hat and I'll meet you at the elevator."

I got an impression that she was angry.

"Come on," she said. "Come on."

We began to walk toward Forty-second Street and the Grand Central Station. She walked fast, staring straight ahead of her, chin up and shoulders back.

"God-damn fool," she said.

She said it between her teeth while she still stared straight in front of her. It surprised me to hear her swear, because I had never heard a nice girl use such language.

"So I can ask for the dirtiest thing in the house to wash, can I?"

"Where are we going?" I asked.

"You and I," she said, "are going to the Bronx. We're not going to accomplish anything except to make Mr. Kaufman happy. He thought I wouldn't do it. I'll do it all right."

"You mean we're going to tenement houses to wash clothes?" I said.

She looked at me again.

"I wonder," she said, "do you know why you're coming with me, or don't you?"

"No," I said. "It all sounds queer to me."

"All right," she answered. "You're coming with me to see that I go through with it. He thinks I'd cheat if I didn't have you along —that I'd make the whole thing up."

When we got off the subway we walked into the dingy vestibule of a yellow-brick apartment house and examined a row of mailboxes with bells beneath them.

"Any of them will do," Marvin said. "We'll try Frenkel."

She rang the bell and a buzzer let us into the main hallway where the air was full of confined odors.

"Come on," Marvin said. "Come on."

Down near the end of the hallway I saw a fat, dark-haired woman clad in a soiled flannel wrapper peering out of a door.

"Good morning," Marvin said. "I hope we are not interrupting you."

"What is it you want?" she asked. "Mr. Frenkel is not at home."

"Don't worry, Mrs. Frenkel," Marvin said. "We're not trying to sell anything."

"Then why are you here for?" Mrs. Frenkel asked. "You better get out of here or I'll call the police. I'm telling you Mr. Frenkel isn't home."

"Now, Mrs. Frenkel," I said, "that isn't the way to talk."

I was surprised that Marvin Myles stared at me and Mrs. Frenkel's eyes grew round and her loose mouth fell open.

"We just came to ask you," I went on, "if we could wash the dirtiest piece of clothing that you have, Mrs. Frenkel."

Mrs. Frenkel made an inarticulate sound.

"Get out of here," she cried, "or I'll call the police!"

Marvin Myles pulled at my sleeve.

"Shut up," she whispered. "Will you *please* shut up?"

"There's no need to call the police, Mrs. Frenkel," I said. "I'm just asking if I can't do a little washing for you. I'm not selling anything. We have a new kind of soap."

Mrs. Frenkel's face looked blank and she began stepping backward.

"My God," she asked, "are you crazy?"

"I don't blame you for asking," I said. "I thought it sounded crazy too when I was sent out here. They want to see what people think of this new soap."

"My God," said Mrs. Frenkel, "you ain't never washed anything."

"That's perfectly true," I said.

"My God," said Mrs. Frenkel, "oh, my God!" And she backed farther away from the door. I followed her into a sitting room filled with bulbous furniture, put the suitcase on a chair and took out a box of Coza Flakes. Then I took off my coat and rolled up my sleeves.

"I'm all ready," I said, "if you'll show me the laundry."

"The laundry!" said Mrs. Frenkel. Then something made her laugh. "If you want to be crazy we can all of us go nuts. You wait here until I get the dishes out of the sink."

She waddled out of the sitting room and I saw Marvin staring at me.

"What's the matter?" I asked. "Have I done anything wrong?"

"No," she said. "I just didn't know there was anything like you and neither did Mrs. Frenkel."

I was only thinking of doing an unpleasant job as well as I could. We stood with Mrs. Frenkel in the kitchen, while she watched me pouring some Coza Flakes into a pan of hot water. Then I washed a pair of Mr. Frenkel's socks, which certainly did need washing Like most things, once you got started it was not so bad.

"Let me do those," Marvin said.

"No," I told her. "It wouldn't look right."

Everything between Mrs. Frenkel and Marvin and me became quite agreeable after that, so it seemed all right to ask Mrs. Frenkel if she did not have any friends in the building who would like something washed. Mrs. Frenkel said that she did have friends — as soon as she put on her dress — and she left us in the kitchen.

"Harry," Marvin said, "I'm sorry I was cross."

I was a little confused that she called me by my first name.

"Harry," she said again, "we're going to have a good time."

That was true, we always did have a good time.

At lunchtime in a drugstore she told me that when Mr. Kaufman had shown me the picture she could not decide whether I was dumb or clever. Then she added something about me that I have never forgotten and that still seems to me the nicest thing that anyone has ever said.

"You're not either one or the other," she told me. "You're just yourself. I've never seen anyone like you."

It was astonishing that I had the same thought about her. Meeting someone, I suppose, is like fractions in school which you try to reduce to some common denominator.

"Would you mind telling me," she asked, "what made you go into Bullard's? You didn't have to, did you?"

I found myself explaining to her how I felt about things and telling more about myself than was really necessary, and answering strange questions. She said I sounded as if I were in the *Social Register*. She wanted to know all about Hugh and about the dances and about Westwood.

"You've had everything I've always wanted," she said, "and now you don't want it."

"What sort of things?" I asked.

She sighed and we looked at each other.

"Money," she said, "security. I'm going to get it someday. I'm good. I know I'm good. Someday I'm going to be making thirty thousand a year."

It gave me a feeling which I have had sometimes in a club where

I have been sitting safe and warm, looking out of the window at people in the street. That idea has often come to me when I have tried to see things through Marvin's eyes, for somewhere something would come down between us, exactly like a window. I used to be puzzled, and I still am, by her sense of values.

Marvin Myles was born and brought up in a small city in Illinois, the name of which I cannot recall. Both her parents were dead. She had a brother married, living somewhere out in California, to whom she hardly ever wrote, and an aunt in Chicago. Her father had owned a furniture store and there had always been trouble with the grocer's and the butcher's bill. Once she showed me one of her high school photographs — a plain girl. Her eyes and mouth were both straight and defiant as she stared into the camera. Her hair was done in hideous bulging pompadour, fastened behind by an enormous butterfly bow ribbon, and she wore a high-necked shirtwaist. She told me once how hard her mother had worked on her party dresses, and about a girl named Lottie Lou whose father owned the bank and who went East to boarding school. Lottie Lou and other girls like her would see Marvin when they came home for their vacations, seeing her always less and less, finally not seeing her at all. She had gone to Chicago after high school; her aunt had sent her to the University. After her father died, she found some work on one of the Chicago newspapers and later brought her mother to live with her in a one-room apartment. Then she got a job writing copy in the Jacobs agency, and when her mother died she was offered a position with an agency in New York. Then Mr. Bullard had heard of her and now she was making seventy-five dollars a week, more money than she had ever seen.

It was six o'clock when we got back to the office and there were dark shadows under her eyes. Nearly all the desks were deserted, but there was a light in Mr. Kaufman's room. Mr. Kaufman was in his shirt sleeves, looking at proofs of footwear advertising.

"We made the calls," Marvin Myles said. "I kept the notes. Mr. Pulham did the washing."

"Let's see the notes," Mr. Kaufman said.

She opened a briefcase and handed him a bunch of printed forms, all filled out in pencil. He ran through them like a paying teller in a bank.

"Did they talk?" he asked, and his eye ran down one of the pages. "Read that to me, Miss Myles," and Marvin picked up the page.

"It's the first time," she read, "that I won't mind when Frenkel takes off his shoes." I remembered that Mrs. Frenkel had said that, but I had not imagined that Marvin had written it.

"That's the stuff," said Mr. Kaufman. "Warmth and color. Have you got any more like that?"

"Plenty more," Marvin said.

"Well, that's fine," said Mr. Kaufman. "Make each interview into a little story. You'd better get going. I'll be here all night. Just wait here a minute, Pulham."

Mr. Kaufman did not speak until Marvin closed the door.

"Now," he said, "just as man to man, Pulham, was there really a woman named Frenkel?" I saw what he was getting at then. "You see, a number of people have been trying to get these interviews. There's a temptation to rely on the imagination."

"You'll have to take my word for it, Mr. Kaufman," I said.

"But what did you do?" said Mr. Kaufman. "Tell me what you said."

"She wanted to call the police and I told her she needn't do that," I said. "I told her I was going to do some washing for her. That was what you wanted, wasn't it?"

"And she listened to you?" Mr. Kaufman said.

"Why, yes," I said. "Why shouldn't she?"

Mr. Kaufman looked interested.

"Pulham," he said, "you must have a human approach. Now go and help Miss Myles with the report."

When I got back to the cubicle where we worked Marvin Myles had taken off her hat and was beating on the keys of her typewriter.

"Is there anything I can do?" I asked.

First she looked annoyed and then she smiled.

"Don't look like a babe in the woods," she said. "If you don't take

151

care a robin will come along and cover you up with leaves. What did Kaufman want?"

"He kept asking questions about Mrs. Frenkel and talking about warmth and color."

"That's his favorite line," she said, "warmth and color, and don't get to thinking that it sounds silly either. You must have made an impression on him."

"I don't see why," I said.

"Never mind," she answered. "You've made an impression on me. I thought you were terrible and now I like you." She pulled a sheet out of her typewriter. "You can go over the grammar of this, and then you can give it to Kaufman's secretary to make a clean copy, and you'd better go out and get some sandwiches and coffee for us and charge it on your expense account. Now, don't talk any more." I had never seen anyone write so quickly.

As time went on, her lips pressed themselves into a thin, stubborn line.

"You can go on home if you want," she said once. "I can handle this. I'm used to it."

"No," I said. "There might be something I could do."

"All right," she said. "Go out and get more coffee."

She finished the report at half-past eleven and stretched her arms over her head and yawned.

"Well," she said, "that's that. God, but I'm tired!" She got up and pulled on her bell-shaped hat. "I'll see you in the morning."

"I'm going to see you home," I told her.

"Don't be silly," she said.

"It's late," I told her. "You ought not to go out alone so late."

"Oh?" she said. "What do you think I generally do?"

She lived in the seventies, between Lexington and Third Avenue, and I took her home in a taxi. She leaned back with her eyes half-closed, looking at the lights.

"I'll have a car of my own some day," she said, "with a chauffeur waiting outside when I do night work; and I'll have a mink coat and a French maid, and I'll ask you up to dinner."

"All right," I said.

"And be sure you wear a white tie and be sure you behave yourself," she said. "There'll be lots of interesting people, all the writers and artists and people on the stage. I'll be a partner in an agency by then. You see, I know I'm good."

"Yes," I said. "I know you are."

"Here we are. Will you come up?"

She asked me as though it were the most natural thing in the world.

"No, thanks," I said. "I'll just see that you get in all right."

We walked up a flight of brownstone steps into the vestibule and she took a bunch of keys out of her bag.

"Curiously enough, I have my keys."

"Well," I said, "good night."

"Good night," and she looked at me in the half-light of the vestibule.

"Good night," she said, "darling," and she kissed me.

I had not expected any such thing at all, but somehow she made it seem the only correct thing for her to do.

"Good night," I said.

I sent the cab away, because I suddenly felt like walking. I have never had anything happen to me before or since which was just like that. I was suddenly more alive to everything—the clearness of the night and the way the street lamps each cut a luminous sphere in the darkness. There was a sense of spring in the air, not like spring in the country, for the seasons in New York are independent of the seasons in the rest of the world. I was sharing something with the city. For once in my life I was where I wanted to be, a part of everything.

As I say, it all seemed perfectly natural. It did not occur to me for quite a while that Marvin Myles might have been in the habit of kissing almost anyone good night who took her home. Even when it did occur to me, it did not bother me. I kept going over, before I went to sleep, what she had said and what I had said, and I remember wondering what I would say to her in the morn-

153

ing, whether everything in the morning would be like the day before. Bill was at his desk when I arrived, but Marvin was not in yet.

"What did you do to Kaufman?" Bill asked.

"What did I do to Kaufman?" I repeated.

"You did something," Bill said. "I've just seen him. He likes your personality."

"Well, I don't like his," I said.

"That's all right. Neither do I," Bill answered. "But if you're getting on with Kaufman it's fine. Now, where is that tabulation on the washrooms? Bullard wants to see it. Hell is going to pop today."

"What's happened now?" I said.

"We're going to sell the Coza campaign today," he said. "It's going to be some party. And what do you think the crux of the campaign is going to be? Who do you think hit the basic idea?"

"I'm sure I don't know," I said.

"Well, I'll tell you who did," Bill said. "I did. It's a great big vital story. Why does mankind use soap?"

"To clean itself," I said.

"There you go," said Bill. "That's it exactly. And why does soap clean? Why does soap get out dirt?"

"It washes it out," I said.

"And why?" said Bill. "Because of an alkaline reaction. And why is Coza better than any other soap?"

"I don't know why," I said. "Is it?"

"Frankly," said Bill, "that's the tough part. Now, why is it better? Because the Coza chemists, after years of work in the laboratory, have developed a cleaning force, an imponderable. And what do we call that force?"

"What do we call it?" I asked.

"We call it Alkalinity Plus," said Bill. "Try this test today. Wash something with an ordinary soap, and then wash the same thing with Coza. Coza cleans because of that added imponderable — Alkalinity Plus."

154

"But is Coza different from any other soap?" I asked.

Bill smiled dreamily.

"It's different — now," he said, "because it has Alkalinity Plus. You can see that in the headlines, can't you? It's easy to remember — Alkalinity Plus. Hello, Marvin."

She smiled at us and took off her hat and put it in the green steel cupboard.

"Hello," she said, and our eyes met for a moment.

"They want to see us up front," Bill said. "They're going to use Alkalinity Plus."

From the way she looked I could tell there was something important in the announcement.

"Bill," she said, "I'm awfully glad."

"And I made it perfectly clear," Bill said, "the idea's mine, but the name's yours — Alkalinity Plus."

Marvin took off her gloves and laid them beside her hat.

"Thanks, Bill," she said. "When did they decide on it?"

"Just this morning," Bill answered. "Bullard called me up at seven o'clock. He had the ideas all in front of him about the pores of the skin and the delicacy of fabrics. You know the way Bullard is. Well, he couldn't decide on anything, so then I gave him ours." Bill raised his arms and let them drop to his sides. "It hit him," he went on, "right in the solar plexus. 'Good gracious,' he said, 'I never thought of that! What does make soap clean?' Well, he's swallowed it, and once you give him an idea, believe me he can work on it. And now we're going to try it on the client. He's going to start with one of those simple reports that you and Harry did yesterday. Just homey, informal stuff. And then he's going to turn to the client and hit him on the head hard. 'Mr. Fielding,' he's going to say, 'what makes soap clean?' Then we bring on the charts and figures. Come on now. Bullard's waiting for us."

"But, Bill," I said, "that isn't the way soap cleans. It is due to its property of emulsifying fats, not due to alkali at all."

Bill sat down on the edge of his desk.

"My God," he said, "where did you get that?"

155

"It's in the encyclopedia," I said. "I looked it up out there in the reference library."

Marvin looked at Bill and scowled. "Do you mean to say," she said, "you got that whole idea without looking anything up?"

"I thought you had looked it up," Bill said. "Wait a minute — wait a minute. The idea is just as good as ever. Here's the way it'll go."

Bill looked at the ceiling and drew a deep breath.

"For years, for centuries, chemists and makers of soap everywhere have gone on the mistaken theory that the cleansing properties of soap were derived from free alkali. Today modern science has revealed a new truth. Leading chemists know today that it's emulsification that cleans — without attacking tender hands and fabrics in the washtubs. That is why the Coza chemists have evolved a soap of a new high emulsifying power, based on the secret property they call Emul. How about that, Marvin? That has eye value — Emul. Coza is rich in Emul. That's why Coza cleans."

There was a moment's silence and Marvin sighed.

"You can talk your way out of anything," she said.

This shows how quickly Bill's mind could work and why I am right in believing that he was a remarkable person, and he was generous too, because he explained to Mr. Bullard that I had studied the whole theory of soap in my spare time. They all seemed to accept me as part of the organization after that. In fact, Mr. Bullard had an interview with me right after the Coza conference was over and his office was still littered with charts and drawings and containers and piles of soap.

"Pulham," he said, "I'm going to call you Harry; that is, if you don't mind. I'm going to call you Harry, because you've made your letter today. You've been a part of the team. Have you ever thought how strange it is that a great idea is always simple?"

"No, sir," I said.

"I'm just playing with words," Mr. Bullard said, "just playing, you understand. We've been the first to get down to the real essentials of a soap campaign, almost the first to consider basically why soap cleans. Your friend Bill King thought of the general idea, which was in the back of my mind all the time, but I give him credit for it. Miss Myles perfected the idea of the chemists working on the formula — and as a matter of fact Coza chemists work very hard — and then you came in with another suggestion that soap emulsifies. Mr. Kaufman and I finally smoothed these ideas and made them presentable. We were given the ball to run with and we put the ball over. Yes, you've earned your letter."

I am sure that Mr. Bullard did not always take himself seriously when he played with words. It was simply the way people talked in those days, and perhaps they talk so still. Yet I know that from the moment he told me that I was a part of the team I began to like the Bullard office.

I began to understand that to sell soap it was necessary to endow it with some unique quality which would appeal to the consumer. What was more, before long they persuaded themselves that Coza had the mysterious, hidden qualities with which their imagination had endowed it. I am quite sure that Bill got himself to believe implicitly that the Coza chemists after years of patient research had developed an inorganic element named Emul. The more he rang the changes on this idea, the more he actually believed in Emul. I like to think that I was the one who thought of the slogan that was used under the word Coza: "Today the Soap of Tomorrow." It pleases me sometimes when I look upon a billboard to discover that my slogan has never been discarded, but sometimes it all seems like a dream that I ever worked in such a place.

I must have begun seeing more and more of Marvin Myles without noticing it much, as spring moved on into summer. We used to do all sorts of things together which I have never done since, such as riding through Central Park in one of those Victorias or rowing on the lake. Later I bought a small runabout and I used to take her to the Long Island beaches, and before long she began to worry about my clothes. She used to pick out neckties for me and she made me order three new summer suits, and she went with me to get a picnic basket so that we could have our own lunch if we motored out of town on Sundays. I never realized to what extent I depended on her company. I never thought anything about it until one week end in July when I asked for a Saturday off so that I could go up to see the family at North Harbor. It was the first time since I had moved to New York that I had seen the family. I had talked to her about them a good deal, and I remember what she said when we had dinner on the balcony that overlooked the courtyard of the old Park Avenue Hotel, before I took the night train. She must have seen that I was looking forward to going.

"I wish you were coming," I told her.

"What would they think of me if you brought me?" Marvin asked. The question had never occurred to me until she asked it, because I had never thought of connecting her with the family.

"They would like you," I said, "as soon as they understood you."

"But what is there to understand?" she asked.

"Nothing, really," I said. "It's only if you see one type of person all your life you judge everyone else by that type. You wouldn't understand them either."

"Maybe I would. I understand you," she said.

Marvin took a cigarette out of her bag and leaned toward me while I lighted it.

"It's easier for one person to understand another person," I told her, "but it's harder to understand two or three. What are you laughing at?"

"At you," she said. "If you'd only just let things go . . . I wonder what you would be like." I did not answer immediately, but I liked it when she talked about me.

"If I were bright like Bill King," I said, "maybe I wouldn't have to worry so much."

"Now, listen to me," she told me. "Bill King isn't running you. I wish you would get over deferring to him."

"Don't you like Bill King?" I asked.

"I don't like what he does to you," she said. "You're just as good as he is. Have you packed your bag?"

I told her that I had not packed my bag, but that it would only take a minute. The train did not leave until eleven.

"Well, I'm going over to see that you get everything in," she said. "You'll be sure to forget something."

"That's awfully nice of you," I told her, "but I don't know what they would say about your coming up to my room."

"What would they say?" she asked. "I have always wanted to see your room."

I had rented one of the front bedrooms in an old brownstone house on Lexington Avenue. The furniture was sparse and simple — an iron bed, a bureau with a large mirror, a small table and two chairs. No one said anything when we went upstairs, but I still had an uneasy feeling that she should not have been there. Marvin took off her hat and dropped it with her bag and gloves on the table.

"Where's your suitcase?" she asked. "It's getting late."

I pulled the suitcase out of the closet and laid it on the bed. Then I noticed that she was looking at the pictures on the bureau.

"Who's that?" she asked. "Your mother?"

"Yes," I said, "that's Mother."

"And that's your father?" she asked.

"Yes," I said, "that's Father."

"And who is the girl? Someone you haven't told me about?"

"I've told you about her," I said. "That's Mary, my sister."

"And what's this picture?"

"The officers in my regiment," I said.

"And who are those boys?" she asked.

"They're in my Club," I said, "my Club at Harvard."

She leaned her hands on the bureau and peered for a while at the pictures.

"All of you is there, isn't it?" she said. "All that you're going back to? It must be queer, being in two places at once."

"I don't know what you're talking about," I answered. "I'm not in two places at once."

"Where are your shirts and socks?" she asked. "If some maid or someone unpacks your bag I want them to know that you're neat."

It was queer seeing her go over my shirts.

"Now, your evening clothes," she said, "and now that other suit I made you buy, and now your white flannels. Doesn't anybody do any mending for you here?"

"The laundry is supposed to," I said.

"Well, it doesn't," she said. "I'll take that up with you some other time."

We called a taxicab at the corner and she rode with me to the station.

"Harry," she said, "you're coming back, aren't you?"

"Of course I'm coming back," I said. "I'll be at the office Monday."

"You're sure?" she said.

"Yes," I said, "of course I'm sure."

She spoke of it again when we got to the gate of the night train.

"Be sure you come back," she said. "Don't let them take you away."

I turned as I walked past the train and saw her standing watching me and I waved my hand to her and she waved back. I did not realize then, or during my visit to North Harbor either, that I was already in love with Marvin Myles.

XVI

I Must Go Down to the Seas Again

The nearest railroad stop to North Harbor was the Junction, at a little town called Hutchins about ten miles away, where the train from New York, one of those week-end accommodation trains, stopped at five in the morning. In the fresh early light all its details possessed the vague excitement of old association, for I had alighted on that platform in summers ever since I was eight years old. The yellowish brown station building and the platform had not changed. In spite of the automobiles waiting, the ghosts of the old carryalls and democrats that used to take us over the long drive to the Harbor still seemed to linger in the driveway. The baggage-master was the same one I had always remembered, squat and fat but growing very gray. In back of the station was the general store and the white Methodist church that looked like something a child might make from a box of blocks, and then there were all the small white houses, each in its yard with its paling fence, and in the air the resinous smell of fir trees which one always associates with Maine. Patrick had come to meet me in the heavy limousine. I saw his round face and his comfortable stomach right away, the same Patrick who used to meet us in the carryall, but now turned into a chauffeur, and not such a very good one either.

"Give me them bags, Master Harry," he said.

I told Patrick I would ride in front with him and he told me I should do no such thing, because it would not look right; I should ride in back, but he would lower the window so that we could talk.

"If you do that," I said, "you'll pull the wrong rein and drive us into a tree."

161

Then I heard someone calling me and I turned back to the platform. For just an instant I was puzzled as to who it might be though the voice and the face were perfectly familiar, and then I saw that it was Joe Bingham. I had not seen him since the war, but there he was, just as he always had been, in a gray flannel suit, holding a suitcase. He must have come on the Boston section of the train.

"My God," he said, "you're looking just the same!" It was incredible that I could be looking just the same. "Are you down for the week end?"

"Yes," I said, "are you?" Then a sort of diffident silence fell between us. I could not think of anything to say, although I liked him as much as ever.

"Where are you staying?" I asked.

"With the Motfords."

"Can I give you a lift?" I asked. "Patrick is here."

"Thanks," he said, "but I'd better go in their car as long as they sent it."

"I'll be seeing you right away," I said. "It's great to see you, Joe."

"It's great to see you, Harry," he said. "I'll see you on the beach."

I climbed in beside Patrick and he threw the car noisily into gear. The sun was high enough now so that the mist was rising over the scrubby woodland of spruces and pine and birch and poplar on either side of the road. It was always a dull drive until you saw the sea. I could remember all the landmarks, although they came and went more rapidly than they had in the horse and carriage days: the yellow house with its arched doorway, the abandoned farm with alders and birch creeping over its fields, the little bridge above the brook.

"How's everyone?" I asked.

"Everyone is well," Patrick said. "Praise be to God!"

"How's Mother?" I asked.

"Your mother," Patrick said, "ain't what she used to be."

I asked him what he meant by that and he said that she was feebler, that the doctor had been coming more often, but she still liked to ride along the shore road in the Victoria, which was shipped from Westwood every summer. He said they had all been missing me, that nothing was the same with me away, but I did not want to go into that. I was beginning to realize, the nearer we came to North Harbor, how much I had been missing them all too, without really knowing it. They must have been in my mind all the time, secure in North Harbor, and I had thought of them that way for a long time — all through the war and ever since.

"How's Mary?" I asked.

Patrick said that Miss Mary was handsome and that there were lots of girls and boys around the house. Then I saw the sea, smooth and blue and gold and misty, with Rocky Point stretching out into the middle of it.

"There it is," I said. We passed the Harbor Inn that still was dozing by the beach, and then turned toward the houses, built in the Eighties and Nineties with porte-cocheres and towers and bay windows, till we came to our own house which looked very much like the rest of them, with luxuriant nasturtiums and geraniums in the window boxes. As soon as we reached the turnabout the front door opened and Hugh came hurrying down the piazza steps and my father, in plus-four golf trousers, followed him.

"Good morning, Master Harry," Hugh said, and I shook hands with Father — not as though I were his son but as though I were somebody his own age.

"Breakfast is ready," he said. "Don't talk too loudly in the hall. Your mother is still asleep. How are you?" The hall had a fresh, soapy smell. The coffee urn in the dining room was ready.

"It's nice of you to get up so early," I said.

"No trouble at all," Father said. "You look a little white around the gills. You ought to get more exercise." He closed the dining room door and Hugh came in with orange juice. "Mary was coming down," Father said, "but she was up late last night. They all keep going to those damned movies."

"How's everyone been?" I asked.

"Your mother isn't very well," Father said. "And Frank Wilding says there's going to be a slump." He paused and drank some coffee. "I'm glad you came here this week end. There's been a devil of a time at the Club."

"What's the matter?" I asked.

"You can't believe it," Father said. "They're going to straighten out the dog leg on the fourteenth hole. That's one of the prettiest, trickiest drives in the country, and they're going to straighten it out."

"Who is?" I asked.

"The Greens Committee. It's that man Field. They've put him on the Greens Committee."

"Who is he?" I asked.

"That's it," Father said. "Just who is he? God knows who, except that he owns a factory in Ohio, and now he thinks he can change the fourteenth hole, because he says it's too hard for a normal player. There's an entirely new element getting in here. You remember the fourteenth hole, don't you? The one just after the water hazard, par five."

"Yes," I said, "I remember. I made a four on it once."

"You did?" said Father. "You never told me about that."

"I got just up to the edge of the green with a brassie," I said, "and then I chipped right up to the pin. They ought not to change that hole."

"Then you'll come down to the meeting before the dance tonight and vote, won't you?" Father said. "I tell you, Harry, this place isn't what it used to be." He looked out of the wide plateglass windows at the sea. "Nothing's what it used to be. It's the restlessness after the war. It's going to take quite a while before we get over the dislocations. Take the income tax. I never imagined that I should live to see the day when some Government whippersnapper could walk into my office and pry into my private affairs. I never thought I should live to see the time when radicals were organizing labor or when a sentimentalist in the White House could almost get us into a League of Nations. I suppose war is disturbing." His eyes were on me and he stroked his graying mustache. "It must be something

164

like going camping. You get used to all sorts of simple things."

"Yes," I said, "you see things differently, Father."

"I can understand that," Father said, "but I'd like to know exactly how. Does it make you restless? Do you want excitement?"

"It isn't entirely that," I told him. "I guess it may be that you get over the idea you're going to live forever or that anything is going to last forever."

Father bit off the end of a cigar and Hugh came forward with a little alcohol burner on a silver tray.

"That's all for now, Hugh," Father said. "You'd better go up and unpack Master Harry's clothes."

"Yes, sir," Hugh said. He closed the pantry door, and Father watched it for a moment.

"That man's always listening," he said. "I can understand what you mean. When you get to be my age you'll know you won't live forever. I suppose it's unsettling, though, to discover it when you're young; but there are some things that I like to think are going to live for quite a while, such as common decency and civilization and human liberty."

Then he looked confused. He was never very good at talking.

"But there's no use in going on," he said, "because you know what I mean: things we don't talk about, but feel; what you feel in a really good book. You get it in Surtees. You get it in Scott and Thackeray, not very much in Dickens, but it's in Charles Lever. It's in what I can understand of Shakespeare. But I like Surtees best of all."

"I don't exactly see what you're getting at," I said.

Father pulled at his cigar.

"It's hard to put these things into words, Harry. It isn't any news that any of us are going to die, but we like to think we're going to be remembered. We don't like to see everything we believe in changing. I should hate, for instance, to feel that the world is going to stay as topsy-turvy as it is. I know it isn't going to. You and everybody else are going to settle down, because certain values *can't* change."

165

I never understood what he meant until recently when I have seen a lot of my own beliefs and standards, too vague to specify, wash overboard.

"Harry," he said, "what the devil is it you do in New York?"

He drummed his fingers on the table while I went into the details of the Coza soap campaign, which sounded out of place in the dining room.

"Thunder!" Father said. "You *can't* like anything like that!"

"I like it," I said, "because something's happening all the time."

Father sighed.

"I can't follow you. I keep trying to think what I was like at your age. I believe I was much the same as I am now. I can't recall ever wanting things to happen. I've spent all my life trying to fix it so that things wouldn't happen. Well, what else do you do in New York?"

"Nothing much," I said. "We generally work late and I'm pretty tired in the evening."

"Don't you ever see anyone?" Father asked.

"Not very often," I said.

"Then you'd better make up for lost time," Father told me. "You'd better see all your old friends, now you're here. The Motfords have asked you to lunch and we're having a big dinner tonight before the Club dance. What's the matter, Harry?"

"Nothing, sir," I said.

"Then, don't look like that," he told me. "I want people to know you're alive. That's all."

The dining room door opened and there was Mary in a blue dress with white dots. She also gave me a queer searching look before she kissed me.

"You look awfully tired," she said.

"It's the train," I told her. "I could never sleep on a train."

She walked upstairs with me to my room with her arm linked through mine.

"He wasn't arguing with you, was he?" she asked.

166

"No," I said, "just talking."

"Because no one's going to argue with you. I've taken it up with all of them. You're just going to have a good time. Everyone's been asking for you."

"Who?" I asked.

"Oh, everyone," she said. "I know a lot of your friends now."

All at once I felt like a stranger, or as though I had never really known my family. It must have been because their interests were no longer the same as mine. I did not even seem to care whether my friends were interested in me or not. In some way we were all like people speaking different languages.

Hugh was waiting when Mary and I got up to my room, and Hugh himself was like a stranger — an oldish, flaccid, pompous parasite.

"Well, well," said Hugh, "so we're working in the city, are we? Advertising! What a thing now for a gentleman to do."

"Shut up and get me out my golf clothes," I said.

"Well, well," said Hugh, "listen to him, Miss Mary. And Mr. Harry used to be a little gentleman."

"You attend to your business," I said. "You're an old fake and you always were a fake."

We were talking as we had always talked, but somehow, though I tried to use the same old tone, my voice had an unfamiliar edge to it.

"Such a thing to say," Hugh said. "I've worked in houses where you would not be permitted to enter, Master Harry. I was in the household in Yarrell Manor in Dorset."

We had all heard about Yarrell Manor before.

"What were you?" I asked. "The boots boy?"

Even that old reply which I had used often enough before had a different ring to it. Instead of grinning back at me Hugh's face grew red.

"If you want anything more, Master Harry, you have only to ring," he said, and he closed the door softly behind him.

"Why, Harry," Mary said, "you hurt Hugh's feelings."

"I don't see why," I said. "It was the way we always used to talk."

Mary sat down in an armchair near the window and I found myself looking at her. She had Father's dark hair and eyes and high color. She had a supple, sensuous sort of grace which I had never perceived before.

"Give me a cigarette," she said and held out a long delicate hand.

"Are you allowed to smoke?" I asked, and she smiled at me.

"What do you think I am?" she asked. "Fifteen? Everybody's beginning to smoke."

"I suppose that's true," I said. I was thinking of Marvin Myles.

"Harry," she asked, "don't you like us any more?"

"Now, what under the sun," I said, "makes you say a thing like that?"

She leaned back in her chair and crossed her knees and clasped her hands behind her head.

"I wonder," she said, "if you and I will ever be the way we used to be? We don't know what to say to each other, do we?"

I walked over to her and patted her hair.

"That's silly," I said. "We're just the same as we ever were."

She shook her head.

"No, we're all grown up," she said. "It's like finishing the *Little Colonel* books and going downstairs to the library and reading something you shouldn't read."

"Do you do that?" I asked.

"Of course I do," she answered. "Not that there is much that I shouldn't read in the library, except the Bible."

"Now, look here, Mary," I said. "There's no use being cheap. When Sir Walter Scott was dying he said, 'Bring me the Book.' He meant the Bible."

"That's what I mean," Mary said. "If you knew me — really knew me — you wouldn't have to talk like that. There's a lot of rough stuff in the Bible, and you know it. Shall I quote you some?"

"No," I said.

"It's all right," she told me. "You were Big Brother and I was

168

Little Sister. That's the way I felt when you went to the war, and even when you got back."

"You're still my little sister," I said.

"Don't be so mid-Victorian," she said. "I wonder if you're really stuffy. I wonder what you're like."

I saw what she meant, but somehow her point of view did not seem correct.

"Maybe a brother and sister never can know each other," Mary said. "They're all so tangled up. But it would be fun if we knew each other — if I could talk to you about boys and you could talk to me about girls. Perhaps if we got drunk together we could say what we really thought."

"Now, look here, Mary —" I began.

"There you go," Mary said. "It isn't any use. And I keep wondering about you. You're able to do what you want, and I sit cooped up here. Do you think I like it? Harry, won't you tell me things?"

"What sort of things?" I asked.

"You know," she said. "Almost anything that you don't ordinarily talk about. It would do you good, because you're so damned tied-up."

"Don't swear, Mary," I said. "Tell me how everyone is," and I tried to think of someone in particular. "How's Albert Oliver?"

"He's in love with me," Mary answered.

"What?" I said. "Do you mean to say that good-for-nothing little squirt is hanging around here?"

"I know you don't like him," Mary said, "but he's told me a lot about you — a lot that you've never told me."

"What's he told you?" I asked.

"Oh, never mind," said Mary. "But there's one thing. Mother's going to try to make you stay here."

She must have seen some change in my expression, because she continued before I could answer.

"And don't you do it if you don't want to," she said. "She makes everybody do everything she wants."

"Now, Mary," I said, "that's no way to talk about Mother."

She got up and tossed her cigarette into the fireplace.

"Just please don't keep correcting me," she said. "There comes a time when I can't stand it. Has Father talked to you yet?"

"No," I said.

"He's probably afraid to," Mary said. "She has him running around in circles, and he's so sweet about it. God, what a life he's led!"

"Now, look here, Mary —" I began.

"Stop it," said Mary, "for God's sake! I know it isn't any way to talk. You don't know anything about any of us. You've always been away from home, except for vacations, and then everyone's been lovely to you. 'Harry must have a good time. We mustn't bother Harry.'"

There was a knock on the door and we both looked startled. It was Father.

"What are you two talking about?" he asked.

"Oh," said Mary, "everything."

"Well, come out of here and let Harry get dressed," he said. "We're going to play golf and you can walk around with us."

"All right," said Mary, "if you want me."

"When can I see Mother?" I asked.

"Not for quite a while," said Father. "Not till twelve. We can go around and go to the beach for a swim. There's lots of time. And, Harry —"

"Yes?" I said.

"Don't do anything to disturb her. She isn't very well."

That golf game was one of the pleasantest I ever had with Father. For a while it got me back into the swing of things more than anything else. I had almost forgotten what a good time we could have taking a shot and walking and talking. I was ragged for the first six holes, but we were even on the fourteenth tee and even again on the eighteenth. He was very pleased when he won that hole.

And then at eleven o'clock we went down to the beach where the whole community always gathered at the latter part of the morning. There was the same hot glare and the same whiteness of the sand and that same smell of wood and bathing suits. The people that were not swimming were in the rocking chairs along the Beach Club veranda, just as though they had never moved from their places. There was Mrs. Frear and Mrs. Frear's sister, each with a good book from the lending library, and old Mr. Jellison was there, in his white flannel suit, waiting until the clock struck twelve so that he could have his whisky and water, and there was old Mrs. Simms talking about her chauffeur, and there was Mrs. Motford, telling, as she always did, what Cornelia had been doing the day before, and there was old Sir Henry on his vacation from the British Embassy in Washington. They were all there, those older people who had been the landmarks of my childhood, but I saw them with a new distinctness, as though my eyesight had altered.

Down on the beach all the kids I had known, who used to run around throwing things, had grown up into what I had been when I was there last, and all the boys and girls I had known were pushed into a different category — two of them with babies capable of crawling in the sand. There was Louise Mitchell, for instance, who had married Wally Joyce and she smiled at me just as though marriage made no difference. They were all glad to see me, but everyone asked the same question — how long I was going to be there, and when I said only until tomorrow night I was conscious that it was a little hard to go on with the conversation. It gave me a feeling that I did not really belong with them any more, that I did not belong anywhere.

Kay Motford was sitting on the sand with Joe Bingham. She jumped up when she saw me and I remember noticing that she was not wearing bathing stockings. Her face was tanned and she gripped my hand hard, almost like a man.

"Gosh," she said, "it's nice to see you, Harry!"

"You're looking fine," I said.

"I'll say she's looking fine," Joe said.

"I'm getting old," Kay said. "Don't you feel old with everybody growing up? You're coming up for lunch, aren't you? One-fifteen sharp."

"That'll be fine," I said. "It's awfully nice of you to ask me, Kay."

"Where's Bill King?" she asked. "Why didn't you bring him too?"

"I asked him but he was too busy," I said. "Bill's pretty important now. He's worrying about soap."

I was not sure whether Kay wanted me to sit there with them, or whether she wanted Joe Bingham for herself. There was something curious in the way she looked.

"I haven't seen you since the war."

"That's true," I said. "It's funny, isn't it?"

"I suppose it is hard to settle down," she said.

"Oh, he'll settle down all right," Joe said. "It just takes time. Have you seen any of our crowd, Harry?"

"Only you and Bo-jo Brown," I said.

"Where have you been keeping yourself?" Joe asked. "Do you mean to say you haven't seen Sam Green, or Steve, or Bob, or Pinkey? Haven't you been up to School?"

Joe looked hurt and it was hideous in a way that everyone except myself was acting properly.

Miss Percival, Mother's day nurse, was standing in the hall in front of Mother's door.

"We've been waiting for you," Miss Percival said. "We've had our nap, but we mustn't talk about anything too exciting."

"How is she?" I asked.

"We are really doing very well," Miss Percival said. "We've been talking about our boy ever so often, our soldier boy, and we've been waiting for his visit, but we must only discuss happy things."

Mother was on her chaise longue and dressed in a lavender negligee fastened by her diamond and sapphire brooch. Her hair was done in the old intricate way she wore it when I was very young — a knot made of careful little braids. It was still dark and beautiful without a touch of gray in it; her skin was as clear as ever, a little too clear, I thought, for it had that half-transparent quality of someone who is not well. On her dressing table, with all the little vases and ornaments she had collected, I saw the callow photograph which had been taken of me in my first officer's uniform.

"Darling," she said, and she held out her arms to me. "Isn't he beautiful, Miss Percival? Now do you see why I am proud of my boy?"

"Yes," said Miss Percival. "We are very proud of our boy, but we must only talk to him for a few minutes."

"Darling," Mother said, "are you having a good time?"

"I am having a fine time," I said. "I have been playing golf with Father and then I have been down to the beach."

"And then you are going down to Kay's for lunch, aren't you, dear?" Mother said.

"Yes," I said. "You mustn't worry about me. I'm having a fine time. It's — "

She raised her hand and touched my head very softly.

"Yes," she said. "It's what, dear?"

"It's just as though I had never been away."

It was hard to talk with Miss Percival sitting in the corner watching us, but her presence prevented our saying too much or thinking too much.

"That's just the way I want it to be," Mother said. "You never have really been away, darling. You are still my little boy. You know what I mean, don't you?"

"Yes," I said, "I know."

"Because we always understand each other, don't we?"

"Yes," I said. I was thinking as I sat there beside her how little words meant. We never had understood each other, and I wondered if she did not know it and if it did not hurt her just as it hurt me.

"You must have such a good time that you won't go away."

I saw Miss Percival move uneasily.

"I've got to go back tomorrow night," I said.

Mother's hands dropped in her lap.

"Darling," she said, "I never thought that you were selfish."

173

"Now," said Miss Percival, "we mustn't have the doctor angry with us, must we? We must only talk about happy things. We must be glad that our Big Boy is with us today and tomorrow."

"Mother," I said, "any time you really want me — "

"I want you now, now, always," Mother said.

"It is time for our boy to be going now," Miss Percival said. "We'll see him in the afternoon."

I closed Mother's door behind me. It had been a good deal worse than I had expected. Mary was waiting for me in the hall.

"Was that old bitch, Percival, in there?" Mary whispered.

I started as though she had stuck a pin in me.

"Where did you pick up that word?"

"Well," Mary answered, "it's what I mean. Did Mother try to make you stay?"

"Yes," I said. "I can't. I'm going back tomorrow night."

Then I forgot that she was my little sister. I suppose that I had to speak to someone.

"My God, Mary, I can't stay," I said.

At lunch I sat at Mrs. Motford's right, and I listened to everyone talking. First we talked about the new Prohibition Amendment and about repression of the rights of the individual. Then we talked about the Bolsheviks and the bombings and about the British dirigible that had crossed the ocean.

"You ought to be staying here," Mrs. Motford said. "Guy is up here every week end. Families should be together."

The men stayed around the table after lunch, and Guy and Joe Bingham began talking about the war.

"You got over, didn't you?" Mr. Motford asked.

"Yes," I said, "I got over."

"Did you see any fighting?"

"Yes," I answered, "some."

"It's too bad we didn't smash the German Army while we had the chance. Don't you feel that way?"

"I don't know," I said.

"You don't know?" Mr. Motford repeated.

174

"It's hard to tell, sir," I said. "I don't know whether it would have been worth while to have killed anybody else."

"You sound like a Pacifist," Mr. Motford said. "The only thing to do with a nation like the Germans is to whip them. That's what they expect, and what they understand."

I always seemed to say something that was disturbing. Out on the piazza afterwards, while the sun was glittering on the sea and the air was pleasantly cool and fresh, they were discussing Woodrow Wilson, who was dragging us without our knowing it into new commitments in Europe.

"I don't see how there can be any possible peace," I said, "if we don't enter the League of Nations."

Everyone looked at me as though I were willfully being difficult. At any rate it was quite plain that no one else believed in the League of Nations. I had a feeling that I did not belong there any more.

I had forgotten how pretty all the girls were. They still wore long dresses at the Club that night, but their dresses had more color to them, and the beat of the music was more pronounced. Instead of all the faces being familiar, there were all sorts of new ones, all sorts of strangers who knew everyone except me.

"Harry," Kay said, "can't you keep time to the music?"

"I am keeping time," I said.

"You're not," said Kay, "and you've been drinking."

"Not any more than anyone else," I said.

"Harry," Kay said, "I don't know what's the matter with you."

"How do you mean?" I asked.

"You aren't the way you used to be at all," she said. "Has anything happened to you?"

"It isn't me," I answered. "It's everything else. Everything —"

Then Joe Bingham cut in on us, and Kay's whole expression changed. Her eyes and mouth were no longer critical. I stood near the wall, watching them dance away, to lose themselves among the other couples. I was thinking that it was about time to cut in on

175

the youngest Frear girl, when Guy Motford came up to me.

"What's the matter with you?" Guy asked me.

"I don't know why everybody asks that," I said.

"Well, you don't act as though you were having a good time," Guy said. "There's a girl that wants to meet you. Did you ever hear of her — Emmy Kane?"

"What's the matter with her?" I asked.

"Nothing," Guy said. "She's one of the best little neckers you ever saw. Come on." He pulled me a few steps across the floor and stopped a couple that were coming toward us. "Here he is, Emmy. Emmy Kane, this is Harry Pulham."

She was one of the new people at the Club, from one of those families that had come there in the war years. She was thin and her dress was a yellowy green. Her hair and eyes were dark.

"I saw you on the beach," she said. "You looked awfully cute in a bathing suit."

Her speech showed that she came from New York or Philadelphia or Baltimore or Washington. Certainly no one nearer home would discuss the way I looked in a bathing suit, and when I put my arm around her I must have hesitated.

"What's the matter?" she asked.

"Nothing," I said.

"I'll bet you've got an awfully good line," she said. "I wish you'd hold me a little closer. I can dance better and it's more cozy."

"All right," I said.

"You act so young," she said. "Is that your line?"

I must have been a good many years older than she. I had been to the war, where I had seen sights which were unbelievable. The bewildering part was that she was a girl in my own social class and I did not know what she expected, or what to do.

"Let's go somewhere," she said.

"All right," I answered. "That would be fine."

We walked out on the veranda with the music playing behind us, and I was thinking of the time long ago when I had walked out there with Kay, when Bill King was visiting us.

"Have you got a car?" she asked. "Let's drive somewhere."

"Yes," I said, "that would be fine — if it's all right." I had never heard of taking a girl out in a car in the middle of a dance, and I was wondering what people would say if we were noticed. I could still hear the music above the crunching of our feet on the blue gravel. The orchestra was playing "Madelon" and "Good-by Broadway, Hello France." The music was all around us in the cool darkness and the stars were out very clear and bright.

"Have you got any rye?" she asked. "I always like rye."

"You mean whisky?" I asked. She began to laugh.

"You have the cutest line," she said. "We'd better go in our car. There's some in the side pocket."

Her car was a new open Cadillac, and she asked me to drive it. She sat close to me, leaning lightly against my shoulder.

"Where shall we go?" I asked.

"Somewhere where we can park," she said. "Out along by the sea. I love the sea, don't you? You're Mary's brother, aren't you? Mary's awfully cute." It was a new word to me — "cute." I wished that I felt more familiar with this sort of thing, and that I knew what to do. I remember thinking that Bill King would have known. We drove through the village along the shore road, past the cottages to the drive along the cliffs where you could hear the sound of the waves coming through the dark. She sat leaning against me, and began humming beneath her breath.

"Let's sing," she said, and we sang "Madelon."

"Let's stop here," she said, and when I stopped the car at the edge of the road near the cliff, she leaned over to the switch and shut off the engine.

"The lights are over there," she said. "You'd better turn them out or we'll burn down the battery." Then she reached into a pocket in the door. "Here it is," she said, and she unscrewed the stopper of a silver flask, and took a drink and handed it to me. I took a drink too because it seemed to me exactly what I needed, and it made me feel a good deal better.

"What are you thinking about?" she asked.

"I was thinking," I said, "that I had never done anything like this."

She laughed at me through the dark.

"Go ahead," she said, "but don't rumple up my hair."

She put her arm on my shoulder, and I saw her face turned up toward mine, white and hazy in the dark, and I bent down and kissed her. I felt her arms tighten about my neck.

"Darling," she whispered, and I kissed her again.

"I've been wondering," she said, "ever since I saw you on the beach what you were like. . . . Do you like it?"

"Yes," I told her. "Very much."

"You're so funny," she said. "You act as though you were worried."

"Look here," I asked her. "Does everyone do this now?"

She pushed herself away from me and looked at me.

"What ever are you talking about?"

"I don't know," I said. "A lot must have happened since I've been away."

"I guess we'd better go back," she said.

"Oh, no," I said, and I unscrewed the stopper from the flask and took another drink, as long as it was the thing to do. Then I tried to kiss her again.

"No," she said, "you act —" her voice broke, "as though —"

"As though what?" I asked.

"As though I was immoral."

"I didn't mean to act that way," I said. "I'm awfully sorry."

"We'd better be going back," she sobbed. "No, don't touch me."

I was sorry and at the same time I was angry at myself, because I knew I had not behaved properly.

"Please listen to me," I said. "I don't know what I did, but I want to beg your pardon."

But she only blew her nose and sobbed.

"Please don't," I said, "please."

"Oh, shut up," she sobbed. "You've spoiled it all. We'd better go back."

"All right," I answered.

I was thinking that had I asked Marvin, if it had been Marvin and I on that road by the sea, whether everyone did that sort of thing, she would have laughed. There was never anything to worry about with Marvin.

"Aren't you going to talk?" Emmy asked at length. "Aren't you going to say anything?"

I have thought often enough of all the things I could have said to her. I suppose everyone has some awkward moment in his life which keeps cropping up uncomfortably through the years, and my ride in the car has always been like that. I have explained to her in my thoughts everything about myself, very volubly and convincingly, but I only said at the time:

"I'm not really as bad as you think I am."

Yet it was true that everything was spoiled.

Father was sitting in the parlor, nodding over his paper, and his head straightened up jerkily when I came in.

"Oh, there you are," he said. "Did you have a good time?"

I wished that they did not all keep asking me the same question.

"Yes, a fine time," I said.

Father sat up straighter.

"You're not serious about going back tomorrow, are you?"

As I stood there looking at him I felt absolutely certain that if I stayed something terrible would happen to me, although I could not tell what.

"I'll have to be there Monday morning," I said.

Father tossed his paper on the floor.

"Harry, when are you going to stop all this damned nonsense?"

"Father," I said, "it won't do any good to argue."

I have never forgotten the way he looked at me, as though he saw something that he could not entirely believe. First his eyes were hard and incredulous, and then he looked older than I had ever seen him. It made me feel that we had met in actual physical collision, and that I had been stronger because I was young. It made me feel sorry for both of us.

"All right," he said. "We won't go over it again, but I'm damned if I know —" He stopped and glanced away from me while I waited for him to go on. "I'm damned if I know what's getting into everybody. I wish you'd talk to Frank Wilding."

He got up stiffly out of his chair and walked over to me.

"Perhaps around October," he said, "you'll feel differently. If you're back around October, and if your mother is feeling better, maybe we could go out after woodcock. When you were born I thought there'd be someone I could take shooting. It's funny, isn't it? Nothing turns out the way you think."

"I wish you wouldn't say that, sir," I said.

"Well, it's true," Father said. "All the things you take for granted — there they are, and then they're gone. There you were, and now you're gone, and I don't know how it's happened."

He stood there staring at the carpet. "We had a good time playing golf, anyway, didn't we? I don't know, Harry, I don't suppose I know much about anything, but just remember I have sense enough to realize it. That's why I'm not arguing with you."

"I wish you wouldn't say that," I said. "You make me feel —"

"I can't help the way you feel," Father said, "and you can't help the way I feel. I guess neither of us is very bright, Harry. We just have to worry on as best we can. Good night."

"You're not angry with me, are you?" I asked.

"No," said Father. "What's the use of talking? I never could talk." He reached out his hand and we shook hands.

I know now why everything went wrong at North Harbor. I did not want to stay there, because I was in love with Marvin Myles.

XVII

When the Girl You Love Loves You

I was back at the Bullard office at nine on Monday morning.
Once I heard the typewriters and saw everyone working, it was
just as though the week end and everything in North Harbor had
been part of a bad night. Early as it was, the day was stifling hot,
and the warm air and the noises from the street came through the
open window; but I did not mind it because I seemed to be wide
awake again. Bill King's and Marvin's desks were still vacant and
I hoped that Marvin would get there before Bill, and when she
did I realized how much I had wanted to see her. I had not thought
much about it — until the light struck her hair when she took off
her straw hat.

"Hello, Marvin," I said.

"Why, hello," she said, and then we both laughed. "Well, here
you are."

"Yes," I said. "It seems so."

"And you don't look any different," she said. "I kept thinking you'd
look different. Did you have a good time?"

I don't know why everyone kept asking me that.

"Where's Bill?" I asked.

"They sent him out to Chicago," Marvin said, "to see the dis-
tributors. Never mind about Bill. We have to see Kaufman at nine-
fifteen. What did they do to you up there?"

"Who?" I asked.

"Everyone — the butler and everyone. Did he unpack your things?
Did he say anything about them?"

"Why, no," I said.

"Oh, he didn't, didn't he?" Marvin said. "He might have said I packed your bag all right."

"Never mind him," I said.

"I do mind," Marvin answered. "Someday I'm going to have a butler and I want to know how they work. Harry, did you miss me?"

"Yes," I said.

"All right," Marvin said. "Now we'll go in to see Kaufman, and remember he's always bad on Monday mornings. Get some paper and pencils. Come along."

"Marvin," I said, "I want to tell you something."

"Well, tell it quickly," Marvin said.

She was bending over her desk, picking up some pencils and copy paper, and everything seemed absolutely natural, absolutely simple. I could hear the typewriters going in the outside office and the motor horns on the street. For once in my life I knew about everything. It was like looking at an examination paper and being prepared for all the questions. It was like hitting a ball exactly right. I had read about such moments, but this was not like anything I had read.

"What are you looking at?" Marvin asked.

"Marvin," I said.

"What is the matter with you?" Marvin asked. "Is it the heat?"

"Yes, it is pretty hot," I said, "but it was cold enough for blankets at North Harbor. It's funny that nothing turns out the way you think it's going to."

"What are you talking about?" Marvin asked.

"I don't know," I said. "Marvin, I love you."

She turned around very quickly, and at first I thought she was annoyed from the way her forehead wrinkled.

"Well," she asked, "whatever put that into your head?"

"I don't know," I said, "just now when I saw you I wanted to tell you."

"Why, darling," Marvin said, and then she stopped. "Well, that's all right. I love you too, but we can't do much about it right now, can we? Come ahead. Kaufman's waiting."

182

There were a lot of details about that period which I thought I would never forget, yet now that I try to recall them, they are all lost. I was perfectly sure that they were somewhere, just the way we were sure last week that the silver cream-pitcher was somewhere in the house, because it had been put away for the summer, and the chore-man would not be apt to get into the third-story cupboard, and the maids would certainly not take it. It would certainly turn up sometime. And that is what I keep thinking of those days that are lost; but they have never turned up. It was the first time that I had ever told a girl that I loved her, and the first time that the girl that I loved loved me. I believe there was a popular tune that went that way in those days.

I know that I was happy, very happy, but there was more to it than that. I was not sure that she really meant it, for she gave no further sign of it, and we were awfully busy that day, so busy that it all became a sort of background. All the time that I was thinking that Marvin had said she loved me, we were discussing the emulsifying properties of soap. My suggestion to Mr. Kaufman that a simple home test could be made to show the powers of Coza was considered a real contribution, and Mr. Bullard paid serious attention to it. I remember now that my love for Marvin Myles was a good deal mixed up with pictures of people washing themselves and with pictures of intimate, filmy garments.

We worked on rough layouts with Mr. Kaufman all that morning and all that afternoon while the perspiration poured down Mr. Kaufman's face, for the office was as hot as a Turkish bath, but the heat stimulated Mr. Kaufman's energy. He sat there, mopping his forehead and tearing things to pieces, looking at roll after roll of drawings.

"The basic idea is all right," Mr. Kaufman said, "but the trouble is there isn't any sex in it."

"Sex?" I remember that I repeated after him.

"Sex," said Mr. Kaufman, and he slapped his hand on the desk. "You can't have a soap campaign without sex appeal. You get my idea, don't you, Miss Myles?"

183

"Yes," said Marvin, "I know what you mean."

"Well, that's what you're here for," Mr. Kaufman said. "I've watched Mrs. Kaufman with soap. It's intimate."

Marvin glanced at me across the room and then looked out of the window. It was the first time that I had heard of Mrs. Kaufman, and I wondered if Mrs. Kaufman loved him. If I were ever married I would certainly not bring my wife's name into conversations about soap. If I were ever married . . . It was the first time that I had ever thought about it that way. If I loved Marvin and she loved me, we would get married.

"Daintiness," I heard Marvin saying, "is that what you mean?"

"Daintiness," Mr. Kaufman said. "Now we're getting somewhere. Wait a minute. I'll see if Mr. Bullard is out of conference."

Mr. Kaufman hurried out of the room, bouncing on his toes, and for the first time that day Marvin and I were alone.

"Marvin," I said, "maybe I didn't understand you when you said — "

"Of course you did," Marvin answered. "How do you think I've been feeling since I first saw you? Here comes Kaufman. Isn't he terrible?"

"All right," said Mr. Kaufman. "We're going to see Mr. Bullard now."

Mr. Bullard was sitting at his desk with the tips of his fingers pressed together.

"Miss Myles," he said, "I hear you have found a word. I want you to tell it to me. I didn't want Mr. Kaufman to spoil it."

"How do you mean I'd spoil it?" Mr. Kaufman asked.

"Now, Walter," said Mr. Bullard, "you know how it was about that lubricating oil. Occasionally you mangle words. You mangle the very web and woof that we're weaving."

"Come off it, can't you, J. T.?" said Mr. Kaufman. "You're not talking to a client. We're trying to get somewhere with that soap and they're screaming for copy."

"Now, Walter," said Mr. Bullard, "what is copy but words? Every word in perfect balance with another."

"Oh, God," said Mr. Kaufman, "come off it, J. T. You're not trying to sell anybody anything."

"What is the word, Miss Myles?" Mr. Bullard asked.

"The word is daintiness," Marvin said.

"Wait," said Mr. Bullard. "Wait, don't speak again. I don't want anyone to speak."

The room was silent.

"Daintiness," Mr. Bullard said softly. "Don't interrupt me. Loveliness. Sheer glowing loveliness. Filminess. Evanescence. Dawn. Mistiness. Don't interrupt me."

Mr. Kaufman stood looking stonily out of the window, his face red and glowing, his shirt sodden and limp. I looked at Marvin. She stood looking straight ahead of her, like a registered nurse in an operating room.

"Daintiness," said Mr. Bullard. "All right. Use it in all the women's copy. Don't plug it too hard. And use all the rest around it. That's fine, Miss Myles."

Mr. Kaufman sighed noisily.

"We can go ahead, can't we?" he said.

"Yes," said Mr. Bullard, "we can go ahead. I think it might be better to put Miss Myles in charge of the women's copy. I'll edit it myself."

"Very well," said Mr. Kaufman stiffly, "if that's the way you want it."

That was all they said, but I had been there long enough to realize it meant that Marvin would no longer have to defer to Mr. Kaufman. Her expression did not change, but there was a change in the way she looked. Somehow, something Mr. Kaufman had said had offended Mr. Bullard. Once I heard Bill King say that he would rather be in a cage with a tiger than be too long with J. T.

"You've got to butter him up," Bill had said. "Watch him when he gets poetic. That's the time when he may do anything, and if he starts to cry you'd better cry too. I had to do it once."

It was after five o'clock when we got back to the room where we worked and Marvin put her hand over mine for a moment.

185

"God, what a day! Everything's happened — everything. I've got to go home and get a bath. Do you see what happened? He told Bullard to come off it, do you remember? He might as well resign."

"Marvin — " I began.

"Darling," she said, "you've got to learn to keep everything in its place. Go home and put on a dinner coat and stop for me at seven. We're going to the Plaza and we're going to have champagne. Go home now and get dressed. I look awful and so do you."

"No, you don't," I said.

Marvin was putting on her hat.

"Don't you see," she said, "we're in the office now? Don't look that way. There's nothing to worry about."

I was not really bothered, because there was never anything to worry about with Marvin Myles.

It was only when I stood in that rented room of mine with the pictures of the family on the bureau that I thought the whole thing through. I had never considered until then what the family would say or what Marvin would say about the family. I did not hesitate about anything for a single instant, and I did not have a moment's regret, but I knew that we would have to think about plans.

I expected her to come downstairs to meet me, but instead the front door clicked and I walked up three flights to her apartment, a furnished one which she had sublet — a bedroom and a sitting room and a little kitchenette. The door was open and Marvin called to me from the bedroom to wait.

"I've got a new dress," she called. "Wait till you see it!"

I sat there in the sitting room waiting, thinking of the times I had been there before; for I had spent a good many evenings there that summer. The furniture, the chairs, the lamp and the studio couch were chintzy and overdecorated — not connected with Marvin. The only things that were hers were the books on the shelves — a row from Everyman's Library, and the Bible and *Bartlett's Familiar Quotations,* and Roget, and a dictionary, and Bulfinch's Mythology, and the *Oxford Book of English Verse*. Then above them were some of the newer books — *The Spoon River Anthology,* two of Dreiser's novels, *Mr. Britling Sees It Through, The Harbor,* a volume of Cabell, and Freud's *Interpretation of Dreams.* Marvin had read a great deal more than I had, and most of those books were strange to me. Now they seemed like my books, simply because they belonged to her. I heard the swish of her dress in the bedroom. I heard her putting things to rights, for she always wanted things in order, and then the door opened. I don't remember what the dress was like, because I can never remember about clothes, but she was beautiful.

"Kiss me," she said. "I've been waiting all day." She pushed me away and held me by the shoulders.

"You've missed it again," she said.

"Missed what?" I asked.

"The back of your head," she said. "You brush your hair hard in front, but there's always a place in back you never touch. Wait a minute. I'm going to put some soap on it."

She went into the bedroom and came back with a washcloth and her hairbrush.

"Now, stand still," she said, "and don't wriggle. There's such a lot I'll have to do to you."

I pretended to think that it was funny, but she must have known that I was pleased.

"Now your tie," she said. "It slides around. I've always noticed that. But you're so wonderful in a dinner coat! You look as though you belonged in it. You don't look like a waiter. You look like a Sargent portrait or like Lou Tellegen."

"It's all right," I said, "as long as I don't look like Francis Bushman — or Rudolph Valentino."

I was moving automatically from everything that I had known into a new and strange adventure. Marvin was a good deal more of a person than I was, more talented, more cultivated, but I realized very suddenly that I was facing something like the Army — a different sort of life — and that my training was entirely inadequate.

"I've certainly got to do a lot about you," Marvin said. "You won't know yourself when you get through."

I stopped the taxi at a florist's to buy Marvin some orchids, not the ordinary purple ones, but some with little brownish-yellow flowers.

It amused me a little to see her when we went downstairs in the Plaza, because she cared about so many things which I took for granted. For instance, I had always thought of the downstairs room as stuffy and complicated, but it meant something else to Marvin.

"Tell the headwaiter we don't want to sit over there," she said. "Tell him we want a good table." And when the waiter asked if madame was satisfied she looked very pleased.

"Darling," she said, "isn't it wonderful?"

"Yes," I said, "it's the first time I ever enjoyed it here."

"Now tell me when you first liked me," she said, and we went over the whole thing, I suppose the way everyone does, remembering this and that, all sorts of little things that she had said and I had said, and the way she had looked and I had looked.

"It all came over me," I told her. "I didn't know what you were like at first and then it all came over me. I wish I could say things nicely."

"You do, when you say what you mean," she said.

"I don't see what you see in me," I told her.

"You wouldn't," Marvin said. "It's because I can do so much for you. That's what a girl really wants. It's going to be like a symphony. You're going to like all the things I like and I'm going to like all the things you do."

"I wish I could be more like Bill King," I said. "I wish I could tell you how I feel."

"Don't be silly," she answered. "That's because no one's ever loved you." Then I began thinking of what I would say when I introduced her to the family.

"Marvin," I said, "when are we going to get married?"

"Why, darling," she said, "do you really want us to get married?"

"Why, yes," I said, "of course."

She looked at me across the table, smiling.

"I was wondering why you were worried," she said. "Don't look that way. Of course I want to, but we ought to see what it's like."

"What it's like?" I repeated.

"What everything is like — you and me — everything. I want you — " She reached across the table and touched my hand — "I want you to want to marry me so much that you don't care about anything else — anything. For once in your life, dear, try to have a good time. Try to think of it all as natural. I'm going to make you do that, if it kills me."

"Marvin — " I began, and then I stopped.

"Go ahead," she said.

"You don't mean, Marvin — " I said, and I felt myself blushing. "You can't mean what I think."

"Of course," Marvin said, "I mean what you think. I want us to be happy, dear. For once in your life I want you to be happy. Have you ever really been?"

"Happy?" I repeated.

"Tell the truth," Marvin said. "Have you ever really been happy?"

"No, I guess I never have," I said.

"Well, from now on," Marvin said, "you're going to be."

Sometimes I can stand away at a distance and see myself as another person back there when I knew Marvin Myles. Everything moved swiftly and strangely. I can think of poems we read and things we saw together, and I can see how callow I must have been; and at other times I can hear myself saying to myself, how could I have done that? There is so much of which I have never spoken, which I have hidden inside myself, and I like it better that way. I like it better when I say to myself, that was that, although it is a poor way to put it. I remember one thing she said to me once, and when I repeat it perhaps I have said enough:

"Now, we can tell each other everything."

Sometimes I begin thinking that I know more than a lot of people around me, because I must know more than anyone else alive knows about Marvin Myles. Somehow I am absolutely sure of that, and perhaps there is a fair exchange, for she knows more about me too, provided that amounts to anything. I suppose that such a thing as that can happen only once in your life, and perhaps it is just as well.

I know the whole secret of Marvin Myles — that she wanted things to belong to her, because what belonged to her gave her a sense of well-being, a sense that had something to do with power, although that is not the proper word. Once something belonged to her, she would give it everything she had. I know, because I belonged to her once.

We rode through the park in a Victoria that night, and afterwards we went in a taxi back to her apartment. It was almost midnight by then. She stood beside me looking at her little living room.

"It looks like the devil, doesn't it?" she said.

"No," I said, "it's awfully nice."

"It isn't," she said. "It's cheap and silly. Some day, I'm going to have a room with nothing but Chippendale in it. You can take me over to England and I'll buy it. Open the window, will you?"

I opened the window and looked out at the street lights and a trolley car went by.

"When do you want to go?" I asked.

"Some day," she said, "some day when there's time. We'll sail on the *Berengaria*. I'll want clothes in Paris too. What do you want?"

"Nothing," I said. "I'll watch you buy them."

"That's because you've always had everything," she said. "I'm tired. Aren't you tired?"

"Perhaps I'd better be going now."

"Now, that's a silly thing to say," she said. "Why do you have to go because I'm tired? I can lie down here on the couch and you can sit beside me, and you can tell me about everything."

"What sort of things?" I asked.

"You know," she said, "the things you always tell me about. Tell me about North Harbor, and you might as well turn out the light."

I sat beside her in the dark and the light from the street was something like moonlight. I have always liked the street lights ever since. It shone dimly on her face while she looked up at me. I must have talked for quite a while about North Harbor and I said a good many things which I had never said to anyone.

"Don't," she said all of a sudden, "don't go on about it any more. I want to know all about them, but not now."

"You're tired," I said. "I'd better be going."

"What are you going to go for?" she asked. "Aren't you going to kiss me?"

"Why, yes," I said, "of course," and then she laughed and I saw that her face was wet. "Marvin, what are you crying about?"

"Darling," she whispered, "promise me something."

"What?" I asked.

"Don't say you've got to be going."

"All right," I said. "I won't."

"Just try to forget that there's anyone but me."

In the years that followed, when I never consciously thought of Marvin Myles, she must have been somewhere in my mind, waiting for me to remember. And now that I start thinking of her it is almost as though it had never ended. Perhaps a lot of things do not end when you think they are over. Lately in those interminable bouts of conversation when people endeavor to be sophisticated, I have heard a good deal of talk about "affairs." It is mostly talk, of course, because not many of us have ever had any, but I have often been interested as I have listened. I have often wondered whether what occurred between Marvin and me could possibly fall into that dreary pattern. Somehow I have never thought so, for it was all new to us both, and somehow it still remains new to me. I am still certain — and my certainty is all that matters — that everything with Marvin and me was unique, not to be placed in any single category, that nothing in this world was ever like it.

XVIII

I Remember Marvin Myles

Next morning the girl at the information desk at J. T. Bullard's did not appear to notice anything unusual about me.

"Good morning," she said. "You're early, Mr. Pulham."

I was wondering what Marvin would be thinking, now that a new day was starting. I was wondering if she would be there already and what we would say to each other when we met. I was wondering if she would ever speak to me again. Bill was at his desk, with his hands in his pockets and with his chair tilted back, looking out of the window, but Marvin was not there. I was afraid she might be staying away because she could not bear the sight of me. I thought that Bill would certainly notice something, but he only waved his hand at me languidly.

"Hello, Bill," I said. "What were you doing in Chicago?"

"The rubber webbing account," Bill said. "We got it. How was everybody at home? How was Kay Motford?"

"Fine," I said. "She asked for you."

"I wish I could have gone up with you," Bill said. "How's your father? Did they want to get you out of this?"

"Yes," I said. "But never mind about it, Bill."

"Well, don't let them," Bill said. "You won't know yourself when you forget the Skipper and the crowd in the entry. Where's Marvin? She's late."

"I don't know where she is," I said.

"Well, never mind," Bill said. "Let me ask you a personal question. How do you keep your pants up?"

"What?" I asked. I was getting used to the speed of Bill's mind.

"I'm just asking," Bill said patiently. "You wear a belt, don't you?"

"Of course I wear a belt," I answered.

"Well, that's just the point," Bill said. "You wear a belt and I wear a belt. Every day you wear a belt, and every hour, every minute, you're unconsciously weakening your abdomen. Those lazy abdominal muscles, each hour, each minute, are becoming more flabby. A hundred hidden dangers lurk about your waistline."

"What are you talking about?" I asked.

"About the Winetka Woven Web Company," Bill said. "They're troubled about their suspenders. American manhood is going to be put back into galluses. Abraham Lincoln wore suspenders. He didn't have a weak abdomen. Nearly everyone in Great Britain wears suspenders. A London tailor never even puts belt loops on his pants. You don't see fat, pot-bellied Englishmen with lazy weakened abdomens. Why? Because they don't wear belts. It's the belt that's ruining the manhood of America. It's going to be a crusade."

"Did you think up that yourself?" I asked. Of course I knew that he had. Already everyone was saying that Bill was a great idea man.

"Anything the matter with it?" Bill asked. "It's going to be a crusade based on fear. If you do it right you can scare off all the belts in the country. A hundred hidden dangers lurk — "

"How do you know there are a hundred hidden dangers?" I asked. Bill could think of something new every minute.

"Suppose there aren't a hundred hidden dangers," Bill said. "Suppose there are only three — or fifty-three. It's good enough for a raise." Bill smiled at me and ran his hand through his light curly hair, the way he did when he was pleased with himself.

Then Marvin Myles came in. As far as I could see, it might have been any other day.

"Hello, boys," she said.

"I've got to be going while I'm enthusiastic," Bill said. "I'm going to take it in to Bullard," and he pushed himself out of his chair. "Every day — every hour — nature's wall of muscle — Marvin, what's happened to you?"

A silence followed that seemed very long, but I don't suppose it was.

"Why?" Marvin said. "What makes you ask?"

"You're looking pretty," said Bill, "awfully, awfully pretty."

"Why, thanks, Bill," Marvin said.

"Well, so long," Bill said. "I'll see you later."

I did not know what to say to Marvin. I did not want to look at her, and everything that Bill had said made it all much worse.

"Marvin," I said, "I suppose you can't help hating me."

Then our glances met and the corners of her lips curled upward.

"Why," she said, "I don't hate you. Why should I?"

"You ought to," I said. "You've got every reason to. It might help you to know that I hate myself. I never knew that I could — "

"Could what?" Marvin asked.

"Forget myself so far," I said.

Then I heard her laugh. I could not believe she was laughing.

"Why, you damn fool," Marvin said, "you sweet, dear damn fool!"

Then everything was all right. It was what I've always felt — that everything was always all right whenever Marvin was there.

One of the few times in my life when I stood on my own two feet was at the Bullard agency, and if I have ever done well at anything since, I owe a good deal to the training I received there. I liked detail and I was a thorough and hard worker, which may have made up for what I lacked in creative brilliance. I never could hit on ideas the way Bill did and I never could write as well as Marvin Myles, but in some ways I could think more clearly than either of them. There is a tremendous lot in the advertising business which requires common sense and a dull sort of accuracy. They put me to work on scientific data and statistics, and some of the things I did formed the background of two or three of the best merchandising campaigns. For example, I wrote a report on suspenders that made the client offer me a job. I was the one who suggested a certain amount of color in the product and the idea of selling a number of braces to go with every suit. Bill may have invented the dangers that lurk about the waistline, but I was the one who thought of the idea that suspenders might be something which you need not be ashamed of when you had your coat off in summer. Though the idea did not go very far, I still think there is something to it. Another thing which helped me, I think, was my habit of not talking too much, rather a rare attribute in an advertising agency; nor did I ever have any great desire to show off when I was in the room with Mr. Kaufman or Mr. Bullard.

This is not an effort to build myself up, but it indicates that the things I achieved began to give me a sort of confidence. I could even listen to Bill's ideas and pick out which were good and which were bad. The belief that I was getting somewhere, that I was learning enough about merchandising so that I could earn my living by it, was satisfying—but any such thoughts are always mixed up with Marvin Myles and Bill.

In those days when the speakeasies were beginning to crop up on Murray Hill and in the old dwelling houses on the west side of Fifth Avenue, we three used to meet at one of them in the afternoon and then have dinner at some queer place—either an Italian restaurant near Bleecker Street or one of the German places in the eighties. I don't know how much Bill knew about Marvin and me then, although he must have seen that we liked each other. As a matter of fact, Bill was a good deal more interested in himself that summer and autumn than in anything else—in himself and in ideas. Whenever I heard him talking with Marvin at one of those restaurants I wondered what Marvin saw in me. Bill had read almost everything and if he hadn't he could make you think he had. He had seen nearly all the shows and the exhibitions in the galleries. He had kept up his contact with newspaper friends and he knew all sorts of people—actors and headwaiters and playwrights and taxi drivers, and when we had dinner he was always waving to someone at another table and going over to talk to someone else.

He used to spend a good deal of time talking about college, because I imagine that he liked to have me argue with him. When he said that Bo-jo Brown and Sam Green and Joe Bingham and Bob Carroll and all the rest of them were stuffed shirts, it always made me angry. I used to tell him that he did not really know what he was talking about, because he never really knew them.

"If it hadn't been for me," Bill said, "you wouldn't be down here, boy. I'm the best friend you ever had."

"There's nothing the matter with where I was," I said.

"Go ahead," Marvin used to say. "I never knew any boys like that."

"You wouldn't, darling," Bill said. "But you know Harry. He's like that."

"No, he isn't," Marvin said, "not really."

I began to be acquainted with other people in the office, men who were married and who lived in the suburbs, or girls who were typing or keeping the scrapbooks and the files. Most of the time I never saw my old friends and when I did I never seemed to have much to say to them.

Once or twice Joe Bingham came to town and called me up, asking me to furnish him with some sort of entertainment. One night I took him down to Greenwich Village. I suppose there is a time in everyone's life when Greenwich Village exerts a peculiar charm. It was like passages from Du Maurier's *Trilby* and a little like something I had seen in Paris once when I was on leave from the front. The ventilation and the food were often pretty bad, and guttering candles on saucers on the table furnished the only illumination, but as a rule everyone could talk to everyone else about subjects which were usually banned at home, such as free love and trial marriage and symbols in dreams, and motion in art, and Marxism. It did not actually matter, however, whether you had ever heard of the subjects, for you could soon pick up the phrases, and there was always someone who was anxious to explain. Marvin pointed out to me that most of the villagers were no good, just on the fringe of everything, but she rather enjoyed it too, and she said that, bad as it was, it did me good. It still gives me a peculiar sort of pleasure to remember that I could call Sonia, the cigarette girl, "Sonia" without her minding it at all, and that I could call Romany Marie "Marie." That was where I saw O'Neill's plays first, down in the stable which had been made into a theater, and once I even met O'Neill. I know it is the fashion to laugh about Greenwich Village and to say hard things about it, but for me it still has an especial sort of beauty, because I associate it with Marvin Myles.

When I took Joe Bingham down there he did not see it at all as I did. Joe just said that it was the damnedest crazy show that he had ever seen. His main idea was to make passes at the girls and to get drunk, and he hurt people's feelings by laughing at their poetry and pictures.

"You wait," Joe said, "until I tell the boys about this when I get home."

When he called me up at the office late one Friday afternoon I took him there a second time, since he was one of my oldest friends. That was how he happened to meet Marvin, and he was almost the only one of my friends who ever did.

"Well, here I am," he called to me over the telephone. "What are we going to do?"

"I'm having dinner with a girl," I said, "but it will be fine if you come along."

"Hot dog! Tell her to bring a friend," Joe said.

"No," I said. "Just come along. I'll meet you at half-past six."

I was afraid that Marvin might mind, but she didn't when I explained that it was Joe Bingham whom I used to room with at college, and that naturally I had to do something about him. She said that of course I had to do something, that we could come and call for her, that she would love to see him. So I met Joe at the Harvard Club and we took a taxi to Marvin's apartment.

"She works in the office," I told him.

"Boy," Joe said, "don't you know better than to step out with any little chicken in the office?"

"Now, look here, Joe," I said, "she isn't like that. She writes copy."

"Yes," said Joe, "I know, I know."

"Damn it, Joe," I said, "it isn't like that."

"So that's what you've been doing here?" Joe said. "Listen, Harry, you'd better tell me about it."

"There isn't anything to tell you," I said.

Joe was perfectly all right with Marvin, once we all met, except that he was different from the way he would have been if Marvin had been one of the girls whom he knew at home. He would not have told the same stories. He would not have drunk as much red wine out of teapots. Though it all made me angry and made the whole evening rather unpleasant, I could understand Joe. He simply had never seen anyone like Marvin Myles. Once long afterwards Joe asked me what had ever happened to her.

"Now, there was a nice girl," he said, "awfully nice. Do you remember Washington Square? Boy, I thought you wanted to marry her."

"Did you?" I asked.

"I used to have a lot of fool ideas in those days," Joe said. "Now, there she was, a great deal nicer than a lot of girls at home, just as much of a lady, intelligent, amusing. Why, she was wonderful."

"Yes, she was," I said.

"And I was just a fool," Joe said. "I tell you what the trouble was. None of us were grown up, were we?"

That was the trouble with a good many people I have known. I felt older than Joe Bingham that night, and I could see him as something I had been once — moving along, not able to see what there was around him; but Joe would have given me the shirt off his back any time and I would have given him mine. I remember what he told us in the middle of the evening when he got used to Marvin and understood that she was a nice girl, even though she did work for a living.

"Now, Harry's my oldest friend," he said to Marvin, "and my best friend, aren't you, Harry?"

"I certainly am, Joe," I said.

"So I want to tell you both something," Joe said. "I want to ask your advice, Harry — "

He glanced at Marvin, hesitated, and went on.

"You won't mind my talking about myself for a minute, will you?" Joe said to her. "It's only Harry's my oldest friend. Harry, how do you think it would be — what would you say if I told you — I was going to marry Kay Motford?"

That was a queer scene as I look back on it now.

"Why, Joe," I said, "that's wonderful," and I remember that Marvin asked me about it afterwards when I tried to explain to her about Joe.

"It was nice to hear you talk," she said. "It made me know so much about you. Who is Kay Motford?"

"Kay?" I said. "Oh, a girl I used to know."

It always seemed to amaze Marvin that I had a few simple accomplishments, and when she was surprised it made me happier than anything else. There was the evening when she found that I could play squash and the time when she discovered that I knew how to sail a boat and the day I took her riding in Central Park. I could never tell why it was that she was so anxious to learn to ride. One Sunday we met Bill in the country and after lunch Bill and I played three sets of tennis while Marvin watched. The games were not exciting, because I was better than Bill.

"You see, I had tennis lessons from the time I was eleven years old," I told her.

"They gave you lessons in everything, didn't they?" she said.

I told her that I could teach her, but she shook her head.

"No," she said, "they've got to catch you young. Darling, they caught you awfully young."

I asked her why she was so silent when we drove back to town afterwards in that little car of mine.

"I was just thinking," she said. "It makes me jealous."

"What does?" I asked.

"Never mind," she said. "Even when I see you drive a car. I'm being nasty. I'll get over it. All women have to be nasty sometimes."

"You never are," I said. "Is it anything I've done?"

"No," she said, "of course not. I've never known you to do a mean thing. You're too uncomplicated."

"Then, what's the matter, Marvin?" I asked. "You know I love you more than anything."

"Harry," she asked, "are you sure of that?"

We were driving down to the ferry, so I could not go on with it until the car was safe aboard and I had cut off the engine.

"I'll tell you something, Marvin," I said. "I wish I could tell you properly. Every time I see you everything is better. It's like compound interest. Everything we do keeps being more so."

"Like liquor," Marvin said. "First you take a drink and then you take another."

"No," I said, "it's not that way at all. There's never any morning after."

"Darling," she answered, "you're awfully sweet, but it's hard to be honest when you're in love. It's awfully hard. Sometimes it hits me all of a sudden. Sometimes I'm frightened."

"You needn't be," I said.

"It makes me frightened when I see you do things that I can't do. They take you away from me, all those little things."

I took both her hands and I laughed at her.

"You see how nasty I am," she said. "Women take everything so seriously."

I remember the queer horsy smell of the ferry boat and the dank smell of the water from the Hudson and the way the sky line moved toward us with all the downtown buildings. I remember how the sun struck them and made the windows glitter.

"Marvin," I said, "let's get married."

Her hand gripped mine tight, but she did not answer.

"I'm not good," I went on, "at this business of pretending."

"Yes, I know," she said.

"I want everyone to know the way I feel about you."

"Darling," Marvin said, "let's not talk about it now. It — might spoil it all."

"It wouldn't," I said. "We've got to talk about it, Marvin; if we don't, this may not last."

As soon as I said it I knew it had been in the back of my mind all the time — that it could not last — that it was impossible that it could.

"I know," she said. "We'll have to talk about it sometime soon. It isn't that I don't think about it all the time, but it's going to be so complicated. There'll be all those people I don't know and all these things I don't know. Someday we'll go down to Maryland or somewhere — and we'll get it over with — and we'll go and see your family — but let's not talk about it now."

I have often wondered what would have happened if I had not kept thinking that there was lots of time. Time has always seemed to me to move strangely, now swiftly and now slowly, and all that time with Marvin Myles gives me the impression of looking from the window of a train which is hastening through some country that I have always wanted to see.

That autumn I took Marvin to the Yale game at New Haven and we sat in the section with my Class, and we met a good many people too between the halves, the way you do at games. That was when Marvin met Kay Motford. Kay had come down from Boston with Joe Bingham. Kay was in a raccoon-skin coat with a red feather in her hat, standing very straight as she always did. Her face still had a touch of the summer tan. Her eyes were bright and she had a grim look around the lips. I heard her calling, "Joe, there's Harry," and I let go of Marvin's arm.

"Harry," she said, "I wondered if you'd be here. Joe can't explain the rules."

"You ought to understand them if you go to a game," said Joe. "It's perfectly simple. One side has the ball for four downs."

"I know," said Kay. "You've tried to tell it to me." She wasn't interested. Everything except the game itself always interested her. I saw her looking at Marvin Myles, in that way that women look when they see a man they know with a stranger — at Marvin's hat and at her gloves — and I suppose Kay felt that everything was too elaborate.

"This is Miss Myles, Miss Motford," I said, and they shook hands.

"Hello, Marvin," Joe said, and I saw Kay look at him.

"Oh," Kay asked, "do you know Joe?"

"Yes," Marvin said, "we all had dinner in New York."

"Oh," Kay said. "You must have Harry bring you up to Boston sometime."

I did not like the way she said it. Something always makes me nervous when women talk together when they first meet.

As we walked down the steps to our seats Marvin said, "Harry, I hope I look all right. Do you think I'm overdressed?"

"No," I said, "of course you're not."

"If I go anywhere I don't dress as though I were going to play field hockey," Marvin said. "Do you think they're engaged?"

"Probably," I said, "if he took her all the way here."

"She's pretty," Marvin said.

"Who?" I said. "Kay?"

"If she knew how to dress," Marvin said.

"I don't see how you can say she's pretty," I told her.

"Her eyes are so clear," Marvin said. "And anyone's pretty if she's having a good time."

"Hello, Harry," someone called.

"Hello, Bob," I called back.

"How's it going, Harry?" someone called.

"Fine, Tom," I called back. "How's it going with you?"

I was glad that I had taken her and glad that they had seen her with me. She was the best-looking girl that I could see anywhere.

"We've got to go to a lot of games," I said.

"Yes," she answered, "lots and lots," and then I forgot all about her. The team was on the field again.

It must have been about two weeks later that Father came to town. He said he had come on business — about a new issue for which the New York branch of Smith and Wilding was negotiating — but I like to think that he came to see me. He came and he brought Mary with him, and I met them at the Belmont for lunch.

When Father saw me he waved and called to me, so loudly that everyone sitting in chairs around the marble pillars looked up at us. I felt responsible for the way he acted, somewhat as though I were still at School and as though he had come to see me there. I actually found myself worrying about the way Father would behave at lunch. Perhaps there comes a time when everyone feels that his father is a little out of touch with the present day.

"Here we are," he called. "Don't you see us?" And then he dropped his cane and stooped to pick it up and then some letters fell out of his pocket.

"Oh, damnation," Father said.

I wondered if he would blow his nose when he picked his letters up — and he did, very loudly.

"I don't see what you see in this town," he said. "Let's go downstairs and eat. Don't you see Mary? Aren't you going to kiss your sister?"

"Father," Mary said, "Harry isn't deaf," and I saw that she felt the same way about him that I did.

I began wishing that Marvin could take Mary out and do something about her clothes. I knew that Mary would like it, because she was trying to be smart and wasn't doing it very well. Her dress had a ready-made look and her coat was not properly tailored — suddenly I felt sorry for her. I wanted her to have a good time.

Downstairs in the grillroom Father asked me what I knew about speakeasies and he suggested that sometime later in the afternoon we leave Mary and go to one of them. You could see that he was awfully glad to have us both all alone with him. He kept looking at us and smiling as though we were children at a party. When he got back home, he said, he was going down to the Cape for duck shooting, if Mother was well enough to let him; it was getting late in the season but the birds were still flying and the club he belonged to had a good warm blind; all you had to do was to play poker and to wait until they called that the birds were coming in. Frank Wilding was coming down for two days.

"I don't suppose you can get off, Harry?" he asked, and I told him that I couldn't, not possibly. Then he told me how Mother was, and then he said that he had had Hugh on the carpet for taking a commission from the butcher.

Mary sat staring about the room, trying to look bored.

"Harry," she said, "tell us about the shows." I told her about "Dear Brutus" while Father lighted a cigar.

"It sounds all right," he said. "Do you think it would be all right for Mary?"

Mary said nothing; she gave me a martyred look.

"The title comes from Shakespeare," I said. "'The fault, dear Brutus, is not in our stars, but in ourselves, that we are underlings.' It's all about having a second chance. The characters have a second chance and they do the same thing over again."

"No one ought to have a second chance," said Father. "That's damned rot."

"Some people," Mary said, "never have a chance at all."

When I looked at the gold watch that Father had given me, it was after two o'clock.

"I've got to be going back," I said. "We're pretty busy at the office."

"All right," said Father. "We want to see where you work."

"Oh, no," I said, "you don't want to do that."

"We certainly do," said Father. "I want to see your boss. What's his name? Bullard?"

"He'll be busy," I said.

"I don't know why it is," Father said, "that you and Mary always want to keep me out of everything. Why shouldn't I see this Bullard?"

When I got them up to the reception room Father looked at the rows of books.

"Maybe you'd better wait here," I said. "I'll see if Mr. Bullard can see you."

"Why should I wait here?" Father asked. "Take me in where you work. I want to see what it looks like."

I took them through the main office back to where it was partitioned off and opened the door of our room. I hoped that Bill King might be there and that Marvin might be somewhere else, but Bill was out and Marvin was writing.

"Where have you been?" she said. "Bullard's looking for you," and then she stopped when she saw Mary and Father.

"This is my father, Miss Myles," I said.

"How do you do," Father said. "Is this where my boy works?"

"Yes," Marvin said, "at the desk over there."

"Well, I hope he's doing well," Father said, and he smiled at her.

"This is Mary, my sister," I told Marvin.

I could see that it was all a shock to Marvin, having them come upon her that way suddenly.

"Oh," she said, "you're Harry's sister. I've often heard him talk about you."

We left Marvin and Mary together when I took Father to see Mr. Bullard.

"Who's that girl?" Father asked, as he walked beside me down the aisle through the main office. "Do all the women in this office call you by your first name?"

"She's one of the writers," I said.

"Do you sit in there alone with her all the time?" Father asked.

"Bill King's in there too," I said.

"Look here," Father said. "She isn't the one you were seen with at the Yale game?"

"How did you hear about that?" I asked.

Before he had time to answer we reached Mr. Bullard's door, and I was just as glad. Sometime I would have to tell him all about Marvin Myles, but I did not want to then. It was difficult, a good deal worse than I had thought.

XIX

It Had to Happen Sometime

As I have said, everything at that time in my life was moving very fast, but of course it had to end, even when I believed it never would. One morning at the office about two weeks later, Marvin was dusting the snow off her hat and there were little drops of water on her hair and face. Bill was sitting with his feet on the corner of his desk.

"They ought to do something nice for us at Christmas," he was saying, and then Marvin said she supposed that I'd go home for Christmas, and then the extension telephone rang on my desk.

"Boston's calling you," I heard the switchboard operator say.

Telephone connections were not as good then as they are now. I could hear the precise, clipped voices of operators on the line saying that New York was ready and saying, "Just a moment."

"I suppose it's the family," I said, "but they've never called me up before."

I imagined that it would probably be something about Christmas, and then I recognized Mary's voice in spite of the bad connection.

"Harry," she said, "is that you? This is Mary."

"Get nearer to the telephone," I answered. "I can't hear you."

"Can you hear me now?" she asked, and I knew that something wasn't right.

"Yes," I answered. "Go ahead."

"The doctors say you must come right away."

"Is it Mother?" I asked.

"No," she said, "it's Father. Harry, they think he's dying."

Her voice went through my head without any particular meaning.

206

"What's that?" I said. "What is it?"

"Can you hear me?" Mary asked. "It's when he came back from shooting, Harry. He has pneumonia. The doctors want you right away."

I pulled out the watch that he had given me; it was half-past nine o'clock.

"All right," I said. "I'll take the ten o'clock. I'll be at the house around three. Tell him I'm coming and give him my love and — Mary —"

"Yes?" she said.

Then I could not think what to tell her. There were a dozen things I wanted to say and none of them made sense.

"Tell him I'm with him all the time."

I hung up the receiver carefully and stood up.

"They want me," I said. "Father has pneumonia. I guess I'd better be starting."

Marvin did not say anything for a moment. Then she said:

"I'll go up with you. I could stay somewhere."

"There isn't any need to do that," Bill said. "I'll go. Come on, Harry, get your coat."

Somehow I still could not understand that anything had happened. I imagine, though, that Marvin must have seen it all without being able to say anything, without being able to tell me anything to do.

"Harry," she said, "have you any rubbers? Well, then, stop at the station and get some rubbers."

"All right," I said.

"And call me up tonight," she said, "any time."

"All right."

Bill put his hand on my shoulder.

"Tell Bullard, will you, Marvin?" he said.

"Good-by, Marvin," I said.

"Harry, don't say that. Don't say good-by."

That ride to Boston has never seemed quite real, in spite of the atmosphere of cold fact which always goes with trains — Stamford, and New Haven, and New London, definite, but difficult to notice. The truth was that I was so withdrawn inside myself that I seemed to be pulled beneath the surface of something like water, except for occasional moments when I emerged for light and air. At such moments I could hear Bill talking to me and I could follow for a while perfectly clearly what he was saying, and then my own thoughts would come over me and cut off his voice. He must have thought that the best thing was to keep my mind off everything by talking. I remember that he discussed a lot of books and plays while I tried hard to listen, because I have always tried to get the most out of it when Bill dealt with a worth-while subject. We walked up and down the platform at New Haven and talked about Yale and wondered why we were always prejudiced against it. You had to admit that they dressed better there than at Harvard. They had a better social sense and a better sense of reality. Bill said if he had a boy, though God knew he did not want to get married and tied up with a family, that he would send him to Yale if he had to earn his living afterwards.

"Harry," he said, "you should have gone to Yale."

I knew that he was joking, but the idea made me wince. I told him that I was certainly glad I had not gone there, that Yale men were always pushing and keeping their eyes on the ball, that they had no true cultivation, and that they were really not gentlemen. Bill kept on teasing me about it, just to get my mind off myself, and then I must have stopped listening. I was back again, wondering how ill Father was and what I should do if he were to die.

Somewhere around New London I was listening to Bill again. He was saying that in some ways he wished he were more like me, because I had a solid quality.

"Don't say that, Bill," I told him. "You know I'm awfully dull."

He said that might be so, but I had tenacity and balance. Everything came too easily to him, so that he grew impatient with what he was doing and moved to something else. He said he was volatile and a light-weight.

"Don't say that, Bill," I told him. "You're the cleverest man I know."

That was because I did not know many clever people, he said, and cleverness was a curse — it made you discontented, and it made you selfish.

Somewhere around Westerly, while we were going through the great Rhode Island swamp, where they had fought a battle in King Philip's War, I was listening to him again. He was talking about our mutual acquaintances at college and the girls we had met. Bill had a sharp, almost unkindly way of discussing them.

"Now, Joe Bingham is just one of your habits," Bill said. "In my frank opinion he's nothing more than a long cold drink of water. Water is the way to describe him — just a long cool drink."

"Now, look here, Bill," I said. "You get fond of people if you've been to school with them."

"If I were to stick a needle in the seat of Joe's pants," Bill said, "it would take five minutes for the sensation to communicate itself to his brain. Even a dinosaur could do better than that and the dinosaurs died because they didn't know the flies were biting them."

"Now, Bill," I said, "Joe isn't as bad as that."

"It gets a rise out of you, doesn't it?" Bill said. "Well, I'll tell you something else. Joe may have had a brain when he was born, but it's just been polished down to a nub. He's just been taught a book of rules — nice people do this, the right people do that — and that's the trouble with all polite society. They may have had brains once, but they're atrophied."

"But what can you live by, Bill, if you don't have standards?" I asked him.

"You can work out the reason for the standards," Bill said.

"Bill," I said, "do you believe in God?" I asked him because I had been thinking a good deal about God, and about prayer and divine mercy. I had been wondering if humbly I could make some sort of appeal to God.

"It depends on what you mean," Bill said. "Do you?"

"I don't know," I said. "I wish I did. Did you ever pray to God to help you, Bill?"

"Once or twice," said Bill, "but I imagine God has other things to think about. Why should you have an idea that God should care?"

"Why, Bill," I said, "the whole Christian doctrine —"

"All right," Bill answered. "A few simple rules would have changed the world, and what happened? The churchmen didn't want them — the one about the camel going through the needle's eye, for instance, and loving your neighbor as you would yourself, and the lilies of the field, and taking up the cross and following. They had to shave off the cross so that it would be light enough to wear on their watch chains when they turned their collars back. They began writing the rules all over to fit human circumstances. And that's what most of religion is — a matter of compromises. I'd read the New Testament instead of the Book of Common Prayer."

I did not answer and I seemed to be pulled under water again, until I heard Bill's voice some time later.

"I can't understand the biological urge that would make a girl like Kay Motford want to marry Joe Bingham. He's a big cold drink of water."

"I don't see why not," I said. "I don't see anything so remarkable about Kay."

Bill sat up straighter.

"You wouldn't. I do," he said.

"But you haven't seen her," I said, "since that dance at North Harbor, have you?"

"But I remember her," he said. "It means something when I can remember anyone so long. She needs someone with imagination, someone who can show her things. God, she could dance!"

"I never thought she could," I said. "She only cares about sail-boats and dogs, and besides she's rather plain."

"Plain?" Bill said. "You call her plain?"

I was not listening to him any longer. I tried to put the idea out of my mind that Father might not be better. I could not recall that I had ever seen him ill, even with a cold, and now there would be trained nurses, and I should have to run things. I had never run anything, except that one time in the war when everyone else was shot.

We came into Providence, and the car grew dark and gloomy because of the train shed over it. Then it moved out into the afternoon and the cold rays of the sun came through the left-hand windows and I saw the state capitol. Once long ago when we had to change cars at Providence on the way to some place like Narragansett Pier, Mother had taken Mary and me into the capitol, and we stood in the rotunda, looking at the flags brought back from the Civil War. I might pass that building a thousand times without ever setting foot in it again.

"Come on, boy," I heard Bill say. "Snap out of it. There isn't anything we can do until we get there."

"I know that, Bill," I said. "I'm thinking about Marvin Myles."

I had talked to him about Harvard and Joe Bingham and God, and now I was talking about Marvin Myles. It must have been because of the strain I was under, and later I wanted to tell him to forget what we had said, but we never mentioned it again. I was saying I didn't know what to do.

"Keep your shirt on," said Bill. "It will all look out for itself."

The porter was kneeling in front of me, polishing my shoes. I have often wondered who thought of that type of service, for there is no reason why your shoes should get dirty in a parlor car.

"South Station or Back Bay?" he asked.

"Back Bay," I told him.

"Boy, you've been a good long way from home," said Bill.

A cold easterly wind was blowing, and the sun, which had been out at Providence, was lost in a gray sky. Heaps of snow along the street showed that it must have snowed that morning, as it had in New York, and now the chill in the air meant that it would snow again. Bill buttoned his overcoat tight and thrust his hands in the coat pockets.

"This place has the damnedest climate in the world," he said.

Patrick in a black broadcloth coat with an astrakhan collar was waiting on Dartmouth Street with the car. The thick smoke from our train curled over the bridge above the tracks, making me cough. Just as soon as I saw the car Bill's remark came back to me that I had been a long way from home.

"Patrick," I asked, "how's Father?"

"He's been the same all day," Patrick said.

"All right," I said. "Let's go."

From the way Patrick looked I knew that things were very bad. The iron and glass door of the brick house on Marlborough Street stood open and I could see the heavy curtains at the windows in the parlor and the rows of plants in front of them. Hugh opened the inner door before I could ring and Mother was standing in the hall behind him. I was surprised to see her there, because she was seldom downstairs. Yet there she was, just the way she used to be when I came home from School.

"Dear, you look awfully cold," she said, and then before I could ask her anything she added, "The doctor's just left. He's a little better."

"I want to see him," I said.

"He's been waiting," Mother said. "He knows you're coming."

I looked at the heavy walnut stair railing and the handsome carved chairs that no one used and at the mirror and the table with the silver card tray on it. The door of the parlor was open, showing the big long room with the silver framed pictures on the table and the books which no one read. I had forgotten that Bill was with me until I took off my overcoat and handed it to Hugh.

"Mother, Bill came up with me," I said.

I was glad that he was there, because Mother might have begun to cry if I had been alone with her. We should have said things which I would rather have kept silent about, although I knew that sooner or later I must say them.

"Hugh," Mother said, "take Mr. King's bag to the front guest room."

"Oh, I'd better not stay," Bill said. "I just came up with Harry."

"Yes, Bill," I said before Mother could answer. "Please stay."

"Here's your Uncle Bob, dear," Mother said.

I saw her brother in the doorway to the parlor — stout, and good-natured, with the light gleaming on his bald spot.

"Your Aunt Frederica is in the parlor," Mother said.

My Great-aunt Frederica, in black with a little ruffle of tulle about the collar of her high shirtwaist, sat on one of the stiff little sofas near the fireplace where a lump of cannel coal was burning.

"How you've grown," Aunt Frederica said. "Don't knock against the tables, Harry."

I stooped and kissed her white wrinkled cheek.

"He looks like John," Aunt Frederica said, "except he has your nose, May."

Ever since I was first brought over to see her as a child, my one idea had always been to get away from Aunt Frederica as rapidly as possible.

"Perhaps I'd better go up and see Father," I said, and I left them in the parlor talking to Bill King.

Up on the second floor beside the library I put my hand on the silvered glass knob of Father's bedroom door and turned it very carefully. Even when the door was open a crack I could hear his heavy breathing. That room, where I had often watched him looking for gloves in the upper drawer of his tall bureau, was full of strange new objects. There were iron cylinders beside the bed and an oxygen tent. All his books and pipes, all the little odds and ends he liked to look at, had been taken away, and he lay in the center of his heavy mahogany bed, breathing in long painful gasps, his head and shoulders propped up among pillows. A nurse was at one side of the bed and Mary was at the other. When I came in, I could look directly into his face; his eyes staring straight at me showed no recognition at first, because all his energy and all his conscious thought were bent on breathing. Then he saw me and I took his hand and stared down at his face. Its self-absorption reminded me of faces in the war. His eyes met mine and his grip tightened on my hand.

"Hello, Father," I said. "I just got here."

I wonder if one always makes some such obvious remark at such a time.

"Don't go away," he said. He spoke with an effort, very huskily and slowly.

"I'm not going anywhere," I answered.

Father moved his head in the pillows.

"It's where you belong," he said, "some man in the house."

"Mr. Pulham," the nurse said, "I wouldn't speak any more."

Father looked at me and frowned.

"Too damned many women — don't let them run you."

"No, I won't," I said. "That's all right."

The nurse put her hand on his wrist.

"Mr. Pulham," she said, "it only tires you out to speak."

Father turned his head toward her with an incredulous sort of look. Then his eyes moved back to me and his whole attention was focused on me, and his grip tightened on my hand again.

"We never did get shooting."

"That's all right," I said. "We'll get there still," but he would not let go of my hand.

"Don't," he said, "put it off. Do what you want to do."

"Yes, Father," I said.

"You know what I mean?" he asked. "What you — want to do."

"Yes," I said.

Then Mary stood up and took my arm.

"Don't talk, Father," she said. "Harry will be back in a minute. He'll stay with you all the time if you don't talk."

Father did not answer. He seemed to have forgotten I was there.

Mary and I tiptoed out of the room, hand in hand like children, and down the hall to the library. I felt cold, as cold as ice.

The library was the room in town which Father liked best. It had the engravings of game birds and all his best books and the only comfortable chairs in the house. His desk by the window was untidy, just as he had left it, for no one dared to touch his papers.

"What's the doctor's number?" I asked.

214

"He's just been here," Mary said.

"Never mind," I told her. "I want to see him."

Suddenly Mary threw her arms around me and began to cry.

"It's going to be all right," I said.

It did no good to sit there waiting, and yet I knew there was nothing to do. I had known it from the first instant I entered the room and saw my father's face.

XX

For I'll Come Back to You

I threw away most of the things that Marvin Myles gave me long ago. It hurt me more to get rid of all those little bits which you can throw into the fire than it did to dispose of the gold cigarette case which she had given me, or the gold and sapphire cuff buttons which I never did care for anyway. Marvin never liked jewelry to be quiet. I suppose that Marvin got rid of most of what I gave her too. There was the white ermine party cloak, for instance, which I should not have thought of buying, if she had not been so anxious for it. I told her that it seemed immoral to buy such a thing for any girl, even for your wife; and I remember how much that remark amused her. She said I could never understand how she felt about clothes and that anyway she was not sure whether she was moral. Then there was a picture I bought for her, and a set of the Aldine poets and a chair which we saw in a window on Madison Avenue. On second thought, she may have kept them all, and I hope so, for chairs and books and pictures have personalities of their own which allow them to stand for themselves. It is only those little things that you bother about most — such as letters which our grandfathers and grandmothers tied up with ribbons and stored away in desks and attics. I think it is better to burn up all of that right away — all the letters and faded flowers and gloves and handkerchiefs. If you keep them too long they become hideous, for they may crop up sometime when you don't expect to see them, or worse still you may see them and be unable to recall just what they were all about.

I was able to give the cigarette case away but when it came to the letters, I thought of sending them all back to her, though at the time it seemed gratuitous, and she never sent mine back either. If you write a letter you ought never to be ashamed of what is in it. Certainly, I have never been ashamed of what I wrote to Marvin Myles; but when it came to burning up her letters there were several which I simply could not destroy and I have kept them ever since — in a furtive sort of way like secret sins, a difficult thing to do after you are married. When I hid them in the back of my desk they kept cropping up whenever I looked for my checkbook, so that I became afraid that Kay or one of the children might come upon them inadvertently, while searching for small change or postage stamps. At last I put them — the only two that I had left — on the upper shelves of the bookcase, between the pages of Volume Three of Plutarch's *Lives*.

One is the note that she wrote me when Father died, in that handwriting of hers which, though it looked difficult, was actually very legible. There is a good deal in it which no one would understand but Marvin or me, and perhaps most letters are like that.

My dearest, dearest darling, I've been thinking of you all day long, and I'll think of you all tonight even when I'm asleep. I keep wondering how you look and what you are saying and whether you are wearing your rubbers. I keep thinking of little things I could do for you. I never knew that you could get into my system like this — so that I don't seem to be one person any more, but part of me always seems to be with you. In some ways I hate it like the devil, but I wouldn't miss it for the world — belonging to someone else. So now when I talk about myself at a time like this you know, don't you, that I'm really talking about you? . . .

It's such a terrible time. I went through it when my mother died. It's so terrible to have someone go and just keep on thinking "I'll have to tell him that when I see him," and then know that never, never, here, will it happen again. Now, if you and I were ever to quarrel — and we never have quarreled, have we — we never have seemed to hurt each other the way other people do — why, if you and I quarreled and said we were never going to see each other again, why, I should always think, "Of course it isn't so. Some day I'll see him — right on the street or somewhere — and he'll take his hands out of his pockets" (I wish you wouldn't always keep your hands in your pockets and slouch), "he'll take his hands out of his pockets," I would think, "and then he would want to kiss me, except that he wouldn't compromise me in public. And then I would tell him I was sorry, and everything would be all right." I would always think that some day, somehow, I could get you back.

You know, don't you, that I'm only running on this way because I love you? And if you love someone and can't do anything about it, it makes you awfully helpless. All I can do is to make you think, when you're up there all alone, that it isn't so bad if you know you have someone, someone forever and always, someone you can always come back to, dear, any time or anywhere. I love you so, and I don't know why, and I don't care. I think you'd better write me again as soon as you can. Don't be too busy. Don't get too lost.

I know what she meant now a good deal better than I knew then, when it was impossible to see anything very clearly. It was hard to realize at first that there was no one else after Father's death to handle responsibilities but me. Mother was splendid through most of it, except that when it came down to such details as the household bills and the lawyers, she did not understand, or try to understand. When they all kept coming to me, even about the routine of the funeral, I would find myself thinking that I could take it up with Father in the morning. At first I imagined that in a week or so, when the house had quieted down and when the lawyers had the details straight, I might reasonably get back to New York. Then I saw there was not a chance — that it would be a long while before I got away.

It touched me that I had been made executor under Father's will, although I found that there was not much for me to do, since the will had been drawn by the Pritchard office and the Pritchard office and I were to act together. Mary and I were each left a hundred thousand dollars outright, and after other bequests to the servants and to charities, the bulk of the estate was left to my mother for her lifetime, to be invested by the trustee. It seemed to me that old Mr. Pritchard worried too much about the state income tax, and that his one idea was to avoid the tax by keeping all the investments in small state companies. I consulted with Mr. Wilding about it and he even went so far as to argue with John Pritchard, but there is no use going into the details now.

I had intended to talk with Mary about it, too, the night I came back from the interview. We sat down to dinner by ourselves in the big dining room, which did not seem to be made for either of us. The room was ornate and shadowy and gloomy. Mary in her black dress, seated at Mother's end of the table, so far away that I nearly had to raise my voice to speak to her, looked very small with the Empire sideboard and all the elaborate silver behind her. When Hugh came in with the soup Mary and I seemed to be like children, furtively pretending to be grown up.

"Will you have sherry, sir?" Hugh asked me.

First he had called me "Master Harry," and now he called me "sir."

"Yes," I said, "and I want to go over the wine cellar with you tomorrow. I want a list of what there is. There may not be any more."

It occurred to me that I sounded a good deal like old Mr. Pritchard when he had taken off his glasses and tapped them on his desk. Mr. Pritchard's whole life had been devoted to saving things for people, because there might not be any more.

"Harry," Mary said, "I'd like to go abroad somewhere."

"You've been," I said. "You went over with Fräulein."

"I'd like to go by myself," Mary said.

"You couldn't do that, Mary," I told her. "But perhaps in the spring someone will be going and you can join some party."

"I don't want to join any party," Mary answered. "I'd like to go alone and pick up people on the boat."

"You never want to do that, Mary," I said. "You can't tell what people are like on boats."

"Now, you needn't try to turn into Father just because he's dead," Mary said. "Sometimes you can be the damnedest fool. I wish you'd please shut up."

We sat quietly eating while Hugh walked around the table. Then when the dessert was finished Mary pushed back her chair.

"Let's go into the library," she said. "I've got to talk to you."

It occurred to me that in the last few days everyone had been talking to me in the library.

"All right," I said. "We won't want any coffee, Hugh."

Mary walked up the stairs ahead of me and our footsteps made dull little thuds on the heavy brown stair-carpet. We seemed to be walking on tiptoe, so as not to disturb the silence of the house, but in the library when the door was closed you could raise your voice. Mary lighted a cigarette with a self-conscious flourish.

"Sometimes you can be awful," Mary said. "Why are you so poisonous tonight?"

I told her I did not mean to be. I told her that I had a good many things on my mind, and this was true. I was usually thinking about something else when Mary was talking.

"Sometimes you're sweet and natural and then you're so obvious that you drive me crazy," Mary said.

I saw as she puffed her cigarette that her lip was trembling.

"You're tired, Mary," I said. "I don't know why women think that someone can be sweet just to order."

"Oh, well," Mary said, "I've got to talk to someone. Harry, I'm in love."

"In love?" I repeated.

"What's so queer about it?" she asked. "Why shouldn't I be?"

"Have you told Mother?" I asked.

"No," she said, "of course not."

"Who are you in love with?"

"You wouldn't know him."

"What's his name?"

"Roger Priest," Mary said.

"Priest?" I said. "What does he do?"

"There you are," she said. "What difference does it make? He wasn't in the war and he didn't go to Harvard, but he's going to Harvard now. If you really want to know, he's in the Harvard Dental School."

"My God," I said. It was the only thing I could think of saying.

220

I tried to think of dentistry as being an exacting and important side of medicine, but it did not seem to help. "He must be perfectly wonderful."

"Harry," she said, "don't tell anyone, will you? It's so awful it's funny, but I can't really do anything about it."

"You know," I said, "it might be a good idea if you did take a trip. There must be some girl you'd like to take with you, Mary. We'll see about it in the morning, or you might go to Florida or California. I've always wanted to go to California. And you don't need to worry about Mother. I'll look after that."

"Harry," she said, "you're not laughing, are you?"

"No," I said. "Of course it isn't as serious as you think it is. These things never are. When you get to California it will just seem — "

I had thought that I was broad-minded, and instead it might have been Father speaking. "Couldn't he stop being a dentist and turn into a doctor?"

"I've asked him that," Mary said. "He wants to be a dentist. Harry, he's awfully proud."

"Well, it's a hell of a life," I said.

"Now you're being nice," said Mary. "You're really awfully nice."

Sometimes I have wondered whether Mr. Priest did not have a good deal to do with changing the course of my life. He was not in the least peculiar, and was the first person I ever saw who was obsessed with a scientific interest, but I have never been able to see why he wanted to be mixed up with incisors and molars. Yet I could not help being fascinated when he talked of the dental development of primitive man and the dental degeneracy of the human race, and since then I have read of the studies he made with certain eminent anthropologists. Roger Priest finally turned into quite a distinguished person. As soon as I saw him I knew that it would be just as well for Mary to see as little of him as possible. He was much too good-looking and amusing.

Though I have often tried to blame the Priest affair for keeping me at home — and he was the only person who could listen intelligently when I talked about soap and suspenders — there were all sorts of other details. Mother and Mary depended on me too much for me to leave them, and then there was the problem of what to do about Westwood — whether we could continue to live there after the estate was settled or whether it would not be better to sell, and then there was Father's property in the Northwest Wharf and Warehouse, in which I was made a director. Someone had to represent the family's holdings. There were dozens of similar complications that seemed to wind around me, but I can think of them all as excuses now and none of them as real reasons why I stayed. I stayed because I was meant to stay.

One afternoon when I was in the customers' room at Smith and Wilding, looking over the news service reports, Mr. Wilding called me into his office.

"How did Motors close?" he asked.

"Strong, sir," I said. "Up two points."

It was just as though I had never been away from Smith and Wilding.

"All right," said Mr. Wilding. "Tell them to give you a desk inside the rail."

"But I'm not working here, sir," I said.

"No," Mr. Wilding said, "but you need a desk downtown. When you go out find the bootblack for me. He's late."

First I had a desk, and then it seemed to me that everyone in the office took it for granted that I'd be sitting at it. Although nothing was said about employment, I kept going down there more and more, because I did not like to stay all day in the house and because it was easier to make appointments downtown. Then I began seeing everyone I used to know, running into them out on the street or at lunch, and the strange part of it was that a lot of them never seemed to realize that I had been away at all.

Then I began making dates to play squash at the Club, and looking up people — all my friends who were married and who were living in apartments.

I wrote to Marvin Myles one afternoon toward the end of January, from my desk at Smith and Wilding, on the Smith and Wilding stationery.

It's funny [I wrote], to be writing you, because you seem to be right here with me — right here at the desk where all the tickers are going and Mr. Wilding is looking out at me, drinking his glass of milk. I can't stand not seeing you, but the way things are going I'm not able to get away, even for a day, and so I'm going to ask you something. I've always wanted you to see it here. We've talked about it so much. How would it be if you and Bill came up next week end? There's lots of room and I can show you everything.

I knew that she would understand about having Bill, since it would look more natural and casual.

I told Mother what I had done when I came home that afternoon, adding it to all the other pieces of news that I usually gave her.

"By the way, I've asked Bill up for the week end, and a friend of ours, a girl named Marvin Myles."

"Why, that's splendid, dear," Mother said. "It's time that you began seeing people. You might take them to Westwood on Sunday. Who is Marvin Myles? I've never heard you speak of her."

"Just a friend of Bill's and mine," I said. "Mary's met her."

XXI

Good-by to All That

Now and then, even as late as 1920, it was not difficult to hear someone humming "Where Do We Go from Here?"

Songs like that used to have a way of running through my head for days at a time, falling into rhythm with my footsteps and actions, as this one did while I waited at the Back Bay Station for Bill and Marvin Myles.

"Where do we go from here?" I was humming. "Anywhere from Harlem to a Jersey City pier." The limits set by that song could not be measured by the words. They were like the limits of the known and the unknown world. Columbus might have sung it aboard the *Santa Maria,* and the truth is you are always going somewhere, even if it's only to hell in a hack.

It was hard to tell what car they would be in, downstairs in the Back Bay Station where the train paused for the shortest possible time. I was wondering what Marvin would be wearing and what she would look like when I saw her.

"Anywhere from Harlem," I was humming, "to a Jersey City pier."

Then I saw the light of the engine and I heard the bell, the light and the sound growing larger every second until they were all around me in a way which used to frighten me when I was young. Then the engine moved past with a hiss of steam and the firebox glowing, and then the baggage car and then the dining car, and then the whole place was full of steam and sulphurous smoke, and the porters were running and the doors were opening and the baggage was coming out. I saw Bill King down at the end of the platform, and then I saw Marvin getting off and speaking to him. She would be saying that it was dirty, but she looked as clean and brushed as though she had never been out of New York. She looked so much better than anybody else that I wondered how she had ever come on account of me. Bill saw me, and then Marvin was staring through the smoke as I ran toward her. Then right there in front of Bill and everyone on the platform she kissed me, threw her arms around me and held me tight.

"Darling," she said, "you look like a Teddy bear."

There was something definite about being kissed there on the station platform in front of Bill. I found myself wondering if anyone else could have seen me, and then I thought it did not really matter.

"Did you have a good trip?" I asked.

"Fine," said Bill. "Boy, you're looking fine."

Marvin squeezed my arm.

"You look just the same," she said. "Are you?"

"Of course I am," I answered.

"Well, where do we go from here?" she said.

"Where do we go from here?" I repeated. "Anywhere from Harlem to a Jersey City pier."

"Come on," said Bill. "Let's push out of this. Oh, joy, oh, boy! Where do we go from here?"

I saw people looking at us and I realized that we were making a good deal of noise. I saw Patrick take a quick look at Marvin when he stood by the door of the car holding the robe. Then inside the car Marvin linked her arm through mine again and I held her hand under the robe and we were all laughing and talking. Bill was explaining Boston to Marvin, pointing out the Library and Trinity Church. I had a feeling that we were all talking a little too much, as though we were afraid that something might happen if we did not all have something to say. I had thought so often of bringing Marvin home.

"Will Hugh be waiting up?" she asked.

"Of course he will," I said.

225

"Yes," Bill said. "He'll want to see what Harry's brought home this time," and I knew that Bill had been telling her all about the house. I didn't want her to feel that anything was really the matter with it. I did not want her to be conscious of it at all. Yet I was more aware of our house when I took Marvin there than I had ever been before.

Mary was waiting for us in the hall and Mary took Marvin up to her room and I carried her bags while Hugh showed Bill where he was going to sleep. Marvin had the big blue room in the front of the house, and Hannah was waiting to help her unpack.

"When you're through," I told Mary, "let's all go down to the library."

I waited in the library alone, just thinking that Marvin was in the house, and imagining how she would look when she came down with her hat off and her gloves off, as though she belonged there. Bill came in before she did.

"Have you got everything you want, Bill?" I asked, and Bill said that he had everything he wanted.

"Bill," I said, "I hope Marvin likes it here."

"Of course she'll like it," Bill said. "Why shouldn't she?"

"I just don't want her to think it's stuffy."

Bill had picked up the paper and was looking at the headlines. Now he put the paper down.

"Listen," he said, "don't act as though you're afraid that Marvin is going to use the wrong fork."

"I'm not acting that way at all," I said.

"You know what I mean," Bill answered. "You used to be like that with me when I came here first."

I did not answer him, because I heard Marvin and Mary coming down the stairs. Marvin was in a tailored traveling suit, all new and perfect, which she must have bought just for the trip. I saw her glance about the room, at the books and Father's prints and at the heavy leather chairs and at the wine-colored curtains drawn tight across the windows.

226

"It's awfully nice," she said. "It's just what I thought it would be like."

"I hope there was everything you wanted upstairs," I said, and I rang the bell by the fireplace. Hugh answered it too quickly, showing that he must have been listening in the upper hall.

"We want some ginger ale," I said, "and Mr. King will have a Scotch-and-soda, won't you, Bill?"

"What about me?" Marvin asked.

"Bring up the tray, Hugh," I said.

"And what about me?" Mary asked. "Don't keep worrying about Hugh."

"Why?" asked Marvin. "What's the matter?"

"There's nothing really the matter," I said, "but it might upset him to find you and Mary drinking highballs. It will be all right just as soon as Hugh brings up the tray. We can wash out the glasses afterwards."

"You mean he will smell the glasses?" Marvin asked.

"Hugh's an awful sneak," Mary said.

"That's right," said Bill. "We'll have to rinse the glasses. You girls don't want to lose your reputations, do you?"

"It isn't that," I said, "but Hugh would tell everybody downstairs and then somebody would tell Mother."

"Oh," Marvin said.

We spoke softly because Hugh was coming back. He set down the tray and the ice and the glasses on the low table near the fire.

"May I help, sir?" he asked.

"No," I said. "That's all for tonight, Hugh."

I took out my key ring and unlocked the cupboard beneath the bookshelves by the window, and took out two bottles and put them on the tray.

"How much do you want, Marvin?"

"Just a drink," Marvin said. "A good stiff drink."

Now that was the way she always talked, but I wished she had not said it until Mary knew her better.

"I'll tell you what we'll do," Marvin said. "Mary, you and Bill can drink out of one glass and Harry and I can drink out of another. Then we can put some ginger ale in two other glasses and throw it out the window."

"That isn't such a bad idea," I said.

Then everyone was laughing, except Mary who looked annoyed.

"You mustn't mind Harry," she said to Marvin. "Harry's always worrying."

"Yes, I know," Marvin said. "Harry's just like that, and he doesn't change. I'm glad he doesn't change."

"You wouldn't think, would you," Mary said, "that Harry had been a hero in the war?"

"See here," I said. "I wish you wouldn't all discuss me as though I weren't here at all. I know what you all think about me."

Yet at the same time I knew that I was perfectly right. Mother would have heard about it and it would have made a lot of trouble.

Sometimes when I am acutely aware that something is worrying me I find that it is actually some stray thought of that visit of Marvin Myles's. Even now I find myself going over all the little phases of it, wondering why I behaved the way I did at such a moment, wondering what would have happened if I had made some different remark. Nothing could have made that visit any better — nothing that she could have done or that I could have done. What gives it such pathos is that both of us tried so hard.

It could not have been anything that she or I said, but rather what we thought. I do not even believe at the time that either of us was conscious of any difficulty; but I know now, and she must know, that there were all sorts of odd little moments, when something discordant happened. She kept looking at everything, which was perfectly natural, since it was all new to her and important, but that attention of hers made me nervous. When she examined the Inness over the mantelpiece and the large canvas on the opposite wall — cows standing in a shallow pool, and when she looked at the paper knives and little books and put out her fingers carelessly to touch

228

things, I kept feeling that she was a stranger. I kept wanting everyone to see her as I did, and yet I knew that everyone we met saw her as a stranger. That was the way Mary saw her — as something desirable and exotic, and Mary was sweet to her. She often told me afterwards how much she liked her. Mother was sweet to her too. She gave her a copy of Emerson's *Essays* before she went away, because they had talked about Emerson. Marvin had the gift Bill had of knowing what to talk about. I don't know why I was continually afraid that she might say the wrong thing, because she never did.

I took her up to Mother's room after breakfast next morning. Marvin must have noticed that I was looking at her to see that she was all right.

"What's the matter?" she asked me in the upstairs hall. "Is my slip showing?"

As a matter of fact, Mother would not have minded at all if Marvin's slip had been showing. It would have given her something homely to work on, because Mary was always having the same trouble. The difficulty was that nothing was showing. I suppose that Marvin must have been working very hard on herself before breakfast, though I did not think of it then.

"No," I said, "it isn't that. It's your nose."

"Why," asked Marvin, "what's the matter? Is it shining?"

It would really have been better if it had been, because Mother would have understood a well-scrubbed, shining face.

"No," I said, "just take your handkerchief and rub a little of the powder off."

Marvin rubbed some of the powder off.

"Now," she asked, "how's that?"

I have often wondered what Marvin really thought about Mother, and that was something which she never told me. I kept worrying about Mother too, hoping that she would not be gushing and sentimental, hoping that she would not begin to cry about Father. As it turned out, Mother was awfully nice. She said she was glad that Harry knew nice girls, really nice girls in New York, although she knew that she ought to trust me to have good taste, since I was just like my dear father. She was sure that Marvin would understand how a mother worries more about a boy than about a girl.

"And now, my dear," Mother said, "tell me about yourself."

I could tell that she did not really want to know. She really wanted to go on talking about me. No matter what Marvin said, Mother would listen very politely, and then go on with her own ideas, just where she had left off.

"She's sweet," Marvin told me afterwards.

I don't know whether she said it to please me or not, but it was sweet of her to say so, and I tried to explain about Mother — particularly that she lived in a little world of her own.

"Why, darling," Marvin said, "everyone does."

Afterwards Mary lent Marvin a pair of arctics and I took her for a walk toward Beacon Hill along the Esplanade. It was a gray sort of morning and the brick buildings on the hill looked old and smoky.

"I like it," Marvin said, "because it makes me understand you."

And then I told her we were going out to Westwood for lunch. I wanted her to see Westwood. I told her I knew that she would like it.

"We're going to have a picnic," I said, "and go coasting."

"Coasting?" Marvin said.

"Yes," I told her, "or else we can chop wood."

"But, darling," Marvin said, "I haven't any clothes."

I told her that Mary could lend her some, that Mary had lots of old tweeds and sweaters and things like that. Later Mary took Marvin up to her room to give her clothes and to get her dressed and Bill and I could hear them laughing about it. All the details of the picnic were a good deal on my mind. I told him that I hoped Westwood would be warm enough, that we only kept a low fire there in winter to prevent the pipes from freezing.

"Is anyone coming with us?" Bill asked.

"There'll be you and Mary," I said, "and Marvin and me and Joe Bingham and Kay Motford."

"Oh," said Bill, "she's coming is she?"

"I asked them," I said, "because you've always liked Kay."

"Yes," said Bill, "that's so. When are they going to be married?"

"Sometime in June," I said.

"Oh," said Bill, "in June. I suppose it's too cold to get married here in winter."

I had so much on my own mind — I was thinking so much of Marvin and how it would be at Westwood — that I did not think much about Bill. What I recall best is the snow, and how it got all over you and melted, and how it kept getting down Marvin's neck, and that Marvin wanted to coast downhill sitting up.

When we all met downstairs in the hall ready to go everyone was wrapped up in sweaters. Marvin was wearing Mary's brown tweed skirt and knitted stockings and one of my old turtleneck sweaters which was too big for her.

"Everything makes me itch," Marvin told me.

"Well, it will do you good to get some fresh air," I said.

We didn't have time to say anything more with everyone else in the hall. Kay always looked well in winter clothes. They seemed to fit her better than summer ones and her cheeks were red and her eyes were bright.

"Look at the snow queen," Bill said.

When she saw Bill she looked surprised for a moment and then she looked happy.

"I didn't know you were here," Kay said.

"Here today," Bill said, "and gone tomorrow."

I picked up the lunch basket and Joe picked up the vacuum bottles. When we crowded into the limousine everyone was laughing and it was just the way a winter picnic should be. It had been quite a while since I had heard Bill be so amusing. When he started to tell about all the hidden dangers that lurked around the waistline and the rest of his crusade for suspenders, I had an idea that Kay would not understand his humor, but everything sounded all right in the car. One thing kept leading to another and Marvin told about how she and I had gone out on the soap survey and how the Jewish lady was going to call the police until I said that I would wash her clothes.

"Why, Harry," Mary said, "you never told me about that."

With everyone laughing and talking it did not matter what anyone was thinking. All the girls seemed to be having a good time, but I suppose that's the way with girls when there are men around.

We ate our picnic in front of the fire in Father's old den at Westwood. Somehow when the fire was burning you did not mind the furniture's being covered with sheets. I managed to bring some whisky and we had plenty of hot coffee and sandwiches and pie, and then we all went out to the barn and got the sleds and dragged them over to the big hill. Joe took Mary down. Joe was always awfully good in the snow. Bill took Kay down and I took Marvin.

"Don't be like Ethan Frome," she said. "I want to live."

Bill and Kay tipped over halfway to the bottom of the hill. They rolled into a snowdrift and Bill got up first and pulled her up.

"That's what comes of not wearing suspenders," I heard him shouting.

Then I saw that Marvin looked cold. We began throwing snowballs at each other, but the snow kept getting down her neck.

"Let's go back to the house," she said. "I want to see it all."

"All right," I said.

I wanted to be alone with her and we had never seemed to be alone. We walked down the lane past the stables and up the terraces where the rose bushes were all wrapped in straw. The house looked sad and deserted, brown and bare among the trees, and I tried to tell her how it looked in summer with the wistaria and ivy over it and all the beeches out. I took her all through the house, telling her little things about it: how I used to slide down the banisters, how I used to think that the back hall was full of ghosts. Her hands were cold when she took her mittens off, so we went downstairs to the den to sit in front of the fire.

"There wouldn't be anybody who could see us if you kissed me," she said, "only the ghosts in the back entry."

When I kissed her it was not like winter at all. I told her it was like May when all the tulips were out in the garden.

"You're so sweet," she said. "I wish I didn't love you so."

I saw her glancing at all the covered pictures and all the covered furniture. I loved the way the fire struck her face, now that the white winter dusk from the snow was coming through the windows. I loved the way she looked in that sweater of mine that was too big for her.

"You look the way I've always wanted you to," I said.

She leaned toward me and rested her hand on my knee and gazed at me, as though she wanted to remember how I looked.

"You're going to stay here," she said. She was speaking softly, but it sounded absolutely final, incapable of shading or misinterpretation.

"If I stay," I said, "you're staying too."

"God knows why it is you're always so," she said. "You never say the wrong thing, even here."

I might have asked her what she meant if I had not heard the front door open. The sound of voices in the hall made me get up quickly from the bench where we had been sitting in front of the fire, and then Mary came in with Joe Bingham.

"Softy," Mary said to Marvin, "didn't you like the snow?"

Joe took off his mittens and blew loudly on his fingers.

"Where's everybody else?" he asked.

"Who?" I asked.

"Why, Bill and Kay," he said. "Didn't they come back here?"

"No," I said. "Why should they have?"

Joe blew on his fingers again, looked at them and rubbed his hands together hard.

"They went walking somewhere. I thought they were coming back to the house."

"They'll be back," Mary said. "There's still some coffee left. Who wants some coffee? Do you want some, Joe?"

"Not right now," Joe said. "I wonder where they are. It's getting sort of late."

It was getting late. Outside the bare limbs of the beech trees seemed to be growing lighter the way they did just before it grew dark in winter.

"It isn't five o'clock yet," I said.

"I'll bet you've never been coasting before like this," Mary was saying to Marvin. "You ought to see it in April. I'd love to take you out in April walking in the mud!"

"I wonder where the deuce they are," Joe said. "I don't want Kay to be catching cold."

"It's all right," I said. "They'll be back in a minute. Bill won't let her catch cold."

"Sometimes for someone grown up," said Joe, "you make pretty dumb remarks."

"Why, Joe's jealous!" Mary said.

"Who should I be jealous of?" Joe asked. "Are you intimating that I'm jealous of Bill King? It's only they may be lost or something in the woods."

"What under the sun," I asked him, "would Bill and Kay be doing in the woods?"

"Walking, of course," Joe said. "Whenever Kay gets anywhere she starts walking. You know how she walks, Harry."

"Yes," I said, "I know. They'll be back in a minute."

Well, Patrick's back here now with the car," Joe said.

Of course there was nothing wrong about Bill's being out with Kay, but I was glad when I heard them outside on the porch. I heard Bill singing when he opened the door.

"Oh, joy, oh, boy!" Bill was singing. "Where do we go from here?"

"Anywhere from Jersey," I heard Kay sing back, "to Harlem with you, dear!"

They stood side by side in the doorway for a moment and there was a sort of pause for no particular reason. I was thinking again that Kay certainly looked better in winter than she did in summer. The scarf around her neck matched her eyes and her cheeks were scarlet and she was out of breath as though they had been running.

"I don't see how you can stick in the house," Kay said, "on a day like this."

"It isn't day," Joe answered. "It's darned near night."

"All right," Kay said, "on a night like this. Harry, do you know where we've been? We went down to the brook."

"This is quite a piece of real estate," Bill said. "I didn't know you had a brook."

"If Patrick's here," Mary told us, "we'd better be going back."

"Here today," Bill said, "and gone tomorrow. 'Tis but a tent where takes his one night's rest."

"Keep the cash," said Marvin, "and let the credit go."

I saw Bill's head turn toward her quickly, and then he laughed.

I was thinking about Marvin Myles. She would be going back on the midnight and I was wondering too, for almost the first time, where we would go from here.

It must have been on Tuesday evening — or close to Tuesday evening — that the telephone rang. Mary and I were having coffee in the parlor after dinner and Hugh came in to say that it was Miss Motford who wanted to speak to Miss Mary.

"What did Kay want?" I asked when Mary came back.

"She wanted Bill's address," Mary answered.

"It's funny she didn't ask me for it," I said. "I wonder what she wants it for."

"She said she'd promised to send him the title of a book that she couldn't remember," Mary said.

"That's funny," I said. "I didn't know that Kay read much," but it all seemed dull. Everything was very dull after Marvin and Bill had gone.

It must have been about Friday when Joe called up and said he wanted to see me about something. I told him to come around to the house and we would have a cocktail. When he got there he said he wanted to see me alone, so of course we went up to the library. I could tell right away that Joe was in trouble. He sat down and rubbed his hands together and lighted a cigarette and threw it into the fire.

"Listen, I've got to talk to somebody," he said, "and you're my

235

best friend. I think I'm going crazy. Do you know what's happened?"

"No," I said.

Joe got up and walked to the window.

"I don't know how to tell you — I didn't know these things happened. Kay's broken her engagement."

"What?" I said.

"You heard me. She's broken her engagement. It happened yesterday."

"You mean, you had a fight about something?" I asked.

"No," Joe answered. "She just said she began to realize I couldn't give her the things she wanted."

"But what does she want?" I asked.

"I don't know," Joe said, "what anybody wants. I was just thinking everything was all right. You don't suppose — something just came into my mind — it couldn't be anything about Bill King?"

"Bill King?" I said. "Why, Kay hardly knows him."

"Yes," said Joe, "that's right and what would anybody see in Bill King? I know he's a friend of yours, but frankly I've always thought that Bill is just a long, cold drink of water."

"Just get that out of your head about Bill King," I said, and then I told him how much better it was if Kay really felt that way to have it all called off. I told him that it showed a good deal of courage on Kay's part. It wasn't anyone's fault if two people did not get on and it was better to know it then instead of later.

"Some day you'll be glad of it," I said. "You get over these things, Joe. Some day you'll find someone else."

I was just repeating what I had heard other people say. The queer thing is that what other people say is so often true, or partly true. If you are young, they say, sooner or later you get over it. They don't say that everything hurts more when you are young. I like to think of that when I hear people talk about lost youth. I am glad that I am through with it and won't be young again.

I never realized that I would say to myself all the things that I had said to Joe and that I would know exactly how they must have

236

sounded to him. When you give advice and consolation it very seldom occurs to you that it may come back to you some day, mockingly, like an echo.

"You're going to stay here," Marvin had said.

I could catch the exact inflection of her voice, again and again, after she was gone. It might have been easier for us both if Marvin had never mentioned it, easier but not any better.

I always like to go over the rest of it quickly, to put it out of my mind, even now, or to scurry around it when it comes up. I feel toward all the rest of it as you sometimes do when you have made a tactless remark or have behaved outrageously in public. You say to yourself afterwards that you have exaggerated the effect, that it was not really as bad as you thought it was. Yet all the time you know that you are only fooling yourself. Nothing that has ever happened to me was ever worse than what happened with Marvin Myles.

I knew when she went away that I wanted to have her always. That was why I went to see her in New York — because I wanted to have her always.

When I called her up after all the times I had thought of calling, I was afraid that she might be away somewhere, until I heard her voice. I sat in the library with the door closed, and I thought while I was waiting that it might have been better if I had made the call from the Smith and Wilding office, in case Hugh might be listening on the extension downstairs, and then I realized that I did not care who might be listening, that it made no difference any longer.

"Marvin," I said, "is that you?"

"Who did you think it was?" she asked. "Harry, are you all right?"

"I'm fine," I said. "It's awfully cold here. The thermometer is down to twenty."

I heard her laugh and then she said, "You'd better put on that sweater, even if it itches."

"Marvin," I said, "how are you?"

"I'm bearing up."

"Marvin, I want to see you."

"Then pack your bag," she said. "Come on right away."

"I am," I said. "I'll meet you at the office this afternoon."

There was a silence long enough so that I thought she was off the wire.

"Hello," I said.

"Harry," she said, and stopped.

"What is it?" I asked.

"Never mind," she said. "Hurry, won't you? Harry —"

"What?"

"How's Hugh?" she asked.

I could not understand why she asked about him until I remembered that she always did.

"Hugh's all right," I said.

"Darling," Marvin said, "don't forget to rinse the glasses."

People who live there keep saying that the great thing about New York is that you can do anything you like there and no one cares. I once told Bill King, when he made that remark, that you could carry the argument further, that no one cared whether you were there or not. When I went back home after having been away for a long while, everything was waiting for me just as though I had not been away, but when I came back to New York nothing had waited.

When I stepped out of the elevator the girl at Bullard's seemed puzzled for a second. She seemed to be thumbing backward through the catalogue of her mind before she retrieved my face from among others she had thrown into the discard.

"Why, hello, Mr. Pulham," she said. "Where are you working now?"

Her manner told me that I was through, through with it all for good. I was nothing but an uninteresting stranger.

"Go right in," she said.

I walked in past the media department and past the closed door of Mr. Bullard's office. It was as though I had been away for years and years. I seemed to have forgotten most of it already, the way you forget an illness and all its details, when you have returned to health.

Back in that room where I used to work Bill was sitting at his desk, looking at some layouts of suspenders, but Marvin was not there. Bill got up and we shook hands, but I could see that he was thinking of something else.

"Where's Marvin?" I asked.

"Out," Bill said. "She left a note. Sit down and don't talk for a minute." I sat down at Marvin's desk and picked up an envelope and Bill began pacing up and down behind me.

Come up to the apartment, darling [she had written]. The butler will let you in. It's nicer than the office.

Bill was still pacing up and down behind me.

"Swansdown — Ocean Breeze. It's got to be virile — Flyweight — Seafoam. . . . Wait a minute," he said. "What's the name of that club you were in at Harvard?"

"The Zephyr Club," I said.

"That's it," said Bill. "There you are. The Zephyr Brace — as chafeless on the shoulders as a summer breeze. That's all right now. How are you, boy?"

"I'm fine," I said.

"What are you doing for dinner?"

"I guess I'll have dinner with Marvin," I said.

He was just asking. He knew that I would want to see her.

"All right," Bill said. "They're running me ragged here. I've got to see Bullard. Call me up tomorrow."

"All right," I said, and I picked up my hat.

"Wait a minute," Bill called. "Have you seen Kay Motford?"

"Oh, I forgot," I said. "Kay and Joe — that's all over."

"What?"

For a second he looked completely blank.

239

"Joe told me," I said, "but it isn't any secret. Kay broke it off."
I thought that Bill looked worried, but it was only for a second.
"Now, what did she do that for?" Bill asked.
"I don't know," I said. "I guess they didn't get along."
"But what did she say to Joe?"
"She just said it wouldn't work," I told him.
Bill drew a deep breath and smiled.
"Oh," he said, "so that's all?"
"Of course that's all," I said. "What else should there be?"
I was not much interested. I wanted to see Marvin Myles.
"Nothing," Bill said, "nothing. I guess it's just as well. Call me up tomorrow, will you?"
He had turned away already and was standing with his hands in his pockets, looking at his desk. Bill always hated to be interrupted when he was in the middle of an idea.

Her dress was new, though I can not recall a single detail of it. Marvin was always more important than her clothes. There was a book on the couch where she had been sitting, but I knew she had not been reading it. There was a bottle of champagne and two glasses, on the low table by the couch, standing on a little silver tray which I had never seen before. I don't know how long it was before we said anything, because words did not make much difference as long as she was glad to see me, and everything was all right as long as she was near me.

"Let's have some of the champagne," she said. "I got it down at Tony's."

"It's a waste," I said. "You and I don't need champagne. We don't need anything."

But there is no use going into what we said. When you are in love with someone, so much you say loses its meaning afterwards, and it always remains a secret that can not be brought back to life.

"He called the suspenders Zephyrs," I was saying.

I worked the cork out of the bottle very carefully while she sat with her fingers on her ears, because she never did like sudden noises.

"So he's going to call them Zephyrs," she said. "Did you see Mr. Bullard?"

"No," I said.

"Well, that's all right. You can see him tomorrow."

"No," I said. "We're getting married tomorrow."

"Why, darling," she said, "we haven't any place to live."

"There'll be room," I said, "until we find some place."

"Where?" she asked. "In a hotel?"

I don't know why I never saw. It all came down like the ceiling above our heads. It all came down like rain.

"Not a hotel," I said. "There's plenty of room at home." I heard her catch her breath sharply; it was just as though a light went out.

"I couldn't," she said. "You belong to me, but I couldn't."

"It would only be for a little while," I said, "until we got a house."

Then she threw her arms around me and I could feel her trembling all over. I could hear the roar of the elevated on Third Avenue.

"Why, Marvin dear, there's nothing to cry about," I said, "just as long as you love me."

"It wouldn't work," she said. "We only belong to each other here. You've got to come back to me here."

Then before I could answer she was saying all sorts of things that hurt me. I was such a fool that I had thought that she liked it at home and instead she was saying that she hated it, that there wouldn't be anything left of her. She was saying that I would be ruined, that I wouldn't be the person she had known, that we would end by despising each other. She wanted me to stay here, right here, where she could take care of me, because I could never take care of myself.

"Darling, I could make you like it. If you only gave me the chance I could make you want to stay."

241

I understood then that it was over, that it had always been impossible.

"I have to live where I belong," I said.

And then we were talking again, interrupting each other. I remember how our voices rose and fell, with neither of us listening to the other, even when there was nothing left to say.

I sat up straight and rubbed the back of my hand across my forehead.

"Perhaps," Marvin said, "it's just as well. You took up a lot of my time."

"You took a good deal of mine," I said.

"Let's not fight any more," she said, and she kissed me, but it was just as though neither of us were there.

Then I got up and put on my coat. I'm glad to think that I behaved myself. It would have been ugly, always getting worse, if I had not.

"Anyway," said Marvin, "it's something to remember."

"I'd better go now," I said.

"Harry," she called, "wait. I want to tell you something. No matter what happens, no matter how long it is —" Her voice broke and she began to cry — "I'll always be waiting for you, if you want to come back — from that damned place where you're going."

"Good-by, Marvin," I said, and then I opened the door.

"Harry," she called. "Harry," she called again, but I knew there was no use going back. The trouble is you can't go back, and besides we had told each other everything. Then the street door was closing behind me, although I had no recollection of having walked down the flights of stairs. I was out on the street alone, and I felt sick and absolutely empty, as empty as that bottle of champagne. It was like her to have champagne.

XXII

Kiss and Don't Tell

I have never talked with anyone about it, because I have never, as Kay sometimes has told me, been able to express emotion. Moreover it was entirely my own business, mine and Marvin Myles's. I was born just early enough to be inculcated with the doctrine of the kiss-and-don't-tell school, a system of manners which I have often heard is entirely out of date. I was taught that telling was one of the things a gentleman did not do, and I still agree. I was also brought up in the intolerant school that has a contempt for crybabies.

This sort of training could lead to only two results: You either got used to taking what was coming to you in a conventional way which troubled nobody — like a gentleman, as the Skipper used to say at School — or else you revolted from it entirely and became what we used to call, among other things, a "mess." You became a Socialist, for instance, the way Bob Carroll finally did, or else you just went around hating everyone and seeing queer people. When I was hurt so badly that sometimes life did not seem worth living I did not want anyone to know it, or even to take it up with myself. That was the reason for a lot I did that winter.

I took the night train home and the next morning when I arrived I went to Smith and Wilding. Mr. Wilding was taking off his hat and overshoes and I told him that I had been down to New York and that I was not going back there again.

"Oh," said Mr. Wilding, "so you're all through with that?"

I always have wondered how much he knew.

"Yes," I said, "I'm all through with that." For once I felt per-

243

fectly able to talk to him, because it really made no difference what happened to me that morning.

"I don't want to sell bonds," I said.

"My boy," said Mr. Wilding, "no one wants to, but that's the way we live."

"If I were a customer here," I said, "do you know what I'd want? I'd want to have somebody who could give me impartial advice about my holdings. There isn't any department here that keeps watch on investment lists."

"No," Mr. Wilding said, "there isn't. I'll see you at half-past three this afternoon."

If I had not worked for Mr. Bullard and listened so often to Bill King's projects, I should never have had such an idea; but a series of little accidents is what leads you into almost everything. I had never heard of an investment counsel service when I went in to see Mr. Wilding that morning, but by the end of the week the partners were discussing it; and it did not matter how hard the work was as long as it kept my mind occupied. I entered the bumping tournament at the Squash Club and began playing regularly for an hour each afternoon so that I would be too tired to think in the evening. I made myself go out and see people, because I never wanted to be by myself.

They say that you can get over anything in time. I don't believe you can, but given enough time you can put it where it belongs — back in your mind beneath the present. All that winter I must have been running away from the shadow of Marvin Myles, and if for a moment I stopped running she would catch up to me. I would wake up in the dark and find myself thinking about her. Those were the worst times — when there was no one else to talk to, and no distraction. All that winter I seemed to be only half alive. I went to the winter dinner of the Zephyr Club and I went to the Motfords' house in the country for a week end and it surprised me on such occasions how smoothly everyone else's life went. Since that time I have always believed that there is nothing worse than being too much involved in yourself.

During that week end with Kay in Concord, where the Motfords had kept their spring and autumn house open through the
winter, I was interested, almost for the first time, in another person.
I thought that she might be going through some sort of experience
like mine, but if she was having an unpleasant time she certainly
did not show it. She looked as though something wonderful had
happened — or was about to happen. We went out to dinner Saturday night and on Sunday morning we went skating, and we
took a long walk on Sunday afternoon. We had one thing in common — we did not want to talk about ourselves. Most of the time
we talked about our friends — about who was crazy about whom
and whether I thought so-and-so was attractive — and after that
we talked about Bolshevism and social problems on which our ideas
were as vague as my ideas are now, and then we talked about the
illness of President Wilson and about what we thought of Presi-
dent-elect Harding. When we took up the subject of Europe I told
her frankly that I could not understand the war debts or exactly
why we had fought the war.

"Here, Rough," she called, "here, Tipsy." Kay always took her
dogs whenever she went walking and most of the time her mind
was on the dogs.

"I asked Bill King up this week end," she said, "but he was too
busy. He's always awfully busy, isn't he?"

"Yes," I said, "he always has a lot to do."

"Tipsy," she called, "come on. He's always so alive, isn't he?"

"Who?" I asked. "Tipsy?"

"No," she said. "Bill King."

"Yes," I said, "he has a new idea every minute."

"He knows a lot about everything," Kay said. "He thinks that
girls are people. Here, Tip."

We were walking in snow through the woods, and the air was
damp and cold, just the way it had been that afternoon at Westwood.
I tried to keep my mind on what she was saying about Bill and
not to think about Marvin Myles.

"When you talk to him, he seems to know all about you."

"He does when he puts his mind on it," I said, "but most of the time his mind is on himself." She had been walking fast with her head up and her shoulders back, but now she stopped and the dogs stopped too. I thought again that she was meant for winter. I wondered if she knew how well her brown tweed coat and skirt looked.

"Harry — " and then she had to call to the dogs, "you don't think that Bill's angry at me about anything, do you? I asked him to the Assembly and he couldn't come, and then, when I went to New York, I wrote him and he didn't answer."

"Bill's always that way," I said. "He hardly ever answers letters, but when you see him he's always just the same."

"We'd better go back," she said. "Here, Rough, here, Tipsy. The dogs have had a good run now."

Somehow she made me wonder why it was that a girl who had broken her engagement should be more interesting than she had been before.

That night when I got home I wrote to Bill King — I had been meaning to for quite a while. In one way I did not want to see him, because he might talk about Marvin Myles, but again, I wanted to hear about her.

"I've just been in Concord," I wrote. "Kay says she asked you out there. Maybe you're right that she's pretty. If you can come up here we'll have her over."

It was quite a while before Bill wrote back. He said that he was too busy to go anywhere, and he did not mention Kay.

Looking back upon it now, that winter of 1920, when I was trying not to think about Marvin Myles, begins to take the form of other winters. There were a few little difficulties about the house — some sort of trouble with the chore-man either about the furnace or the sidewalk, and a frozen pipe in Mary's bathroom one night when she left the window open. Then Mary had another caller instead of Roger Priest, and Mother was asked to join a new reading club, which she refused. It seems absurd that I should recall events such as these in the light of my own sorrow.

246

What helped me most was seeing Joe Bingham. We began playing squash together nearly every afternoon and usually he would stop a while at the house before he went on home. I was fascinated by the frank openness of his suffering and at the ease with which he spoke of it, for he made it sound like an operation or a railroad accident when he discussed his symptoms. What seemed to hurt him most was that any girl who had cared for him should have stopped before he had stopped caring for her.

"Do you know what I think?" Joe said. "I don't think Kay has any real balance. I'm beginning to think that maybe I'm just as well out of it."

"Of course you are," I said.

"Now, look here," said Joe. "I'm only talking like this to you, Harry. I'm telling everyone else that Kay's wonderful, but just between you and me, she could have made it come gradually, couldn't she, instead of just socking it at me all at once?"

"You must have seen it coming, Joe," I said.

"I tell you I didn't," Joe answered. "Everything was fine. Why, look at the time we all went coasting. Everything was fine then — except Kay had a headache that night."

"There's no use going over it, Joe," I said.

It was a comfort to see the way his mind was working, but what amazed me most was his resilience. After a month or two I saw him walking with Madeline Bush on the Esplanade.

"Well," he said, when I asked him about it, "why shouldn't I? You don't know Madeline well, do you?"

I didn't know her very well.

"You can't tell anything about a girl," Joe said, "until you know her. Now, I know what you think when you see her. You just think, 'Oh, hell, there's Madeline Bush.' I used to think that myself — 'Oh, hell, there's Madeline Bush.' Now, you wouldn't know from looking at her how much Madeline knows."

"About what?" I asked.

"About life," Joe said. "We've had some pretty serious talks about it. Do you know what happened to her when she was ten?"

247

I certainly did not know.

"When Madeline was ten she was making fudge in the kitchen and she got her sleeve caught in the saucepan and it went all over her arm, and she had to go to the hospital. That's how she knows what pain is — real pain. You wouldn't think to look at her that she could talk that way, would you? Frankly, Madeline Bush has made me think."

"About what?" I said.

"That's right," Joe said. "Go ahead and laugh at it. The trouble with us, Harry, is we take life as it comes without thinking. Now, when I got engaged to Kay I simply wasn't thinking. Madeline made me see that."

"Maybe she's right," I said.

"You see," Joe said, "it isn't that I really like Madeline Bush — not that way, I mean. When anybody's been through what I have you can't get over it, but it makes me feel better when I do nice things for Madeline — taking her to the movies — that sort of thing. I don't suppose you realize that you can like a girl simply for her mind. She understands all about Kay. She's made me see Kay the way she really is for the first time. Madeline's got a wonderful mind."

Not long after that — it must have been April — the Motfords asked me to dinner. They had all been very kind to me after Father died. Just a family dinner, and I was so early that Mr. and Mrs. Motford had not come downstairs and Kay was alone in the parlor, sitting looking at the fire. Her arms were bare and her dress was cut lower than usual.

"Kay," I said, "that's an awfully pretty dress."

"There isn't much to it," Kay said. "I keep thinking it's going to fall off."

"Well, it's awfully pretty while it's on," I said.

I was afraid that I might have gone a little too far about the dress, but Kay was smiling. It was a queer sort of smile, which made me think that she was practising before a mirror.

"I suppose you've heard the news," she said.

"No," I said. "What news?"

"About Madeline and Joe. They're engaged."

"They can't be," I said. "Joe never told me."

Kay laughed.

"Maybe Joe doesn't know it yet," she said, "but Madeline does. She called me up at six. It's still a secret, but she wanted me to be the first to know."

"That wasn't nice of her," I said.

"That's all right," said Kay. "That's fair. I'm awfully glad, really. Harry, have you heard anything from Bill King?"

"No," I answered, "not for quite a while."

"Oh," Kay said, "well. I'm awfully glad you like my dress."

It may have been true that Joe Bingham had not known it, and perhaps girls always know beforehand when such a thing is going to happen, because when Joe told me the news a few days later he looked shy and bewildered.

"You know, Harry," he told me, "I just don't see how it happened. I just went to call on Madeline to kill time around five o'clock, and there we were engaged. Do you know what Madeline has done? She's saved me from myself. Do you know what I think? I think I've loved Madeline for years without knowing it. That business about Kay Motford — Madeline says it didn't really mean anything, and it doesn't. It's funny about women, isn't it? And it's funny about love. I tell you, Harry, the trouble with you is you've never been in love. You'll know what I mean some day." Fond as I was of Joe Bingham, I could not listen to him talk about love. It was the last thing I wanted to think or hear about at the end of that winter. That must be why I went up to School for a night in the spring.

As the weather began to be warmer I kept thinking about the Skipper, but Sam Green was the one who suggested that we ought to go out to look the old place over. Although Sam was working downtown in the cotton business, somehow we had not seen each other much. Then one day we found ourselves side by side on two stools at one of those four-sided lunch counters on Washington Street, where a girl stands in the center, serving coffee and pie and cake out of the dumbwaiter to a circle of eating men. It was a pleasant arrangement to be able to stop eating and to look up at a pretty girl.

"You're looking fine, Sam," I said.

"I didn't know you ate with Tillie," Sam said.

"When I come here," I told him, "I always eat with Tillie."

"Well, how have you been anyway?" Sam asked. "Have you been out to School?"

When I told him that I had not, Sam looked serious.

"Well, you ought to go. The Skipper's been asking for you. It hurts him when the old boys lose interest. You're not losing interest, are you?"

"Why, of course not, Sam," I said.

"That's right," Sam said. "Look here. The Skipper wants to see me Saturday. I've got my car. Why don't you come out with me?"

No matter what has happened to you, it is always a little better in the spring. It was the middle of April and the sun was out and the day was almost warm. Sam said that it was great to be out-doors and that once we got through Worcester it smelled like School already. He kept going back to all the things we had done there, which I had almost forgotten, and when he wasn't talking about School he was talking about Harvard. I asked him how he liked the cotton business and he said it was perfectly all right, as good as any business.

"All that's wrong," said Sam, "is that there are so many nickel-plated muckers in it. Haven't you ever noticed how many of them there are? I guess I'm not made for business."

"I know what you mean," I said.

"It's great to be getting away from it," Sam said, "to be getting back to something worth while." I knew how he felt. Back at School and in college, Sam had been an important man. It must have been an anticlimax, trying to learn about cotton. When we saw the buildings on the hill, with the grass around them just turning green, Sam stopped the car.

"Look at it," Sam said. "There it is. I wish to God we both were back."

"It doesn't do any good wishing, Sam," I said. "It wasn't meant for that."

"The trouble with you," Sam said, "is you never made a team."

They were knocking out flies down in the lower field. You could hear the sharp crack of the bats long before we stopped to watch. Sam got out of the car and took off his overcoat.

"Hey!" Sam called. "Give me a bat." Everyone knew who he was — he was Green, Sam Green.

Then a few minutes later, while I stood there watching, the study bell began to ring. In spite of all the time that had passed the bell made me want to hurry. When the Skipper asked me into his study before dinner it did not seem to me that a picture or a book had been moved.

"All that changes is the boys," the Skipper said, "and they don't change much either — not even when they're grown up."

We had supper at the high table. I sat on the Skipper's right and Mr. Folansbee, who used to teach me mathematics, was beside me. The dessert was rice pudding and the Skipper tapped his glass after we had finished eating.

"Two old boys are back with us tonight," he said. "You have seen Sam Green here before, but you have not seen Harry Pulham, only his name on the war tablet in the great hall — our boy who won a medal."

I had not known that my name was on any tablet.

"But he comes back here," the Skipper went on, "as one of us."

Then that strong, sonorous voice of his stopped, and he put his hand on my shoulder.

"Get up," he said, "and speak to them, Harry."

I found myself on my feet, looking into their faces. Never in my wildest thoughts had it occurred to me that I might address the School.

"I'm not good at speaking," I said. "All I can say is this: It's

251

pretty hard to forget anything you have learned here. It all keeps coming back to you. You'll see — you won't forget."

The Skipper there beside me might have been holding a book ready to tell me to sit down and to walk twelve times around the track if I did badly. The faces of big boys and little boys made me feel that I was speaking to myself, somewhere in the past. Then as I started to go on with it, I had the queerest thought that Marvin Myles was listening. It seemed to me that I had come back there on account of her, just to get everything straight.

"I'm not referring to the books," I said. "I never was much good at them, was I, sir? But outside — " I stopped, not very well contented with the word. "When you get out of here, you'll find that other people have different standards. It's puzzling sometimes. Now when I was in the war," — I had not meant to speak about the war, — "there was one time when I was afraid to go ahead, because I thought that I'd be killed." I gripped the edge of the table, and it still seemed to me that Marvin Myles was listening. "I went on because it was the right thing to do. I guess it was something that was kicked into me here. That's what I mean by things you learn that you can't forget."

I sat down and listened to them clapping and when I took a drink of water I saw that my hand was shaking. I was never good at speaking, and I had not intended for a minute to show off in front of everyone.

"Harry," the Skipper said, when I was leaving in the morning, "that was a great speech last night."

"I'm sorry it wasn't better, sir," I said. "If I had been prepared — "

"You were prepared," the Skipper said. "It shows that I've turned another boy into a man, and that's what I'm here for."

I'm glad that Bill King did not hear him say that. I wished that the Skipper did not sometimes sound that way.

"It's made me feel better to come here, sir," I said.

"Harry," the Skipper said, "if you ever need any help and advice, you know where to come."

I wished that he had not said that either, because it made me feel that I should have asked his advice and I knew exactly what he would have answered without my asking.

"That's awfully kind of you, sir," I said. "I'll certainly remember."

When we left the school grounds I had the feeling of being outside, and I wished again I had not used that word the night before. All the part of it that was simple and easy was disappearing.

"It never fails," Sam said. "I'm always better when I go there."

"He's just the same," I said.

"That's exactly it, he's just the same."

When I came home that evening Kay Motford called me up.

"Harry," she asked me, "where have you been? Would you like to go for a walk in the country tomorrow afternoon? The dogs ought to have a run."

I told her that I was busy, that there was a lot of work at the office.

"You're just like Bill King," she said. "You're always busy."

When spring came I thought about Marvin Myles just as much, but there was a lot to do at Westwood — the trees and garden had suffered badly from the ice storm and the walls had begun to leak, and I was the one to whom everyone came for decisions. When I found that the days were long enough and when the tennis court was in shape, Mary and I began asking friends out for the night so that we could play doubles. One of them, Cecilia Leverett, played a beautiful game of tennis and we played mixed doubles in the spring tournament that year. It never occurred to me that Cecilia was around much until Mary asked me if I wanted Cecilia for over Sunday.

"She's your friend," I said, "not mine."

"But you like her, don't you?" Mary said.

"Yes," I said, "of course I like her. I like all your friends."

"Oh, Harry," Mary said, "I'm awfully glad."

"What are you glad about?" I asked.

"Well," Mary said, "I wasn't sure that you really liked her, and I was just thinking this Sunday I was going to ask a boy out and I wouldn't have so much time for Cecilia."

"What boy?" I asked.

"Don't worry," Mary said. "He's perfectly all right. He went to Harvard three classes below you — Harrison, Jim Harrison."

"Harrison?" I said. "He didn't go to School, did he?"

"Everybody can't go to your damned old School," Mary said.

"I was just asking about him," I said. "Have him out. That's fine."

"Then you'll look out for Cecilia, will you?" Mary said.

I had never heard about Harrison, but he sounded better than Roger Priest. He did not look so well when he came out on Saturday night. He was a rather heavy, dumpy-looking boy, with a dinosaur on his watch chain, and after dinner he did a trick of making an egg drop into a milk bottle. He was selling bonds for one of the big houses, so we were able to talk about the market, but most of the time he played little jokes on Mary that made her laugh. The next morning she took him riding and I took Cecilia up to the Purcells' for tennis. Then after lunch Mary took Jim Harrison somewhere else and Cecilia and I were left alone. It was quite different, now that I had her on my hands — just as though we were getting to know each other for the first time. I remember her saying that my eyes were sad.

"It's funny," she said. "I've always just thought of you as Mary's brother. I've never thought of your eyes."

"When you come right down to it," I said, "I've never thought of yours."

It was strange to be on the piazza in the June sun talking to a girl, when all the while I kept thinking of Marvin Myles and what she would have said if she had been there. If Cecilia had not gone abroad that summer, we might have really grown to know each other — have kept on playing tennis and being thrown together, as they put it. I don't remember that I even touched her hand, but I might have.

"Harry," she said the last time I saw her, "I'm going to miss you," and I told her that I'd miss her too.

"Harry," she said, "I'll see you in September, just after Labor Day."

She sent me a post card from London, saying just when she was getting home, but I never called her up. On Labor Day I'd gone sailing with Kay Motford at Northeast Harbor.

All the boys and girls I knew who weren't married already seemed to be getting married that June. Neither Madeline Bush nor her family believed in long engagements, so she and Joe were married early in the month. I was best man at the wedding, which was held on the lawn of Madeline's grandmother's house in Peabody. Joe, who was recovering from his ushers' dinner, was rather pathetic that day — a gray, chilly day which was not meant for a country wedding.

"We'll keep right on being friends, won't we?" Joe said. "It will just be the same as ever, only better. That's what Madeline says."

"Yes, of course," I said. But we both were wrong about that. Friends do not always last through a marriage, and when I saw Madeline's hard little eyes watching me I knew that she was thinking that I had a bad influence on Joe. Now that she had Joe, she would want him for herself.

I was an usher at several other weddings, so I kept seeing the same faces and going through the same routine — dinners where we drank too much and threw glasses on the floor, guest rooms where we unpacked bags and got into cutaways. Kay's brother, Guy, got married, and Kay wore blue. Then Kay's best friend, Lorene Wills, married a man from Baltimore and Kay and all the other bridesmaids wore orchid-colored organdy which made Kay look very badly. Then Bob Carroll married a dark-looking girl from Keene, New Hampshire.

Bo-jo Brown's wedding was the biggest of them all. He married Gay Paisley in the little church in the town where the Paisley Spinning Company was situated. The Paisleys were always married and buried from the old Paisley house which looked as though it had not been used for anything else for quite a while. Jack Purcell told me that the champagne came right over the border in two trucks. Wherever it came from, there was plenty of it. Jack Pur-

255

cell was Bo-jo's best man and Bo-jo spoke to me particularly about my not being an usher; it wasn't that he didn't want me, he said, it was just that Gay had so many cousins and there had to be somebody from the football team. Gay Paisley was a pale little girl who looked frightened when Bo-jo lifted her up and sat her on his shoulder.

"Come on now," Bo-jo shouted. "Three times three for Gay!"

Then he wanted to get all the Class together, and all his old form at School, and the crowd at the Club. As old Mr. Paisley sat in his wheel chair watching at the party I heard him make a remark which was quoted quite often afterwards.

"I'm damned if that boy doesn't think my daughter's wedding is a football game."

It was true that Bo-jo seemed to think his marriage was closely connected with college activities. The only thing that disturbed him was that it was already too late for them to have the class baby, although naturally he only mentioned this to a small group.

"It isn't right," Bo-jo said. "Do you know who has the class baby? A guy named Weinberg who lives in Galena, Illinois. Whoever heard of Weinberg? I ask you, is it right?"

We told him that it was not right.

"If it had been any of the old crowd," Bo-jo said, "I wouldn't say a word, but how's it going to look at the reunion? When we have to give a loving cup to a little kid named Noel Weinberg!"

We moved up to North Harbor as usual in July and finally around the first of August Bill King came up for two days.

It seemed to me that Bill was looking white and rather tired. He told me that he had a new job with another agency at twice his other salary, and it looked as though they were going to get the Coza account away from J. T. Bullard.

"How's Marvin Myles?" I asked.

"She's fine," he said. "She struck Bullard for a raise. You can't keep that girl down."

He looked as though he were going to say more and I was glad he didn't.

"I'm awfully glad," I said.

"Marvin's all right," Bill said. "You needn't worry about her."

That was all he said, but something in his attitude hurt me. He did not want to talk about himself any longer and he no longer seemed interested in what I was doing. He seemed to say, without saying it, that he had spent a good deal of time and thought upon me and now he had given up; but I was determined to have him still like me. I don't know what I did or said, but I think at the end he saw how hard I was trying, because he began to laugh at me the way he used to, and to make jokes about me with Mary.

"Bill," I said, "you're not mad at me, are you?" I felt about him, I suppose, much the way Joe Bingham felt about me.

"I was," Bill said; "not any more. Forget it, Harry."

Then he began telling about the people he had met in New York, lots of writers and artists. Bill always liked to use big names.

"It's just you're one kind of a person," he said, "and I'm another. Forget it, Harry. The thing is, you want to settle down — and you're certainly settling."

"I suppose that's true," I said.

"Now, when it comes to me," Bill said, "all I want is variety. I don't want to be tied to anything. I want to see people boiling around. It's the way I get ideas."

When we went down to the beach Sunday morning Kay was there. She looked very surprised when she saw Bill, and I left them talking while I swam out to the float. Bill always wanted to put off until the last possible moment jumping into the water. When I got ashore again they weren't saying much.

"Don't be so silly," I heard Kay saying. "That's perfectly all right."

Then when she saw me she got up.

"Come on," she said. "Who's going out to the float?"

"I didn't come here to freeze to death," Bill said.

"Come on," Kay said. "Come out again, Harry." We swam out to the float and back. Kay had learned the crawl that summer and she did it very well.

"Why didn't you tell me he was coming?" she asked, and I told her he had just wired the day before.

"It's too bad," Kay said. "I like to do something for your friends. I'm going out to lunch, I'm going out to dinner, and I'm going away all tomorrow."

Bill was sitting on the beach, just where we had left him.

"Good-by, Bill," Kay said.

Bill sat watching her as she ran up to the bathhouses.

"Does it strike you," he said, "that she's mad at me about something?"

"Why should she be mad at you?" I asked.

Bill picked up a handful of sand and watched it run through his fingers.

"There's absolutely no reason at all," he said. "I suppose girls around here haven't got much to do except build incidents out of their imaginations."

"Incidents?" I asked. "What sort of incidents?"

"Nothing," Bill said. "Absolutely nothing. They just don't seem to realize that you're here today and gone tomorrow."

XXIII

Frankly, Only a Symbol

We were beginning to get away from the war that summer and back to normalcy, as President Harding put it; there were signs of a business upturn and the League of Nations was becoming a dead issue. My whole generation, except me, seemed to be happy and sure of itself. I had a feeling that my whole life meant nothing, while all the other people I knew were building their lives about something worth-while and permanent. I imagine it is some such line of thinking as this that makes most people marry. Romantic novelists have created the illusion that it is hard to find someone to marry. From my own observation I think they are mistaken. There is nothing easier than doing something that nature wants you to do, and there is always someone ready to help you. Before you know what it is all about, you are selecting cuff links for the ushers. I was amazed when Kay Motford told me that she felt much the same as I did. That autumn marked the first time that we really talked about ourselves — or at any rate about certain aspects of ourselves. It might have been better for us both if we had been frank instead of each nursing a sort of reticence, and a fear that one would be defenseless if the other knew too much.

If Erick Munne had not asked me to Northeast Harbor on Labor Day I might never have been interested in how Kay Motford felt, and there we would have been — Kay and I — just as we had been before, impersonal. It was only by accident that he happened into the customers' room at Smith and Wilding and that I was looking at the board, watching the trade in Motors. Erick Munne did not ask me because he knew and liked me as an individual, but simply because he wanted an extra man, someone whom he could ask home without bothering about, someone whom he would not have to explain to everyone.

"Why don't you come to Northeast for Labor Day?" Erick said. "The family wants me to find an extra man," and then he told me who would be there, and I knew everyone. The more he spoke of it the more I could see that he liked the idea, that I was just the sort of person he was looking for, certain to fit in.

"Kay Motford's coming up," he said. "Come ahead. Don't think about it. Say you're coming."

"All right," I said. "I'd like to very much."

"Take the boat on Friday," Erick said. "You'd better make a reservation right away."

About half an hour after the boat sailed Friday afternoon I saw Kay standing in the bow, looking at the green and peaceful islands in the harbor. The wind was blowing at her dress, and she turned around quickly as though she had been thinking about something so hard that she had forgotten where she was.

"Why, Harry," she said, "I didn't know you were here."

"I'm going where you're going," I said, "to the Munnes'."

"I didn't know you knew the Munnes."

"I don't very well," I told her, "and I never knew you went away from North Harbor on Labor Day."

"I'm sort of tired of North Harbor," she said. "It will be fun to see someone new."

"And here I am," I told her.

"Yes, that's true," she said, "but then there will be different people; perhaps that will make us different."

We had dinner together and then we changed at Rockland, at four in the morning, to the little steamer with a walking beam th: : went up among the islands, and we stood watching everything grow clear and bright as the sun drove the mist off the water. We did not talk much, but I was glad she was there, because I had never visited the Munnes and I have always felt ill at ease going to some unfamiliar place.

"Going on a visit," Kay said, "is like going to a dance, isn't it? You never know whether you'll have a good time, and if you don't you can't get away."

"I didn't know anyone else felt that way," I said.

"I always do," Kay said. "Harry, if everybody knows everybody else too well, let's try to do things together."

"Yes, of course," I said.

"That's just like you," Kay said. "You always say, 'Of course.'"

That was why I took her sailing in one of those little knockabouts, because everyone knew everyone else a great deal better than they knew Kay or me. There were all sorts of local jokes that only people who had been there together could understand, and there was that sort of mutual sentiment among them that comes over people who have spent the summer at the same place and who see that it is almost over.

"Harry," Kay said when we were in the knockabout, "you'd better trim in the jib. You never keep it flat enough."

"You'll do better if you keep her off a little," I answered.

It was a light breeze and there was not much to do, except sit and watch the islands and the streaks on the blue water, and what made everything pleasant was that neither of us had to make any effort. There was the first chill of autumn in the air, the end of summer. Kay was in a tennis dress with a soft brownish orange sweater pulled over it. She braced her legs against the seat opposite and held the tiller under her left arm. Now and then she brushed the hair away from her eyes, when the breeze blew it over her forehead. Her face had been pudgy when she was a little girl, I was thinking, but now that she was older all the pudginess was gone. Her face was light and active like all the rest of her.

"When the air is like this," Kay said, "and everything is bright and still, it's like a period and a paragraph."

"That's true," I said. "You feel that something's over."

"Harry, we're not either of us happy, are we?"

I had been looking at the jib as she spoke. I still thought it was trimmed too flat, but I turned around when she asked that question and was surprised to see that she had been watching me and not the sail.

"What makes you ask that?" I said. "Kay, have I been acting badly?"

She smiled. I had often thought that her smile was mechanical and hard, but now her lips, her whole face, looked delicate and sad.

"It isn't anything in the way we act, but if you're unhappy you can tell when someone else is. It's rather nice to find someone else. That's all I mean."

In all the time I had known her she had never said so much. Of course I knew she could not have been happy, or she would not have broken off with Joe Bingham, but I had not thought of it particularly from her point of view.

"Everybody else is so damned contented," she said, "it makes me sick."

"I know what you mean," I said.

"No, you don't," she said, "not really. They don't seem to want anything except what they have or what they can get."

"Maybe they're right about that," I said and stopped. "I never thought of you as wanting something you couldn't get."

"Haven't you?" she asked.

"It's no good to try to be different from what you are," I said. "Did you ever try?"

"Yes," she said, "I've tried."

"Well, it doesn't work," I said.

"Oh, well," she said. There was something in her voice that made me turn sideways to look at her.

"Why, Kay," I said. She was biting her lower lip and rubbing the sleeve of her sweater across her eyes.

"Don't look at me," she said. "I'll be all right in a minute. It's just — it's just — I feel so — damn futile."

"You'd better let me take the boat," I said.

Instead of taking the tiller as I intended I found that I put my arm around her.

"Kay," I said.

She did not draw away from me; she did not seem to mind.

"I'm so tired of it," she said, "so sick of it."

"It's all right, Kay," I said. "I know."

"I didn't mean to come out here and make a scene," she said. "I hate people who do that. Do I look all right?"

"Yes," I said, "you look beautiful."

"You never told me that before," she said. "I didn't mean to be such a fool."

"You haven't been," I began. "It's made me feel a whole lot better seeing someone else —"

I stopped and we did not speak for a moment.

"We ought to be going back now. I'm going to pay her off and jibe."

We did not talk about ourselves any more, but about the boat and the channel, and I found a chart and we looked over it together. I was thinking about Marvin Myles, but she was in the background when I looked at Kay. We kept looking at each other and looking away again.

"Harry," she said, "maybe people you've always known are better. You know what they're going to do."

"Yes, that's true," I said.

"Well," Kay said, "you'd better get up in the bow and take in the jib, and get the boathook ready. I don't know how far she's going to shoot when I put her in the wind."

"All right," I called to her, "put her over."

"You mind your own business," Kay said, "and catch that mooring."

Now that I try to look at it honestly, I frankly think that Kay was only a symbol in a problem and that I was the same to her. It may not pay to look at life that way, and it probably does not matter much, since it is what happens after marriage, the method two people finally find of getting on with each other, that is really important.

Even during that autumn Kay was honest about it, and it all must have puzzled her a little. Once when we had got to seeing a great deal of each other and had begun to take it for granted that we would, Kay asked a question which used to bother me.

"Harry," she asked me, "do you think we're falling in love with each other — or trying to fall in love?"

I don't know how Kay got into the habit, in October, of calling me up at the office, except that a good many casual impulses seemed to turn into habits with us before we knew it. I don't know when I began to wait for her to telephone or when I began to feel that something was wrong when she didn't.

"Hello," she would say.

"Why, hello, Kay," I would answer, just as though I were surprised to hear her. "What are you doing?"

"I've just finished my orange juice," Kay would say, "and Rough's been sick on the dining room rug."

Quite a lot of our conversation used to be about Rough's insides.

"Harry," she would say, "what did you do after you went home?" And I would tell her what I had done.

"Well, I kept on with Wells's *Outline of History,*" she would say. "I'm up to the Chinese Empire now. Harry, what are you doing this afternoon?"

"Nothing much," I would say. "I'm going to play squash later."

"You'll stop in, won't you, on your way?"

It began to be a habit for me to stop in at the Motfords' on my way home, and they seemed to expect me to do it. The teatray would always be ready in front of the fire, and sometimes Kay would be alone, and sometimes Mrs. Motford would be there with her. Mrs. Motford would ask how Mother was feeling and then she would discuss some article she had read in the *Atlantic Monthly,* and if I had not read it she would give it to me to read. We were on less difficult ground when we discussed Kay in a playful sort of way. Mrs. Motford would tell Kay she thought her dress was too short, even if dresses were getting shorter, and she would ask me to use my influence on Kay about this or that, because she had tried and tried herself, but Kay was very hard to manage. When Kay would ask me how much sugar I wanted in my tea, Mrs.

Motford would tell her that she ought to remember. She told Kay that she must be very unobserving if she had to ask questions about cream or lemon when I came there tired from the office; Kay should remember that men in the afternoon were always tired from the office; some day Kay would think more about other people and less about her own amusement. Then sometimes if I stayed late enough Mr. Motford would come in from the club where he always stopped in the afternoon, and Mr. Motford would always shake hands with me as though he were very pleased to see me there but had not expected to see me in the least. Then he would tell what he had heard at the Club. When he did so Kay and her mother would look at their teacups and you could tell that they had heard it all a great many times before, and they would suggest that perhaps I had heard it also, and Mr. Motford would say he was sure I hadn't and I would say that of course I hadn't. Then Mr. Motford would ask where his book was, the book he had just been reading, and once he told me that Kay was just like her mother — she was always putting things away.

This all sounds dull enough, but there was never any effort about it. They just took it for granted that I was there to see Kay and that I liked to be there. When Kay and I were alone she would talk about her family as though I knew them as well as she did and we would talk about Mary and Mother. She would try now and then to be interested in Smith and Wilding, and once I tried to teach her a little about bonds and stocks, because she said it was so unintelligent of her not to know — but she never could understand them. We used to go on walks out in the country and on walks all over town. We always seemed to be meeting at someone else's house at dinner, and gradually we seemed to be asked to the same places on Saturdays and Sundays. When Christmas came Kay gave me some things that she said she thought I needed — a pair of socks she had knitted herself and some neckties, because by then I was out of mourning. I was puzzled at the thought of what I should give her. I wanted to give her something she would like, but which at the same time would not look so expensive that it would worry her. I could not think of anything for a long while until I remembered a pair of German field glasses which I had picked up in the war, officer's glasses in a field-gray case.

Christmas, I suppose, is always a time when a good many inhibitions and barriers break down. That year it made me think of all the Christmases when Father had been alive and it made me think of Marvin Myles. She seemed more real to me than she had been for a long while when I saw the crowds in front of the shop windows. The morning before Christmas when I went downtown to work I carried the field glasses with me, wrapped up very badly, ready to leave for Kay on my way home. There were some letters on my desk, one of them in Marvin's writing. It was so unexpected that I thought everyone must be looking at me when I opened it. It was a card with a picture of a great star over a village, presumably Bethlehem, and under it she had written:

Darling, aren't you coming back?

I wished she had not sent it. She should have known, if she had not heard from me, that I could not come back. She should have realized how much it all had hurt me, without adding to the hurt. She might as well have come right in there to see me. I seemed to be telling her that this was not the time or place — right outside the customers' room, with the market opening in half an hour — but her voice kept rising.

"Darling, aren't you coming back?"

It was just as though she did not want to listen to me, but kept repeating that same appeal, regardless of all the sights and sounds.

"Darling, aren't you coming back?"

Then the telephone on my desk rang. I was relieved to hear it, because once I was speaking I was back where I belonged. It was Kay.

"How are you?" she asked. "Busy?"

"No," I said, "there isn't much to do before the holiday."

"Come over early this afternoon. It's an awful mess over here. We're putting candles in all the front windows."

"All right," I said. "I'll be over early."

"I wish you would," Kay said. "I always get lonely on Christmas Eve."

When I hung up the telephone Marvin's card was still staring up at me. I picked it up and tore it across and tore it again and dropped it into the wastebasket. Even so I could not get away from it for quite a while. When Mr. Wilding called to me, it took me a moment or two to concentrate on what he was saying. First he talked about some bonds of a small manufacturing company and then he asked me if I would not come to luncheon at the Club, the usual lunch which he gave to the partners before Christmas. I was not a partner yet, he told me, but he would like to have me there because I was my father's son.

"It will be the next best thing to having John," he said.

I was very pleased, because he would not have asked me with the partners if he had not thought that I was doing well and that there was a possibility of my being a partner some day. I thought how pleased Mother would be when she heard about it, and I wanted to tell Kay.

There was holly on the table and all the best Club silver. There was turtle soup and wild duck and venison and hot spiced wine. It was like a family rather than a business lunch with everyone making fun of everyone else. They all began talking about Mr. Wilding's rubbers and asking the waiter to give him a glass of milk and finally, right in the middle of lunch, the door opened and Tony the bootblack came in to shine Mr. Wilding's shoes. It turned out that it was Tom Wade's idea to bring in Tony, and Tony was given a glass of wine and he made a speech in Italian. It was pleasant to see how much everyone really liked everyone else. We knew we were sharing in an institution and in a great tradition, for Smith and Wilding was a gentleman's banking house run by gentlemen, a fine house with a sense of honor. As we stood there in silence to drink to the lost and the absent I could forget the difference in our ages.

"*Darling,*" she had written, "*aren't you coming back?*"

267

When I drank the hot spiced wine, that was all fantastic and impossible. I was not coming back because I had never been away.

It was dark when I left the office, being nearly the shortest day in the year. There was no snow, but there was a feeling of snow in the air — that cold, expectant sense of silence in the clouds above the city. They were already lighting the candles in the windows along the street where Kay lived.

"Is that you, Harry?" Kay called.

She was alone in the parlor. Some logs were burning in the fireplace and brackets had been put along the windows with rows of candles standing on them, already lighted.

"We don't need any other light," Kay said, "with the fire and those candles." The room had a soft warm glow of friendliness. All sorts of lights and shadows danced across her face when she smiled at me.

"We've been having the darnedest time," she said, "fixing the candles and getting buckets of water in case the curtains catch fire. Mother's upstairs watching and I'm down here watching. I'm awfully glad you're early."

"I'm glad too," I said.

"Harry," Kay said, "you look tired."

"No," I said, "I'm not tired. You just think of lots of things at Christmas. Here's a present for you, Kay," and I handed her the package with the glasses.

"Why, Harry," Kay said, "what is it?"

"It isn't anything much," I said. "I found them in a dugout."

She bent her head over the package and untied the ribbon.

"You wrapped it, didn't you?" she said and she laughed. "No one else could have done it," and then she was looking at the field-gray case. "Why, Harry," she said, "you shouldn't have given me anything like that."

She looked shy and I felt shy.

"They aren't anything much," I said.

I stopped and we stood there. It was suddenly still and mysterious and beautiful. The light from her eyes was lost in shadows beneath

268

her cheekbones. Her lips were parted, not exactly in a smile, but as though something surprised her.

"Kay," I said, "I'm awfully glad you called me up this morning."

"I like to," Kay said. "I like to hear your voice."

"Kay," I said, "I never realized — "

"What?" she asked.

"How much it meant," I said.

"It just happened," she said, "didn't it?"

I still don't know, for so much in life turns upside-down when you least expect it. It had just happened — perhaps the way it always happens. There was no one else but Kay — no one in the world but the two of us. It was like struggling through a wood and coming out into the sun.

I don't know which of us moved first or what it was that broke our stillness, or why any of it was. She turned her face toward me and I kissed her.

"I forgot about the windows," she said. "They'll see us from the street."

"I don't care," I said. "It's all right now."

"Yes," she answered, "dearest. It's all right now."

After a while Kay put on her hat and coat and called Rough and put him on a leash and we walked arm in arm over Beacon Hill, looking at the candles in all the windows. Kay was worried because I had no rubbers and only low shoes and thin socks. I told her that she ought to be wearing some sort of scarf and she said that she had had so much on her mind that she had forgotten it, so I lent her mine and stopped and knotted it around her neck. Then we talked about being engaged, because she said that she supposed that we were engaged, and I said I supposed so too. She didn't want to tell anyone for a while until we both got used to it, which seemed to me a good idea. She didn't want to go through being engaged until we both were sure, perfectly sure, that it would work. That was the way we left it. People could guess all they wanted, but we were not to speak of it to anyone until spring.

I have always been rather pleased that we did it that way. I have heard it said again and again that a long engagement is unnatural and a strain, but I think this is only true if it is conspicuous and you know that people are watching you; and no one seemed to worry much about Kay and me, with the exception of Mrs. Motford. Kay used to laugh about it occasionally, saying that her mother was feeling the strain. By the middle of February Kay said that Mrs. Motford was wondering why I did not propose and she was beginning to do things to throw us together. She used to send us to the country for long walks. She used to talk to me about Kay, and Kay told me that she used to give her advice about ways to catch me.

"I ought to have a little dignity," Kay used to say. "I ought not to throw myself at your head. That's what Mother says. I ought to have other nice young men around or else I'll be conspicuous. Do you think I ought to have other nice young men around?"

"No," I told her.

"Do you want me to throw myself at your head?" Kay asked.

"Yes," I said. "I like it."

XXIV

I Break the News

One of the nicest times I ever had was when I was engaged to Kay without anyone else's knowing it. There was no sense of responsibility, and the more we saw of each other, the surer we were it was going to work. We used to wonder why it had not happened long before. We used to sit looking at the fire, talking about where we were going to live and what we were going to do. There was nothing vague and uncertain, as there used to be when I talked to Marvin Myles. Kay wanted us to work out everything between ourselves before anyone interfered, and I knew how wise she was in doing this when our engagement was finally announced, for once you are engaged everyone thinks for you. Kay and I sat down with a paper and pencil and figured how much we would have to live on. There was the income from what my father had left me, my salary from Smith and Wilding, and Kay had something of her own from her grandmother's estate.

It seemed like plenty then — enough for a house and two maids and a house for the summer at North Harbor. The best part of it was that Kay and I seemed to have a good many of the same ideas — the same tastes in furniture, the same ways of spending our time. We both wanted a boat and we each wanted a car. We both liked unsalted butter and a lot of cream, and we agreed that it would be fun to have a farm and horses some day.

All the time, I suppose, we were thinking of ourselves in terms of ourselves when we thought we were thinking of each other. Perhaps that is so with everyone who is engaged. If it all moved fast before, it all moved faster still when our engagement was announced in March.

"You see," Kay told me, "it's what I was afraid of. Now there'll be people. It won't be you and me at all until it's all over."

She was right. Until June I can only remember all sorts of people. First there was Mr. Motford, whom Kay said I ought to see at his office. And then there was Mrs. Motford, who kissed me and said I would never know how long she had hoped for this, that I must be very patient with Kay. I could not expect Kay to be practical, she said; she and I would have to be practical for her. Then I went downstairs with Kay to the Motfords' kitchen, to shake hands with Norah, the cook, who had been in the family for twenty years. Then Kay and I were in Mother's bedroom, kissing Mother. Then we were shaking hands with Hugh and with Lizzie, our old cook, and with Patrick. Then we were out in Roxbury visiting Kay's old nurse and having tea with Great-aunt Frederica, and tea in Hingham with Uncle Bob and all his family, and tea with Kay's Uncle Jackson and her Aunt Geraldine. Then Kay and I were standing side by side at her announcement tea, telling everyone how lucky we were. I think Kay really liked it, although she said she didn't. I don't know why Mrs. Motford said she wasn't practical, because she kept everybody's name straight.

"Harry," she asked me once, "did you like Uncle Jackson?"

"Why, yes, I thought he was fine," I said.

"I thought you wouldn't like him," Kay said. "He always spills. Aunt Geraldine never takes the spots off him."

"I thought he was fine," I repeated.

"What did you talk to him about?" Kay asked.

"About Indian arrowheads," I said.

"Harry, are you sure you aren't sorry? If you want to back out I won't mind."

"Do you want me to?" I asked.

"I'd feel sick if you wanted to," she said. "I'm so proud of you."

I loved the way she talked to people and looked them in the eye. I liked to think that we were doing it all together.

"Let's not mind if we get cross and tired," Kay said. "After a while they'll all be used to us, and then there will be just you and me."

I don't like to feel that at any time there was any indecision in my mind and I don't honestly believe there was. Yet I remember that I did not know exactly what to answer when Kay took it up a long while afterwards. Kay has always had a habit of stretching her hand restlessly into the past, picking up a piece of it and juggling about with it for a while before throwing it back into the past again.

"Don't say you didn't want to back out of it," Kay told me not so long ago, "and don't try to act as though you were perfect, either. You were scared before it was announced. You may not have said anything — you never do — but you wanted to back out of it."

"I never did," I said.

"I don't see why you have to be so secretive," Kay said, "when it's all over and done with. I don't see why it would hurt you to admit that you had a few doubts. I've admitted it, haven't I? I wasn't at all sure, and neither were you. Something was bothering you."

"Nothing was bothering me," I said. "That is, nothing that had anything to do with anything."

"But something was bothering you."

When she was in a mood like that she always liked to pin me down.

"It wasn't anything," I said. "No one is entirely natural or normal at a time like that — no man is."

"Do you know what I thought once?" Kay said. "I'd think it still, if it weren't you. I thought there was another girl — perhaps that girl you brought up from New York. You acted that way, Harry."

"Now, look here, Kay," I said. "From the minute we were engaged, right down to now, I have never looked at anyone else and you know it. I don't believe in that sort of thing."

"Oh, Lord," said Kay, "I know you haven't. And half the time you've never looked at me."

I never told her about Marvin Myles and I think perhaps it was just as well; and I never asked her and she never told me anything about Joe Bingham, either.

No matter what anybody says, there is something positive about marriage that must make anyone falter. There is a sort of feeling that a book is closing. Early in March before our engagement was announced I had a strange, sad desire, which I fought against, to look back again through the pages before it was too late. I fought against it, but before everything was absolute I wanted to see Bill King. There was no real reason for it that I could ever see, because I was awfully glad that I was going to marry Kay. Nevertheless it seemed to me that if once I saw Bill King I would be absolutely sure. I could not understand why I did not let it go with writing him one of those letters that everybody writes about wanting him to be among the very first to know, but instead I told Kay that I had to go down to New York just for a day on business. This was true as far as it went, for Mr. Wilding wanted me to go over some figures with the statistician in the New York office, but I was not wholly frank about it — not even with myself.

"I'll just be gone for a day," I said. "I'll come back on the midnight. You don't mind, do you? I suppose I'll see Bill King."

Kay had been holding my hand and she drew hers away when I finished.

"That's fine," she said. "Go ahead and tell him, and tell me what he says."

"Bill won't say much," I said. "Bill's awfully clever, Kay, but he doesn't often say much when I tell him about myself."

And then she did something that surprised me. Instead of sitting with her hands clasped about her knees she turned around to me all of a sudden and threw her arms around me. It surprised me because she was not an impulsive person.

"Harry," she said, "just don't feel so inferior when you speak about him. You're so much better than he is — ten times nicer. You're so darling to me — always."

The new firm where Bill was working was on the twentieth floor of a building on Forty-second Street. The reception hall, when you got out of the elevator, reminded me a little of the Bullard office. There was the same sort of girl, but instead of shelves of books behind her there were some Byzantine arches with ivy growing up the columns. Bill had a big office of his own, with a tapestry on the wall that showed a rather plump Saint George on a horse, running a spear through a sick-looking dragon. Bill had a Jacobean table with three telephones and his own secretary typing in a little cubbyhole.

"Hello, Harry," Bill said. "Just sit down and wait a minute," and he began pacing up and down on a soft carpet.

"Why didn't you tell me you had a place like this, Bill?" I asked.

"It's quite a layout, isn't it?" Bill said. "It's all eyewash, though. It gets the boys from Detroit. Don't interrupt me."

Bill began pacing up and down the carpet again.

"Miss Prentice, come here a minute. This is Mr. Pulham, Miss Prentice. Take a memo to get Burton's *Arabian Nights* — every driver his own Caliph of Bagdad."

"Bill," I said, "are you going crazy?"

"Listen, Harry," Bill said, "you've got to get out of here. You know how it is when I'm working. Come around to the apartment at half-past five."

"What apartment?" I asked.

"My apartment. I'm living in town now — an apartment and a Jap. His name is Horuchi. Call up the apartment, Miss Prentice, and tell Horuchi that Mr. Pulham's going up there. Tell him to shake up some Martinis. I'll be there at half-past five, and we'll get Marvin. Marvin's down at Bullard's, and then we'll go down to the Algonquin. I'm meeting some of the boys there tonight and then we'll all go to a musical show — any musical show. Give Mr. Pulham the address of the apartment, Miss Prentice . . ."

"Bill," I said, "never mind about Marvin Myles."

"Don't you want to see her?"

"I just want to talk to you, Bill," I said.

275

"All right," Bill said. "Just snap over to the apartment, Harry. I'll see you at half-past five. . . . Where was I now, Miss Prentice?"

When I saw his apartment I knew that he must be making a lot of money. There was a big theatrical studio sort of room with a bedroom off it and a Japanese in a white coat. Before Bill arrived a blond girl came in. She said her name was Franchine Parke, but I could call her Franchine, and I told her I was a friend of Bill's.

"Bill does have some of the damnedest friends," she said.

"Bill must be doing awfully well," I said.

"I'll say he's doing well."

"Bill's awfully clever," I said.

"Clever? Why, Bill's as slick as an eel. You can't two-time Bill."

Horuchi gave us each a cocktail, and then another.

"I certainly don't want to two-time Bill," I said.

"Who said I said I wanted to?" Franchine asked.

"I didn't say you said you wanted to," I said.

"Well, then what have you been saying?"

"God knows," I said.

"You're kind of dumb," Franchine said, "but you're kind of sweet."

"You know that's funny," I told her. "A lot of girls have said that about me."

"That means you're that way with girls. Are you that way with girls?"

Just then Horuchi hurried to the door and let Bill in. He tossed his hat and coat to Horuchi and then he looked at me and laughed.

"Hello, Billy," Franchine said.

"Hello," Bill said, "how did you get here?"

"Because you asked me," Franchine said, "you big bum."

"I remember now," Bill said. "I can't remember everything," and then he looked at me and laughed again. "Well, well, here we are."

"And what do we do now?" Franchine asked.

"Listen, sweetie," Bill said, "just run into the bedroom and powder your nose. Harry's an out-of-town boy and I want to talk to him."

"I want to talk to Harry too," Franchine said.

Bill walked over to the couch and picked Franchine up. Horuchi opened the bedroom door.

"Go in there and stay there," Bill said. "Lock her in, Horuchi."

He rubbed the palm of his hand over his hair.

"This has been quite a day," Bill said.

"Who's Franchine?" I asked.

"Oh, she isn't anything," Bill said. "You've got to relax when you work the way I do and the boys from Detroit all like Franchine. Don't look so worried, boy."

"I'm not worried," I said.

"Oh, yes, you are," said Bill. "You've got to learn to take things like this. Be tolerant, boy, be tolerant."

"I'm perfectly tolerant," I said.

"Well, that's fine," Bill said. "How are you?"

"I'm all right, Bill. I'm awfully happy."

"Why?" Bill asked. "What should make you happy?"

"Because I'm engaged, Bill," I said. "It's going to be announced next week."

"Engaged?" Bill repeated. He stopped. Franchine was beating with her fists against the bedroom door. "Do I know her?"

"Yes," I said, "you know her. It's Kay."

Bill walked over to the table and set his glass down.

"Kay?" he repeated. "You're engaged to Kay?"

I was surprised that he was so slow about it, when his mind usually worked so fast.

"Yes," I said. "You remember her — Kay — Cornelia Motford."

"Naturally I remember her," Bill answered. "You've certainly tied yourself up if you're engaged to Kay."

Bill put his hands into the pockets of his carefully creased trousers. Then he took one hand out of his pocket, and spread his fingers apart, and stared at them.

"Yes, you've certainly tied yourself up."

His whole attitude, his clothes and his apartment, made me angry.

"If you want to know," I said, "I'm glad that a girl like Kay wants to marry me."

Bill's cheeks grew redder and the lines deepened about the corners of his mouth.

"Harry," he said, "I don't know why, but I'm awfully fond of you."

"That goes with me, Bill," I said. "You'll be my best man, won't you?"

Then Bill held his hand out to me.

"Don't think I'm not glad," he said. "Kay's a great girl. Be sure to give her my love."

"Yes, I will," I said.

"It's just hard to get it into my mind," Bill said. "The more I think of it the better I like it. Let's have another drink, and I'll let Franchine out."

I was glad that I had come down. Now that I had seen Bill I didn't have any doubts any more. I wanted to get back to Kay — back where I belonged.

"Harry," Bill asked, "have you told Marvin Myles?"

"No," I said.

"All right," Bill said. "I'll tell her."

XXV

It's a Long, Long Walk

Ever since Christmas Eve, as I see it now, I was not moving events, but events were moving me. The whole world had made up its mind that Kay and I were going to be married and everyone was pleased about it. The girls I used to know, friends of mine and friends of Kay's, were just as cordial as they could be, but a sort of interest which they used to have in me was completely gone. When I spoke to Kay about it she said it was the same with the men she knew. Everyone had moved away from us, leaving us entirely alone. When I saw Cecilia Leverett, for instance, she was just as nice as she could be. She said that Kay was such a fine girl, although Kay was older than she was — she remembered when Kay was a big girl at school and how well Kay played field hockey; but Cecilia never asked me to come around any more. There was nothing left but Kay and me.

When you came down to it, there wasn't much chance to see Kay either. She was out with her mother, buying clothes or sheets or towels, or else we were going around with Mrs. Motford, looking at houses or apartments. We kept wondering whether we ought to live in Cambridge or Brookline or in town, and finally we rented a little house near the Esplanade. After that I would go with Kay and Mrs. Motford to look at roll after roll of wallpaper and bolt after bolt of material for curtains. I tried to say that Kay could pick out the papers and the curtains, that she knew more about it than I did; but instead of making it easier Kay would grow exasperated. She said that it was my house as much as hers and that I ought to realize that she wanted it the way I wanted it. Then I would suggest, perhaps, that the living room be done in green. Then Kay and Mrs. Motford, who had been arguing for an hour, would agree at once that green was an ugly and difficult color and not Kay's color. Then Kay would get tired and Mrs. Motford would get tired and the next day they would start all over again, looking at wallpapers and at colors.

I was never reminded so much of death as I was when we were engaged. There were certain pieces of furniture that we could have now, but it was necessary to remember that there were lots of other pieces — rugs and sofas and tables and pictures — which we would have when Mother and Mrs. Motford died. When Mrs. Motford died we could have the large Persian carpet with the Tree of Life that was in the parlor. When Mother died we could have the Inness, and it would be much better to plan on having these things some day; and yet when we actually did plan, both Mother and Mrs. Motford would always resent it. They would say that Kay and I talked as though they were dead already, and neither of them was going to die just to please Kay or me; and once Mother said that I wanted her to die, and Kay told me that Mrs. Motford had said the same thing.

"Harry," Kay said, "let's talk it over by ourselves. Do you like that wallpaper with stripes for the living room?"

"Which one?" I asked. "They all had stripes."

"You can be maddening sometimes," Kay said. "Don't you remember the one with the little thin green stripes? You said you liked green."

I am afraid that I was not much help. I never could visualize how paper would look. Sometimes when Kay was not tired she would laugh about it and say that everything would be all right when it was all over. I felt that way too. I wanted it to be over. I wanted to be alone with Kay and I used to tell her so when I kissed her good night.

"Yes," she used to answer me, "we'll get away from everything, won't we? I'm so tired I just can't hear myself think."

When the wedding presents began to come in Kay pasted numbers on them and kept a little book. I could not understand how so many people of whom I had never heard could know about me. Now, of course, I know that most of it was a worldly sort of game, which Kay and I have played ever since. I can imagine, now, all sorts of people saying: "The Pulham boy and the Motford girl are going to be married. We've got to do something about it. The Motfords gave our Beatrice a green glass bowl — and what was it the Pulhams gave her? They gave her something." First the presents filled the sewing room in Kay's house and then the upstairs sitting room. There were a good many sets of beautiful leather-bound books by writers hitherto unknown to me — solid, shy Victorians, lost in the postwar shuffle. There were histories of England, excerpts from great orations, famous homes and gardens, and some memoirs. They have been on the library shelves ever since and they still look well. Then there were dozens and dozens of plates, and of course the silver and the linen. But Kay kept track of them all and even began to write letters of thanks immediately in order to get them out of the way.

"Harry and I simply adore the little tea cozy and all the beautiful little napkins that go with it. How did you ever find them? You must come to see them yourself on the tea table when we are in our new house."

Kay began to get pale and tired, and Mrs. Motford and I kept asking her to go upstairs and take a rest, but I suppose that only great minds can delegate authority, and I have never known a woman who could. Kay wanted to know if I had bought presents for the ushers and if her father had done anything about champagne, and if I really knew anybody who could help me about the steamer tickets. We were going to Europe on our honeymoon and she wanted to know exactly where we would be from day to day. She wanted to know whether I had enough luggage and whether I had been sure to remember to engage a hotel room in New York and whether I had seats on the five o'clock train.

"That's all right, Kay," I said. "I'm looking after that."

"I know you are," Kay said; "but if I don't remember, somebody's going to forget. Have you heard when Bill King's coming?"

"Yes," I said. "He's coming up the night before."

"Well, do you think we can catch our train?" Kay asked. "What will we do if we don't? And have you got a gold piece to give Dr. Mowbry?"

"Don't worry so, Kay," I told her.

"Suppose when we get to the Biltmore," Kay said, "they think we aren't married?"

Mrs. Motford said that there was nothing like a country wedding and so we were going to be married at the Motford family place at Concord. It was not far from the bridge where the battle was fought, and the land where the house stood went straight down to the edge of the river. The house itself had a bullet hole near the second story, pierced by a British musketball, and carefully marked by a marble tablet. I had never taken the bullet hole or the house very seriously until my wedding; I had never realized until then how seriously Kay and all the Motfords took it.

Bill King came down a day ahead, in time for the ushers' dinner. "You needn't think of anything," he said, "and the less you think, the better." He went over all the tickets and took charge of the ring and the gold piece for the minister. He saw about having my trunks and bags checked and he helped Guy take care of Kay's and he helped Mother and Mary make arrangements to motor out to Concord in the morning.

"Won't your Club be having one of those ceremonies?" Bill asked.

"Oh," I said, "why, I'd forgotten about that."

"When is it," Bill asked, "that they get you in a corner and sing a little song and give you a coffeepot or something?"

"Don't worry about that, Bill," I said. "Are you sure you've got the ring?"

"Keep your pants on," said Bill, "and say what the man tells you out of the book."

I had been over the service carefully, so as not to make a mistake.

"If this ever happens to me," Bill said, "I'll do it before a New York judge somewhere downtown."

"Maybe you're right," I said, "but Kay couldn't do that."

"That's so," Bill said. "Kay couldn't — or she wouldn't."

Bill and I spent the night before the wedding in Concord in a house belonging to one of Mrs. Motford's cousins, whom I had not met before and who said, after this, I was to call her Cousin Violet. Bill had two silver flasks with him and rinsed out the glass in the bathroom every time he took a drink without my telling him to do it, but I did not take any. I wanted Bill and everyone else to see that I did not have to take a drink to marry Kay.

The Motfords asked us over to dinner the night before, just Bill and me and the immediate members of the family.

Though Bill had had a few drinks in our room beforehand, just in case there might not be anything at the Motfords', he took several cocktails, but it only made him pleasanter and gayer. He told Mrs. Motford that he loved her dress and he wanted to know all about the bullet hole in the house, because his business was largely made up of shooting holes in things.

"And everybody shoots holes in me," Bill said. "You wouldn't know it, Mrs. Motford, but my heart is full of holes, like a piece of cheese."

Mrs. Motford looked puzzled at first, but she told me later that she never thought that I would have such a witty friend. All the out-of-town aunts and cousins were laughing at something he had said, when Kay came in.

Bill took her hand and suddenly bent forward and kissed her cheek. I could see that no one had expected it, not even Kay.

"You're looking wonderful," Bill said.

"It makes me feel a whole lot better if you think so," Kay said.

Then she held out both her hands to me, and her hands were cold, and everybody moved away, leaving us together.

"Harry," she whispered, "do you want to back out?"

"No," I said. "Do you?"

Her hands gripped mine still tighter and she smiled.

"You've been so sweet. You won't get tired of me, will you?"

Bill was singing an old song which wasn't so old then, from a musical comedy which I had seen before I had gone to the war.

"First they say, here comes the bride," as nearly as I can remember it, "and then she's off to Reno."

Kay turned her head to listen.

"Don't you remember the rest of it?" she called across the room. " 'I want to be a good little wife, in the good old-fashioned way.' "

"That's right," Bill called back. "That's it."

The party broke up early so that Kay and I could be rested. I remember that Bill did not say much when we got back to our room in Mrs. Motford's cousin's house.

"Bill," I said, "I'm awfully lucky."

Bill was leaning over his suitcase. He pulled out a flask and shook it beside his ear.

"What's that?" he asked.

"I'm awfully lucky, Bill," I said.

"That's right," Bill answered.

Then he took a small white pill out of a bottle.

"Take this," he said, "and take a glass of water and maybe you'll get some sleep."

"What is it?" I asked. "I don't need any drug to make me go to sleep."

"You take it and like it," Bill said. "I don't want to listen to you pitching around all night."

I got into bed and Bill crawled into the twin bed beside me and switched on the light and began to read *The Trojan Women,* which he had brought with him. It seemed to me that he looked a little pale and tired, now that he was reading. After a while he closed the book and looked up at the ceiling and began to talk. He began to tell me about all the things he had been doing in New York and about all the people he was seeing — artists and actors and writers.

"It's different," I heard him say, "not one of them is married — not seriously. I suppose it's what I'm meant for — here today and gone tomorrow." I must have gone to sleep while he was talking.

Mrs. Motford's cousin sent us up our breakfast on two trays, and when we were dressing all our pajamas and collar studs and collars seemed to get mixed up with eggshells and pieces of toast and empty orange-juice glasses.

"You'd better take a drink," Bill said.

"No," I said, "and at any rate I never drink in the morning."

"Well, if I were going through what you're going through I would," Bill said, and he went into the bathroom for a glass. Then he began worrying about the ring and the gold piece and I had to help him find his tie and his socks.

"You act as though you were getting married yourself," I told him.

"Maybe I am," said Bill, "by proxy."

It amused me, until I remembered how much he had been drinking the day before and that he had not been able to eat much breakfast.

"Bill," I said, "you aren't feeling sick or anything?"

"Me sick?" Bill said.

Bill and I were out by the altar and everyone was standing up and all the ushers and bridesmaids were walking up the aisle. I saw Mother standing beside Mary and I saw that she and Mrs. Motford were both crying. The clergyman, who wore glasses with heavy lenses and had an Adam's apple, swallowed twice and opened his book. Then I saw Mr. Motford, and Kay, holding her father's arm and looking straight ahead. Then the music stopped and the clergyman swallowed again and began to read.

"Dearly beloved, we are gathered together here —"

The air was heavy with flowers, the way it always is at funerals and weddings, and as I stood listening to the cadence of the words, I was thinking of something that Kay had said, a long while ago, about a period and a paragraph. Those sentences were like closing doors, shutting out all sorts of things that might have happened, and I wondered if Kay thought so too, as she stood beside me.

"I do," I heard myself saying.

Then I was only thinking about Kay — that from now on I

must look after Kay; no matter what else there was, Kay and I were there.

We stood side by side at the reception surrounded by everyone who was glad that it was over, talking and laughing, shaking hands, trying to remember everyone, trying to say something adequate.

The Skipper's face was in front of me for a moment, and I heard him tell Kay that he had done his best and that it was her turn now. Then I saw Mr. Wilding and my Uncle Bob and my Great-aunt Frederica, and then I saw Major Groves with whom I had served in France. He moved in front of me out of that sea of faces.

"Why," I asked him, "how did you get here?"

He said that he had come from Toledo and that he would not have missed it for the world. Then there were lots of children, distant cousins of Kay's and mine — shy little girls with straight long hair and little boys in hot blue suits, who looked the way Kay and I must have looked once. Later Kay and I and all the ushers and bridesmaids sat at a table, eating chicken salad and bricks of ice cream — layers of vanilla, orange sherbet and chocolate. Then I was up in a guest room and Bill was helping me get into some other clothes. Bill had brought up two bottles of champagne and we both had a drink and while I was dressing Bill sat on the window sill, finishing the second bottle by himself.

"I'm damned if I see how you got through with it without pooping out," he said.

"Have I got everything in my bag?" I asked.

"Have you got everything in your bag! Don't ask me that again. Everything's in your suitcase and your suitcase is in the car and your tickets are in your pocket."

Then when I was getting into my trousers there was a knock on the door.

"Oh, my," Bill said, "it's the Zephyr Club."

"Bill," I told him, "if you don't mind, you'd better go out for a minute."

"All right, boys," Bill said. "I don't belong to any lodge, but if

286

I go out you see that Harry buttons his pants, or do you want to wrap him in a sheet?"

"Go on out, Bill," I said. "It won't take long."

"Don't be embarrassed, fellows," Bill said. "I'm leaving right away."

I wished that the Club had not come in just then, because Bill made us all seem a little foolish.

Even when Kay and I were on the train in our drawing room, we did not seem to be by ourselves. Kay was in her "going-away" dress, but as far as I was concerned she was still in her white satin wedding gown. All we could talk about was the wedding. All the way to New York and over the dinner we had served in the drawing room, but which neither of us really wanted to eat, we talked about what had happened, and each of us had noticed something which the other had not. Every now and then our glances met in a strange sort of astonishment, and I remembered that we would be going away tomorrow on an ocean voyage. I had heard that times like this frighten girls, and I hoped she was not frightened. I wanted to tell her not to be, but she seemed to be taking it all for granted, still talking about the wedding. When we began to see the city lights in the dark outside the windows little silences fell between us which we both joined in struggling against. I reached for her left hand where it lay in her lap with her engagement ring and her wedding ring on the third finger — a plain gold wedding ring, because she did not believe in platinum.

"Kay," I said, "I'm awfully glad we're married."

"So am I," she said. "I wonder what's happened to Bill? I'm afraid he's got awfully drunk."

"Bill's all right," I said.

Then the porter pressed the little button by the door and Kay pulled her hand away.

"Harry," she said, "have you got all the ribbons off the bags?"

"Yes," I said.

The porter came in smiling. We would be at the Grand Central in a few minutes now.

"He knows we're just married," Kay said. "I hope everybody isn't going to think that we're just married."

"There's no reason why anyone should," I answered. "I feel as though we had been married for quite a while."

Kay looked at herself in the mirror and straightened her hat and pulled on her gloves. I still had the feeling that when we got off the train I should be seeing her to some friend's house.

"Harry," she said, "the hotel—"

"Lots of people stay at hotels," I said.

"I'm glad you reminded me," Kay answered. "When we get there I'll take off my glove so they can see my ring."

"It's going to be all right," I said. "You just stay with the bellboys and the bags and I'll go up to the desk."

"Harry," she said, "won't you please kiss me?"

"Why, yes, of course," I said.

"Don't say 'of course'! Just kiss me."

When we walked up to the desk together—with the cashier's cage and the telephones and all the pigeonholes full of letters—I hoped that we both appeared bored and casual. The clerk was talking to a fat man holding a smoldering cigar and we had to wait until he was finished.

"There is a reservation for Mr. and Mrs. Pulham," I said, and then I signed the card—Mr. and Mrs. Henry Pulham.

"I hope the room isn't going to be noisy and near the elevator," Kay said.

I knew she was saying it because the bellboys were there.

"Oh, well," I said, "it's only for tonight."

The remark did not make much sense. Both of us must have known it was not only for tonight but always. I gave a quarter to each of the two boys who carried our bags, and they closed the door and left us. My suitcase rested on the luggage stand in front of one twin bed and Kay's was on the other with her new initials C. M. P. upon it. Beside it was her round hatbox with the same initials. I stood there with my overcoat over one arm and my hat

288

in my hand and Kay stood beside me. The bedroom was clean **and** impersonal. The bathroom was white and shining.

"Well," Kay said, "it's awfully nice," but she didn't look at **me.** She sat down in front of the dressing table and took off her hat with a quick decisive little jerk. Then she took off her gloves more slowly and raised her fingers to her hair, and then she stood up.

"Well," she said.

"Here's the sitting room," I said. "We haven't seen that yet." **We** walked into the little sitting room.

"Oh," Kay said, "it's lovely."

It really had the colorless elaborateness of any sitting room in any good hotel — a sofa covered with brocade, two brocade armchairs, one or two other stiff-backed chairs and two tables with contorted-looking lamps. On the wall were a French mirror and imitation French prints of decorous doings in Versailles. I have often thought that there must be a factory somewhere that turns out those prints like postage stamps.

"It isn't bad," I said. "You must be awfully tired."

"I'm not tired exactly," she answered, "but I suppose we'll have to get up early tomorrow."

"Well," I said, "I'm not tired at all. I think I'll sit here and read for about half an hour — in case you want to go to bed."

Kay had been examining one of the scenes at Versailles very carefully; when she turned away from it she was smiling.

"Harry," she said, "I'll bet you've been thinking of that speech for hours. Is that why you took the sitting room? Is it?"

"Well, in a way," I said.

"All right," Kay said. "I'll call you."

I sat down and opened a book, but I did not have time to **begin** reading before she called me from the bedroom.

"Yes," I said, "what is it, Kay?"

Something in her voice had startled me, but nothing was **the** matter.

"Do you mind leaving the door open so we can talk?"

"Of course," I said. I heard her draw her breath in sharply.

"Harry—" she began. "Oh, never mind."

"Go ahead," I said. "What is it?"

"Harry, I'm not sure we love each other."

"What?" I said.

"I'm not sure. Wouldn't it be awful if we thought we loved each other and really didn't? What I really mean is—if we only got married because we thought we ought to!"

She was thinking just what I was thinking and she had not been afraid to say it.

"Kay," I said, "maybe everybody feels that way. Maybe millions and millions of people always have," and then I put my arms around her and kissed her. "Don't worry. Everything's all right, Kay."

"Darling," she said, and I kissed her again. "I didn't want to be silly—but I suppose all girls are."

"No, you're not," I said.

"It's all right as long as you're here," Kay said. "You won't leave me, will you?"

"No," I said.

"Not ever?"

"No," I said.

"And you'll leave the door open, won't you, while you're reading?"

"Yes, of course," I said.

"Darling," Kay said, "it's just a little thing, but could you just stop saying 'of course'?"

"Why, yes, Kay," I said, "of course."

XXVI

The Music Goes Round and Round

It has always seemed to me that whenever I have wanted to get away by myself to read or to think, all the rest of the family have always found out where I was. In North Harbor there was a room upstairs called my dressing room with a single window that looked over the latticed clothesyard and the service entrance. I could never imagine why that room could be attractive to anyone except to me, but once I got in it everyone else came there. That was where I had the mission desk which used to be in my room at college and where I kept my checkbook and papers. There was an armchair and a radio and some tobacco and a closet, theoretically for my clothes, but half of it filled with old evening dresses which Kay could not decide whether or not to give away. When I was at North Harbor, particularly on my vacation, I used to try to get off into my dressing room to read the newspaper and to pay the bills.

There was a bill I had to pay for George's tennis lessons, $16.50, to the order of the professional at the Harbor Club. When I took up my checkbook I was not sure of the date, for days had a way of slipping into each other when I was out of the office. I looked at a tin desk calendar, first recalling the day of the week, a Thursday. The calendar had been sent me by my classmate Robert Ridge, and on the metal work was stamped: "With the hearty best wishes of Robert Ridge — Life Insurance," and beneath in quotations was stamped: "Fleeting days." It was a Thursday near the end of August, 1939, half-past nine in the morning, a clear, warm day.

Beneath me I could hear Jerry, the chore-man, carrying out the wastepaper and the ashes, and I could hear the maids on the kitchen porch quarreling about the Irish Free State. I wrote out the check, and addressed the envelope.

There was nothing to do until I went down to the beach with Kay at twelve, and so it seemed to me that I might be able to make a start at writing my Class life. I had thought about it a good deal, but only up to the time when Kay and I were married.

There did not seem to be so much worth writing about in the succeeding years. I could not understand it, because they were the years on which my life was built, and yet they seemed to be crowded all together in a much more confined space than that earlier time. It all made me try to think of something that would represent it, of some sort of simile. I looked out of the window at the clothesyard where my shirts were drying, all mixed together with garments of George's and Gladys', and with some slips and tennis dresses of Kay's; I watched them all dancing in the breeze, thrown together in an aimless sort of plan over which they had no more control than Kay or George or Gladys or I who would wear them when they were ironed, and then I had it — a simile for my life. Sometimes at parties in town Bob Carroll would bring his big accordion and he would stand up and play all the old tunes on it. Sometimes when he was playing the accordion would all be creased up tightly at one end, while the other end was all pulled out, and all the music would be squeezed out of one end while the other was still full of sound. Now, my life was rather that way too. The years of the latter twenties and the thirties were telescoped together, while the years before them were stretched out, still playing a sort of music. What happened later may have been important, but it did not seem to matter, because I had grown used to all of it. I knew what Kay would say, for instance, and what I would answer, without having to think about it. Perhaps all years close in together when you grow more capable, but back there when I knew Marvin Myles and when I was engaged to Kay I did not know the answers. That must have been why this time was mysterious and arresting whenever I went back to it.

It gave me a guilty conviction, sitting alone in my dressing room, trying to piece such thoughts together: that it was all a waste of time and that I should be doing something else — reading a good book, for instance. Somehow there never had been time to read, for something always came up which I had to attend to. Back in the twenties the children were being born, or being ill, and there was Mother's illness and death, and the time I had to untangle the estate after the Pritchard office had got through with it, and then there was Mr. Wilding's death, and the crash, and then the trouble when Smith and Wilding had nearly gone to the wall. It always seemed that, when I finished with one particular problem, there would be time to read or time to think — but there was always something else. There would be a dinner party or Gladys would fall downstairs or the cook would have a gall-bladder attack. Now just last week, when I had thought that I could get away from the office, the European situation started up again. I had to decide whether or not to sell out pound accounts that some clients were holding in Barclay's Bank. It surprised me that several clients felt that I was letting the British Empire down when I advised them to sell, but it was just as well that I advised them. There was always something that I had to cope with, when I least expected it. For instance, there was the time when Gladys' nurse was thrown down by her boy friend and Kay found her in the bathroom drinking iodine. You never could tell what was going to happen in a house, whether you were going to be a figure of fun or a doctor or a veterinarian.

Outside the window Jerry, the hired man, was lifting a galvanized ashcan up the bulkhead steps from the cellar. There was a sudden crash and the whole thing fell back into the cellar. Something like that was always happening. I wondered if Jerry were covered by the new liability insurance.

"Jerry," I shouted out the window, "what's the matter?"

"It's all right, Mr. Pulham," Jerry called back. "It just slipped out from between my hands."

Then I heard a knock on the dressing room door. It would be Ellen, the maid, because no one else would knock.

"It's Mrs. Frear on the telephone to speak to Mr. Pulham," Ellen said.

"Harry," Mrs. Frear said, "you and Kay haven't bought tickets for the minstrel show tomorrow night for the library — you know — we have it every year."

The day was going to turn out the way every other day on my vacation turned out as soon as I got into the dressing room and tried to read and think.

When I put up the telephone George appeared. He pushed the door open with a bang, hit against a small table and knocked two books and a pipe off of it.

"Pick those up," I said, "and look where you're going."

"Hey, boss," George said.

It was often difficult for me to understand what had happened to George. A few years ago he had been a little boy with a pail, who kept slipping off the rocks into the water. Now he was nearly as tall as I was and his arms were too long and his nose was too big and his face was marred by that adolescent disease known as acne. I tried to remember whether I had ever been like George and I could not believe it.

"What do you want?" I asked.

"Have you got the keys to the Ford?" George asked.

"What do you want the Ford for?"

"I just want to practise running it around," George said.

"Your mother and I have told you that you can't run it around," I said, "unless someone is with you."

"Well, how can I ever get a license if I can't learn how to drive?" George asked. "I just want to practise backing."

"You know what happened the last time," I told him. "You ripped off the garage door and it cost me fifty dollars."

"Well, it wasn't my fault," George said. "The wind made that door slam just when I was backing."

"Now, listen, George," I told him, "when I was your age —" and then I stopped, because George was not much interested and I was not interested either. "Go on and get out of here," I said.

294

"Well, boss," George said, "can I have a dollar?"

"What do you want a dollar for?" I asked.

"Well, some of us are going out to the movies," George said, "and I borrowed a dollar from Gladys. I've got to give it back, haven't I?"

I felt in my pocket for a dollar. I was wearing some old tennis flannels which were turning slightly yellow and there was no money in them. I got up and opened the closet door. My wallet was not in my gray suit or my blue suit.

"Where in hell has my wallet gone?" I said.

"It's on your bureau," George said.

"Well, take a dollar out of it," I said, "and leave it just where it is."

"Say, boss," George said, "sometime I'd like to have a talk with you about money. If I had a bigger allowance I could buy my clothes and I wouldn't have to keep asking. It's humiliating."

"Get out now," I said. "I'm busy."

"Well, this is your vacation, isn't it?" George asked.

"Get out," I said. "I'm busy."

George hit against the table again. Two books and a pipe fell off, but I did not bother to pick them up.

I realized that sometime I ought to have a good long talk with George. When he was back from school, either he was busy or I was. I had heard a good deal about being a companion to one's son, about being pals and doing things together. Perhaps it was my fault that George and I were not exactly pals, but I was not sure. It seemed to me that George did not particularly crave my company, and that his world only touched mine when he wanted something or made too much noise eating. To reach a basis for companionship I had to thumb back through my memory to the time when I had been George's age and all I could recall was that I had been sensitive and shy and not in the least like George.

"George." I could hear Kay's voice somewhere out in the front hall. "Do you know where your father is?"

Then I heard Kay walking through our bedroom with quick,

295

brisk steps. Kay was in a white tennis dress with a green eyeshade pulled over her forehead. She was holding a pad and pencil which indicated that she was on her way to the kitchen to see about the ordering.

"Harry," she said, "have you seen Gladys?"

"Gladys? No," I said.

"Did you see her at breakfast?"

"Yes," I said. "She was going out to study insects."

"I wish she wouldn't do that," Kay said. "I don't think it's normal."

"It won't do any harm," I said. "Maybe she's a genius."

"It isn't normal," Kay said. "They say at school that she does too much imaginary play."

"When that school teaches her long division and how to spell," I said, "I'll listen to them."

"You don't know anything about it," Kay said, "and you don't try to learn."

"The year before last," I said, "she was an Eskimo and the year before that she was an Indian and this year she's a Viking, and she can't do long division and the tuition is seven hundred dollars."

"Let's not go into it," Kay said. "It's easy to be cheap and cynical and funny."

"All right," I said. "Let's not go into it."

"What are you doing up here anyway?" Kay said suddenly. "Why aren't you outdoors?"

"I'll be out pretty soon," I said. "There are just some things I wanted to attend to."

"When I finish the ordering," Kay said, "suppose we go out and play some tennis."

"I'd like to," I said, "but not right now. I've got to call up the office, and then there're some bills."

Kay sat down in the Morris chair and sighed.

"I wonder why it is," she said, "when we're alone together we always start talking about bills and money."

"I don't know," I said. "It's the way it always is."

Kay sighed again.

"This room is an awful mess," she said, "because you won't let anyone move anything. I don't see why you want to sit here when you have the whole house. Harry, do you love me?"

"What?" I said. "Of course I love you."

"Then don't look so nervous," Kay said. "What's so funny in my asking if you love me?"

"I didn't say there was anything funny about it," I said.

"I don't see," Kay said, "why we can't talk naturally and not argue."

"Listen, Kay," I said, "I'd love to talk, but I just came up here to be out of the way."

"Harry," she said, "come and get your racket. Let's go out and play some tennis."

"This afternoon maybe," I said. "I'm really busy now, Kay."

It was like a thousand other conversations. I knew what she would say before she said it.

"All right," she said again. "Just don't say we never do things together."

"We never want to do things together at the same time," I said, but her mind was already on something else.

"You know we're going out to lunch?" she said. "Harry, have your clothes come back from the cleaner's?"

"Yes, they're back," I said.

"Then wear some other trousers," Kay said. "Those are awfully tight for you and, Harry — is Bill King coming tomorrow morning?"

"Yes, Bill's coming," I said. "I just got a wire."

"I wish I didn't have to think of everything," Kay said. "Have Bill and Elise really broken up?"

"Yes," I said, "I guess so."

"I wonder what was the matter," Kay said.

"I don't know," I answered. "You never can tell about things like that."

"Harry," said Kay, "can't we *ever* talk about *anything?*"

I got up and took her hands and pulled her out of the chair.

"Come on," I said, "and get your racket. I'll play if you want."

She looked happy when I put my arm around her. She laughed and rubbed her cheek against my shoulder.

"I don't know how I've stood you so long," she said, and then she added quickly, "I don't mean that. It's just awful living together in a house so long."

"I don't know," I said. "I've had a pretty good time, take it all in all."

"Harry," Kay said. "You're worried about something. Are you thinking about Bill?"

"No," I said. "I was thinking about the war. I want to listen to the news at twelve o'clock."

"I know," Kay said. "It's awful, isn't it?"

"It's like an accordion," I said.

"Like an accordion?" she repeated. "What is?"

"Time," I told her. "It's all squashed up between the two wars."

Kay laughed.

"There's one thing anyway," she said. "I never know when you're going to be funny."

She stood in the hall, swinging her tennis racket.

"Go out and get the Ford," she said. "And don't start pulling things around in the garage or else we won't get a court. You know how it is at the Club with all those college boys."

I walked past the clothesyard toward the garage and found Gladys lying on her stomach in the long brownish grass.

"What are you doing?" I asked.

She turned her head around without getting up or even getting off her stomach. I saw her eyes watching me sideways with an expression of patient resentment that I should have interrupted her.

"What are you doing on your belly in the grass?" I asked her. "If you lie there long enough you'll get a stomach ache and ants will get into your clothes."

"I'm studying nature," Gladys said.

She said it as though I were an outsider who could not understand, and it was true. I could not understand.

"Well, what about nature?" I asked.

She told me that she was looking at a spider through the magnifying glass.

"I used to like spiders," I said. "Let me look." I crawled over beside her, although I knew that she did not really want me there, because it was her spider, not mine.

"He's got bristles on his legs," she said.

I was very much pleased when she said it and I tried to think of something suitable to reply.

"All spiders are covered with bristles. It must be so birds can't eat them."

Then I heard Kay's voice speaking above us.

"Harry, I thought you were going to get the car. What on earth are you doing?"

I pulled myself to my hands and knees.

"We were looking at a spider," I said.

"You know we won't get a court if you don't hurry," Kay said. "Gladys, I thought you were going to play with Alberta."

"I don't want to," Gladys said.

"Why not?" Kay asked.

"Because she's all wet," Gladys said.

"Then go down to the beach," Kay said, "and stop lying in the grass."

I felt embarrassed that Kay had found us there. I should have gone to the garage for the car. I should have known that I could not get back to a world which I had left forever — one which Gladys would be leaving soon, before she knew that she was leaving it.

I backed the car out of the garage and Kay got in.

"Why is it," Kay asked, "any time you start doing anything with me you always end by doing something else?"

"You always do the same thing," I said. "You always forget your purse or you have to telephone someone."

299

"Harry," Kay said, "let's not fight."

We drove for a while without speaking, past the bathing beach where the automobiles were already beginning to gather and past the new houses on the cliff. It was a beautiful clear day with a touch of coolness in the air. Autumn always came early in North Harbor. I glanced at Kay, who sat looking straight ahead holding her racket between her knees. I was wondering how it would be if Kay and I did not know exactly how everything would react upon each other. I was wondering how it would be if without knowing each other so well we both tried to be agreeable. Then I knew it was impossible. Simply by having been together so long we could never get back to that.

"I don't know why everybody says you have a faculty with children," Kay said.

"I didn't know everybody said so."

"Oh, yes, you did. That's why you always keep acting like Uncle Remus."

"I just wanted to see what Gladys is like," I said. "I don't see the children very much."

"That's why they like you," Kay said. "You're a novelty. I'm not."

"I know," I said, "that's true. But let's not argue about it, Kay."

"Why is it," Kay asked, "that any time I say anything to you you say I'm arguing?"

I did not answer.

"What are you thinking about?" Kay asked.

"I'm thinking about Hitler," I said.

"Oh, God," Kay said, "Hitler!"

Kay was almost right about the tennis courts. By the time we had got to the Club and parked the car there was only one left — the worst one in the far corner. Nearly all the others were filled with boys and girls who looked at Kay and me peculiarly and called me "sir." I saw George playing doubles with the little Goodwin girl who had a wall-eye. I could not understand what there could possibly be about her that was attractive. George looked at us much

300

the way Gladys did when I saw her in the grass and I heard him say to the Goodwin girl, "They still play all right."

"George is out there again with that Goodwin girl," Kay said.

"Well, never mind about it," I told her.

"Now, go ahead," said Kay, "and smash them! And don't try to be gallant. You're perfectly maddening when you try to be gallant."

Kay always played a hard fast game. I could beat her, but it was never easy. We played for an hour hardly speaking and by the time we got through I think we both felt a good deal better about each other. We walked to the clubhouse like friends who did not know one another too well.

"You're awfully good," Kay said. "Your backhand's better."

"So is yours," I said.

"You know darned well," Kay said, "I always had a good backhand. You used to tell me so."

I'd entirely forgotten that I used to tell her so, but now that she reminded me I remembered.

"Where are we going to lunch?" I asked.

"We're going to the Buhlfields'."

"The Buhlfields'?" I repeated. "Who are the Buhlfields?"

Kay shrugged her shoulders and made a cut at the air with her racket.

"Don't try to pretend that you don't know who they are," she said. "They've come up here every summer for the past ten years and you're the one who always says it's nice to be gracious to new people. They've asked Mary and Jim and now we've got to go."

"All right," I said, "all right."

"It isn't all right," Kay said. "I don't like it any better than you do. That Ethel Buhlfield's voice goes right through my ears."

"All right," I said.

"Please," Kay said, "don't keep saying 'All right'!"

XXVII

We Westerners Like Our Fish

I could not seem to remember very much about the Buhlfields, except that they came from some place near Chicago like Lake Forest, but it was not Lake Forest. Evan Buhlfield had made a lot of money in 1929, and judging from his house he must have kept some of it. It was one of those new stucco houses that were built in that period in an attempt to bring a California Spanish influence to the coast of Maine. There was a court in the middle of it which Mr. Buhlfield called a "patio" and a terrace overlooking the sea where we had cocktails. It was true what Kay had said about Mrs. Buhlfield's voice. It had a way of going through you and it sounded a little bitter.

"Why, Mr. Pulham," she said, "I'm glad you managed to come."

Mary was drinking a second Martini. I had not seen her in quite a while.

"What are you doing here, dearie?" Mary said.

"How about you?" I asked. "What are we both doing here?"

"Oh," Mary said, "never mind. How's Kay?"

"Kay's fine," I said.

"I know," Mary said. "Kay's always fine."

Two maids in lavender uniforms with frilly aprons came passing cocktails and little sandwiches shaped like hearts and pieces of smoked salmon on crackers. Mary finished her cocktail and took another.

"Mary," I said, "those are double Martinis. I wouldn't take any more."

"Stop being my brother," Mary said. "I can drink you under the table."

"Well, don't do it here," I told her.

Mary finished her third cocktail.

"There's Jim looking at me," she said. "Jim says you have a bad influence on me, darling. I hear Bill King's coming up this week."

"Who told you that?" I asked.

"Kay did," Mary said. "She was worrying as to who was going to meet him at the Junction."

"Why," I said, "I'll meet Bill."

By that time everybody was making a good deal of noise and Mary had disappeared. I found myself talking with a man I knew named Albert Thwing. We met sometimes at just such parties. Albert was several classes ahead of me at college but as life went on the age group shifted.

"Let's see," Albert said. "You were three years behind me at Harvard, weren't you? That means you're going to have your Twenty-fifth next year."

I wished that people would not keep talking about my Twenty-fifth.

"Yes," I said, "I wish I didn't have to go."

"Now," Albert said, "that isn't the right spirit. It gave me a sort of jolt when I faced it. I didn't want to go either. I thought it would be depressing, but it isn't when you get into the spirit of it. Frankly, it does something to you. I don't know what, but it certainly does something."

"What about everybody's wives?" I asked. "I don't want to see their wives."

"I know," Albert said. "I felt just that way about it. But I'll tell you something. After a minute or two you just don't notice them. They all fit into the picture. It's a great experience! I didn't know you knew the Buhlfields."

"I didn't know you did," I said.

"He has something to do with soap, hasn't he?" Albert said. "That soap that's all over the place — Coza soap?"

"What?" I said. "Coza soap?"

I sat at lunch on Mrs. Buhlfield's left. There were two kinds of wine and a good deal too much to eat. I knew I would fall asleep in the afternoon, and I always hated sleeping in the daytime.

"I didn't know your husband had anything to do with Coza soap," I said.

Mrs. Buhlfield's laughter sounded like jangling chimes.

"Evan gets his fingers into all sorts of things," she said.

"Years ago," I said, "I used to do some advertising for Coza soap. I used to know a girl who worked on it. Her name is Myles — Marvin Myles."

"Now, come," Mrs. Buhlfield said. "I don't believe you ever did, but it's awfully funny."

"Yes," I said, "it is funny."

"We're going to have deviled crabs," Mrs. Buhlfield said. "We Westerners love our fish when we get to the shore. Evan went out with a man and caught them the day before yesterday."

"You mean, they've been sitting around since the day before yesterday?" I asked.

"Yes," said Mrs. Buhlfield. "In a pail of wet seaweed, blowing bubbles. Here they come now. Don't take one. Take two, Mr. Pulham!"

It was just as I had thought. I was sleepy after that lunch and didn't feel like doing anything all afternoon. Kay went out somewhere and then we went for a rock picnic that evening and ate broiled live lobsters and drank beer. Kay did not talk about the Buhlfields until we were going to bed that night.

"What was it that you and Mrs. Buhlfield were talking about?" Kay asked.

"About crabs," I said. "Buhlfield caught them the day before yesterday."

"No, you weren't," Kay said. "You were talking about something else. What was it you were saying that made Mrs. Buhlfield laugh?"

"Why is it that you're always listening to me?" I asked her. "I wish you wouldn't, Kay."

"You always make me nervous," Kay said. "I'm always afraid you're going to be tactless. What was it you said to Mrs. Buhlfield?"

"I was talking to her about soap," I said. "Coza soap. Someone told me that Buhlfield had something to do with it."

"That's just like you!" Kay said. "Of course it embarrassed her. Harry, have you got the alarm clock?"

"No," I said. "What do we want the alarm clock for?"

"Don't you know that you have to get up at half-past five to meet Bill King at the Junction?" Kay said. "Now I'll have to go into Emma's bedroom and get that alarm clock."

"I can wake up without it," I said.

"Oh, no, you can't," Kay said. "Harry, what are we going to do about Bill when he comes? We'll have to think of something. We don't want him to be bored."

"Oh, Bill's all right. Let's go to sleep," I said.

There always seemed to be a time just when we put out the light when Kay's mind moved restlessly and erratically through all the present, into the past and into the future.

"Harry," Kay said, "did you put Bitsey out?"

"Yes," I said. "I always do."

"You don't like Bitsey," Kay said. "I don't think you like dogs at all. I wouldn't have married you if I'd known you felt the way you do about dogs."

"I've always liked dogs," I said. "Father always had them. Let's go to sleep."

"You don't really like them," Kay said. "You don't really understand them."

"I do understand them," I said. "Let's go to sleep."

Kay was silent for a while and I closed my eyes. My stomach was not feeling right.

"Harry," Kay said.

"Yes," I said.

"I wish I knew whether you've really given George a good talk about sex."

305

"Why do you keep asking that?" I asked. "I talked to George two years ago about it when you told me to. If you've heard it once it isn't so important to hear it over again."

"Oh," Kay said, "so you don't think sex is important?"

"Listen, Kay," I said. "Please let's go to sleep."

"I don't believe you really told him anything about it," Kay said. "You're always so reticent, Harry. Did you tell him about it or didn't you?"

"Yes," I said, "I did, Kay. They tell him at School anyway — with pictures and diagrams."

"How perfectly disgusting," Kay said.

"When the Skipper was there — " I began.

"For heaven's sakes," Kay said, "don't begin talking about the Skipper. Just try to remember he's been dead for ten years."

"All right," I said. "Kay, have you told Gladys the facts of life?"

"Of course I haven't," Kay said.

"They say now a child is never too young," I told her.

"Harry," Kay said, "I wish you'd please be quiet. You're so boring when you're analytical. Can't we ever go to sleep?"

"All right," I said.

Kay was silent for a while and I could hear the waves lapping against the rocks through the darkness beyond the open window.

"Harry," Kay said, "what makes you keep tossing and pitching around?"

"I don't know," I said. "It's something I've eaten."

"Eaten?" Kay repeated. "It's something you've drunk, you mean."

"I'll be all right," I said. "It's something I've eaten."

Now that we had started talking again it would be a long while before we went to sleep.

"Why is it," Kay said, "we always seem to end up talking about indigestion or drains?"

"I guess that's true of everyone," I said.

"Oh, no, it isn't," said Kay. "Take the Trilbys — "

I stirred uneasily. Kay was always taking the Trilbys.

306

"Did you see Egbert help her over the rocks?"

"Damn the Trilbys!" I said. "You don't like to be helped and you know it."

"I'd like it if you'd try sometimes," Kay said.

"I do try," I said. "And I don't like the Trilbys."

"That's because they're interesting," Kay said.

We were silent for such a long while that I thought she had gone to sleep.

"Harry," Kay said, "I wonder why Bill left her. I never liked her much. She was never up to Bill, but she was awfully pretty."

"Who?" I asked.

"Elise, of course," she said, "Bill's wife. I don't know why he ever married her. I wonder if he's unhappy about it."

"I don't know," I said.

"Of course you know," Kay answered, "but you've always been so loyal about Bill."

"Bill's never talked about it much," I said. "I don't know much about divorce."

Kay was quiet again. We did not speak for a long while, but I knew she was lying there thinking, as I was, in the dark.

"Harry," she asked, "are you feeling all right?"

"I'll be all right in the morning," I said.

"Harry, you forgot something. You forgot to kiss me good night."

I got out of bed and stubbed my toe against the table and leaned over the twin bed beside it to kiss her.

"Good night, dear," I said.

"I always like it," Kay said, "when you call me 'dear.' You know I love you, don't you?"

"Yes, of course," I said.

Her arms around me tightened and she drew me toward her.

"Oh, Lord," she said, "don't say 'of course'! It always makes me happy when you kiss me good night. You'll be sure to wake up in the morning, won't you? So I won't have to think about it."

I woke up long before morning with violent cramps, feeling deathly sick. I did not call Kay, because I've always felt ashamed when I'm ill, and I tried to make as little noise as possible in the bathroom. I thought for a while that I was going to die. It was something you could not fix up with soda, and I went into Gladys' bathroom for castor oil. I swallowed half a bottle, but it seemed to me that I was getting sicker all the time. I was getting so that I did not notice things around me until I saw Kay in the bathroom in her green silk dressing gown. She must have been frightened by the way I looked.

"Harry," she said, "Harry!"

"It's those damned deviled crabs," I said.

"It couldn't be," Kay said. "It was something you drank. I ate the crabs."

"Please, Kay," I said. "I'm going to be sick again."

"Darling," Kay said, "I'm going to call the doctor. You look all green."

"Don't," I said. "We have too many bills. Just go away and leave me."

I began to hope she was going to get the doctor. It was hard to think about anything except the way I felt. It was humiliating — awful — but I hoped she was going to get the doctor. I had never liked him much. He was one of those seaside physicians with a bedside manner. Nothing was very clear again until Kay and Dr. Broderick were both in the bathroom.

"Well, well," the doctor said, "you must have eaten something."

"It's clever of you," I said, "to find that out!" It made me angry when Kay and the doctor laughed.

"Harry, you poor darling," I heard Kay say, "just when you're having your vacation!"

I said it was a hell of a vacation, that something always happened on my vacation; and then they got me back to bed. I could hear the doctor speaking to Kay.

"We'll have a nurse in an hour," the doctor was saying, "and we'll give him a high colonic."

"Look here," I said. "I don't want any nurse. I'll have to get up at half-past five and meet Bill King at the Junction."

"Someone else can meet him," the doctor said. "You'll be right where you are for a while."

I knew it and I knew that I was acting badly. Doctor Broderick was sponging off a place on my arm. He was asking Kay for a little warm water. He had taken a syringe out of his bag.

"You'll be better when you get this," he said.

"You're giving me a shot," I said. "It's like the war." But I did not care what he gave me as long as I stopped feeling the way I did. I heard him speaking to Kay but I did not care what he was saying, and then he was gone and Kay was sitting beside me. I had spoken about the war and I was thinking about the war.

"They're going to fight," I said. "It's the same thing all over."

Kay was sitting beside me holding my hand, and I felt very grateful to her.

"Never mind, dear," she said. "Don't talk."

"George mustn't go," I said. "Don't let George go."

"Of course he won't," Kay said, and she put her hand on my forehead.

Something was mixing itself in my thoughts and I was moving away from it, but I wanted to speak about it before I moved away.

"Kay," I said, "call up the garage. I guess I can't meet Bill."

"I'll meet him, dear," Kay said. "Don't worry."

"When he comes I won't be able to do anything with him."

"Don't worry, dear," Kay said. "I'll look after Bill."

Then everything was growing blurred. Now that I was thinking of Bill I was thinking of New York. It would be hot down in New York, the way it was when I was working there, when I used to take Marvin out in the car somewhere in the country for supper. Marvin used to love broiled live lobsters. I felt a slight spasm run through me.

"What is it, dear?" Kay said.

"We used to eat lobsters — broiled live lobsters," I said.

"Who used to?" Kay asked. "Not you and me. I've always hated them."

"No," I said, "not you. I'm not making any sense, am I? Kay, don't go away."

"Of course not," Kay said. "I'm right here."

"All right," I said. "Did I let Bitsey out?"

"Yes," Kay said, "you're always sweet about letting Bitsey out."

"I wish I could say something interesting," I said. "I know I'm awfully stupid. But Bill — he'll be interesting."

"You're darling," Kay said. "I always love to talk to you. You're darling."

"That's because I threw up," I said. "Kay, I think I'm going to sleep."

I felt weak, but a good deal better, by the middle of the morning. The nurse went away at eleven o'clock and I wanted to get up, but neither Kay nor the doctor would let me. I was to stay in bed for twenty-four hours at least, they told me, eating nothing but liquids. I lay there for a while, trying to read *The Education of Henry Adams*. It had sometimes seemed to me that the rare times when I was ill should have offered a chance to finish some book or other. The only difficulty was that things always seemed to keep right on happening when I was sick in bed. I would begin worrying over what I might have forgotten — details about the office or whether the car had been greased. Now I began worrying about Bill. I didn't want him to spoil his good time, seeing me when I was not all right, but I wanted to be with him as soon as I felt better. In the meantime I kept wondering whether he had had a good breakfast and whether he had everything he wanted in his room. Although Kay told me not to bother, of course I kept on bothering. When Kay came in for a few moments at about eleven o'clock I asked if Bill was all right.

"Don't keep worrying about him," Kay said. "Bill's fine."

"Well, is he cheerful?" I asked. "We want to do everything we can. We want to cheer him up."

"Don't you worry about Bill," Kay said. "He's been asking about you. I'm going to take him to the beach."

"Well, he ought to have some exercise," I said, "and you'd better show him where the whisky is in case he wants a drink."

"He doesn't drink in the morning, does he?" Kay asked.

"He might," I said. "I don't want him to feel we're stuffy about it. I want him to feel he can have anything he wants. You know the way you are about drinking."

"I'm not that way at all," Kay said. "I'm just that way with you because it gives you indigestion."

"It wasn't anything I drank," I said. "It was the crabs."

"Well, don't keep telling me what to do about Bill," Kay said, "because Bill's perfectly all right. I'm going to take him down to the beach now and then we're going to the Sutherlands' to lunch and then we're going sailing."

"Bill doesn't like to sail," I said.

"Oh," Kay said. "Well — Bill said he wanted to go sailing."

"Well, don't make him do anything he doesn't want to," I said. "Has he talked to you about Elise at all?"

"Yes," Kay said, "quite a lot. He seemed to want to talk to someone."

"Well, what's happened?" I asked.

"It's all over," Kay said. "They've signed an agreement and she's going to Reno next week. I'll tell you all about it later. Bill's waiting downstairs now. We're going to the beach."

I lay back and watched the breeze waving the green chintz curtains. There was very little one could do about a thing like divorce, but I knew it must be a time when you needed friends. I tried to imagine how I should feel if Kay and I were ever to break up. I watched Kay as she moved swiftly around the room, taking a compact out of her upper bureau drawer, giving her hair one final brush, getting her light polo coat out of the closet.

"You've got everything, haven't you?" she asked.

"Yes," I said, "everything."

Then she was gone and I was left alone with *The Education of*

Henry Adams. I was reading about his days in Washington when George came in. He opened the door and moved furtively into the room.

"Gosh," George said, "you look awful."

"What do you want?" I asked.

George stuffed his hands in his pockets and balanced himself on one leg.

"Don't do that," I said. "You make me dizzy. What do you want?"

"Could I borrow a necktie," George asked, "one of your snazzy ones?"

I don't know why it should have given me a feeling that I was already dead and that George was going to go over my things.

"What about your own ties?" I asked him. "What do you want one of mine for?"

"I just wanted to look keen this afternoon," George said. "I've got a date."

"If it's that Goodwin girl," I told him, "you can take one of your own ties."

"Now, listen, boss, you want your son to look properly dressed, don't you? Ease up on the ties, boss."

"Take one and get out," I said. I did not feel like arguing.

"Say," George said, "I wish you could have some ties like Uncle Bill's."

"I'm not in the advertising business."

"He knows everybody on the radio," George said. "Do you know he knows Bergen?"

"Who's Bergen?" I asked.

"Bergen? You don't mean you don't know the Charlie McCarthy hour? I wish we knew interesting people like Uncle Bill does."

"I wish you'd learn to speak grammatically," I told him. "Maybe they're not so interesting. Why should a ventriloquist be interesting? It's Uncle Bill's business doing those advertising hours on the radio."

"Well, I wish you had a business like that," George said. "He

312

knows Dragonette. He takes her out to dinner. And he knows Rudy Vallee. That's more than you do, boss."

"I don't want to know Rudy Vallee," I said.

"You ought to get out more," George said, "like Uncle Bill. You don't understand my generation."

"Rudy Vallee isn't your generation, and neither is Mr. Bergen."

"That may be," George said, "but they interpret my generation."

"To hell with your generation," I said.

"I guess you're feeling pretty sick, aren't you, boss?" George asked. "Well, I'll be going now. You don't want the radio, do you? Maybe you want to listen to the news."

I pulled myself up straight in bed. I had forgotten about the news, and now it was all mixed with Charlie McCarthy and George's generation. The war was all starting again, just as it had started twenty years ago. They were all saying the same things and none of it made sense.

"Take your tie and go away, George," I said, "and try not to spill ice cream on it."

"The Germans are going into Poland," George said.

"Yes," I said, "I suppose they are. Go on out, George, and have a good time. I'm sorry I was cross."

It was always like that with George. I always wanted to have a good talk with him, but somehow one of us was always in a hurry. If I had told him what I thought about the war or about the Goodwin girl, George would not have listened. If I had tried I could not have explained to him why the war made me feel futile and empty. If it lasted for four years — and it might — George would be able to go.

I was annoyed by something almost patient and patronizing in his manner, and I tried to think whether my attitude had been the same toward my own father. I certainly would not have borrowed his necktie. I certainly would not have spoken so familiarly, and yet I must have felt about the same toward him as George did toward me. I had also treated him with a patient tolerance, secure in

313

the knowledge that he did not understand me, confident that he was a stuffed shirt. It was all repeating itself — another war and another boy. I closed my eyes, and my stomach and my head felt empty. I wondered if Father's thoughts had been the same as mine, if when people reached a certain age all points of view were not alike. Yet Father had led a secure and certain life. He had not lived through the panic of '29 or the depression. He had not lived to see Smith and Wilding sink into almost nothing, like so many old banking houses. He had not lived to see what old Pritchard had done to the trust estate, but I had been all through it. I still was going through it, and if my guess was right worse times were on the way. I lay there now, as I did sometimes at night, piecing facts together. Following this war, whether we were in it or not, there would inevitably be inflation. Taxes could not be raised to pay the national debt. The whole thing had started when I was nearly George's age and it still was moving. In their own small ways Bergen and Dragonette were a part of it, a part of peculiar new ideas, of peculiar humor. It was amazing how many unpleasant things you could think of when you lay in bed. I must have dozed off thinking of them, because they all were vague. Then before I opened my eyes I knew that someone was watching me. I opened them and saw Gladys. She must have entered the room on tiptoe and perhaps she had been there for quite a while. She was holding a letter in her hand.

"Look," she said.

"What?" I asked.

She thrust the letter toward me and I knew from her expression that it contained something wonderful, because her face was exalted and completely happy, like the face of a dreamer who has seen the vision of another world.

"Look," she said. "It just came this morning."

"What is it?" I asked.

"Look," she said again. "It's from Uncle Fuzzey."

"Who?" I asked.

"From Uncle Fuzzey," she said, "Uncle Fuzzey on the radio. I wrote him and he answered it." It was a typewritten form letter with a printed signature.

"Dear Little Tuffy-Eater," I read, "I am so glad to welcome you with all the other boys and girls into the club that eats a big hot plate of Tuffies every morning. On another sheet of paper you will find the club password and enclosed also is your Uncle Fuzzey button. When you see other boys and girls wearing it you will know they are in the Tuffy Club and you can give them the password. With all best wishes — Uncle Fuzzey."

"I thought you'd like to see it," Gladys said.

"Yes," I said, "I'm awfully glad to see it. It makes me feel better."

"Well," she said, "I'd better be going now," and she turned and ran away.

It must have been a good deal later when I opened my eyes again. Kay was back in front of her bureau, brushing her hair and putting some powder on her nose.

"We're just going out to lunch," she said. "You're going to have some clear broth and a glass of milk and some dry toast. You're looking better."

"Yes," I said. "Kay, you're looking awfully well."

Kay turned and examined herself in the mirror and then glanced back at me and smiled.

"Bill's really a lot of fun," she said.

"I can see Bill later this afternoon, can't I?" I asked.

"Yes," Kay said, "late. Have your lunch and try to take a nap. The doctor says you'll be better if you sleep."

"I can't keep awake," I answered. "I'm all full of dope. Kay, I'm awfully glad you're having a good time."

She bent over and kissed my forehead.

"I've got to go. Bill's downstairs waiting. We're taking the Packard."

"You drive," I said, "if Bill starts drinking."

"Now, don't keep worrying," she said. "Have the children been bothering you?"

"Not much," I told her. "Gladys is in the Tuffy Club."

"What in heaven's name," Kay asked, "is the Tuffy Club?"

I found it a little difficult to tell her; she was not listening carefully, because she was in a hurry to go out.

"That's awfully childish for a girl her age," Kay said.

"I don't know," I said. "Maybe everything that you and I do is childish. I don't know."

Kay turned toward the half-open door, but her mind was somewhere else. She still looked awfully pretty.

"Don't try to generalize," she said. "You're always so awfully obvious."

I was feeling sleepy again, but it seemed to me that I had never seen her look so pretty.

"Maybe everyone's obvious," I said.

She was moving toward the door, but when I spoke she turned around as though I had startled her.

"Now, what on earth are you trying to say?" she asked.

"Why, nothing," I said.

"Harry," she asked, "you're not being jealous, are you?" Kay smiled.

"Jealous?" I repeated. "Jealous of what?"

"Why, of Bill and me, of course," she said. "You're not being silly, are you?"

"Of Bill and you?" I repeated. "Why, I wasn't even thinking of Bill and you. I was thinking about my intestines, if you want to know."

"Oh," Kay said.

"And what's more," I told her, "why should I be jealous of Bill and you? Have I ever been jealous?"

"No," Kay said, "of course you haven't. It was just something in your voice, but as long as it was just your stomach . . . You don't think we're mean to leave you here, do you?"

"Of course I don't," I said. "I want Bill to have a good time."

XXVIII

It All Adds Up to Something

Bill came in to see me at five o'clock when the sun was soft on the sea outside the window. He had been out in the boat with Kay and his face was sunburned, but the burn was becoming. He was dressed in tan-colored flannels and a gabardine coat and an odd sort of shirt, and he was wearing canvas shoes with rope soles. I told him he looked like a picture in a movie magazine and Bill laughed.

"You hit it that time, boy," he said. "As a matter of fact, I bought this outfit when I was out on the Coast. I wore it when I was photographed with Myrna Loy."

"Well, it looks that way," I said.

"I knocked their eyes out on the beach," Bill said. "Do you see this shirt? It's what they call a rogue shirt."

"A rogue shirt?" I repeated.

"No buttons on it," Bill said. "It just folds around you. You can relax in it. They wear them on the Coast. How are you feeling, boy?"

"I'm feeling better," I said. "Would you like a drink?"

Now that I saw Bill there was something gay about him that made me want to have a drink myself, even though the doctor had forbidden it.

"Where's Kay?" I asked.

"Kay?" Bill said. "Why, I've worn Kay all out. She's taking a nap in the guest room or something. We're going to the dance tonight."

"Then I guess I can have a drink too," I said, and I rang for Ellen and told her to bring up some Scotch and ice and glasses.

317

Bill began talking about everybody he had seen on the beach, while we waited, and about George and Gladys and about everyone he had seen at lunch, and when the whisky came he poured himself a stiff drink and a smaller one for me. He said never to mind what the doctor said, that a drink would do me good, and he was right — I felt a whole lot better. I told him about the crabs and about all the things the doctor had done to me the night before and that morning.

"If it's that way," Bill said, "maybe you ought not to be drinking whisky."

I told him never to mind about it. I wanted to make the effort to talk to Bill. It took my mind off my own troubles. That was the way it always was with Bill. As soon as I began talking about the doctor and the nurse, Bill started thinking it was funny, and I saw it was amusing too. I began to forget the impression that Bill's espadrilles and rogue shirt had made upon me. No matter how Bill dressed he was always just the same.

"I don't know why it is you make me laugh," Bill said, "because, frankly, you've always been a straight."

"What's a straight?" I asked.

"A straight," Bill said. "Don't you know what a straight is? A straight's someone in a skit who has all the jokes thrown at him. I start to tell you a joke. I say, 'I was walking down the street the other day,' and you say, 'Yes, you were walking down the street? Go on.' And I say, 'I met a dame,' and you say, 'Oh, you met a dame, did you?' That's what a straight is."

Bill always had something to say that was new and interesting.

"I see," I said. "I guess I've always been a straight."

I thought Bill would laugh, but instead he finished his drink and poured out another one.

"Maybe, but maybe it's better than being the smart man. He's mighty lonely and there're lots and lots of straights."

I could see that something was bothering him. I did not like to bring the matter up, but I knew I should, because I was his friend.

"Bill," I said, "I'm awfully sorry about Elise."

Bill shook the ice in his glass. I could not tell whether ne wanted to talk about her or not.

"Elise," he said, "oh, yes. We never should have got married in the first place. I don't know whatever got into me to marry her."

"She was awfully pretty," I said. "I know I never got along very well with her the few times I saw her, but I always liked her."

Bill sat scowling into his glass.

"She was spoiled," he said. "She couldn't understand that I had my work. Oh, hell. What's the use of going over it? All these bust-ups are alike. Boy, if I started to tell you about Elise — do you know what she did? She tried to stab me with a paper knife."

"Why, Bill," I said, "why did she do that?"

Bill took several swallows of whisky and looked more cheerful.

"We were just talking," he said. "It didn't really mean anything. It was just the way we were — and the things I used to do for Elise! Palm Beach! Hollywood! She's an artist — a great artist — you wouldn't understand."

"She must have been awfully selfish, Bill," I said.

"Naturally," Bill said, "but then look at me — I'm selfish. The best way to treat those things is to laugh at them. It's like what happened to you, only you ate crabs and me — I married Elise!"

Bill looked at the ceiling and smiled, but I could see that he was hurt and I hoped that he would change the subject.

"Oh, hell," he said. "She was a nice girl. She is still. It wasn't anybody's fault."

"I don't suppose those things ever are," I said.

Bill sat for a while without speaking, but I knew he was thinking about it. In spite of his sunburn he looked thin and tired, completely sick of himself and sick of everything.

"Bill," I said, "you'd better get it off your mind."

Bill shook the ice in his glass and set his glass down. Then he pulled a gold cigarette case out of his pocket, looked at it and put it back in his pocket again.

"Hell," he said, "she gave me that. That's the trouble with it, things keep coming up—what she did, what I did, what we used to do."

"Bill," I said, "you know Kay and I are right behind you."

Bill looked as though he did not hear me and took another drink.

"She never understood me," he said, "but everyone says that. Maybe I never understood her either. I'm damned if I know what it was all about. Maybe I'm just a plain heel. I don't know."

"No, you're not," I said. "It just didn't work. That isn't anybody's fault."

Bill took another drink and smoothed his coat.

"I'll tell you one thing," he said, "that always comes out of a mess like this. There's nothing more dangerous than a man who isn't happily married. He just goes around getting into trouble. Boy, the trouble I've been in the past two years! You wouldn't believe it,—" and he began to smile,—"and the trouble Elise's been in!"

"I suppose," I said, "if you'd ever had a baby—" Bill looked startled.

"A baby! For God's sakes, why a baby?"

"Well," I said, "I don't know." Bill was staring at me and I was glad to see that he was looking better.

"Go ahead, boy," Bill said. "Why a baby?"

"Well," I said, "I don't know. Of course I suppose everyone has difficulties. I know I do lots of things that make Kay mad. I suppose I'm awfully stupid sometimes, but after Kay had George, why, everything was a whole lot better. And I think Kay and I are pretty happy. We've always been happy."

Bill lifted up his glass and set it down without drinking.

"Would you mind saying that again?" he asked.

"I don't see what's so queer about it. Taken all in all, Kay and I have really been happy."

"All right," Bill said gently. "Just tell me how you and Kay have been happy."

Bill had a way of being amused by things which I could not understand.

320

"It's a little hard to explain," I said. "It's like taking a lot of numbers that don't look alike and that don't mean anything until you add them all together."

I stopped, because I hadn't meant to talk to him about Kay and me.

"Go ahead," Bill said. "What about the numbers?" And he began to smile.

"I don't know why you think it's so funny," I said. "All the things that two people do together, two people like Kay and me, add up to something. There are the kids and the house and the dog and all the people we've known and all the times we've been out to dinner. Of course Kay and I do quarrel sometimes, but when you add it all together, all of it isn't as bad as the parts of it seem. I mean, maybe that's all there is to anybody's life."

Bill poured himself another drink. He seemed about to say something and checked himself. He kept looking at me.

"Well," Bill said, "maybe you're right, but you sound like the Oxford Group."

"Well," I said, "I'm awfully sorry, Bill. I didn't mean to talk about Kay and me. I was just thinking of it this morning when Kay was putting powder on her nose."

"What?" Bill said.

"When Kay was fixing herself over there by the mirror," I said, "before she took you down to the beach."

"Hell's bells!" Bill said, and he ran his hand over his hair. It was still blond and curly. "What time is it?"

I looked at the watch on the table by the bed.

"It's two minutes after six."

"Good," Bill said. "Have you got a radio?"

"Yes," I said, "right on the table over there. Do you want to listen to the news? The Germans are going into Poland."

"News?" Bill said. "To hell with the news. It's the Coza hour. We're putting on Bill Bingo and his new swing orchestra and Larry Leach is the new host and I want to hear how that damned fairy comes across."

"Who's Bill Bingo?" I asked.

"What?" said Bill. "Haven't you heard of Bill Bingo? He's top on the KC rating, and costs us five thousand dollars for half an hour and he has blackheads and wears smoked glasses. Wait a minute. Here he is. There goes Larry. I wrote the continuity."

Bill stood by the radio holding his whisky glass with one hand and raising the other hand so that I would not speak. A mellifluous voice filled the room, against a background of soft music.

"And now once again," the voice was saying, "Cozaland greets you."

"It's better," Bill said, "without any plug for the soap. It's proved on the KC rating. Just music from Cozaland."

"And as we sit and watch the sunset, Bill Bingo and the Bingo Boys swing it for you, with the compliments of the manufacturers of Coza Soap."

"No more plug than that," said Bill, "and it pulls. That voice has personality, hasn't it? There they go."

The room was filled suddenly with strident music that George had learned to call "hot."

"Turn it down lower, Bill," I said. "It goes right through my ears."

Bill turned it lower, swinging his shoulders rhythmically. "I'll shut it off in a minute," he said. "That boy Bingo certainly can give."

He turned the radio down lower so that the music became very faint.

"Even as low as that," Bill said, "he still pulls."

"Bill," I said, "I didn't mean to talk about Kay and me. It must have sounded as though I were preaching to you."

"Oh, that," Bill said. "It sounded fine. Wait a minute. I'm thinking of something."

Bill began pacing up and down softly in front of my bed.

" 'Please keep me happy,' " he said softly. "No, that isn't right. How's this one? 'I want to stay married.' "

"How do you mean, Bill?" I asked. "What are you talking about?"

"A series," Bill said, "when we get through with Bingo. That little squirt will try to up us another thousand on his next contract. 'I want to stay married'—a series of fifteen minute skits at six o'clock, just when the woman's serving supper—problems of married life—music, a voice—'I want to stay married'—more voices 'I want to stay married.' Then in it comes—'Fifteen minutes in the Coza Theater, May and Tom in their daily drama of married life.' It isn't new, but it has something."

"You mean, you're thinking of having that every night?"

"Every other night so they'll wait for it," Bill said. "A good marital quarrel always gets them. 'I want to stay married'—the voice of America, from Maine to California."

Bill began pacing the floor again, rubbing his hands slowly over the back of his head. The music was all around him.

"Bill," I said.

"'I want to stay married,'" Bill said softly. "Yes, what is it, Harry?"

It must have been the music that made me think of it—the music and a world I never knew.

"Bill," I said, "last spring Marvin Myles called me up. She's married. Someone in our class named Ransome. Did you ever know him? I didn't."

Suddenly I wanted to talk about her, but Bill kept on pacing.

"Oh, yes," Bill said, "I remember now. She told me she'd called you."

"Bill," I said, "do you think she's happy?"

"Who?" Bill said. "Marvin? It's all coming Marvin's way."

"Ransome? I can't remember him," I said.

I had been thinking about it a good deal and wondering what he must be like and where Marvin had met him.

"Oh," Bill said, "John Ransome? There isn't any reason why you should have remembered him. He's one of those rich boys with a complex about being rich. Marvin's pretty good with John."

"But what's he like?" I asked.

"What's he like?" Bill repeated. "He's a straight. He wouldn't

323

wear a rogue shirt, for instance. Wait a minute. I never thought of it that way. Ransome — why Ransome's something like you."

It gave me a feeling which I could not analyze, with the music of the Bingo orchestra and with Bill standing there, holding his glass, his face shiny and red with sunburn. I wanted him to go on, but instead he seemed to have forgotten all about it. He had turned on the radio louder.

"Wait," he said. "Larry's coming in with the plug. I want to hear it. There it goes."

The music had died down and I heard the announcer's voice.

"And so goes Billy Bingo's music in the Coza hour," he was saying, "subtle, soft and penetrating like the foam of Coza Soap, scintillating like Coza Bath Salts. On it goes."

"I wish you'd shut that off, Bill," I said.

I was not feeling as strong as I had when Bill came in or I should have got up and thrown that radio out the window. There was nothing about any of it that was real — not the Bingo orchestra or Bill or Marvin Myles or that man she had married who was just like me.

Bill turned the radio down again.

Kay was standing in the doorway looking at Bill, smiling. I was afraid that she would be cross about my having had a drink, but instead she looked happy.

"Swing music always makes Harry nervous," she said. "Turn it off, Bill. How many highballs have you had?"

"It's just the sunburn," Bill said. "You ask Harry."

I saw Kay glance at the whisky bottle the way she sometimes did, and I knew that she was estimating just how much Bill had taken and I was afraid it might make her cross, but instead it only seemed to amuse her.

"We've got to be getting dressed," Kay said. "It's late. We're going to the Club for dinner, and then we're going to dance."

"I hope we dance for a long time," Bill said. "That's fine with me."

"As long as you don't get tight," Kay said.

"You've always liked dancing with her, haven't you, Bill?" I asked.

"Go on, Bill," Kay said. "Hurry and get dressed."

"All right," said Bill. "I'll be seeing you, Harry. I hope you're a whole lot better in the morning."

He waved his hand and walked into the hall, but even when the door was closed it seemed to me that Kay and I were not alone. That swing music was still coming faintly from the radio.

"Kay," I said, "would you mind turning that thing off?"

"Why, yes, of course," Kay said. "Ellen's bringing you up an eggnog and some toast." When she turned off the radio the whole room seemed suddenly stunningly silent. I must have been awfully tired, because I was glad that Bill was gone.

I could hear Kay singing while the water was running in the bathtub. It often surprised me how she liked to go to any sort of party. She always seemed to keep the illusion that something interesting and exciting would happen at a party. Now I could hear her splashing in the tub, and now I could hear her stepping out of it.

"The hot water's awfully rusty," Kay called. "It's beginning to look like tea."

My mind was getting away from Bill. I had noticed the same thing about the water.

"Next year," I answered, "we'll put in copper piping."

"Harry," Kay called back, "has anyone checked the oil in the Packard? It made a funny noise."

I began to reconstruct the Packard in my mind.

"That must be one of the tappets," I said. "What are you laughing at? What's so funny about a tappet?"

"It's just that you have the queerest names for all sorts of things," Kay said, "that no one else knows anything about."

Kay opened the bathroom door and came out, still rubbing her face with her towel. She had on her shorts. Her legs and arms and shoulders were tanned and all the rest of her was white.

"You look as if part of you had been in that water and as if part of you hadn't," I said.

Kay examined herself in the mirror.

"That's true," she said. "It does look sort of queer. I hadn't thought of that."

As a matter of fact, Kay did not look queer. She looked lithe and straight, and having the children had never hurt her figure. She made me think of a young girl, just getting ready for a party.

"It doesn't," I said. "It ought to, but it doesn't."

Kay was opening and closing her bureau drawers.

"Where the devil are my stockings?" she said. "Oh, here they are."

She sat on the edge of her bed and began pulling them on carefully.

"If they get a run in them I'm going to scream," she said. Then she went over to the bureau and began combing her hair and said that the salt air made it look terrible, but it did not look terrible.

"What do you think I'd better wear?" she asked.

"The dress with stripes," I said, "that makes you look like a stick of candy."

"No," she said. "I'll wear the green one and the green slippers." She pulled the green dress from the closet and began tossing it over her head.

"Look here," I asked, "aren't you going to wear a girdle or a slip or anything?"

"Not with this dress," Kay said. "I don't need them with it."

"I just thought you might be cold or something," I said.

"You know what it's like," Kay answered, "when you get in there dancing." She was looking for her lipstick in the bureau drawer. I could see her in the mirror, pursing her lips and moving her head from side to side. I remembered how plain she used to be when she was seventeen but ever since then she had kept on looking better. She began humming a tune and looking for her green bag in the upper bureau drawer.

"Kay," I said, "I've been talking to Bill."

326

She stopped humming and I could hear the breeze rustling the chintz curtains.

"What do you mean," she asked, "you were talking to Bill?"

"It was sort of silly of me," I said, "I don't know how I got started, but I was telling him that you and I had been happy. I don't know why I thought of it, but when I saw Bill — "

"Happy?" Kay repeated. "Why, Harry — "

"I mean," I said, "when you add it all up, all the things we've been through together."

Kay turned around and looked in the bureau drawer again.

"I don't know why it is," she said, "you say the smuggest things sometimes. Here comes Ellen with your eggnog. Ellen's going to move me into the spare room, so I won't wake you up."

Kay bent over and kissed my forehead.

As Ellen opened the door I could hear George and Gladys laughing in the hall and I could hear Bill telling them some sort of story.

"Good night," Kay said. "Bill's downstairs waiting."

XXIX

What Did I Do Wrong?

By noon the next day I managed to get downstairs, but I was too weak to be good for anything. That was the way it was all the week end. When we had guests for Sunday lunch I could not eat any of the food and I had to go upstairs to rest afterwards. Though I tried to be as amusing as I could about what had happened to me, I hated it because I could not do anything for Bill and because I was afraid that Kay would get very tired entertaining him steadily for two or three days. When Kay told me that she did not really mind it, I thought at first she was just being nice about it and trying to make up in every way she could for my being sick, but when I saw that they really enjoyed each other and that neither of them seemed to get tired of the other, I began to like the week end. I never saw Bill nicer. It made me secretly glad that his marriage had broken up, because he was more a part of the family than he had ever been before, more like the old days. I told him that he must come up from New York whenever he had a chance, whenever he felt worried or lonely, and Bill said he would. Of course we were all very old friends, but we seemed to be discovering all over again how valuable and how really splendid that friendship was. We knew each other so well that we had all sorts of little jokes that old friends have, and Bill could see exactly what there was about me that half-exasperated and half-amused Kay. They would laugh when I began to explain about the tappets on the car, for instance, and somehow it did not annoy me at all. We had all sorts of jokes that would not have been amusing to anyone else. I remember that Bill told me that I looked as though I had been through a good deal.

"You mean I look as though a good deal had been through me," I said.

That was the sort of thing that I should never have said in any other company, but between Bill and Kay and me it was definitely funny and we kept laughing about it a long time afterwards. It only goes to show that we really were having a good time.

It would have been hard to imagine two sorts of lives as completely diverse as Bill's on one side and Kay's and mine on the other. I used to tell Kay, and Kay agreed with me, that I could not possibly have led Bill's life, but it did not mean that I did not admire it. Sometimes I had felt, particularly after Bill had married Elise Megg, who was after all a very important singer, that he considered Kay and me an effort, although Bill and Elise always told us to be sure to call them up the very first thing whenever we came to New York. And now all at once, all of that constraint was gone completely.

In the times when Kay was ordering the meals or seeing about the children Bill really made me feel that he liked to listen to my ideas. He was keen and lucid about the war and about the political and business situation. It was like going out into the world myself to hear him talk and he gave me some very good lists of books and magazines.

I tried to make Bill stay on for a week because the change had done him so much good, and he and Kay had been going around to so many places while I had to be quiet in the house that we had not nearly talked things out. I kept waiting for an opportunity to ask more about Marvin Myles, but somehow the chance had never come. He had to get back to New York, he said, because he had a hundred things to do, but he wanted Kay and me to come down to see him and to see the town.

Usually when a guest left after a visit, no matter how much I liked him, I always had a guilty sense of relief. It would mean that life settled down again without any additional effort and planning, but Bill had fitted in so well that there had been no effort. I was awfully sorry to have him go and Kay was awfully sorry. His train would leave the Junction at half-past eight, so we had an early supper, just the three of us without the children. We had cocktails and we had champagne because Bill was going.

"I've had a swell time," Bill said. "I can't begin to tell you what it means to me to know I still have friends."

"Why, Bill," I said, "you have hundreds of friends — hundreds in New York that we don't know."

"It isn't the same," Bill said. "Not real friends — just table-hoppers."

"What are table-hoppers?" I asked.

I wanted to change the subject. I did not want the last few minutes to seem sad. Bill grinned at Kay.

"We've got to take him around more," he said, "so he can see some table-hoppers."

"Kay doesn't know what table-hoppers are either," I said. I knew she didn't, but she looked annoyed.

"Harry," Kay said, "Bill's finished his champagne. I wish you wouldn't always keep holding back. There's another bottle in the icebox. Go and get it and hurry up. Bill's got to go."

I hadn't the slightest idea of "holding back" on the champagne. I would have given Bill all the champagne in the house and I wanted him to know it, but I did not want him to think that Kay and I were always arguing. I went out into the pantry for another bottle and got the wire off and worked out the cork. When I got back to the dining room Bill must have been telling Kay again what a good time he had had, because they were both sitting saying nothing. Whatever it was that Bill had said, it made Kay look awfully sad.

"Come on," I said. "This isn't a funeral. Bill's coming back, aren't you, Bill?"

Bill straightened his shoulders and smiled.

"There never was anyone whiter than you, Harry," he said. "I mean it."

330

I began filling up the glasses.

"Are your bags all packed, Bill?" I asked.

"Of course his bags are packed," Kay said. "Don't ask such silly questions."

Bill was still there, drinking his champagne, but the house seemed quieter already, and gloomier, the more we tried to talk.

"Well, I'll go and bring Bill's bags down," I said.

"No, you won't," Bill said. "You're not feeling well enough."

"I'm feeling fine," I said. "Just when you're leaving I'm cured."

"Let him get them if he wants to, Bill," Kay said.

Bill's two pigskin bags were in the guest room and I lugged them to the front door. The exertion took more out of me than I thought it would, although the bags were not heavy. I stood for a minute getting my breath back, looking out of the open door at the drive-way. The Packard was outside already. It was a starlight night, very clear and almost cold. Kay and Bill were still in the dining room. I had not heard either of them speak, but something made me think again that Bill had been speaking. I wished that they would cheer up. After all, Bill was only going to New York.

"There's forty minutes to get to the Junction," I said. "We'd better get going, Bill."

Kay pushed back her chair and stood up.

"I'll just get my coat," she said. "I'll drive Bill over."

"Oh, no, Kay," I said. "I'd like to drive."

Kay shook her head.

"It's been enough your being sick once, Harry. You stay right here."

"Then let's all go," I said. "You can drive if you want to, Kay."

"Now, Harry," she looked the way she always did when she considered I was being stubborn, "I wish you'd try to do what the doctor wants."

"But it's only going over to the Junction, Kay," I said.

Bill slapped me on the shoulder.

"Listen, boy," he said, "you've been pretty sick. You just stay right here."

"All right," I said. "I just don't like Kay driving back alone at night."

"Darling," Kay said, "half-past eight isn't really night. You haven't read the morning papers and you haven't been over the bills. We'd better start along, Bill. I'll just get my coat."

While we waited for her the house seemed quieter than ever. Bill and I began talking about Pullmans. I told him that they switched the cars all over the place and Bill said he knew it, but he always slept well on a train. Then Kay came running down the stairs with her brown polo coat over her arm.

"Harry," she asked, "where is Bitsey?"

"He must be in the kitchen," I said. "He generally is at meal-time."

"Well, see where he is, will you?" Kay asked. "Come on, Bill."

"So long, Bill," I said. "I'll see you soon."

"That's right," Bill said. "I'll see you soon."

It was cold enough, when Kay and Bill had gone, to start a fire in the living room. Even with the logs burning the chintz-covered furniture looked cold. The bare light-colored walls, with only a few etchings on them, all arranged by Kay to give an impression of coolness and restfulness, were cold too, reminding me that summer was about over. Even under the new chintz covers the furniture looked battered and out of shape and the hooked rugs which we used to buy at auctions were pretty well worn down. Kay always said that you couldn't do much with a house when there were children in it. When George and Gladys were younger they used to bounce on the big sofas and they used to drag all the chairs and pillows onto the floor to play games of train and dragon. It was the same way with the house in town. Kay always said that when the children got bigger we would have to do both the houses over so that our nice things would really "stand out and show for something." George was still hard on furniture and he had not lost his habit of fingering books and of testing the tensile strength of small articles such as pewter ashtrays, but he would grow out of

332

it in a year or so. Gladys, being a girl, was not destructive. In a year or so we could do both houses over, and I might start now building up a fund for the purpose. Kay used to say that I was always building up funds. Nevertheless she could see the sense in it.

The logs snapped in the fireplace, but the chimney did not smoke even though it had not been used since the foggy weather several weeks before. I stood there looking at the flames until I felt warmer. Then I sat down and picked up a book off the table. Kay always made a point of having a few of the latest books around the living room. The one I happened on was a new novel, and, frankly, I never liked new novels. The characters in them, ever since the twenties, were always struggling with internal emotional conflicts that revealed themselves in sexual irregularities, and they were never like anyone I knew. They were farmers in the Dust Bowl or traveling salesmen or people who lived at Palm Beach or on the Riviera, never decent, honest-to-goodness men or women. I could not put my mind on the story. *The Education of Henry Adams* was upstairs in our bedroom, but I was not in a mood for that either.

I had never known the house so still.

"Before you know it," people used to say, "the children will be all grown up."

It had sounded like a silly remark when George was in his play pen or roaring in the nursery, but it was true. All sorts of things happened before you really knew it. You got married and had children and then the children grew up and left. Some day Kay and I would be alone and I was certainly alone now. I rang the bell near the fireplace. I had never believed in having bells in the house, but Kay had wanted them.

Ellen came in, wiping her hands on her apron. Ellen had stuck by us for a good many years, the only servant who had ever stuck.

"Ellen," I asked, "where are George and Gladys?"

Ellen said that Master George was on a beach picnic and that Miss Gladys had gone out to supper with one of the Frear girls, and that Jerry was going to call for her in the Ford and would then pick up George.

"Where's Bitsey?" I asked.

Ellen said that Bitsey was asleep under the kitchen stove, and then she inquired whether there was anything else I wanted. I looked at the clock over the mantelpiece, the clock that used to be in Father's study. It was nearly half-past eight. Kay would not be back for three quarters of an hour, but there was nothing else I wanted.

"No," I said, "that's all. I was just wondering where the children were."

"I hope you're feeling better, sir," Ellen said.

"A good deal better, thanks," I answered. "I'm sorry I made such a lot of trouble."

"Sure, sir," Ellen said, "you weren't any trouble and it was nice having Mr. King. He's such a jolly, generous gentleman."

It had been a long while since I had missed Kay so much. I paced up and down the room. I went out on the porch and looked at the sea and listened to the crickets in the grass and looked at the lights in the other houses. I picked up the book again and tried to read it. Then I heard the car in the driveway and I heard Kay run it into the garage and shut off the motor. I opened the front door and waited for her. Kay came in with her hands in her coat pockets. Her hair was blown and her face looked clean and clear.

"Well," I said, "you're back."

"Yes," Kay said, "where else would I be?" She pulled off her coat and tossed it on a chair with a little sigh. "I've put the car in. Aren't the children back yet?"

"No," I said, "but Jerry's going to get them. It's been awfully lonely with no one in the house."

"Lonely?" Kay repeated. "You always say that if you could be left alone for a minute you could get some reading done."

"I know," I said, "but I'm awfully glad you're back. Did Bill get off all right?"

"What?" Kay said. "Oh — oh, yes, Bill got off."

334

"No matter what happens," I said, "Bill's always just the same."

"Yes," Kay said. "Let's not talk about it now."

"How do you mean?" I asked. "Not talk about what now?"

"Oh, about Bill, or about anything," Kay said. "Harry, I've got a headache. Do you mind if I go up to bed? Will you wait for the children?"

"Why, yes, of course," I said. "Is there anything I can get you, Kay, an aspirin or something?"

"No," Kay said. "I'll be all right when I get to sleep. Don't bother to come up, please."

"You've worked too hard over Bill," I said.

"Oh, Harry," Kay said, "please. I'll be all right in the morning."

The coldness next morning and the heavy haze over the sea marked the end of the summer as surely as a fall of snow. I found myself, by the time I was shaved and dressed, in what I might term the autumn frame of mind. It was an attitude that was made up of all sorts of old associations with the autumn — the smell of rain on fallen leaves, the smell of wood smoke, new clothes and packing up for school, the Skipper, football. There is nothing like our autumns. Instead of being sad they are the pleasantest seasons in the year, a period of hope, of getting everything cleaned up before the winter and of going on. Of late years they meant moving the family and the maids back to town, a process so complicated that I always hoped to arrange my vacation to coincide with those few days when Kay and Ellen and all the rest of them were closing up the house and opening up the other one.

Kay usually liked to go to town two or three days beforehand with Ellen in order to hire two or three individuals whom she called "cleaning women." Kay often tried to explain to me what she did in those three days with Ellen and the cleaning women, and it always seemed to me that she did a great deal that was needless. For the life of me I could never imagine why Kay and the cleaning women always cleaned everything in our house in town when we left it in the summer, if they had to clean it all over again before we got back in the autumn; but Kay used to say that I did not understand, that you could not have summer dirt piling on top of winter dirt. It did no good to tell her that the cleaning women kept coming every week, keeping out the winter dirt. Whenever I reached town with the children and all the things in the car the house would be spotless, but Kay would be exhausted. Every autumn I used to hope that Kay and I could talk it over and invent a better system, but in the end every moving day was like every other one.

As I say, I could feel it all coming over me again as I got up that morning. It was time to start getting organized, time to do all the things that we had meant to do all summer. Kay was still in bed, but she was awake. She pushed her hair out of her eyes and sighed when I got up.

"Harry," Kay called when I was shaving, "please don't whistle. I'm trying to think."

"I'm trying to think too," I said. "We've got to get organized, Kay."

"Get organized for what, for heaven's sakes?"

"For getting back to town," I told her. "I suppose you'll be going down with Ellen on about the twelfth."

"Yes," Kay said, "but let's not talk about it now, Harry."

"If we just went over it beforehand," I said, "and if you could make me a list of what you wanted brought back in the car, we wouldn't all be mixed up in the end."

"Jerry will take the heavy things down in his brother's truck," Kay said. "You only have to take the children and the cook in the Packard and Bitsey and the electric iron and the electric toaster."

"We don't need to have great stacks of junk piled up in the car," I said.

"Has the car ever been hurt by anything that's been put in it?" Kay asked.

"Kay," I said, "there isn't any reason to get excited about it. If we just arranged it all in time — "

"Let's not talk about it now," Kay said. "Let's not always be so boring, Harry."

"I don't see that it's boring," I told her, "to try to make a few consistent plans."

"Oh, Harry," Kay said, "please! No sooner do we get settled here than we have to think about moving back. We're always moving and we never get anywhere."

"But everybody we know always moves from the country to the city and back," I said.

"That's just it," Kay answered. "I'm tired of being everybody. And why do I have to be waked up to discuss every simple little detail?"

"I haven't done anything wrong, have I, Kay?" I asked.

"No," Kay answered, "no, no, no! Just go down and get your breakfast and ask Ellen to come up here. I think I'll have my breakfast in bed."

I knew it was a mood of Kay's. It was the reaction after that long week end of entertaining Bill. Bill was so restless that he was tiring; sometimes he even made me tired.

"Just as soon as I've had some coffee," she said, "I'll be all right."

XXX

They Possibly Might Start Talking

I had been telling myself for quite a while that I ought to have a
talk with my sister Mary, and North Harbor during my vacation was the place to do it, for Jim would be back in town working
and he wouldn't interrupt us. It was something that I didn't much
want to do, but I was the one to do it. I was not greatly disturbed
by anything that Kay had said. I certainly had not gathered the
idea from Jim or from anyone else, and yet I did have the impression that people were talking about Mary. All that summer whenever I had wanted Mary for anything she had always seemed to
be at the Riding School, and there had been talk before about
Mr. Rigal who ran the place. It was simply that he wasn't the
sort of person that one had for a friend. It was all very well to
sit on his veranda up by the stables, but not many people asked
Rigal to dinner, although Rigal was always careful to point out
that he had come from an old Dorsetshire hunting family and that
he knew everyone in his county back at home. The first time I had
seen him at Mary's house having cocktails it had not really bothered
me; it was only when I saw him on a second occasion that something made me think that he had been around there a good deal.
It was not because Mary called him "Rig." It was rather in the
way he passed things, and when Mary had sent him out to the
pantry for more ice cubes, Rig had known exactly how to get
into the pantry without being told. Of course it was simply that
Mary had not thought, but I did think that I might speak to her
about it, so I called her up as soon as I had finished breakfast.

It was always pleasant to hear her voice. It was always clear and strong and it always made me wish that she and Jim and Kay and I got on better together.

"Are you out of bed?" she called over the telephone. "Are you cured?"

I told her I was feeling fine, that I just wanted to see her.

"If it's about those estate papers," she called, "Jim took them with him."

I told her it wasn't about the papers. I just wanted to see her.

"Well, it's a tough time to see me," Mary said. "There was a big party here last night and somebody broke three of Jim's dinosaurs. Jim's going to have a fit."

"I shan't blame him," I said.

"Well, come on over, darling. I'd love to see you."

When Mary and the executors and I were making the division after Mother's death, we had agreed to sell Westwood and the house on Marlborough Street as places too cumbersome for either of us to handle, particularly after what had happened to the trust estate. At the time, Mary and Jim had both wanted the house near the point at North Harbor. It puzzled me that Mary was so fond of it and that Jim liked it, as it was big and rather ugly. My memory of it, and the way it looked now, always made the house confusing, for Father and Mother and I never seemed to have left it entirely. I asked Mary once if none of this ever bothered her and she surprised me by saying that she rather liked it.

"We used to have a darned good time here," she said. "I like to be with it still."

I imagine that she was always a happier person than I. All I could remember of the house were awkward moments; and what I could never get away from was a memory of the time when I came there from New York, just before I told Marvin Myles that I loved her. Marvin Myles had never seen the house, and yet I always associated it with her, because I had wanted to take her there. I had imagined her in the halls so often and on the porch. I had thought that she would like it. Perhaps that was why I never wanted to go back there. It always gave me a guilty feeling

339

that I was not being exactly fair to Kay, although of course this was absurd.

It seemed to me when I opened the front door — I never liked to ring the bell, since it used to be our house — that I was beginning already to go back and to think of things as they might have been before either Mary or I was married, when we could look forward into a mysterious future. I could hear the vacuum cleaner going behind the closed doors of the living room. The damp salt breeze was blowing through the hall.

"Mary," I called just the way I used to call her, "where are you?"

She came running down the stairs, dressed in riding breeches and boots and a polo shirt, her hair done straight in a "page boy" cut.

"Hello," I said, "are you going riding?"

"I give you three guesses," Mary said. "Why don't you come too? Rig can lend you some boots and breeches up at the stable. You're just about Rig's size."

"I can't today," I said. "I'm just trying to wind things up. You don't have to go right away, do you?"

"Why, no," Mary said. "Let's go out on the porch."

"You'll catch cold in that shirt," I said.

I wanted to see her where we would not be overheard, so I asked if we couldn't go into Father's old study. Of course the study was Jim's room now, but Mary had left some of Father's stuffed birds on the wall and the four-pound trout he had caught. I had always wanted that trout. I had even thought of asking Mary for it, but if she had given it to me I should not have known what to do with it. Mary and I sat down on the sofa in front of the fireplace and I saw that there was a whole row of china and clay and ivory dinosaurs upon the mantelpiece.

"There you are," Mary said, "more of those damned things of Jim's — jade ones, china ones, clay ones, and there's one made out of soap, and there's his latest made out of a piece of toast. I wish to goodness Jim's Club had some other symbol. I'd like to smash them all."

340

"Now, Mary," I said, "Jim naturally thinks a lot of his dinosaurs."

"Well," Mary answered, "I think it's arrested development."

I had not come to talk about Jim. In fact, I never approved of talking about Jim with Mary.

Mary slapped her hand on my knee and smiled at me.

"Gosh," she said, "it's nice to see you! Even at half-past ten in the morning, even when I have a hangover. That party last night started before Jim went to the Junction and it went right on."

"You ought not to do that sort of thing, Mary," I said.

"Now, listen," Mary answered. "I love to have you tell me things, but you know I hold my liquor. How's Kay?"

"Kay?" I repeated. "Kay's fine."

"She certainly was stepping out all week end."

"She was awfully nice," I said, "looking after Bill. She's sort of tired this morning. You know Bill — he sort of gets you down."

"What?" Mary said.

"You know the way Bill is. He sort of gets you down," I repeated.

Mary took a cigarette out of a box on a little table and tapped it on her red thumbnail. I always wished that Mary did not have so much color on her nails.

"I should have gone to see you," she said. "I didn't know you were sick until yesterday, dear."

"Well, I'm feeling all right now," I said. Mary lighted her cigarette and threw the match into the fireplace. It fell on the carpet and I got up and kicked it onto the hearth and sat down again.

"Harry," Mary asked, "you're not here because you've had a row with Kay or something?"

"Now, look here, Mary," I said. "Have I ever had a row with Kay?"

"No," she said, "I don't suppose so, but then why are you here at half-past ten in the morning?"

"It's just that we don't seem to see much of each other," I said. "You're my sister, aren't you?"

"Darling," Mary said, "please sit down, and don't twist up your

341

face. You wouldn't say that if something weren't bothering you."

"Well, it really isn't anything," I said, and I sat down beside her. "It's just that we know more about each other in some ways than anybody else. I always feel responsible for you, because I'm fond of you."

Mary sighed and threw her cigarette in the fireplace. Like the match it fell upon the carpet.

"Never mind the damned thing," Mary said. "Don't keep bobbing up," but I got up and kicked it onto the hearth and stepped on it. "Sit down. I feel responsible for you too. I used to feel responsible when you spilled at table and when you went to the war and when you brought that Myles girl home."

"Never mind about me," I said. "Mary, you don't want people to talk, do you?"

"Darling," Mary said, "sit down. What are people talking about now?"

"It isn't really anything," I said. "I don't think anybody really has, but don't you think you're seeing a little too much of Rigal? I mean, it's fine you're going to the Riding School, but you're always sort of riding with him, aren't you?"

I had only seen her angry once or twice. At such times her face would lose all its expression and become "dead pan," as the current phrase has it. Now it was like a bad photograph. She sat absolutely still, staring at the fireplace, and I was afraid that she was going to put a lot of words into my mouth that I had never said or intended.

"Mary," I said, "don't get mad. Of course there isn't anything in it."

Then her cheeks grew red. She looked all right again, but she had difficulty speaking. She started to speak and stopped and cleared her throat.

"I wish you weren't always so damned decent," she said. "You've always been so sweet to me."

It did not seem to me that I was being either decent or sweet, saying something which hurt her.

"I'm not mad," she said. "I don't mind telling you. There is something in it."

"Good God," I said. "Why, Mary!"

I tried to remember what Rigal looked like. I tried to tell myself that I must not be stuffy and provincial.

"Mary," I began, "you haven't — " I felt that I was blushing.

"Slept with him?" Mary asked.

"Good Lord, Mary!" I told her. "I never said anything like that."

"Well, I haven't, dear," Mary said. "Now are you feeling better?"

I told myself that it was unfair to feel so completely relieved.

"It wasn't what I meant at all," I said. "I was just going to ask if you'd told Jim."

"Told Jim?" Mary repeated.

"Well," I said, "perhaps you ought to."

"Well, I haven't," Mary said, "and I won't."

Perhaps she should have, but I was glad she hadn't.

"As long as it's this way, you ought not to see so much of him, Mary."

Mary looked a good deal the way Kay had sometimes after I had said something that I had not intended to be amusing.

"Sometimes," Mary said, "I seem so much older than you."

"It doesn't do any good to start on that," I answered. "There are some things that people like you and me don't do — that's all."

"Darling," Mary asked me, "what do you know about what people do?"

"I know that a girl like you — a nice girl — shouldn't be playing around with Rigal."

"Has it ever occurred to you," Mary asked, "that married people can't just stay in love with each other always?"

"You've got to cut it out with Rigal," I said. "He isn't even a gentleman."

"That's just it. Maybe I've seen too many gentlemen," and she began to smile. "Rig doesn't need me, but he wants me. Did you ever hear anyone say that a woman's desire is to be desired?"

"Look here, Mary. Don't say things like that."

"I'll tell you something else about Rig," Mary said. "He doesn't collect dinosaurs. He collects women, and it's mighty pleasant for a change."

"I always knew he wasn't a gentleman," I said.

"That's what I mean. If you could ever stop being a gentleman and if I could ever stop being a lady — but we haven't got the guts to be anything else, have we? Darling, we were overtrained."

She stopped. She seemed to be curious as to what I would answer, and I answered nothing.

"That's it." She put her hand on my knee. "We haven't got the guts. We won't do anything that's really wrong, because our inhibitions will stop us, darling. You don't have to worry about me and anyone like Rig. It's all too late. If I had the guts I'd run off with him and see what it was like, but don't worry. All I'll do is to think about it. And when Rig makes too big a pass I'll ask him how he could ever have thought such a thing and I'll cut him dead."

"Mary," I said, "it doesn't do any good to go on."

She threw her head back and laughed. Mary was essentially an awfully nice person.

"You feel better about it now, don't you?"

"I wish you wouldn't talk that way," I said.

"But you do feel better. You had a moment's doubt. I'm awfully glad you had. Harry, I wish you'd tell me something, just between you and me. Harry," — she smiled at me, — "did you ever sleep with anyone besides Kay?"

I took my hands out of my pockets and rubbed them carefully on my knees.

"That's none of your business," I said, "and I refuse to answer it one way or the other."

"There!" Mary said. "That means you have. When was it? Please, please, tell me, Harry."

"It had nothing whatsoever to do with Kay," I said, "and I refuse to answer it one way or the other."

"Harry, I'm awfully glad."

344

"Now, look here, Mary," I said, and I got up. "I've never looked at anyone since I've married Kay."

"No," Mary said, "I didn't say that. Who was it? I'm going to guess."

"No, you're not. I'm going now."

"Oh, please don't," Mary said, "just when we've begun to have a good time. What about Kay? Has Kay ever looked at anyone else?"

"Kay?" I said, and the idea made me laugh.

For a moment Mary did not see the humor of it.

"What about Bill King?" she asked.

"Why, Bill King's my best friend. Don't be so silly, Mary."

Then Mary was laughing too, and she threw her arms around me.

"Oh, Harry," she said, "I hope you'll always stay like this. I hope to God you will."

I got home at a quarter before one, in time to find George throwing a tennis ball up on the roof and catching it when it came back. Kay was in the living room with a pad and pencil.

"Hello," she called. "I'm beginning to think about putting things away. I'm going to take down some of the curtains tomorrow and you and Jerry can wrap them up. Harry, where have you been?"

"Just over to see Mary," I said.

"Why?" Kay asked, and her voice had a little edge to it. "What did Mary want to see you about?"

"Nothing," I said. "I just dropped over to see her. Are we going anywhere to lunch?"

"No," Kay said. "Harry, I've just been telephoning. I'm going down on the tenth. I've got the cleaning women — and you can leave on the morning of the thirteenth. Is that all right?"

"That's fine," I said. "I've got to be back at the office on the fourteenth." And then I went up to my dressing room to listen to the news broadcast before lunch.

XXXI

Yoicks — and Away

It was a busy time as it always was — getting ready to go away. It was the time when one came most in contact with those people whom we called the "natives." Since North Harbor had been a summer resort for almost two generations the natives now lived off all the rest of us in many different ways. Father had always made it a point, and so had I, to be friendly with them and to make that friendship a part of the summer life. When it came time to go away, I had to have a number of talks with Mr. Alfred Boost, who was our general contractor. Everyone used to say that Mr. Boost was a fine Down East character who could turn his hand to everything, and this was true if you personally checked everything to which he turned his hand. It was necessary to show Mr. Boost all the valves for turning off the water. Then I found myself climbing up on the roof with him to show him about new flashings and how to get the dead leaves out of the gutter. Then Mr. Boost brought in Mr. Meigs, the painter, who called me "Harry" because he used to know me as a boy.

Mr. Meigs told me that he had once read in a trade magazine that it was the duty of a good house painter to tell his clients frankly just what work needed to be done; and so Mr. Meigs told me frankly that the whole exterior of the house should be repainted for three hundred and fifty dollars if I wanted to save any of it. He knew it was a lot of money, but it was better than having the whole house rot away. When I pointed out to him that he had painted the whole outside of the house two years before, Mr. Meigs said that no matter what quality of paint was used the salt air would peel it. I could see for myself how it was peeling already.

Mr. Boost said that Mr. Meigs was perfectly right about the salt air. If you lived by the sea you had to pay for it. In Mr. Boost's opinion all the chimneys should be repointed and it was about time to put on a whole new roof. Of course the present roof could be patched up, but we would always run the risk — Mr. Boost usually got down to the collective pronoun — of having ugly inside leaks, and then where would we be? I knew what had happened to Mr. Frear's house last winter, didn't I? Now, Mr. Frear was a fine man and he wouldn't say anything against him, but I knew and he knew that Mr. Frear was tight with his money. As a result Mr. Frear had lost two ceilings and a wall, although Mr. Boost had warned him. Now Mr. Boost knew very well that Mrs. Pulham and I were not that kind of people. We were the kind of people who wanted our house tight and shipshape. He and Mr. Meigs had been having a talk about it. Mr. Boost hadn't wanted to say that we needed a new roof, because he was afraid that I would think he was looking for business. Mr. Meigs told Mr. Boost that it was only friendly to tell me about it and he wanted to be friends with the summer people. New roofing would cost five hundred dollars.

Then Mr. Mack who ran the nursery came around. Mr. Mack said that he loved trees and that he knew I loved them. He had looked after our trees so long that they were like friends. Only God, he said, could make a tree, and he often thought that trees were God's most perfect work. Mr. Mack wasn't much on religion, but he felt that he was helping Our Creator when he and his boys were up in the trees getting the parasites out of the bark, and it made him feel good always, on long winter evenings, when he knew that the trees, his trees, were storing up health and energy out of a good dose of patented fertilizer inserted around their roots, and he knew I felt the same way about it, because the Pulhams loved their trees. He and the boys weren't very busy now and they could fix every tree on the place for four hundred and fifty dollars. I may not have noticed the lawn either, Mr. Mack said;

the sea air was awfully hard on turf. What the lawn needed was a good hand weeding and a fine lot of leaf mold rolled into it. Mr. Mack and the boys could do that too since they weren't busy for only a hundred-dollar bill.

Then Mr. Boost took me aside, about another matter that he wanted to discuss in private, not in front of Mrs. Pulham. He had noticed that the toilet in the downstairs lavatory was getting noisy. He knew the way it was. He had children himself and children were hard on toilets. A whole new outfit installed by him and decorated by Mr. Meigs would only cost me two hundred and seventy-five dollars and now was the time to do it before it was too late. This all meant a long period of discussion since Kay wanted it one way and I wanted it another and Mr. Boost and Mr. Meigs and Mr. Mack had ideas of their own. As usual, Kay and I would start arguing in front of them and sometimes Mr. Mack took her side and Mr. Boost took mine and then before I knew it they would all shift around.

Then Kay and Ellen began getting together the essential articles which would have to go in the car when I drove it down, piling them up in the front hall. I pointed out that Jerry was bringing down a truck and Kay pointed out that there were some things that were too delicate to go in a truck and I said what I had often said — that the Packard was not a truck. Then Ellen brought out the ice-cream freezer. We had been dealing with the ice-cream freezer for the past five years. Kay said it was getting pretty rickety and Jerry would break it if he put it in the truck. I said it couldn't go in the Packard with the children and the cook and the dog. I said we ought to have two freezers and if we didn't have one in town that I would buy one. Kay said she was trying to save me money, that we weren't millionaires, and at least we could save on an ice-cream freezer. I said it wasn't any saving if the car was wrecked and Kay told me that we would have to start saving somewhere.

It was all building up to the sort of climax with which I was familiar. When Kay and Ellen left to open the house in town there was a lull, but it was like a lull before a storm. There was no place to sit, there was nothing to do when Kay was gone. A day seemed like a week and another day seemed like a month. I called her up each evening to ask how everything was going. The first evening Kay said that it was all right and dictated to me a list of things to do. The second evening Ellen answered the telephone and said that Kay was out.

I found myself trying to interpret Kay to Gladys and George, so that I seemed to be two people.

"Your mother wouldn't want you to take those dungarees to town," I told them.

Then George and Gladys would interpret Kay to me. It seemed that Kay had distinctly told them that they were to bring all the odds and ends in the house.

"You don't understand," George would say. "Mother distinctly told me."

"Well, your mother isn't here now," I told George. "You'll do what I say."

"All right," George said. "Just don't blame me. That's all. I can't help it, can I, if Mother distinctly told me?"

The cook and the other maid and Mrs. Meigs and her daughter began wrapping the furniture in sheets on the last day, and rolling up the rugs and wrapping the andirons in newspapers and Jerry began loading the truck and I began loading the Packard. Kay had given me a list of what to leave out if it was absolutely necessary. Even when I added a good deal more to the list there was no room for the cook, so I arranged with a taxi to take her to the Junction for the evening train. George and Gladys and the dog and I would leave early in the morning — I told them so at supper. We were each having a chop and a glass of milk and a baked potato. That was all the food there was left in the house except a little something for breakfast.

"Now, listen," I said, "we're going to do this right tomorrow morning. You, George, and you, Gladys, are both old enough to pack your own suitcases without bothering anyone. We're all going to turn out at six. We're going to get through before there's any traffic. Remember, six in the morning."

They looked at me blankly.

"Mother distinctly said that she didn't want us to come too early," George told me. "Six o'clock is awful early."

"It will do you good," I said. "Now, don't argue."

"Where are we going to have lunch?" Gladys asked.

"I don't know," I told her, "somewhere. You always get car-sick if you eat too much."

"Gee, boss," George said, "not six o'clock in the morning! Mother distinctly said — "

"Don't argue," I told him.

"Gee, boss," George said, "there isn't any reason to be sore."

"I'm not sore," I said. "I'm just telling you."

"Well, it isn't my fault," George said.

That had been a favorite phrase of George's for some time. I told him it was not anybody's fault; it was just life. I told him I didn't enjoy moving any more than he did, but sometime when he grew up he would have to do the same thing, provided there was any money left when he grew up. I told George and Gladys that they were pretty lucky, that lots of children were starving to death, and here they were going for a nice ride tomorrow to the city! It ought to be fun for them, it used to be fun for me when I was a kid. Then I wondered to myself if it had been.

When the children went to bed, I walked through the pantry and the kitchen, looking for an alarm clock. A tap on the laundry tubs was leaking, but it made no difference now, since Mr. Boost would turn off the water in the morning. I found a clock on the top of the icebox and brought it upstairs to my room and I brought Bitsey up with me too and let him sleep on the foot of Kay's bed. I turned on the radio while I was packing, but pretty soon I turned it off because the news was terrible. Then I opened the window and looked out. It was getting cloudy and a breeze was coming up from the northeast.

Then I got into bed and started in on *The Education of Henry*

350

Adams. Instead of finishing it on my vacation as I had intended, what with one thing or another I had only done about twenty pages. Kay always seemed to interrupt me just when I was in the middle of a paragraph and now, without her, I seemed to expect I would be interrupted. I was wondering whether I had actually been weak with Mr. Boost in letting him rip out all the plumbing in the downstairs lavatory. Although it was all very well to give work to the natives in hard times, it occurred to me that Mr. Boost went down to Daytona Beach every winter with his wife and mother-in-law and two daughters, which was more than I ever did. I suddenly found, while I was thinking, that I had read five pages of *Henry Adams* without knowing what it was about. When I tried to begin again I was too sleepy to get on with it.

When I finally went to sleep, it was a sort of rest which did not do much good. In the back of my mind there must have been a feeling that tomorrow would be a trying day, that Gladys would stand more than an even chance of being overcome with nausea. The trouble with Gladys was that she would never say anything about it until it was too late. It would be up to me to watch her while I was driving the car, but maybe George could do it. All the other times that I had moved from North Harbor, from childhood on, gathered cloudily about me in a queer dreamlike confusion. I remembered the things Father had said when the lid of a trunk went down on his fingers and how Hugh had sat down hard when a trunk strap had broken. And when I went to sleep, the ice-cream freezer came into it. I dreamed that Kay was walking to Boston, carrying the ice-cream freezer on her head and saying that it was all right, that it was really economical.

Then the alarm clock was ringing. It was one of those clocks that started with a whisper and ended with what its maker called "a cheerful good-morning shout." I had put it somewhere across the room so that I would be sure to get up to turn it off when it rang, and now I stumbled about trying to control it. It was dusky and cold and it was raining. I went into the hall and began knocking on the children's doors. Gladys was up and dressed already with

351

her hat and coat on. Her bag was closed and she was holding a candy box with holes punched in the top.

"What have you got in there?" I asked.

"Spiders," Gladys said.

"Well, let them out," I said. "We've got enough to bother with without a lot of spiders."

Gladys looked as though she were about to cry.

"It's part of my Natural History," she said.

I wished that Kay were there.

"All right," I said, "but don't tell your mother."

I never knew a boy who could sleep like George. I had to shake him and half pull him out of bed and then he began to complain. He said it was raining. I told him I didn't give a damn if it was — he ought to get used to taking it. I told him it was like the war; it always rained in the war.

"But we're not going to the war," George said. "We're going to Boston."

"Never mind," I said. "It's like the war to me."

I had always believed in assuming that a motor trip with the children would be pretty bad, but actually that trip was worse. I was stopped by a state trooper outside of Portland and then Gladys was sick. I picked up a nail outside of Saco and had to get out and change the tire. I tried to be nice to the children, but they began to wear me down. They began playing alphabet games and picking letters off the signs; then, when Gladys went to sleep, George began telling of his social triumphs among his own contemporaries. I tried to be as nice as I could about it. The one thing I wanted was to get to Boston and to get a hot bath and a drink, but I kept telling myself that I was fond of the children.

"When are we going to have lunch?" Gladys kept asking.

"Yes," George kept saying, "when are we going to get lunch? There's a Dixie stand. . . . There's a Tootsie stand. . . . Let's have lunch at Joe's Place. . . . Let's have lunch at Daddy and Ann's. . . .

352

Let's have some fried clams. Say, boss, don't you want some nice fried clams?"

In the slightly fetid air of the closed car, the thought of fried clams made me ill.

"We'll be at home in time for you to get something there," I said.

"Oh, gosh almighty," George shouted, "we don't want to eat at home."

"Don't yell at me," I shouted back. "You'll eat at home and like it."

We got home at half-past twelve, still in the driving rain. I was wet from changing the tire and I was tired. The first thing to do was to get the children inside, then to unload the car. I found my keys and opened the front door, and when I did so, I felt a great sense of peace. I seemed to have been through a good deal and now life could begin again, the steady, sensible life of autumn and winter. Tomorrow I would be back at the office and I could start in again with squash. The house was fresh and clean, solid and comfortable. Ellen hurried into the hall.

"Why, Mr. Pulham," she said, "we didn't expect you till evening."

"We started early," I said. "It's a great idea to get it over with."

Gladys was running upstairs quickly with her spiders before anyone could see them. I was telling George to take Bitsey around the corner. Ellen was saying there wasn't any food in the house. Then I heard Kay calling down the stairs.

"Harry," she called, "why on earth did you come so early? Why didn't you call up?"

Her voice was sharp. I suppose I should have called her up. When I hurried upstairs, Kay was in the hall in front of the living room.

"I had a hell of a time," I said. "We picked up a nail outside of Saco and then Gladys was sick."

"Well, you might have telephoned," Kay said. "Bill's here."

"What?" I said.

"Bill's here," Kay said. "He was just going to take me to the Ritz."

353

Then Bill came out of the parlor, and I was awfully glad to see him.

"Why, Bill," I said, "where did you drop from?"

Bill smiled.

"I'm indispensable," he said. "When the boys need me, I just drop everything. Harvard — rah-rah — Harvard!"

"What are you talking about?" I asked.

"The Play Committee," Bill said. "The Twenty-fifth Reunion. Our old friend Bo-jo Brown, he got me."

"Bo-jo?" I repeated. "Bo-jo said he didn't want you."

"Maybe he didn't," Bill said, "but he wants me now."

Then Kay was speaking.

"It's pretty nice of Bill to come away up for that," she said.

"Why, yes," I said, "it's wonderful. It's mighty good of you, Bill, to give them the time."

"Somebody had to do it," Bill said. "Who else could they get? What are you laughing about?"

"And you always said the Class gave you a pain!" I said. Just seeing Bill there had made me laugh.

"Harry," Kay said, "Bill and I were going out to lunch. It's sort of mean of us running away, but you didn't telephone."

"Oh, that's all right," I said. "You go ahead and I'll take the kids out somewhere and then we can all have dinner, can't we?"

"Harry," Kay said, "what *are* you laughing at?"

"I just can't get over it," I said, "Bill's getting himself roped into the Reunion!"

I stopped, because Kay looked at me. It was one of those looks that meant that she would take up what I had said sometime later and would ask me how I could possibly have been so rude and stupid. I stopped, though I could not see what on earth I had said that was disturbing, except that I may have sounded a little forced and flat, because I was overtired and wet. Nevertheless, when I looked at Bill, I knew that I had certainly put my foot in it. I had always thought that Bill was able to stand a lot of good-natured give and take, and I had never minded — indeed, I had rather liked

354

it — when Bill used to put me over the jumps in front of Kay. Yet Bill had a peculiar expression, not exactly annoyed, but as though he were really worried about what I might say next, when all I had done was to intimate that Bill was not particularly loyal to his Class. I still could not see what was wrong with it, since Bill had gone out of his way for nearly twenty years to make gibes at class spirit and at all our classmates who tried to do their part in making things go when we got together. It all made me feel confused, as though I had not come into my house at all, but into someone else's.

"What have I done now?" I asked.

Then Bill laughed, as though he had seen the joke for the first time.

"All you've done is get home in time for lunch," he said. "You're coming with us, aren't you?"

It was all right as soon as Bill began to laugh.

"No, no," I said, "you go ahead. Somebody's got to feed the kids and I've got to get the things out of the car. I'll take them somewhere down the street. No, no, you and Kay go ahead."

"You don't think it's mean of us, do you?" Kay asked.

Making so much of going out to lunch began to make me a little impatient. I did not see why Bill and Kay seemed to be underlining everything, as though we weren't old friends.

"Of course it isn't mean of you, Kay," I said. "Now let's not bother about it. By the way, I brought the ice-cream freezer. It's tied on in back."

"What ice-cream freezer?" Kay asked.

It surprised me that she seemed to have forgotten all about the ice-cream freezer, when we had been all over it only three days before.

"What ice-cream freezer?" I repeated. "Why, *the* ice-cream freezer, that one we argue about every year. You don't mean to say you've forgotten all about it?"

"Oh!" Kay said, and she looked as though she remembered. "That was awfully sweet of you, darling. Did you all have a good time while I was away?"

"No," I said. "Come back pretty soon, won't you? The kids are sort of getting in my hair. I don't see how women stand it."

"You're sure you don't mind?" Bill said.

"Mind?" I repeated. "Haven't I been telling you, Bill, I don't mind? I think it's swell! You can have the car as soon as I take the things out — and give Kay a good lunch. She deserves it."

"I'll help you unload the car," Bill said.

It was nice of him to offer to do it, because Bill had never cared much about useful manual labor and he had on a navy blue pin-striped suit all nicely pressed.

"Oh, no," I said, "this isn't your funeral. You're not married."

Then I knew I'd said something else that was dull. I had completely forgotten that Elise was out at Reno and I hadn't meant it that way.

"Boy," Bill told me, "that's the truest thing you ever said. I am less and less married every minute."

"I didn't mean it that way, Bill," I said, and then I saw Kay watching me again.

"Harry," Kay said, "I wish you wouldn't always bear down on everything. Bill, you don't have to help him really. He'll get everything out of the car in just a minute, and Harry knows where everything belongs. Harry loves to pack and unpack cars."

That was what Kay always said when someone else was around. She always said that Harry would love to do it. She was always telling Mrs. Jones or somebody not to let the hired man carry down the trunk or not to let the maid pick up the broken pieces of the goldfish bowl — that Harry would love to do it. She told me once that it was all unconscious on her part, that she only wanted people to see how nice I was. I went downstairs and opened the front door.

"Ellen," I called, "where's Master George?"

She didn't know. He had gone away somewhere, which was not strange, because George always faded out when there was any work. I asked her where the chore-man was, but he was not around anywhere either. I had never known him to be, when anything really had to be done — but after all, I had not telephoned.

I put on my raincoat and my hat and went out to the car. First I unlocked the luggage compartment and hauled out all the suitcases, finally getting into the rhythm of walking from the car and up and down the steps. I piled the suitcases in the hall and then I barked my knuckles on the ice-cream freezer. Then I hauled out a box of assorted canned goods, most of which we had brought up with us five months before, because Kay always wanted to have something in the house in case people dropped in unexpectedly. Then I lifted out a cardboard box, filled with half-empty tins of baking powder and spices and condiments which had been cleaned off the kitchen shelves. I had suggested to Kay that it might be just as well to leave them for Mrs. Meigs, but Kay had said we could use them ourselves — that we ought to try to save money. Halfway across the sidewalk, the bottom fell out of the box, and I had to spend several minutes gathering tins up in my arms. Even when I had finished, the sidewalk was covered with salt and cloves and cocktail wafers. Then I got out my account books and Kay's box of jewelry and George's radio and Gladys' microscope and Bitsey's rubber bone and comb and brush, two boxes of candles, an enema bag, a motion-picture projector, one rubber, a sneaker and three bars of Old Lavender toilet soap. George came up from somewhere down cellar.

"Where in thunder have you been?" I asked. "Why didn't you help me unload the car?"

"Oh," George said, "were you unloading the car, boss? I didn't know it."

"Just who did you think was going to do it?" I asked. "What have you been doing?"

"I was just down trying to find my electric train," George said. "Say, boss, can we go somewhere to get hamburgers?"

I did not answer his question. Instead, I called up the stairs.

"Kay," I called, "the car's all ready now."

Kay came down, in a new coat, with fur around the edge, carrying a brand-new handbag. She looked very pretty and not tired at all. I was surprised that she had found time to do any shopping.

Bill followed her. He might have been coming out of a club car after the porter had brushed him.

"Fast work, boy!" Bill said. "You certainly brought everything except the kitchen stove."

"Harry," Kay said, "what have you done to your face?"

"What's the matter with my face?" I asked her.

"It's all grease and black," Kay said. "You've been rubbing your face with your hands."

Bill laughed.

"Spit on your handkerchief and take it off," he said.

"Say, Mother," George said, "when do we eat?"

"Your father will take you out in just a minute, dear," Kay said, "and Uncle Bill and I will be back pretty soon. We won't be gone long, Harry," and then they were gone.

"Hey, boss," George said, "when do we eat?"

"When we get cleaned up," I told him. "Now go upstairs and get washed and tell Gladys to get washed."

Now that I had arrived, with the car unpacked, North Harbor and the summer were slipping out of focus and blending in with all the summers I had known, and the reality of winter picked me up bodily in its arms. I had a comfortable sense that everything in the hall was in its place. The mirror, the table and the chairs were all fresh and clean, and exactly where they should be. Ellen was already arranging the silver on the sideboard in the dining room — Mother's teaset in the center, ornate and overdecorated, on either side the two enormous *bonbonnières* that used to be on the dining room table in Marlborough Street, and in the back the candelabra and the two knifecases. The decanters were on the low serving table beneath the portrait of Kay's grandfather, old Colonel Motford who fought in the Civil War, and between them was the silver pheasant. I was glad to see that the landscape by Henry Inman, which my grandfather had bought, was back from the gallery, freshly cleaned and varnished. Kay used to say that it was about the most stuffy dining room that anyone could find, that it was like living in someone else's shell; and this was why she had bought the Chinese screen and had put in light curtains, to try and brighten it up. I saw it all in a single glance, the way you see rooms that you know.

The stair carpet was very badly worn. It was one of those furnishings which we were going to change when the children grew up, but I was glad to see that it was all tacked tight. Up in the second-floor hall, the wall paper was dingy. No matter how often Kay and I had told George and Gladys, they always rubbed their hands over it. But the parlor looked splendid. Kay called it our only successful room, for somehow all the possessions we had bought and inherited fitted together. The Persian rug, which came from Kay's mother, was not too large for it and it went well with the Motford armchairs.

The Inness was over the fireplace, a restful canvas of hazy, rolling country. As long as I could remember, Mother and Father had talked about the Inness and it was the only item from the house in Marlborough Street over which Mary and I had argued. We finally had agreed to match for it, three times out of five. The brasses in the fireplace were all freshly shined. The secretary desk that came from the Motfords was waxed and so was Kay's piano, a baby grand. Neither of us was musical, but Kay always said that no room looked well without a piano — so there it was, for Gladys to practise on at two in the afternoon.

There were fresh flowers in the boxes by the windows — cyclamen, ferns and begonias. It was really Kay's room more than mine. Even with Kay out of it, I thought of her walking back and forth in it arranging this and that. The cushions on the chairs and sofas were all neatly plumped out and dusted, except for the sofa near the fireplace, where Kay and Bill must have been sitting when I arrived. One of the pillows had fallen on the floor and there were some cigarette ashes on the carpet. The other pillows were all bashed in.

The library had been cleaned too. As always happened when the cleaning women got at the books, Thackeray was mixed in with Jane Austen and my college textbooks were in with the histories. I would have to straighten them out as soon as I had time, perhaps that afternoon. The flat-topped desk, which Kay had bought me

359

once in England, was covered with all the second-class mail which had accumulated during the summer, mostly charity appeals — for Spanish orphans and blind children and Chinese victims of Japanese aggression and Jewish victims of German aggression and homeless waifs and fallen women and cancer clinics and epileptic clinics. There was never any way to escape from that background of misery, all packed into neat envelopes.

I actually just walked through the parlor and through the library, only a hasty detour on my way upstairs. Our bedroom was in the front of the house, a large room with comfortable twin beds and a chaise longue which nobody ever used, because Kay hated resting, and a highboy that had come from the Motfords and the bureau that had been my father's and the dressing table that I had given Kay. All our tastes were mingled there into a sort of compromise. I was the one who had picked out the water carafe on the table between the beds and I had insisted on having two Currier and Ives prints of early locomotives. Kay was the one who had wanted two pastels of flowers in vases and the flowered chintz window curtains that went with the spread.

Like all the rest of the house, the room was fresh and spotless, silently waiting for Kay and me, although Kay must have slept there. Yet as I looked around, I knew she had not. It was all just as the cleaning women had left it, without any of the little things that Kay always brought with her to change that look. Her silver traveling clock was not on the bedside table. Not even her combs and brushes were on the dressing table. The bag she had taken from North Harbor, the little overnight case I had given her for Christmas the year before last, was not on the chaise longue where she would have tossed it. At first I was only aware of a sterile sort of vacancy. In fact, I did not notice any of this until I had begun to change my clothes. It was just as though someone had played a bar of music that was off key. There was no untidiness — her slippers were not in the closet and her wrapper and dressing gown were not hanging on the hook on the bathroom door. The bathroom was just as impersonal as our bedroom, no toothbrush, no bath salts, no tooth paste. When I knotted my tie in front of the shaving mirror on my bureau I was sure of it. I was the first to come in the room. Kay had not been there.

The radio was playing in the library and George and Gladys were waiting.

"And now you can hear for yourself," a voice was saying, "how Aunt Mamie makes those fluffy cookies that are all full of good rich crunchiness."

"Turn that thing off," I said. "We're going to lunch."

"Well, it's about time," George said.

"Can I have a quarter?" Gladys asked.

"And what do you want a quarter for?" I asked her.

"She wants to buy doll's didies," George said.

"No, I don't," Gladys said. "Shut up!"

Both of them were getting cross and I did not blame them.

"Everybody stop," I said. "Come on."

I was getting cross myself. It was after two o'clock. Ellen was still working in the dining room.

"Ellen," I said, "wasn't Mrs. Pulham here last night?"

Ellen rubbed her hands on her apron.

"No," Ellen said, "she wasn't here, Mr. Pulham. There was so much cleaning going on. She has been spending the nights out in Brookline."

"In Brookline?" I said. "Oh, that's it — she must have been staying with Mr. Guy."

The children were standing behind me with their coats on.

"Come on," I said, "let's go!"

I was glad that Kay had been staying with Guy. She would have been lonely by herself, with only Ellen in the house. Then, as I was opening the door, I saw Kay's suitcase with its canvas cover and with her initials, C. M. P. She had left it under the hall table that morning and had not had time to bring it upstairs. Kay had been awfully busy.

XXXII

Pale Hands I Love

The only place available for luncheon in our neighborhood was the Bob Cratchit Tea Roome and Coffee House, an establishment run by a group of dour-looking ladies who also sold cakes and cookies at the change desk — tea thirty-five cents, luncheon fifty-five cents and dinner seventy-five cents. On the whole, it always seemed to me that the Bob Cratchit Tea Roome was a sensible, nice place, patronized by people who did not care to pay any more for simple wholesome food, and by people like me who were driven there when there was no food at home. In the years since Kay and I had bought our house in town I may have been there four or five times — especially just after George and Gladys had been born — when the house was so filled with trained nurses that either the cook must leave or I must; and once Kay and I had gone there when the boiler at home had exploded. Every time we went, we always remarked that the blue and orange tables were most attractive and that the food was tremendously good, but we never became regular customers.

The girl who took our order said that they were out of beets and out of spinach, that the chicken pie was out, and that the luncheon hour was pretty well over. This was obvious enough, since George and Gladys and I were the only customers, with the exception of a mouse-colored man, who was reading a book on *The Measurements of the Great Pyramid,* and he got up and left by the time our beef stew appeared.

"Gee," George said, "this food is worse than school!"

Gladys did not say anything, but she did not each much. I told

George that it was time for him to cultivate a few thoughtful manners. This was one of the days, I told him, when we all were out of luck. When he grew older, I said, he would find there were lots and lots of times when things did not go right, when you must take them in your stride, making the best of them cheerfully, without griping and bellyaching. I asked him what he would have thought of me and what his mother and everyone else in the house would have thought, if I had begun whining and complaining when I had to unload the car and could not go to the Ritz with Mother and Uncle Bill, because I had to take two little brats out to lunch instead. I thought this example might hold them for a while, but Gladys asked:

"Why couldn't we all have gone to the Ritz?"

For some reason, this was hard to answer, but soon I began to think of a great many very good reasons why we couldn't have, and I pointed them out to Gladys and George while the waitress brought me a pot of stale coffee and brought each of the children a glass of milk flavored with chocolate. In the first place, I said, we could not have gone to the Ritz because Uncle Bill had asked Mother and had not asked us.

"Why didn't he ask us?" George said. "We were all there before they went out, weren't we?"

"He didn't ask us," I said, "because grown people like to be together sometimes and because he didn't want to have lunch with a lot of little brats who make noises with their soup."

"You make noises with your soup. Mother says so," Gladys said. George began to laugh so loudly and immoderately that the ladies behind the cake counter frowned.

"Listen to the boss," George said. "He's making noises with his stew!"

I told George to shut up and behave himself, but Gladys had not lost her train of thought.

"Why couldn't you have taken us to the Ritz?" she asked.

"Oh!" I said. "Why couldn't I have taken you to the Ritz?"

Then I explained to them that it was time for them to learn that most people can not afford to do silly, extravagant things. This lunch here would cost fifty-five cents, whereas lunch at the Ritz would cost two dollars and fifty cents apiece and there would be no large tip here for the service, either, because gratuities were not allowed in the Bob Cratchit Tea Roome. I told them they might as well get it into their heads now as any other time that neither their mother nor I was made of money. We were doing the best we could to keep them dressed and to give them the advantages of an expensive education and this meant that their mother and I had to do without a great many things which we really wanted. They did not seem interested; they ate their stew slowly, but I kept on telling them. I told them they might not know it, but that they were mighty lucky—luckier than ninety-four out of a hundred other children. Here they were, with a comfortable home and comfortable beds, eating a good meal of wholesome stew with lots of fresh milk and bread and butter, when lots of other children right here in town were cold and hungry. Lots of other parents were on the WPA because they could not get a job. They were lucky and instead of knowing it, they wanted to go to the Ritz.

"Why don't you believe in the WPA?" George asked.

It surprised me sometimes, that George was old enough to read the papers.

"Whether I do or not," I said, "the WPA is here, and never mind about it!"

Gladys stared at us with wide, dreamy eyes.

"I thought you didn't like Mr. Roosevelt," she said.

"A lot of people don't like Mr. Roosevelt," I answered, "for a lot of different reasons, but Mr. Roosevelt's here, like the WPA."

"If I wrote Mr. Roosevelt, would he write me?" Gladys asked.

The conversation was making me confused, and convincing me that I had been with George and Gladys for altogether too long a time.

"You write him," I said. "You write him and tell him you're a big girl who still collects spiders, and misspell it, the way you've been taught to misspell at your school, and either Mr. Roosevelt will answer it or Mrs. Roosevelt will. Now both of you shut up! I want to eat."

George and Gladys did not shut up, but they changed the subject. They began to play what is known among progressive educators as "a game of the imagination." It had been amusing when they were younger, but now they were too old for it. Gladys was Mrs. Brown and George was Mr. Brown, and Mrs. Brown was telling Mr. Brown how to pack things in the car and Mr. Brown was complaining. It was a clumsy and humorless parody of Kay and me which made me wonder whether we really appeared that way through our children's eyes. It made me see that they did not know what we were like at all. I could hear their voices going on around me while I sat and ate, and my mind moved away from them.

Since the war had started all over again, I was more conscious than I had ever been of the misery around us. Yet most people I know were removed from it, insulated from all understanding of it, like figures under glass. The awful thing was that there did not seem to be anything much that a person like me could do. I had a feeling, which I had known when I was younger, that I had never really seen the world. I was closer to it there with George and Gladys than I was at the office. It occurred to me that I had been leading two lives — my business life and my private life, which I suppose must be true with everyone. Your business life, your activities and Clubs were what you talked about and put down in a Harvard Class Report.

After leaving Harvard, I was employed by the firm of Smith and Wilding. At the conclusion of the war, I spent a year in New York in the advertising agency of J. T. Bullard. I then returned, rejoined the firm of Smith and Wilding, where I stayed until shortly before its dissolution in 1933. I then formed, with an associate, my own investment counsel service, where I am today.

What was really important were the human contacts I had made. There was my life with Kay and the children, and what did it amount to? As I finished my vanilla ice cream with maple walnut sauce over it and listened to the rain lashing against the windows of Bob Cratchit's Tea Roome, I could not give a very encouraging answer. I began thinking about Dickens' *Christmas Carol*. That work of fiction was read annually to Mary and me from the time we were old enough to listen — and now I had been reading it ever since George and Gladys could listen. I would read it again this Christmas, as a duty, like writing checks for charity appeals, but I could not say that I had ever really appreciated the Cratchit family and Tiny Tim's thin voice joining in the chorus — "God bless us every one." The way the world was going now, Tiny Tim should have been saying, "God help us, every one!"

"Say, boss," George said, "do we have to sit here all afternoon?"

"No," I said. "Let's go."

It was nearly four o'clock and I was arranging books in the library when Kay and Bill got home. They called to me from the hall downstairs and I called back, telling them to come on up. They came in, and sat on the library couch as I worked, and once again, Bill offered to help me, but Kay said he mustn't bother, because there was nothing that I loved better than puttering around arranging books. I told Bill I was sorry that everything was all upset here, but that it would be quieted down by dinnertime.

"You're staying to dinner, aren't you?" I asked.

"No," Bill said, "I'm taking the five o'clock. There's a big conference in the morning. I've got to get some sleep."

That meant he was going away in half an hour and I had hardly seen him at all. If he had only told me that he was leaving so early, I should have let the children have lunch alone and I should have gone with them to the Ritz.

"Go ahead and take the midnight," I said. "I've hardly seen you, Bill."

"You'll see plenty of me," Bill said. "I'll be up for the Yale game. That isn't so far off now."

"You'll stay with us, won't you, Bill?" I asked.

"That would be swell," Bill said, and he looked at his wrist watch. He was worrying about the train already.

He seemed preoccupied as he sat in the library beside Kay. That conference must have been on his mind, and somehow it kept us from reaching the common basis that we always had before.

"Come on," I said again, "and go on the midnight, Bill."

"No," Bill said. "But I'll be up for the game. It was just an accident that I came this time, anyway. I thought you were still up in Maine."

"Yes," Kay said. "He just happened to call up and the telephone was just connected."

"It's good luck you called before Kay went out to Brookline," I said.

It seemed to me like a perfectly casual remark, but from the way Kay looked, I must have been tactless again. Just for a second I wondered if she had not wanted me to know, for some reason, that she had been in Brookline. Then I knew that this was absurd.

"Brookline?" Kay said. "Oh, yes, I meant to tell you. The house was all torn up; the beds weren't made."

"It certainly was torn up," Bill said. "I'm afraid I've been an awful nuisance butting in."

"No, you haven't, Bill," I said. "Everything's organized now. I wish you'd take the midnight."

Bill got up. He had a vague, distracted look.

"The midnight?" he said. "No, I couldn't do that. I've got to go to the office and go over my mail. I have to digest a report." Then he smiled. "That's a funny way of putting it, isn't it? Digesting a report? Well, I'll see you soon, Harry. Good-by. Good-by, Kay."

"Wait a minute, Bill," I said. "I'll take you to the station."

"Oh, no," Bill answered, "don't do that. You've had enough of a beating today."

"Oh, no, Bill," Kay said, "Harry would love to take you to the station." And Kay gave me a little push and a meaning glance.

"No, you don't," Bill said. "I'll get a taxi on the corner. I've got to pick up my bags. Good-by, Harry. Good-by, Kay."

I went down to the door with him.

"But you will be up for the game?" I said.

"Up for the game, or sooner," Bill answered. "So long."

When I came upstairs again, Kay was still sitting in the library, looking at the piles of books on the floor.

"Why didn't you take Bill to the station?" she asked.

"Because he didn't want me to," I said. "Kay, that's an awfully pretty dress you have. I've never seen it before."

I had been afraid that we would have an argument about the station, but Kay looked pleased.

"It is pretty, isn't it?" she said. "I've decided to take more trouble about my clothes and I'm going down to New York shopping the first of the month."

"Well, that's fine," I told her.

All at once everything was better, now that the day was over and the house was nearly settled. We could have a quiet dinner, with nothing to do until tomorrow. I put my hands on Kay's shoulders.

"It's certainly swell to have the moving over," I said, "and to be back here, just you and me."

"Why, Harry!" Kay said, and she actually blushed. "Do you like it as much as that?"

"Yes," I said, "of course."

"Well," Kay said, "don't kiss me now. There isn't time. Let's pick up the books."

I started arranging the Thackeray on the shelves.

"Can you hand me Volume II of *Pendennis*?" I asked. "We ought to read *Pendennis* aloud sometime. . . . You know there's one thing I never thought about."

"What?" Kay asked.

"How awful it must be sleeping in this place, when you're moving in," I said. "I'm awfully glad you went to Brookline. Who did you stay with, Kay?"

"Oh, Harry," Kay said, "never mind about it now. I'll tell you all about it, but let's get the room picked up."

And then the telephone rang and Kay ran into the parlor to answer it.

"There we go!" she called. "There's the telephone! Everything's starting all over."

I have often wondered what life would be like without a telephone, or even a day without its steady and insistent interruption. I understood just what Kay meant when she said that everything was starting all over. There would be the same quick, heated conferences, held in an undertone while the receiver was off in the other room.

"It's the Joneses. They want us to dinner."

"Do we have to go?"

"They're your friends and not my friends."

"They're not my friends any more than they are yours."

"I thought you always liked it at the Joneses'."

"Of course I do, but I don't like to have to think of it all at once."

It was necessary to make your mind up quickly when the telephone was ringing.

"It's the man who wants to kill all the mice in the house."

"Which man?"

"I don't know which. There aren't two, are there, who kill mice?"

"Yes, there are. One does mice and cockroaches together and the other does just mice."

"Well, I can't help it, Harry. He wants to talk to you. He's been calling up all day."

"Well, tell him I've just gone out."

"Harry, you've got to talk to him. You've got to get it over with."

There was no way of getting away from the telephone, but perhaps it helped to keep your mind alert. Suddenly, without ever knowing when, you would have to shift from *The Education of Henry Adams* to chatting about clean, safe methods of killing vermin or the problem of whether you wanted a little life insurance, or whether you wanted a vacuum cleaner, or Virginia hams, or a case of Florida grapefruit, or whether you would like

369

to be an end man in a minstrel show for the benefit of the Little Wanderers' Settlement House.

On this occasion the call was no problem of mine. It was Susy Prohill, an old school friend of Kay's, who wanted to know if Kay was going to join the Social Science class. It had always seemed to me that if Kay had read the Sunday supplements, she would have found out for herself everything that Miss Reisit gleaned from interesting books and contemporary periodicals, but Kay said that Miss Reisit had a vital and universal mind. I could hear her discussing the details as I kept on rearranging the books.

She sighed and slumped down heavily in a chair when she had finished.

"Oh, Lord," she said, "it was the Social Science class."

"But you've always said it was interesting," I said.

"Oh?" Kay said. "Do you think it's interesting to hear a lot of girls comment on a lot of things they don't know anything about?"

"But they're your friends," I said.

"That's just what you would say," Kay answered. "I wish that sometimes, just once in a while, we could ever see people we haven't always known."

"Strangers?" I said. "They're harder to get on with."

"Oh, Lord," Kay said, "that puts your whole philosophy in a nutshell, Harry: always being careful, always being safe, only wanting to see the same people because it isn't any effort, always being dull."

I began to pick up the last of the books, Father's set of Plutarch's *Lives*. I knew that she was tired or she would not have spoken that way, and I suppose I was tired too or I should not have resented it. For some reason nothing that I had done that day was right. Ever since I had arrived, before Kay and Bill had gone out to lunch, there had been something vaguely wrong between us, something in the way she had looked at me, something in the way we had both spoken.

"Maybe I am dull," I told her, "but you've had an interesting day. Bill King isn't dull, is he?"

"What do you mean by that?" Kay asked.

"I don't mean anything, Kay," I answered. "Except I've been being a chauffeur when I haven't been a handyman and a nurse-maid."

"And what do you think I've been," Kay asked, "for years and years and years?"

I picked up two of the Plutarch volumes and got up on a chair and put them on the shelf. Kay was sitting with her hands clenched in her lap, looking back over the years, and I certainly did not want to start going over them.

"Well, you've certainly had time off," I said.

"How do you mean, time off?"

"Well, take today," I said. "You've been having lunch with Bill King." Kay began to speak and I raised my voice. "Now wait a minute, Kay," I said. "I'm not finding any fault. I'm awfully glad you had a good time with Bill, but that doesn't mean I wouldn't have liked to have seen him too. Now, wait and just think if it's fair. I do all the work, and then you complain that I'm dull. Maybe I am, but some people don't think so."

"Why can't you ever let anything go?" Kay asked. "I just make a perfectly casual remark, and then you bring in Bill King for no reason at all. If I had thought for a minute that you minded, I'd have taken all those damned things out of the automobile myself. I'd have taken the children to lunch. You could have gone to lunch with Bill."

It was like so many other quarrels. Now that we were right in the middle of it I could not understand exactly how it had started.

"I didn't say I minded it, Kay," I said. "If Bill's more interest-ing than I am, I can't help it, can I?"

"Then don't keep going on about it," Kay said. "You make an issue out of everything."

"Now, Kay," I told her, "I'm not making an issue out of any-thing. You won't let me finish what I am trying to say."

"You've said it all hundreds of times, thousands of times. You're right and I'm wrong. You're sweet and patient, and — "

"Kay," I said, "please let's stop," and I closed the door into the hall. I suppose I shouldn't have, because of course it made her angry, since it implied that she had lost her temper and that I hadn't.

"Open that door," Kay said. "Don't try to make a scene."

"Kay," I said, "please, let's stop."

Kay drew a deep, harsh breath, and we both stopped, and there was something that was sad in the silence. I could hear the clock on my desk ticking and noises in the back yards. It was beginning to grow dark and I pressed the light switch for the table and desk lamps.

"My God," Kay said, "I wonder why we ever got married."

We had said it all before. We had wondered before, again and again, why we had ever got married.

I was holding Volume III of Plutarch's *Lives*. It seemed to me that its binding was getting shaky, though goodness knows, I had hardly looked at Plutarch since I was in college. I opened the book, and two leaves of writing paper fluttered onto the carpet.

"Why, it's a letter," Kay said. She picked up a page, and then I remembered. That was where I had kept those two letters from Marvin Myles which I should have burned up long ago. Kay was holding the sheet of paper under the light. Her face had changed. Her voice had changed.

"Why, Harry," she said, "oh, Harry! *It's a love letter!*"

I might have known that she would find out about those letters some day, because Kay always found out everything which I tried to hide. It was just what had happened when I had bought her a jeweled wrist watch once for Christmas. Just by accident she had thumbed through my checkbook, and just by accident she had run upon the jeweler's name and price and everything. It was the same thing when I had tried to surprise her with a new fur coat. The furrier, in a state of mental aberration, sent the bundle to me at the house instead of to the office, and Kay opened it without thinking. There would always be some little accident which turned up anything I tried to hide.

But when I saw her holding that letter, it certainly did not seem like an accident, but rather as if it were always meant to happen.

372

"*My dearest, dearest darling,*" Kay was reading. "Why, Harry, who ever sent you that?"

If her voice had been kind, I might not have minded.

"*I've been thinking of you all day long, and I'll think of you all tonight even when I'm asleep.*" Kay paused and gave a quick, sharp laugh. Her reading became mincing and precise. "*I keep wondering how you look and what you are saying and whether you are wearing your rubbers. I keep thinking of little things I could do for you. I never knew that you could get into my system like this, so that I don't seem to be one person any more, but part of me always seems to be with you . . .*"

"Kay," I said, "give me that letter."

Kay stood up and put the letter behind her back.

"Why, Harry," she said, "I wish you could see yourself! Why, what did you do to her to make her write to you like that?"

"Give me that letter, Kay," I said. "It hasn't got anything to do with you."

She backed away when I reached out my hand.

"Oh?" she said. "I suppose that's why you hid it."

I spoke slowly and distinctly.

"It's none of your business and I won't have you read it," I said.

I could tell from the way she looked at me that I had lost all sense of perspective and proportion.

"Oh, won't you?" she said. "Well, I'm going to find out who it is."

"Kay — " I began.

"Well, who is it?" Kay asked.

"Never mind who," I said.

"Well," Kay said, "I know who. It's that thin, overdressed girl from New York, isn't it?" Kay's voice broke into a strident laugh. "And she wondered if you wore your rubbers!"

She had only seen Marvin Myles once at a football game and once that time at Westwood. It had never occurred to me that anyone could possibly remember. Marvin and I had been by the fire at Westwood and Kay had been walking in the woods with Bill King.

"Kay," I said, "I should have burnt that letter long ago. Now, give it to me, please."

"Why, Harry," Kay said, "you're still in love with her!"

"How do you mean," I asked, "I'm still in love with her? Why, I haven't seen her for years."

"Do you think you'd act the way you are if you weren't?" Kay said. "Why can't you be frank and confess you're in love with her? She's crazy about you. She's always been."

"Look here, Kay," I said. "How do you know? Who ever told you anything about Marvin Myles?"

"That's just like you to be surprised," she said.

"Go ahead," I said. "Who told you?"

"Why, Bill King of course," she said.

I could not believe it. She had obviously said it only because she was angry and I could see already that she was sorry.

"He never did," I said. "Bill's a gentleman. Give me that letter."

Kay backed away from me. I did not want to be rough, but she was not to have that letter. I took her hand in both of mine and began opening her fingers.

"You're hurting me," she said.

"Then give it to me," I answered.

It was the first time that Kay and I had ever been through anything like that. The letter fell on the floor and she wrenched her hand away.

"Oh, take your damned letter," she said.

Before I could speak she had jerked open the library door. Then she was in the hall and she had slammed the door in my face. I heard the telephone in the parlor ringing. It rang four times before Kay answered it.

"Oh, Mrs. Smithfield," Kay was saying, "I'm so glad to hear your voice. No, I'm not a bit busy. . . . Yes, we had a *lovely* summer. . . . Why, let me see — Friday? . . . Why, no, we're not doing anything at all. We'd love to come to dinner."

XXXIII

Rhinelander Four —

I stooped and picked up the letter. I could not remember ever
having been so angry. It was like pulling a thread and having
a whole piece of cloth unravel.

What shook me most, however, was not my anger. It was not
conceivable that I could be in love with Marvin Myles after
twenty years. For periods of months I had never thought of her.
It was preposterous to suppose that I could keep on loving someone who was so little in my thoughts. I had finished everything
with Marvin when I married Kay, erased it all from my mind, like
a problem in geometry from the blackboard at school. I had never
looked at anyone else after I married Kay, but perhaps even when
I had not thought of her Marvin had been there; and then there
had been times when I had called her back deliberately into my
thoughts. She had come to me on sleepless nights. She had walked
with me invisibly, and I had lived over every hour we had known
together. Perhaps this had been wrong, but I do not see how I
could have helped it. She was with me again now that I held the
letter, and the strange, the awful thing about it was that Marvin
Myles, whom I had not seen for nearly twenty years, was more
real to me at the moment than my own wife. This did not seem
possible with Kay still talking in the parlor, but it was so. Marvin
Myles seemed to be so close to me that I could touch her, and
now I wanted her to be there. I knew every word of that letter
of hers by heart, and now I found myself reading over a part of
it I liked best, and I could hear her voice speaking all the words.

You know, don't you, that I'm only running on this way because I love you? And if you love someone and can't do anything about it, it makes you awfully helpless. All I can do is to make you think, when you're up there all alone, that it isn't so bad if you know you have someone, someone forever and always, someone you can always come back to, dear, any time or anywhere. . . .

Now Kay had never said anything like that to me. I wondered if it were true that she was still waiting for me — any time or anywhere. It was as though I were back already, as though nothing else had mattered, as though the only time that I had ever lived was that little while. I folded the letter carefully, and then I kissed it. The pages smelled old and musty like the pages of the Plutarch.

I knew it was time for me to take hold of myself when I found myself kissing that letter, but I wanted to look at her again and to talk to her again — just once.

When I realized what I was thinking, its absurdity began to bring me to my senses. Yet I could reach for the telephone and call her. . . .

What I needed was some exercise and a good cold shower. I straightened my coat and put up the last volumes of Plutarch and opened the library door. Kay must have been waiting for the door to open, because she called as soon as she heard me. She was sitting on the parlor sofa with her engagement calendar on her knee.

"Harry," Kay asked, "where are you going?"

Her voice meant that she was going to be nice again, but somehow it made no difference.

"I'm just going over to the Squash Club," I told her. "I want to get some exercise."

"Why, darling," Kay said, "you've been exercising all day."

"I have to sign up for the autumn bumping tournament," I said.

"But, Harry," Kay said, "it's nearly half-past six. You'll be late for dinner."

"I'm going out for dinner," I said.

"Oh, Harry, dear," Kay said, "please! Please, don't take it out on me. We're having a very special dinner. We're having a big steak."

"I'm going out, Kay," I said.

"Oh, Harry," Kay said, "please!"

She was implying that I was being unreasonable, and I suppose I was. Given a little time, I should come back as though nothing had happened and pick it all up again.

"No," I said, "I'm going out."

"Oh, all right," said Kay, "if you want to act like a child. But, Harry — "

I did not answer her, because at the moment there was nothing I could say. I wished that she were not being so nice about it, but there was nothing I could say. Most of the bundles I had taken out of the car were still piled in the front hall. Bitsey was waiting at the door to go out, but I did not care.

"Kay," I called.

"Yes," she answered, "yes, Harry."

"Bitsey wants to go out," I called. "You'd better take him."

"Yes," she called, "all right, Harry."

I could not help thinking it was very unusual. It was very nice of Kay.

The rooms of the Squash Club had been freshly decorated downstairs and they were deserted, as I supposed they would be, since it was so early in the season. In the main room the heads of a moose, an antelope and a zebra looked down on some comfortable chairs and on a big table, covered with newspapers and periodicals. The headline of the evening paper showed that the Poles were getting whipped. The German Army was rolling them up and the Allies weren't helping. Unlike home, the room had no difficult associations, no reminders of duty or responsibility. I did not know where the moose- and antelope- and zebra-heads came from and if the moths began to eat them up it would not have mattered. It was a healthy and pleasant feeling just to be out of the house and over at the Squash Club. I rang the bell by the fireplace and when no one answered I began shouting for Louis. Pretty soon Louis came in a clean white coat and I asked him how he was and what kind of summer he had had. Louis said the summer had been fine, but it was nice to get back to town.

"Is anybody here?" I asked.

"No, sir," Louis said, "except Mr. Boomer. Mr. Boomer might give you a game."

"No, no, Louis," I said. "Is Gus upstairs? Just call up to him that I want to play for half an hour, and I want to stay for dinner."

My sneakers and shorts were wrapped in newspaper and my racket was in good condition. Everything was always all right at the Club. I carried all the things into the dressing room, and there was Mr. Boomer sitting on one of the benches in his shorts pulling on his socks. Mr. Boomer was always working to keep his muscles in tone and to keep his weight down. He was burned a mahogany color by summer sun baths, but sun baths or exercise, Mr. Boomer's weight was catching up on him. I wondered if it would ever be like that with me.

"Hello, Harry," Mr. Boomer said, and we shook hands. "Just back, are you? Did you have a good summer?"

That was what everyone would be asking me for the next two weeks, and what I would be asking everyone else, and every one of us would have had a good summer.

"Yes," I said, "a fine summer."

"So did I," Mr. Boomer said. "There's nothing like the sun. I took off two inches."

Mr. Boomer did not look as though he had taken off anything.

"What are you looking at?" Mr. Boomer asked. "I suppose you think it doesn't show. Well, I only weigh fifteen pounds more than I did in the bow at New London."

The one thing I did not want was to hear Mr. Boomer talk about that boat race.

"And I'm going to have another inch off by the first of the month," Mr. Boomer said. "I've been on the rowing machine all the afternoon. Are you staying for dinner?"

"Yes," I said.

"I thought you were married. How did you get away?"

"We're just moving in," I said.

"Oh, that's it, is it?" Mr. Boomer said.

I felt that I ought to explain it a little further, so that Mr. Boomer would understand that it was absolutely a matter of household convenience that made me come for dinner, but I had no time because Gus came in. Gus was a first-rate squash professional whose nose showed that he had once been a pugilist. I shook hands with Gus.

"We'll take Number One court," Gus said. "She's got all new lights. Did you have a nice summer, Mr. Pulham?"

"Yes," I said, "a fine summer. Did you?"

"Yeah," Gus said, "fine. The wife had twins."

"Well," I said, "that's something."

"Yeah," Gus said, "I'll say so. All ready? Let's go, Mr. Pulham."

We trotted up the stairs through the corridor to the Number One court. I still could not stop thinking about Marvin Myles, and what I needed was a good stiff workout, and Gus was the boy to give it to me. The black ball went up against the white wall, whang, whang, whang, like a bullet.

"Six-five," Gus said, "let's go, Mr. Pulham."

I could see Gus out of the corner of my eye. I had always been able to give him a good game. I was not, thank God, getting fat and heavy. The ball came off the back wall and I slammed it into a corner. It pulled Gus out of position and I passed him on the next shot.

"Yow," Gus shouted, and rapped his racket on the wall. I could not tell whether Gus had let me get the point on purpose or not, but I did not think so. I remembered what the Skipper said. He used to say, When you play a game, play it with all your heart and soul. I was playing it that way, but just the same part of me was somewhere else with Marvin Myles. Wham, the ball went. It bounced off the back wall and the side wall. It came out of the corners to my forehand and my backhand, but she was always there.

I remembered the time that I had told her that I loved her.

"*Someone you can always come back to, dear, any time or anywhere.*"

"Yow," Gus shouted.

I was wondering what would happen if I called her up, just casually, to ask her how she was. After all it would not be such a peculiar thing to do. On the contrary, it would be thoughtful and kindly, seeing that she had called me up last spring.

"Thirteen–twelve," Gus called. "Let's go."

I could not understand what was possessing me. In the first place, she was married and I was married and you did not call up married women long distance to New York.

"*Darling,*" she had written on the Christmas card years and years ago, "*aren't you coming back?*"

"All right," Gus said. "One more."

Gus was paid to be enthusiastic.

"All right," I said. "Another one, Gus. Let's go."

Wham the ball went. Squash was a noisy game, but it could give you a better workout in a shorter time than any other. Gus was pushing me up toward the front wall and I was trying to get back. Marvin Myles probably wouldn't remember who I was and if she did she would think I was drunk or crazy.

"Fourteen–twelve," Gus shouted. "Game point. Let's go," and he rapped his racket on the wall. The thing to do was to forget about it. I must be going crazy.

I was dripping wet and out of breath when I pulled on my sweatshirt.

"Thanks, Gus," I said. "That was swell."

"Thank *you,* Mr. Pulham," Gus said.

Then I turned on the cold water hard, and when it struck me it nearly took my breath away. I stayed under it until I was icy cold, but when I was out the blood raced through me. When I stood by the open fire, drying myself, I felt tired and pleasantly relaxed. Mr. Boomer was waiting for me and he began to tell me about how the Elis were one length ahead at the halfway buoy and then they raised the stroke, and he asked me if I wouldn't like a Martini and I said I would — but only part of me was there. It was a quarter after seven o'clock. The toll rates would be low. It was a silly thing to think of, that the toll rates would be low.

"There was a fine crowd in the boat," Mr. Boomer was saying. "Nothing like the water to make friends."

I cleared my throat and looked at the moose-head over the fireplace.

"Louis," I called, "have you got a New York telephone directory?"

"Yes, Mr. Pulham," Louis said, "a last year's one."

"Oh," Mr. Boomer said, "so you're going to call up New York?"

I cleared my throat again.

"Yes," I said, "a call I have to make."

I could not understand why I seemed to be doing a shady thing when I simply told him that I had to make a call. I began turning over the pages of the book. The name was Ransome — John Ransome; business address, Broadway; residence, Park Avenue; Rhinelander 4. . . . Now that I had said I was going to make a New York call, I had to.

"Louis," I said, "give me another Martini."

"That's right," Mr. Boomer said. "You can talk to Central better with another." I was ordering another drink, because I did not have guts enough to go to that telephone booth without it, and after all what was it? Nothing more than calling up an old friend of mine in New York. The number was Rhinelander 4- . . .

"Just leave mine on the table, Louis," I said. "I'll be right back."

The number was Rhinelander 4- . . . I was in the booth in the hall dialing the operator; it was too late to stop.

"New York City," I said, "Rhinelander 4- . . ."

"Hold the line, please," the operator answered. Then there was a little buzz. "RX, New York — Rhinelander 4- . . ."

Suppose she was there, what under the sun was I going to say to her? How in God's name could I explain to her why I was calling her up? If I just asked her how she was she would think I was crazy.

"Ready with New York," the operator was saying. "Boston calling Rhinelander 4- . . ."

381

I heard a resonant, fluty voice, saying: "Hello, Mr. Ransome's apartment."

It would be the butler. Marvin had always said she was going to have a butler.

"Is Mrs. Ransome in?" I asked.

"Mrs. Ransome is at dinner."

I felt steadier.

"Oh, well, if she's at dinner," I said, "I won't disturb her."

"Who shall I say called, sir?"

"Never mind," I said. "I won't disturb her," and I hung up.

Then I pulled out my handkerchief and mopped my forehead. I remembered how I felt once in a dentist chair after I had been given a whiff of gas. First the whole world had been cloudy and I had been thinking the most outrageous thoughts, and then it had all come back with a click, and I was in the dentist's office and he was leaning over me.

"That didn't hurt much, did it?" the dentist was asking.

When I stepped out of the telephone booth it was just like that. It was all over, and I had done what I was going to do — I had called her up. It was all over — and that was that. I would never have to go through that again. All of a sudden I felt fine. I began to wonder what Kay was doing and what the war news on the radio was. My Martini was waiting for me in the big room.

"Well," I said, "that's that." I could give Mr. Boomer my full attention now. I had never been through anything like it before, and it was over.

"Did you get your call?" Mr. Boomer asked.

"Oh, yes," I said, "I got my call. They were at dinner."

Of course I could call her up in an hour when she had finished dinner, but I knew I would not. I had been on a long and dangerous journey and now I was safely back, and Marvin Myles was gone.

I had been careful, as soon as I got back to town, to put my ring of town keys in my left-hand trousers pocket. A good deal of my life seemed to consist of reminding myself of such small details — to be sure I had my keys, to be sure I had my wallet with my automobile license, to be sure to stop at the drugstore to get some more shaving cream. I patted my pocket at least three times, because there would be trouble if I came home without my keys. Once when I returned from a Club dinner, perhaps having had a little more to drink than was necessary, I had been obliged to ring the door bell for nearly half an hour before anyone woke up. Although that was a good many years ago, Kay had never forgotten it. The last thing I wanted that night, on top of everything else, was to have Kay think that I had gotten mad and had gone off and gotten drunk, like other people's husbands she had heard of. When I walked home from the Club the rain had nearly stopped, and the whole city was bright and brisk as it always was in early autumn. There were all sorts of window displays of new dresses and blue and red and green hats and hunting costumes, and the florists' windows were filled with house plants. I stopped and bought a dozen pinkish-yellow roses for Kay, in case she was still awake, so that she would know I had been thinking of her.

All the lights were out except the one which we always kept burning in the hall. I set down the roses in the vestibule and got out my keys. There was the key to my locker at the Squash Club and one for my locker at the Country Club and one for the cash box in my desk at the office, and the safe deposit key, the automobile ignition key, and the front-door key, and the basement key, besides a lot of others which seemed to have no purpose at all, but which I was afraid to throw away. I could not recall distinctly what the edges of the house key looked like, so I tried three others before I found the right one. The hall inside was close and stuffy, and Bitsey began to bark.

"Shut up," I said.

He knew me perfectly well, but he always barked. I took off my raincoat and my hat and walked upstairs very quietly. When I opened the door of our bedroom I heard Kay move, so I knew that she was awake before she spoke.

"Harry," she said, "is that you?"

"Yes," I said.

I heard her yawn, and then she switched on the light beside the bed.

"What on earth were you doing rattling the front door?" she asked. "I thought you were a burglar."

"I couldn't find the right key," I told her.

"Oh," Kay said, and I handed her the roses, all wrapped in green waxed paper.

"Oh," Kay said. I thought she would be pleased, because she always was when I brought her flowers, and in a way she was, but somehow not exactly in the way I expected. Instead, she looked a little bothered as though she were thinking of something else.

"They're so darned innocent, aren't they?" Kay said. "Even though they were grown in a hothouse. You'd better put them in the washbowl." Her voice was soft and sweet, but somehow I was vaguely disappointed.

"Kay," I said, "I'm awfully sorry I was cross."

I wanted it all to be finished, the way it always was after she and I had quarreled — clear with nothing left. Kay moved uneasily and clasped her hands behind her head.

"Oh, that's all right," she said. She sounded tired and resigned. "It was all my fault."

"Oh, no," I said, "it wasn't, Kay. I didn't mean to take that letter away," and I reached into my inside pocket and drew Marvin's letter out. "I wish you'd read it now."

Kay shook her head quickly.

"Oh, no," she said. "It doesn't make any difference."

"I hadn't any business being angry. It was just that it hurt me when you laughed, because I was in love with her and she was in love with me."

"Harry," Kay said, "let's not go into it any more."

"It was a long time ago," I said, "an awfully long time ago. I just don't want you to think that there's anything in it, because there isn't."

384

"I know there isn't," Kay said. "There wouldn't be with you."

I sat down on the edge of the bed and took her hand and kissed it.

"All right," I said, "but you're not angry with me any more, are you, Kay?"

"No," she said, "of course not."

"Because it doesn't do any good," I said. "When it's all over, there you are and there I am. I don't know how to put it, but it all comes out in the wash."

"Please!" Kay said. "Please, don't say any more, and get me an aspirin — and then let's go to sleep."

"It's awfully nice we're both here, Kay," I said. "Last night and the night before and the night before that — I was awfully lonely without you."

"Oh, Harry," Kay said, "please, let's go to sleep."

We were back where we always were, just Kay and I, and I was wondering if the children were all right and whether I ought to get up to see if they had enough over them. I was wondering if the market would still be going up tomorrow and whether my partner, Tom Maxwell, had done what I had asked him about General Electric. I could feel myself sinking off to sleep. Thank Heaven, I had not spoken to Marvin Myles.

XXXIV

With Pleasure Rife

Yes, autumn was always a busy time. The war had brought about a brisk rise in the stock market which was quite a responsibility. Tom Maxwell and I had to decide whether to advise our clients to take profits or to let them ride. I finally got Tom to sell out some steel and commodity stocks right on top of the bulge, though I agreed with Tom that this was not usually good practice for investment lists which were essentially long-term, but, as I pointed out, there had not been an opportunity to take a profit for quite a while. I was asked to sit on the investment board of one of the larger trust groups, and though I could not do it, it made me feel that I was getting somewhere. It even made me wonder what might have happened if I had started out in a large bank like the National City or the Chase. It was conceivable that I might have had a vice-presidency by now. Yet I was contented with what I was doing. I rather liked running my own show as long as my clients were satisfied, and they must have been because we were getting more business.

Yes, superficially everything was going well that autumn. George had gone back to school and was playing on the second team and Gladys was getting good reports and several stocks in the family estate which I had thought were worthless had begun to come to life. Nevertheless, something at home seemed to make me restless. Kay and I were with other people very often, but when we were alone and talking everything over, she never seemed to concentrate. She seemed to have a hard time that autumn working out plans, and now and then she acted as though they bored her. She seemed bored, for instance, when Bo-jo Brown's wife asked her to be on the committee for the entertainment at our Reunion. I was very pleased that Kay was asked, and I thought she would be. Instead, she forgot to go to the get-together tea.

"You know, Kay," I said, "when I think of you with all those other girls it makes me awfully proud."

"Proud?" Kay said. "How do you mean?"

"You look so much better than any of them," I told her, "so much prettier."

"Well, that isn't saying much," Kay said.

"I know what you mean," I told her. "A lot of them look discouraged and tired."

"It isn't that," Kay said. "They all look frustrated."

"Maybe everybody gets frustrated after a while," I said. "Perhaps it's part of life."

"Yes," Kay said, "but life is meant to live."

It occurred to me that Kay was always talking about living that autumn. Several times when we were out at dinner I heard her saying something about the right to live, and I imagined that she got it from some book at the Book Club. It always seemed to me that living was just living, but when I said this once at dinner Kay did not like it. Kay went down to New York in October to see about her clothes, and when she came back she seemed a whole lot happier. She began to talk about the Yale game and she did not seem to be absent-minded any longer. Bill King was definitely coming for the game and we would have a party. I was awfully glad that Kay was interested in the game, but I did wish she would pay a little more attention to our Class.

Nearly every Twenty-fifth-year class has a tea right after the Yale game. It had been found from the experiences of other classes that it was much better if we all saw as much of each other as we could before the Reunion. Lucy Green, Sam's wife, was in charge of the tea and at the end of October she asked Kay to help her. The note came at breakfast time, just as I was leaving for the office.

"Who is she?" Kay asked. "She signs herself 'Cordially, Lucy,' and I don't even know her."

"It's just that you don't remember, Kay," I said. "She's Sam Green's wife. You remember Sam. He was at our wedding."

"I don't remember," Kay said.

"Sam?" I told her. "Sam is one of my oldest friends."

"Well, I've never heard you mention him," Kay said.

I had not even thought of Sam for several years. That was the way it was with a lot of my oldest friends. For no good reason they seemed to disappear, but it did not change the way I felt about Sam.

"That's true," I told her. "I don't know why it is that we haven't seen anything of Sam and Lucy. Sam was in my form at School and he was in my entry at college. I don't ask you to like Sam but there he is, and he gave us that after-dinner coffee set for a wedding present."

"Which set?" Kay asked.

"The one you didn't like," I said, "the one with butterflies that you couldn't change because it came from Philadelphia. Now, Kay, it isn't going to take long to go to that tea."

"I married you," Kay said. "I didn't marry your college class."

"I'm only asking you," I said, "to try just for an hour to be nice to them."

"Now, Harry," Kay said, "I'd like you to name a single instance when I haven't been nice to your friends — yes, a single one!"

I began one morning in November to go over our security list for tax-loss sales. Since Tom Maxwell was never as good as I at detail, I closed myself up in our conference room and told Miss Rollo that I did not want to be disturbed by anyone until lunch. I had just got the papers out on my desk and everything ready when Miss Rollo opened the door softly and adjusted her glasses on her nose.

"It's Mr. Brown and Mr. Purcell," Miss Rollo said. "They say they have to see you."

She did not have time to say any more, because the door opened wider and Bo-jo Brown came in with Jack Purcell just behind him.

"Why, hello," I said. "It's awfully nice of you to come in." It was nice of Jack, because he was always very busy, and it was nice of Bo-jo too, just to drop around.

"Come off it now," Bo-jo said. "Why weren't you at the committee lunch yesterday? Are you going to work for the Class, or aren't you? What about the Class Reports?"

"What Class Reports?" I asked.

"God almighty," Bo-jo said, "the Class lives, the big anniversary book! You said you were going to help me with it. We went all over it last spring at lunch."

"See here," I said. I had almost forgotten about that lunch last spring. "I never really promised, Bo-jo. I only said I'd help you if I could."

Bo-jo slapped me on the shoulder.

"Now, look," Bo-jo said, "you're not going to be a yellow-belly, are you? We've got to get this Reunion going, and it's getting stalled. Now look at me. I've got as much to do as you, haven't I? And Jack has just as much. Well, I can't do this whole job alone and neither can Jack. You've got to help and Cynthia's got to help."

"Who's Cynthia?" I said.

"Hell's bells," Bo-jo shouted, "she's your wife! Don't you know your own wife?"

"That isn't her name, Bo-jo," I said. "It's Cornelia."

"Now, don't you kid me," Bo-jo said. "Her name is Cynthia. Isn't it Cynthia, Jack?"

"No," Jack answered, "it's Cornelia."

"Well, it doesn't make any difference," Bo-jo said, "and we haven't any time to argue. We've all got to pull at this together — wives and kids and everybody. Look at Bill King. Now, I never thought much of that squirt, but he surprised me. He's been breaking his neck over the Class play. You've got to snap into it, Harry."

"Now, wait a minute, Bo-jo. I didn't say I wasn't going to help."

"Then snap out of it," Bo-jo said. "*I* can't keep going around and seeing the printer about that book. *I* can't write come-on letters and go over the details. Are you going to do what you promised, or aren't you?"

"Why, if you really think I promised, Bo-jo."

"Now you're talking," Bo-jo said. "Come over to the office at four o'clock and we'll go over it, and get Cynthia stirred up. Attaboy! You can have him now, Jack. Get in and shake him up."

Jack Purcell pulled some papers out of an envelope. Bo-jo sat down and I sat down and Jack pulled a chair close to mine.

"This problem of raising money," Jack said, "for the usual gift and the entertainment — I don't suppose you've read my letters?"

"No, Jack, not very carefully."

"That's all right, Harry," Jack said. Well, here's your pledge all filled out and ready for you to sign."

Jack passed me a slip of paper and handed me a fountain pen.

"Attaboy," Bo-jo said. "Shake it out of him."

"Now, wait a minute, Jack," I said, and I laughed feebly. "You've got exaggerated ideas. I hadn't planned to give nearly that much."

"It's what you're down for, Harry," Jack said. "Out of the fifteen I've seen already fourteen of them have signed in full. You can take it off your income tax."

"All right, Jack — but I'll have to pay it gradually."

"Attaboy," Bo-jo said. "Harry always comes across."

Jack Purcell put the paper carefully back in the envelope and drew out another paper.

"I know Bo-jo's got you sewed up for the Reports," Jack said, "but I wonder if you could help me out a little on the Special Gifts Committee. What we want now are three or four gifts of over five thousand dollars. Have you heard of a man in our class named Ransome, John Ransome? Maybe you have, Bo-jo."

Bo-jo clenched his fist and beat his forehead softly.

"I never heard of him," he said. "Ransome? And you've got him on the first list? All right, Jack. We've got to shake it out of him."

"It's a little hard if you don't know them," Jack said. "I don't think this man Ransome has ever been much interested in the Class."

"That's all right," Bo-jo said. "We'll write him. We'll give a little dinner for him after the Yale game. That'll sweeten him up. What's his first name?"

"John," Jack said, "John Ransome. He lived in Dunster and specialized in Economics."

"What's his nickname?" Bo-jo asked.

"I'm sure I don't know," Jack answered.

"All right," Bo-jo said. "It doesn't make any difference. Call him Johnny. Just write him something like this." Bo-jo beat his fist softly on his forehead. " 'Dear Johnny, I haven't heard of you for a long while and we ought to get together. You'll be coming up to the Yale game of course and Bo-jo Brown (you remember Bo-jo?) and I want to have you beside us down in front of the cheering section and after that just four or five of us, some of the old football crowd, are going to have a little dinner, to talk about old times and the Class, and we want you to come along. It will be swell to see you again, Johnny.' "

Bo-jo paused and looked at us.

"Naturally, I'm putting it a little roughly," he added, "but nothing shakes them up like football and some of the old songs. Maybe he's a pansy, but he'll like it all the better."

"Yes," Jack said, "maybe. Harry, did you ever hear of Ransome?"

"I never did know Ransome," I answered, "but I know his wife." Jack Purcell looked interested. Bo-jo hitched himself forward in his chair.

"Well, why the hell didn't you say so in the first place? How well do you know his wife?"

"I don't know her now, Bo-jo," I answered. "I used to know her quite a while ago — pretty well."

"What was her name?" Bo-jo asked. "Did I ever know her?"

"No," I answered, "I don't believe you did. She comes from New York."

"All right," Bo-jo said, "all right. Now we're getting somewhere. Was she an old girl of yours?"

"Now, wait a minute, Bo-jo."

"Listen," Bo-jo said. "I'm not going into your private life, but we can't pass up a contact. Haven't you seen her since she was married?"

"No," I said. "It was all a long time ago, Bo-jo. I don't want to be mixed up in it."

"Come on. Snap into it."

"No," I said. "Get all the money you want out of Ransome, but you needn't think I'm going to use my friendship with her to do it."

"Haven't you got any class spirit?" Bo-jo asked.

Then Jack Purcell interrupted us.

"Harry's perfectly right," he said. "The other way's the best."

I had not seen much of him for years, but I had always liked Jack Purcell.

Now, Bill and I had always been awfully good friends and he had done a lot for me, but even so, I did not see why Kay should make quite all the preparations she did for his coming up to the Yale game. I had known Bill a good deal longer than Kay had and I had seen a lot more of him, but Kay seemed to set herself up as an authority on what Bill would like and what he wouldn't like — whether he liked gin cocktails or rum cocktails, whether he liked soft bath towels or scratchy ones. I ought to have been pleased that Kay was so interested, and inside myself I suppose I was, yet at the same time it began to look as though I were going to have nothing to do with Bill, although I had always felt that Bill was my responsibility. I don't mean to imply in any way that I was jealous, because nothing was too good for him as far as I was concerned. Yet I wished that Kay had ever given as much thought to my personal comforts and conveniences as she seemed to be giving to Bill's. I even joked with her about it.

"Bill isn't so soft," I said, "that he's going to mind Gladys' china animals on the mantelpiece in his room. He won't mind her micro-scope either."

"You don't understand," Kay said. "Bill mustn't be made to feel that he's driving Gladys out."

We didn't have any regular guest room, because we usually did all that sort of entertaining at North Harbor. Gladys had the room and the bath next to ours; George had the small back room on the third floor during his school vacations; and when we did have a guest, Gladys had to move into George's room, or into the old nursery, which we never had got around to fixing over. It was all informal at best, and there was no reason for anyone staying there over Friday and Saturday to be worried about Gladys' china ani-mals, or her Maxfield Parrish pictures, for that matter.

"There are a lot of buttons off my shirts," I told Kay. "I wish you'd give me a little service instead of using it all up on Bill."

I just said it as a joke, and I expected her to laugh, but lately Kay had been awfully touchy.

"Why don't you ever say something when your buttons come off," she asked, "instead of making a grievance of it?"

"Oh, that's all right, Kay," I said. "I'm just being funny."

"If you didn't want Bill to come," Kay said, "why didn't you tell me frankly?"

"But I do want Bill," I said.

"Then don't criticize me when I'm doing the best I can. There's Bill and the dinner party, and then there's that damned tea."

"I know, Kay," I said. "You're awfully nice about the tea."

On Thursday morning Kay got in the cleaning women. They went all over the dining room, the parlor and Gladys' room and her bathroom. They cleaned everything out of Gladys' closet and out of her bureau and Kay unearthed some long-lost Japanese prints of shaven-headed men carrying things over bridges in the snow. They were valuable, but we had never found any place to put them and they had gradually disappeared. When Kay and the women were finished, I must say you wouldn't have known that Gladys had ever slept there.

"Those prints are awfully attractive, aren't they?" Kay said. I had to admit that they were; and after the chore-man and I had carried Gladys' writing desk temporarily down into the cellar I had to admit that Kay had done a good job.

"We ought to keep this as the spare room and do the nursery over," she said.

Although it was a perfectly sensible suggestion, I hated the idea of doing the nursery over, but I suppose Kay was right.

On Friday, when we were half-through breakfast, Kay found out the size of my gift to the Class. Kay was planning the dinner party that we were going to give for Bill. She said there was only one bottle of champagne left down cellar and she wanted to know if I would order another case. It was not that I was not perfectly glad to give Bill champagne, but I did not want to get a reputation for having champagne at dinner. It was obviously the sort of gesture which would imply that we were in a financial bracket in which we did not belong.

"They'll all have cocktails, Kay," I said, "and we'll have brandy and Scotch-and-soda after dinner if they want it. Don't you think a little Bordeaux would be all right at dinner?"

Kay frowned at me across the table and put all the letters she had been reading into a careful pile.

"I don't see why we can't ever do anything chic," she said. "Besides, Bill loves champagne."

"For heaven's sakes, Kay," I said, "how do you know Bill loves champagne?"

I was really curious, because I had never known Bill to drink it much.

"Oh, never mind," Kay said, "if you want to be stingy — but I don't know why we can't stop thinking about money sometimes."

"It's simply a matter of proportion," I told her. "It looks so obvious, having champagne."

"Obvious?" Kay looked startled. "How do you mean, obvious?"

"We don't have to make an impression on Bill," I answered,

"and there are the repairs at North Harbor and the children's tuition."

"Well, if you're so worried," Kay said, "I'll buy the champagne myself."

If Kay really wanted something she would always offer to get it herself, and then it would make me feel mean.

"It isn't that, Kay," I said, "but there's my contribution to the Class this year."

I stopped. I had not meant in the least to bring it up.

"Harry," Kay said, "how much did you give the Class?"

"Well, it was more than I had planned to give," I said. "You see we have to raise a hundred thousand dollars."

"What for?" Kay asked. "For paper caps and whistles? For all those little cakes we're going to have at that tea tomorrow?"

"If you'd been in the Class you'd understand. Jack Purcell's raising the money and Jack's having a pretty hard time."

"I'm glad he is," Kay said. "I never liked him."

"That's because you don't know him, Kay," I answered.

"My dear," Kay said, "you don't really know him either. He came around and dunned you, didn't he? And you were impressed. Why can't you ever say no to anything? How much did you give? You've got to tell me, Harry."

I told her. I hadn't meant to tell her, and there was no use trying to explain it either.

"Why, Harry," Kay said, and she laughed in that way of hers that was not funny, "and we can't have a new stair-carpet, and I have to shop at the A and P! What's the use in our trying to save?"

Kay continued for quite a while. She had reacted just about the same way when I bought the Packard, and when I bought the gas stove with the refrigerator in the bottom of it. There wasn't much for me to answer, because I knew she was right. I had given a good deal too much.

"It's all right," I said. "Go ahead and order the champagne."

I thought Kay might change her ground and say it was impossible, after what I had done, to have champagne, but instead she was awfully nice about it.

"Darling," she said, "I didn't mean to go on so. You're awfully kind to me — always."

I walked around the table to her chair. The day was going to be all right. It always was when Kay was like that. We were going to have a fine time all week end.

"I'm awfully glad I told you, Kay," I said. "It's always better, no matter what fool thing I do, to tell you everything."

Her cheeks grew redder and she reached out and took my hand.

"You make me feel awfully mean sometimes," she said.

"That's the last thing you are," I told her.

"Oh, yes, I am," she said. "I'm rotten to you, Harry."

"I'm going to send you some flowers to wear tonight," I said, "gardenias — or yellow orchids if you wear your yellow dress."

"Oh, no," Kay said. "Oh, please don't, Harry."

XXXV

He Was Certainly Low in His Mind

It was a fine day outside, more like the middle of October than late November. The leaves were off the trees, but the sun was bright and warm, and the paper said that it would be a good day Saturday. Downtown everyone was talking about the game.

I was glad our office was not like a New York office where everyone rushed around whether there was anything to do or not. There might be a war in Europe, but it hadn't caught us yet. It made me think of college, the way everybody began dropping in from the other offices to talk about the game. I began to be glad we were having a dinner the night before, glad about the champagne.

"Mr. Pulham," Miss Rollo said, "Mr. Brown is on the telephone."

"Hello," Bo-jo called. I had to remove the receiver a little farther from my ear. "We got him. He's coming."

"Who?" I asked.

"What's the matter with your mind?" Bo-jo asked. "Ransome — we've got him."

"Oh," I said, "well, that's fine, Bo-jo."

"And there's a little dinner," Bo-jo said. "Just six or seven of the boys — and Ransome — up at my house after the game, seven o'clock and you don't have to dress."

"That's awfully nice of you to ask me, Bo-jo," I said, "but I can't come — really."

"You can't?" Bo-jo shouted. "Why the hell can't you?"

"We have a guest," I said. "Cornelia has some other plans."

"Then you come," Bo-jo said.

"I don't think I possibly can, Bo-jo."

397

I never could understand why it was so hard to say no to Bo-jo. Perhaps it was because he never expected you to. At any rate I did not have the slightest intention of going to the dinner.

Bill arrived at half-past five. Kay was in the kitchen and I carried his bag up to his room, and explained to him about turning on the hot water slowly in the bathroom, because, if you weren't used to it, it had a way of bursting out with a rush. Then I showed him about opening the inner window and the storm window and where he could get extra covers for his bed if he should be cold, and finally I asked him if he had everything he wanted.

"It's awfully nice you could come, Bill," I said.

Bill seemed a little remote when he came down to the parlor, and I wondered whether I had said anything or done anything that had hurt his feelings. I could not put my fingers on it. He looked tired and drawn and his color was not good and I poured him a drink.

"When we get through with this dinner," I said, "we can all sleep late. There's nothing to do until the game — unless you'd like to get up and go to the Club and play a little squash."

"Squash?" he said. "Good God, no! What I need is a rest. How's Kay?"

I told him that Kay was fine, that she was down in the kitchen, showing the extra waitress the right dishes and all that, and I began telling him how glad everyone was that he was taking an interest in the Class.

"Yes," Bill said, "one and all we must do what little we can — " and he lighted a cigarette.

"You needn't be so grim about it, Bill," I said.

He got up and walked about the room.

"Bill," I said, "are you worried about anything?"

"Who?" Bill asked. "Worried — me?"

"Because if you are," I said, "I wish you would tell me. There might be something I could do, Bill."

Bill looked down at me quickly and for a moment we were friends again.

398

"It's just Life," he said. "That's all," and he poured himself another drink. "I've been thinking about Life quite a lot lately."

"So have I," I said. "Have you written your Class life yet?"

"Oh, hell," Bill said. "Let's not talk any more about that Reunion. What is it anyway but a lot of artificial, infantile stimulation?"

"I know what you mean," I said, "but it's something to think of — all of us going through life together and here we are."

"If you'll excuse my saying so," Bill answered, "people can go through life together without being in any confounded college class. We all go through it and then we're dead — and so what?"

Bill was certainly low in his mind.

"We're not dead yet," I said. I had never felt so much alive. I had never felt so little like giving up.

"There you are," said Bill. "You put your finger on it exactly. The trouble is that we're not dead yet."

The great thing about Bill was that he was always interesting. He was almost the only man I knew who could talk on general subjects.

"Well, life hasn't messed you up much, Bill," I told him. "Now look at the rest of our Class — "

"Would you mind," Bill asked, "not talking about that damned Class? Life is made up of working and living and loving, of women and money, and God knows what! But it hasn't got anything to do with what you learned when you were a boy."

"I don't know," I said. "I suppose you'll think this is funny, but a good deal of life is playing the game."

Bill looked at me as though I had said something astonishing. He passed his hand softly over his hair and patted the back of his head.

"My God," he said gently, "like tennis?"

"Well, not exactly," I said, "but there are rules in it. You can take the Decalogue, for instance — about coveting your neighbor's wife and his ox and his ass."

The animation had left Bill's face. It looked tired and drawn again.

"I never coveted anybody's ox," he said, "nor anybody's ass

either, but a good many rather decent people commit adultery. You know the rules and you break them. Boy, you'd be surprised."

Bill's voice sounded patiently incredulous as though he were talking to someone who was not grown up, and I did not like it.

"That isn't what I meant," I said. "Of course there are all sorts of exceptional circumstances. I simply mean that you and I, Bill, we have rules."

Bill whistled softly.

"I don't know whether you're being serious or not," he said, "but, honestly, you'd be surprised! You ought to get out and travel around more. How did we get on this subject anyway?"

"I don't know," I said. "It is a sort of funny subject."

"You're wrong there. Nothing about it is funny," Bill said. "You know, there's one thing about you, Harry —"

"What about me?" I asked.

"You're the only man I know who isn't afraid to say what he thinks. Sometimes I think you're a damned fool and sometimes I don't. I'm just not man enough to handle you."

"I make an awful fool of myself sometimes," I said.

"Now and then," Bill said. "Not always." His face lighted up. He was thinking of something else. "What sort of seats have you got for the game?"

I told him that they were somewhere down in the bowl. Ever since I left college, they had been in the bowl or in the wooden stands. I always had rotten seats. Bill seemed still more cheerful.

"Well, that's the way they break," he said. "I got a good single seat — never mind how — and I'll tell you what I'll do. You can have it and I'll take Kay to the game and we'll sit in the bowl."

"That's awfully nice of you, Bill," I said, "but I don't think Kay would like it."

"How do you mean, she wouldn't like it?"

"Well, it's silly," I said. "It's just a sort of piece of sentiment. Kay and I go to the game together. We always have."

And then Kay came in. Her cheeks were flushed and she was out of breath from running up the stairs.

talking about Bill's being with us, just before they rang the bell.

"Tell Kay to hurry up," I told her. Then the doorbell was ringing again, and Ellen was bringing in the cocktails, and the doorbell was ringing again.

"Well," Jim said, "here's looking at you."

"Happy days," Bill said.

Everyone was saying the same thing that everyone always said at dinners.

It was all over at a quarter of one. Kay and I were alone again — just she and I — and Kay was yawning and taking the bird out of her hair. I don't know of anything that draws two people together more closely than the end of a dinner party — at any rate, it always did that with Kay and me. It was like talking over one of those amateur plays in which everyone had tried to do his best.

"Harry," she asked, "do you think everything went all right?"

"Yes," I said. "Everyone seemed to have a good time." I was taking off my collar. It had been chafing my neck all the evening.

"It was the champagne," Kay said.

"Maybe it was," I answered.

"Ellen got mixed up with the oysters."

"Yes," I answered, "but I don't think anybody noticed."

"And the soufflé fell," Kay said.

"Yes," I answered, "but I don't think anyone noticed."

We were like two children alone telling each other that this or that may have been wrong, but that really no one had noticed.

"It's awfully nice doing things together," I said. "It makes everything worth while." Kay turned away from the dressing table. "I hope Bill had a good time. I think he did, don't you?"

"Yes," Kay said, "I think he did."

"It's sort of mean," I said, "Bill's going to the game all alone. He said he'd sit in the bowl with you. I told him we'd always gone together. Maybe I was selfish."

"Oh, no, you weren't," Kay said. "Harry — I'm a mixed-up sort of person. I'm all mixed up tonight."

404

"Oh, Bill," she said, "I've been awfully busy. I'm trying to get the table worked out right. Harry, you'd better go down and see about the cocktail glasses. That extra woman doesn't understand them." She looked from me toward Bill. "What have you two been talking about?"

"About Life," Bill said.

"Oh," Kay said, and they kept on looking at each other. "Well, we've all got to go and get dressed. Dinner's at seven-thirty."

While I dressed my mind was absorbed with all those intricacies which always come with a dinner party at one's house, and I wished that it were all over and that we had never started it. I was trying to recollect the people that Kay had asked, and as usual I could not remember all of them and I knew that as usual she would have asked too many.

But Bill King remained in the back of my mind, because he had looked so entirely alone and so deathly sick of himself. It did not seem right to be feeling so happy myself, interested in all the details of the house, proud of the way Kay had fixed the table. After that talk with Bill all sorts of small nonessentials made me happy and all the mechanics of existence became significant. Bill King had said that life was made up of loving and making money, but it was a good deal more than that. Life was made up of letting the dog out, of hitting your thumb with the hammer when you were driving nails, of getting someone to fix the washer in the laundry faucet, of Christmas and friends to dinner — of thousands of things like that, all added up together.

"Bill looks awfully tired," I told Kay while we were getting dressed.

"Oh," said Kay, "does he?"

"Kay, I don't believe Bill's happy," I said.

"That isn't remarkable," Kay answered. "Maybe no one's happy."

"I don't know," I said. "We're happy quite often."

"Don't let's talk," Kay said. "Hurry and get your studs in."

It was ten minutes past seven, and our guests were asked for half-past. I would have to get dressed and mix the cocktails.

401

"What do you suppose Ellen did with my studs?" I asked.

Kay did not answer, nor did I expect her to. She was sitting at her dressing table working on her hair. Her arms and shoulders were bare and I noticed the right hand strap of her slip was secured with a safety pin. She had spilled powder over her silver-backed brush and over the framed photographs of her father and mother and George and Gladys and me, which she always kept on the dressing table. She had opened one of the side drawers, displaying the box which contained all the artificial flowers and synthetic birds that she occasionally put in her hair. It made me think of all the different things that Kay had done to her hair since we were married. First it had been long, almost down to her waist, and then she had bobbed it, and then she had let it grow long again, and then she had cut it and curled it, and then she had let it grow half-long with just a curl on the end. Then she had thinned it all out, and after that she had "upped" it and had worked on it with hairpins, and now it was down again in some sort of bob with a fresh new permanent.

"Are you nearly dressed?" Kay asked.

I was working at the neckband of my shirt. The hole for the collar stud gave way and I pulled the shirt off and threw it into the wastebasket.

Kay was pinning a red bird in her hair. I was looking for my studs in a box that was half-full of laundry pins.

"I don't know what's the matter with Bill," I said.

"Harry," Kay said, "be sure to hang up all your clothes in the closet and close the door. The girls will have to leave their things here."

"Who's going to sit next to me?" I asked. Kay leaned back in her chair and looked at the ceiling.

"Beatrice Rodney is on your right."

"Does she have to be there?"

"Are you dressed or aren't you?" Kay asked.

"I'm more dressed than you," I said.

"It's getting the things fixed underneath that takes time," Kay said. "Don't just stand there."

"Well, what do you want me to do?"

Kay sighed.

"Pick up all your things," she said, "and then go downstairs and ask Ellen to air out the dining room so that it doesn't smell of fried chicken — and wait a minute. Where's Bitsey? Did you take him out when you got home?"

"No," I said.

"Then go and find Gladys and tell her to take Bitsey around the block. Have you done anything about the champagne?"

"Yes," I said.

"Wait a minute," Kay called. "Has Bill got everything he wants?"

"Bill always has everything," I said.

"Please, Harry," Kay said, "don't just stand there."

The dining room smelled of fried chicken and candied sweet potatoes, and I opened the windows. It was a relief to get upstairs to see Bill. His pigskin dressing case from London with all the gold-topped bottles in it was open on Gladys' bureau. His wine-colored brocaded dressing gown was thrown over the foot of the bed.

"Come on down when you're ready," I told him, "and help me with the cocktails."

When everything was finally in order, it seemed to me that we were going to have a good evening. When the doorbell rang I hurried down into the parlor. It was Mary and Jim. They were always early.

"You can leave your clothes in our room," I told Mary, and I kissed her.

"I suppose Bill King's here," Mary said.

"He's going to sit next to you," I said. "Try to cheer him up, won't you?"

"If he's here," Mary said, "he'll cheer up without my helping." From the way she glanced at Jim I imagined that they had been

"Why, Kay," I said, "what are you mixed up about?"

"About you," Kay said, "and everything."

"Why, Kay," I said, "did I do anything wrong tonight?"

"No," Kay said. "I just sort of hate myself tonight."

She rested her head on my shoulder for a moment and her arms tightened about my neck.

"You've been so sweet all day," she said, "and I've kept ordering you around."

"Well," I said, "that's what I'm meant for."

"No, it isn't," Kay said. "Tell me that you love me."

I could not understand why she wanted to know.

"Of course I love you," I said.

"No matter what?" and she clung to me again.

"Yes," I said, "no matter what."

I could not understand what was on her mind.

"Harry."

"Yes?" I said.

"Do you suppose you can love two people at once?"

"What?" I asked her.

"Do you suppose you can love two people at once — in different ways, I mean?"

"Now, Kay," I said, "don't worry about that letter any more. That was written twenty years ago."

"Oh, that," she said. "It isn't that, Harry."

I waited for her to go on, but she stopped.

"Nothing, dear," she said. "It's awfully late. Everything's locked up downstairs, isn't it?"

"Yes," I told her.

I did not know what it was she was going to tell me, but it disturbed me — that business of loving two people at once. I wished she had not brought it up, because now I had to forget Marvin Myles all over again.

405

XXXVI

Two in the Bowl

The next day started like any other Saturday before a game. We went to Mary's house for one of those early lunches, where everybody stood up and ate creamed chicken. Then there was the business of getting out to Cambridge and of finding some place to park the car and of arranging for Bill to meet us afterwards at Zangwell Hall where we were having the Class Tea. It all reminded me of the books I had once read by Ralph Henry Barbour: *"The day of the big game,"* the chapter always started, *"dawned crisp and clear."*

As Bill and Kay and I walked to the stadium I realized that I was doing most of the talking.

"It always makes me feel like an undergraduate again," I said, "walking to the game. I don't care if I live to be a hundred, I'll feel that way about it."

"Yes, Harry," Kay said. "Yes, we know you do."

Kay and Bill both looked as though they belonged on the Yale side more than on ours. Bill had on a Homburg hat and a brand new coat lined with mink, and yellow kid gloves. Kay was dressed in a new tan broadcloth suit that made even the mink coat that she wore over it, the one that she had done over after she inherited it from her mother, look new. When it came to me, I looked pretty shopworn. I was wearing the old raccoon coat which Father had given me at college. The hair was getting thin in back, but I had never wanted to give it away. As I watched them, I wondered if Bill felt hurt because I was not taking his seat in the cheering section.

"Do you still want to change seats, Bill?" I asked him.

"Oh, no," Bill said. "No, thanks."

406

"Bill doesn't want to," Kay said. "Don't go on about it, Harry."

We were at the gate that led to the cheering section by then, and Bill waved his hand at us.

"So long," he said. "Take care of yourselves. I'll see you later." And Kay and I kept walking.

Kay was not like herself, and she had not been last night. It made me a little impatient, because I wanted to have a good time. I tried to think whether I had ever seen her just that way, and I remembered once years before when I had gone to see her off with her father on a trip abroad, after George was born. When it was time for all to go ashore who were going Kay seemed to realize that I was going too, that she would be on the boat and I would be on the shore, and she had held onto me for a minute in just the way she had last night.

"Kay," I said, "what is it that's wrong?"

"What?" Kay said.

She turned around when I spoke to her and she looked startled.

"You're unhappy. You weren't happy last night."

"Oh, Harry," she said, "never mind it. I can't be happy all the time."

I forgot all about it when we were up in the stands. There were lots of people we knew and Kay looked interested, and football could take me out of any mood, away from anything, just as soon as the whistle blew. I do not know why it was that Kay, who was always athletic and who had been brought up on Harvard football since childhood, could never seem to keep her mind on the game, when I could live over so many of the games I had seen. The sound of everyone yelling was a little like the war. I found myself standing up and shouting.

"Block that kick," I shouted. "Block that kick!"

Kay pulled at my coonskin coat.

"Who is that over there, just in front?" she asked. "The man with the woman in the red hat."

"Never mind it now," I shouted. "Block that kick!"

407

"I wonder whatever happened to the little fat man in the red sweater with the white gloves," said Kay, "who used to come out in the middle of the field and wave his arms."

"What?" I said.

"Can't you listen to me?" Kay asked. "The little man who used to wave his arms. What did he used to wave his arms for?"

"He used to signal to the scoreboard," I said. "Come on, Harvard!"

I wished that someone like Bo-jo Brown were in there, or Sam Green. As usual, it was a rotten team. They were slow on their feet, slow at getting started, slow at seeing anything.

"Hold 'em," I shouted. "Hold 'em! Watch that pass!"

"Harry," Kay asked, "who *is* the man with the woman in the red hat?"

"Oh, hell," I shouted. "Hold 'em Harvard! Don't stand there fiddling!"

"You're not listening to me," Kay said. "If you didn't want Bill to sit with me, at least you might listen."

"I did want Bill to sit with you," I said. "I asked him."

I did not hear what she answered, because there was too much noise.

"Somebody's hurt," Kay said. "They're bringing all those little paper cups. They used to drink out of a bucket. I don't suppose it was sanitary."

"To hell with the paper cups!"

"Harry," Kay said, "it doesn't do any good to act like that."

I knew that it did not do any good, but it did make me feel better.

"I don't know what's the matter with the team," I said. "I'm glad Percy Haughton can't see them."

"Harry," Kay asked, "where is Zangwell Hall?"

"What?" I said. "Oh, look at that! Look out!"

"Won't you listen?" Kay said. "Where we're going to that tea."

"Kay, I'm watching the game."

"Then what did you want me for?" Kay said. "You said you wanted me to come."

"Of course I wanted you to come — so we could see the game."

The team was not what it should have been, but it got better in the second half. It was growing dark when it was all over and we stood for a while watching them light red flares and watching the procession on the field and I threw my arm around Kay's shoulders.

"Well, that was quite a game," I said.

Her face was shadowy in the dusk, but I could see that her lips were half open the way they always were when she was thinking of something.

"That was quite a game," I said again.

"Well, I might just as well not have been here," Kay said. "I guess you don't need me much."

Now that everyone was going home somehow the darkness and the crowd made me feel discouraged.

"Kay," I said, "I'm sorry. I forget when I watch them play."

"Oh, that's all right," she said.

It occurred to me that it was better for women not to go to football games.

The tea party was in what was known as a Common Room in one of the Houses — buildings they did not have when I was in college. When Kay and I came in, all sorts of men I should have known and could not remember came trooping in too, with women and children.

"Harry," Kay asked, "how long do we have to stay here?"

I did not blame her much for asking, for we did not seem to know anybody. A long table at one end of the room was covered with tea cups and cakes. Through the clatter of voices the women and children were pushing near the table while the men all moved in another direction.

"I'm going to get a drink," I told her. "There must be some over in that corner."

"No, you're not," Kay said. "You're not going to leave me here alone."

"All right," I said, and we stood there, while I kept trying to change the faces back into faces of boys I had known in their teens.

"Oh," Kay said, "there's Bill!" And then I saw Bill edging his way toward us across the room!

"Hello, boy," he said. "How do you like the classmates and the kiddies?"

"I'm going to get a drink," I said.

Kay put her hand on my arm and stopped me.

"Before you go, give me the keys to the car," she said. "Bill can take me home."

"Now, Kay," I told her, "you're on the Committee. You ought to go and speak to the others."

Kay looked across the room at the tea tables. I knew from her expression that there was not much use arguing. Nevertheless, it did not seem fair.

"I'll just speak to them," she said, "but I have a headache, Harry. Just give me the keys, and you can stay."

"Why, of course, I'll go too," I said, "if you have a headache," but I did not believe for a minute that she had one.

"No," she said, "you stay."

"Kay," I asked, "can't you just wait for half an hour?"

"Let's not argue," Kay answered. "Just give me the keys. Bill will take me home."

I gave her the keys, because I did not want to have an argument in front of Bill.

"I don't ask you to do much, Kay," I said. "I really think you might —"

The room was getting crowded. We had to raise our voices to make ourselves heard.

"Oh, Harry!" Kay said. "Don't be so tiresome. Just come when you get ready. Come on, Bill," and she took Bill's arm.

"All right," I said. "I'll come when I get good and ready."

It did seem to me that the least she might have done was to stay a little while. It was not fair of Kay. She was simply taking out some irritation she had with me on the Class. She wanted to have a good time with Bill and so did I, but that was no reason why she and Bill should have left me flat. It took away all my enthusiasm and all my interest.

Everyone looked tired and unattractive and lost and bewildered. I ran into someone's daughter who was carrying a cup of tea; part of it spilled on the floor and I said, "Excuse me." Then I ran into someone's son who had pimples like George, and I realized that we were all in the same boat together and that I ought to be nice to my classmate's son.

"It's quite a crowd, isn't it?" I said.

The boy gulped and said yes. I never did know what to say to anyone else's son. I had seen plenty of them at friends' houses and only a little while ago they had been in rompers.

"It was a great game, wasn't it?" I said.

"Yes, sir," he said and looked around him wildly. He wanted to get away and so did I, but there we were.

"Where do you go to school?" I asked.

"Exeter, sir," he said.

Someone else bumped into him and he got his feet twisted just the way George did. He was bored to death and so was I. I could put myself right in his place.

"Well," I said, "have a good time," and I began pushing myself toward a corner near the piano where most of the men were going. I was halfway there when someone stopped me — my classmate Bob Ridge. I never could understand why it was that I always found myself thrown with Bob Ridge in any sort of a crowd.

"Harry," Bob said, "I didn't know he was as big as that."

"Who?" I asked.

"Your boy," Bob said. "He looks just like you, too. Harry, have you ever thought it's about time —"

"Time for what?" I asked.

"Time for you to take out something on him at the low rates!" Bob said.

"He isn't my boy," I said, "and I want a drink."

Then I saw Bo-jo Brown in the corner near the piano. Sam Green was near him and Bo-jo had his arm around the shoulders of a pale thin man, who looked confused.

"Well, there you are," Bo-jo called. "Get a drink into Harry, Sam. All the old crowd's getting together."

Bo-jo slapped the pale man on the back and pushed him toward me so hard that we nearly collided.

"Isn't this a swell party?" Bo-jo shouted above the noise. "Say, Johnny, you remember Harry, don't you? This is Johnny Ransome, Harry Pulham," and then I realized that I was looking at the man whom Marvin Myles had married.

He had never seemed real to me before, but there he was, being pushed right at me, and I remembered that Bill had said he was like me. I only hoped I was not like him physically. He had a long nose and pale gray eyes and thin lips. He made me think, I don't know why, that he must have been the sort of boy who would have been educated by tutors, the sort of boy whose father would have owned a private car. His clothes were quiet and inconspicuous, but they were beautifully cut. He looked at me as though I were the first comprehensible person he had seen for a long while. He was grasping my hand like a man on a turbulent sea grasping at a plank.

"Marvin's told me a lot about you," he said.

I wondered just what it was that Marvin had told him and for a moment I forgot about the noise.

"I'm awfully glad to meet you," I told him. "Marvin — Marvin used to be quite a friend of mine." I was wondering what there was in him that Marvin liked. Then I thought he was probably wondering what she had seen in me. I raised my glass and took a few quick swallows.

"I wish we could all have a talk sometime," he said. "You've got to look us up. I never knew anyone much in college. I — you see, I wasn't very well."

I did not know what to say to that. It would sound a little queer to say that I was sorry. Bo-jo had been listening to us and perhaps he thought things were slowing up a bit, because he thumped John Ransome on the back again.

"Well, you know the whole crowd now, don't you, Johnny? All the best boys in the Class and it's the best damned Class that ever came out of Harvard. Come on, Sam, and give Johnny a drink."

"I've had plenty, really," Ransome said.

"Come on," Bo-jo called. "Come on."

I told myself that it was just as well we didn't get together often, but we all were trying hard.

"It was a great game, wasn't it, Bo-jo?" I said.

Bo-jo scowled at me and then he put his arm back around Ransome's shoulders.

"Now, what do you know about that, Johnny?" he said. "He says it was a great game. Now, you and I know it was lousy."

A number of people around us stopped talking. Everyone always wanted to hear what Bo-jo said about a game and Bo-jo began to tell us. The Harvard team was shot in the pants with luck, he said; the trouble was that all the boys were suffering from mental hebetude. I finished my drink and took another. Everything was getting easier, coming back into something like old times.

"They haven't got any guts now," Bo-jo said. "Now, I don't want to boast about ourselves, but we definitely had. Now, take that time when we were out there on the five-yard line. Yale's ball, first down, and it came to Dunbar and Dunbar fumbled. That was quite a game. You were there, Sam. You remember."

"Yes," Sam said, "I remember."

"Well, let's tell Johnny about it," Bo-jo said. "Do you remember, Johnny? Third quarter, Yale's ball on the five-yard line, first down, and that Eli, Dunbar, he was going to take it around end, don't you remember?"

"No," Ransome said, "I don't think I do, Brown."

"Now, listen," Bo-jo said, "how do you get that way? My name's Bo-jo. It was this way — if you boys aren't bored."

Of course no one was bored.

413

"All right. It was this way. Sam was over there and I was over there and you're the Eli center, Johnny, and Dunbar's right back of you, there, and you snap the ball back and Dunbar drops it."

I felt rather sorry for Ransome. He was trying his best to follow it, but he looked blank.

"That was all there was," Bo-jo said. "I came through that hole over there and picked it up. If it hadn't been me you'd have had it, Sam. You were over there, over by the piano, and I was over here."

"As a matter of fact," Sam said, "you were a little more to the left, Bo-jo, going at a diagonal. If we had a pencil and paper — who's got a pencil?"

Then I saw Bob Carroll. He walked over to the piano and sat down and began to play. It made everything better as soon as the piano was going. First he played "Hit the Line for Harvard" and everybody began to sing.

"Sing 'I Want to be a Yale Boy,'" someone said.

It occurred to me it was not exactly a proper song with all the wives and children present, but nevertheless I found myself shouting at the top of my lungs, "Mother, if I can, I want to be a man, but I want to be a Yale boy, too."

Then Bob began to play "Old New York" and then someone asked for "The Girl on the Magazine Cover," and then they were singing the caisson song, but I never did think much of the caisson song, having been in the infantry myself. It was singular, once you started, the songs you could remember.

"Come on, boys," Bo-jo shouted. "'Good-by, Girls, I'm Through.'"

"Wait a minute," Bob said. "How does that go?"

There was a pause as we all tried to remember, and then Ransome spoke diffidently, "'I'm done with all temptation, you've no more fascination; good-by, girls; good-by, girls; good-by, girls, I'm through.'"

"Attaboy, Johnny," Bo-jo called. "You tell 'em."

XXXVII

Home from the Hill

It was getting late, time to be going home, and I edged my way out of the crowd by the piano. Then suddenly I saw her. It had never occurred to me that she had come with her husband. I was face to face with Marvin Myles, and all the noise and all the other people seemed to have dropped away from us. I could hear them in the distance shouting out that song again — "Good-by, Girls, I'm Through." I don't know how long we stood there looking at each other, but I remember that I felt cold for a moment and not at all like myself. She was standing there, aloof and puzzled. Her face was just as I remembered it and so was her hair. She was carrying a mink coat over her arm. She had on a pearl necklace and a diamond bracelet and a diamond ring on her engagement finger, and she looked awfully trim and awfully well.

Then I heard her speak to me, just as she had in my thoughts, when I had met her in my thoughts.

"Harry," she said, "why, Harry, darling!"

"Why, hello, Marvin," I said.

And then she kissed me. I had not expected that at all and it startled me. It was the first thing that made me remember where I was — her kissing me — and I wondered if anyone had noticed and would tell Kay about it. Nevertheless, I was awfully pleased she had, because it was just like her.

"Why, darling," she said, "you're just the same!" And I saw that she was laughing at me.

"It's awfully nice to see you, Marvin," I said.

The voices around us were growing louder. We seemed to have

been away somewhere, just she and I all alone, and now we were back. I must have always known that we would meet sometime, and there we were. She and I had snatched an instant out of time. We had snatched it out of all the noise of that steamy, stuffy room. For an instant we had belonged to each other again.

Her eyes, when they met mine, were trying to see what had happened to me, not inquisitively but kindly.

"Is Kay here?" she asked.

She must have seen that I looked surprised, because she spoke quickly before I could answer.

"I knew her, don't you remember?"

"Oh, yes," I said. "No, Kay's gone home. She had a headache. Bill King took her home."

"Oh," Marvin said, "Bill." I could see that she was thinking, remembering all sorts of things. "Bill and I have always talked about you."

Her eyes had grown narrow. Her forehead puckered into a little frown, just the way it used to.

"This is all so peculiar," she said. "I still don't know how to act. It reminds me of when you took me to that football game. I was awfully puzzled then. Do you remember?"

"Yes," I said, "of course."

"It's really funny. It's just as though — "

"Just as though what?" I asked.

"Oh, never mind," she said. "Have you seen John?"

"Why, yes," I said. "He's over by the piano with Bo-jo Brown."

"Bo-jo?" she said. "He's the one you used to talk about, and who was that other one, who had dinner with us once? He was out there with us in the snow."

"Oh," I said, "Joe Bingham. Joe's in Chicago now."

It made me a little sad to think of it. Somehow I wanted to think of something else.

"All of that — " Marvin said, "that's why I married John."

I could not understand why she wanted to explain to me why she had married John.

416

"When I first saw him he looked like you. He had that worried look. Tonight he's going out to a men's dinner."

"Yes, I know," I said.

She frowned again, just the way she used to, and she looked around the room just the way Kay had. I could see that she did not like any of it, that she wanted to get away.

"Harry," she said, "why don't you and I have dinner — up in our room?"

"What room?" I asked, and Marvin laughed.

"Our parlor," she said, "at the Sulgrave."

At first I thought of a lot of reasons why I ought not. For one thing, I ought to be back entertaining Bill, and for another I should probably be expected to call somewhere for Gladys, but then again I did not see any valid reason why I shouldn't, and besides I wanted to.

"Why, yes," I said, "I'd love to — that is, if it's all right."

I had never imagined myself dining alone with someone else's wife and I wondered just what I would say to Kay about it, and then it occurred to me that I might not have to refer to it at all.

"I knew you'd say that," Marvin said. "Of course it's all right, darling. Let's get out of here," and she put her arm through mine. If she had been Kay she would have told me not to be silly, but Marvin had never been like that.

"We can get a taxi somewhere," I told her.

"We don't need a taxi," Marvin said. "Adolph's right here outside. John had the car sent up."

Then I was sitting beside her in the car with a robe thrown over our knees and Marvin took off her hat.

"God," she said, "I'm glad to get out of that! Darling, do you remember when you met me with your car?"

"With Patrick? Yes," I said.

I wished that she had not brought it up. It still hurt me to think of the time when I met her. We did not speak for a while, but simply sat there in the darkness of the car, watching the lights go past. I was thinking of how she called me "darling." It had sounded differently the first time she said it — just when we saw each other. Now it sounded the way Mary might have said it — sweet but different.

"Do you remember when I used to read poetry to you?" Marvin asked.

"Yes," I said.

"You always liked Tennyson," she said. "I never could get you to like real poetry."

"I still like Tennyson," I said.

"'Blow, bugle, blow,'" Marvin said. "Do you remember? 'Set the wild echoes flying, Blow, bugle; answer echoes, dying, dying, dying.'"

Her voice was the same, musical and clear.

"That's awfully sad," I said. "I wish you'd quote something that isn't sad."

"Why," Marvin said, "it isn't sad, really. Darling, I wish you'd hold my hand."

I took her hand under the robe. It was not the right thing to do, but I held it tight.

"Isn't it queer?" Marvin said.

"Yes," I said, "it is."

"And we've got such a lot to talk about," Marvin said. "Like the hunter 'home from the hill.'"

"Yes," I said, but we just sat there, holding hands. I knew the poem she meant. I had not done much about poetry since I had last seen Marvin Myles, and now it made me sad, quiet and sad, and I did not want to be, because I was awfully glad to see her.

But there was nothing sad about the Sulgrave. The lobby was full of the Yale crowd, all milling around the palm trees, and I saw a good many people looking at us. It made me wish I had on something better than my raccoon-skin coat, and then something else began to bother me. I did not want John Ransome to pay for the dinner and I told Marvin so, but Marvin only laughed. It all gave me an excited, guilty feeling, going up with her in the elevator to the fifth floor, and waiting while she looked for her key and unlocked the door. I was hoping that no one I knew would see us or misinterpret my being up there with Marvin. I recalled stories I had heard about house detectives, the truth of which I could not vouch for, since I had never seen a house detective. Yet, though I was partly worried, I partly did not mind at all.

"Come on in," she said, and she closed the door.

We were in one of those ornate hotel sitting rooms. Its sofas and chairs and tables were in a decorative style which had been popular about twenty years before. It seemed as though I had been in just such a room once, and then I remembered. It was just like the hotel room that Kay and I had taken on our wedding night.

"Well," Marvin said, "here we are."

"Yes," I said, "here we are."

Marvin tossed her coat over a chair.

I laid mine beside hers. I wished that I could have thought of something bright and amusing to say to her, but my mind was filled with old thoughts, like the pages of a scrapbook. The way she had tossed her coat on the chair, quickly and impulsively, reminded me of days in the Bullard office when Marvin used to come in late and of times when we used to come up to her apartment after dinner and the theater. When she took her coat off I had always kissed her. I wondered if she were remembering that, and I wished that I could think of something to say to get my mind off it or that she would say something, but she did not speak. We just stood there, looking at each other.

"It's been a long time," she said, and I knew that we were thinking exactly the same thing, just the way we used to.

"Yes," I said, "awfully long."

We should have been talking about the weather or about the war or what plays there were in New York or about what she had done or I had done — anything that would make us natural and sensible. Instead of that we just stood there.

It hurt and yet I could do nothing about the silence. It seemed to say, There it was. It seemed to say, We had wanted to see each other and there we were — and what of it? I knew if I wanted to

I could take her in my arms and kiss her. Perhaps she wanted me to and wondered why I didn't, but if I did — what of it? Everything I had thought about her was there — grim and absolute. It made my eyes smart. It made a lump rise in my throat. I could not take my eyes away from her. Her lips were trembling.

"Harry," she said. Her voice was shaky and uncertain.

I waited for her to go on. I did not want to try to answer her and I heard her voice again, slow and insistent.

"Harry, dear, have you been happy?"

I had to answer, but how could anyone answer that?

"Yes," I said, "yes, I've been happy, Marvin." It was as near as I could come to it. I could have gone on a good deal further. I could have asked her what she meant by happiness. The question in itself and the answer had no particular validity. I was struggling with what had come between us, and I knew what it was. It was time. There had been so much time, a whole road of it.

"How about you?" I asked.

"Me?" said Marvin. "I've had everything I wanted — nearly everything."

Nearly everything, but then you couldn't have everything. Marvin drew a quick breath. It was almost like a sob.

"Darling," she said, "we —" and she choked on what she was trying to say. She reached out toward me as though she were frightened and her cheeks were wet with tears.

"Marvin," I said, and her head was on my shoulder.

"Darling," she said, "we can't go back."

That was the answer to it. That was what we had been trying to say all the time — the truth, absolute and perfect. I must have always had the idea somewhere in the back of my mind that we could, if everything were terrible, that we could go back — and now it was an ending. I had never faced an ending so complete, except death. She was crying and I was crying. I was ashamed of myself when I realized it. I had not done such a thing for years and years.

"It wouldn't have worked," I said.

I knew it was time for me to pull myself together Suppose someone came in — a waiter or someone — and found us like that. You have to go on and it doesn't do any good to bawl about it. Perhaps I was not bright or quick or clever, but I could take what was coming to me. It was finished nearly twenty years before.

"Darling," Marvin said, "I used to love you so."

"The same here," I said, and I blew my nose.

"Give me that handkerchief," Marvin said, "for a minute, will you?"

"It's awfully dirty," I said. "Ever since I've been married I've never had enough handkerchiefs."

"That's all right," Marvin said and she took it and dabbed her eyes. "Harry — Harry, you'd better call up Kay and then we'll order dinner."

"Yes," I said, and I didn't mind the idea of calling up Kay at all.

When I left I kissed Marvin good-by, not that it meant any more than kissing Mary, and if I ever met her again I would kiss her, no matter who was there, Kay or anyone else. Although I felt tired, I felt peaceful. I was glad to walk home by myself and to go over it all, to walk slowly, breathing the cold night air. I was glad that I had seen her now, because it was out of my system like an operation, cut clean out. This was so simply because we had not stopped living. We had lived and we had grown and that growth had not been entirely a process of growing older. Everything I had seen and done had left some sort of mark on me. I felt a good deal stronger, a good deal more sure of myself, than I had felt years ago. I was not sorry that I was changed, because the change had been worth while. It was true what I had told her — that it would not have worked. I had lived, on the whole, the only sort of life for which I was really fitted. Perhaps there is some needle inside everyone which points the way he is to go without his knowing it. I had never known, not really until now, how fond I was of Kay. I could not have gone back if I had wanted to, because Kay and I had been so long together, and perhaps that was what love really was — not passion or wish, but days and years — and now I was going home.

If you fall down flat and knock your breath out you can pick yourself up and go ahead, and finally you forget that you have fallen down. I was wondering whether the gas stove were still leaking. The gas company had assured me that it was fixed, but it had never been a satisfactory stove. The pilot lights had never operated properly. It might be better if they were shut off entirely and if we used matches on the burners. I had not been down cellar for quite a while either. I had been meaning to look at the ashcans, which were pretty well battered out of shape. I was wondering what the market would do on Monday. That was one of the subjects I wanted to take up with Bill. He saw so many people and heard so much gossip that he sometimes gave me very good ideas. I wondered if Kay had arranged to have people for Sunday lunch, or if she thought that the maids had done enough for the week end after the dinner on Friday night. There were cars parked on both sides of our street, a solid line of them, and most of them stayed for hours in front of all our doors, with the police doing nothing about it. On second thought, perhaps this was just as well, because our Packard was probably in front of our own door. Kay never could remember to call up the garage and have it taken away. I wondered if Kay had thought of giving Bill anything to drink. It might be just as well if she hadn't, because Bill had been drinking a good deal too much lately.

I would be getting George's report card within the next ten days for the first month of the new school year. I hoped it would only be a report, without a letter from the new headmaster discussing deficiencies in George's attitude and personal habits. When any such difficulty arose, the school would always blame Kay and me for lack of oversight and Kay would say that all of George's personal difficulties came from me directly. On the other hand, if George won a prize, which he had done once or twice, Kay would say that his mind or his physique, whichever it was that was responsible, came directly from the Motfords. Yet if you looked at it in the right way all of this was amusing, as long as you understood that nothing was ever perfect and that nothing ever could be.

Youth, after all, in spite of the efforts which everyone made to keep young, was a turbulent and terrible period, parts of which kept clinging to you like old clothes that you never wore out and did not want to throw away. There was my silk hat, for instance. I had not worn it for twelve years, and it was still right upstairs in a leather box on the top shelf of the closet, right next to the box that contained my Sam Browne belt and my overseas cap. I would never wear any of them again, but I could not throw them away. There were the linen plus-four knickerbockers and my brown tweed knickerbockers which had matched the tweed coat that was now worn out, and all those heavy knitted golf stockings. For some reason no one wore them much any more, but they were all in too good condition to throw out. Now youth was like that. You kept coming upon it unexpectedly in corners in the closet and when you did it would give you a twinge sometimes. You had to clean it out and get through with it.

After all, home was all that mattered. I remembered a line of a poem by Edgar Guest which Kay and I had both laughed over: "It takes a heap o' livin' in a house t' make it home."

I would know about the stove as soon as I got into the front hall. For some reason the odor of gas was always there when it was not anywhere else. Sometimes Kay said that it was all my imagination, that she could not smell gas, and once I had bet her five dollars she could if she came down in the front hall and stood right by the closet below the stairs where Gladys kept her roller skates, and I had been right. I patted my left-hand trousers' pocket to be sure I had not forgotten my keys. I remembered now what the front door key was like — a big notch at the base and then two little notches. As I had thought, the Packard was still by the front door, close against the curb. The lights were on in the parlor where Kay and Bill would be sitting. I wondered if Kay had remembered to water the plants.

Just as soon as I got into the front hall and closed the door I smelled it. The pilot light was out again and I would have to fix it before I went upstairs. I listened for a minute, thinking that Kay

423

might call to me as she did sometimes when the door closed, and I wanted to tell her that the stove was leaking again, but she could not have heard me come in. There was no sound from upstairs Bitsey must have gone to bed in Gladys' room or he would have barked. The enameled kitchen table was bright and bare; and when the light was on there was that sort of heavy, secret solitude which had always met me in the kitchen when I had come down to get ice cubes late in the evening, or when I had gone down in my wrapper and slippers to heat hot water when Kay or one of the children was ill. I was right. The second pilot light in the gas range was out. I took a knife from the table drawer and adjusted the burner so there would be more gas, and finally I got it lighted.

Then I went back to the ground floor through the pantry and through the hall and I began to think what I would say to Kay, for of course she would ask me where I had been, since I had told her over the telephone only that I was staying out for dinner if she did not mind. Instead of minding she had been nice about it, perhaps because she had been sorry already about the tea. Perhaps she would start to bed pretty soon and Bill and I could talk for a while. I certainly did not want Bill to get the idea that I was neglecting him. We would talk about the war and what under the sun the Allies were going to do, and why they had not pushed at the west wall when Germany was busy in Poland. Bill might even know whether the Russian Army was good for anything or not, because Bill knew a lot of White Russians. At any rate I wanted to talk to him, just to get my mind off myself and to get the day straight.

The house had been absolutely quiet until I began walking up the stairs, but when I was halfway up I could hear Bill and Kay talking through the closed door of the parlor. At first their voices were indistinct, but they were plainer when I stood in front of the door. I paused there for a moment before I went in, not because I was curious about what they might have been saying, but because I had never realized that anyone could hear from the hall when the parlor door was closed.

"We were crazy — both of us," Kay was saying.

424

"Don't be so involved," I heard Bill answer.

And then I heard Kay's reply. It sounded just as though she were speaking to me, instead of Bill.

"Let's not go all over it again. We can't go back."

"I thought you said —" I heard Bill's voice again.

As I stood there, I had a thought of which I was almost immediately very much ashamed. It must have been all that had happened that day which put the idea in my head, because I actually found myself wondering if there could possibly be anything between Bill and Kay, such as people talk about sometimes. I confess it did flash across my mind, and then I knew that I had no business having such an idea even for a second. Bill King was my best friend, and besides he was a gentleman, and Kay was my wife. As I say, I was ashamed of myself. It made me feel like apologizing to both of them when I opened the parlor door, and I told myself I must never consider such a thing again — not ever.

"Hello," I said.

The lamp that stood on the table by the sofa was on, and the lights were on above the mantelpiece. Bill and Kay were standing up. When someone is startled by a sudden noise there must be a sort of contagion in it. There must have been something in their manner that startled me too. Bill's lips were half open and Kay's right hand was pressed against her throat. She tried to laugh, but instead she caught her breath.

"Why, Harry," she said, "I didn't hear you."

I had an idea for a moment that they did not expect me at all, although I could not understand why, since I distinctly told Kay that I would be back early.

"Why, hello," Bill said, and his voice did not sound exactly natural. "So there you are."

"Of course I'm here," I said, but Bill did not seem to think it was funny. His face looked flushed and his voice was hoarse. He must have done a lot of cheering at the game.

"Yes," he said, "naturally. Where else would you be?"

It seemed to me that he sounded a little rude and out of sorts, but then he was probably tired. I looked at Kay and wondered whether she were still angry about the tea, but when she spoke, I realized that she must have forgotten all about it.

"Harry," she said, "where under the sun have you been?"

Of course I had known that she would ask me. I had intended to tell them both, perfectly casually, that Marvin Myles had asked me to dinner with her, but as soon as she asked that question I knew that I would never tell her, never, because it was something that was gone, and it was something that belonged to me and to no one else. It seemed to me that it was the only thing I possessed which was entirely my own.

"Oh," I said, "I just met some people there and we had dinner. I thought as long as you had a headache — I hope you didn't mind."

"Why, no," Kay answered, "of course I didn't mind."

I knew by the way she spoke that she did mind, really, but for some reason she didn't want me to go on about it. I waited for someone to say something, but neither of them did, and then I remembered about the stove.

"When you came in did you smell any gas?" I asked.

"Gas?" Bill said hoarsely. "What gas?"

"You don't mean to say that you didn't smell it in the front hall?" I said. "It's that pilot light in the range downstairs, Kay. It was out again, but I fixed it."

"Oh," Kay said, "was it out again?" But she did not seem interested. She never was interested in anything mechanical, but for some reason they seemed to expect me to go on with the conversation.

"Well," I said, "what are we all going to do tomorrow?"

They made me a little impatient. I wanted to get something organized and moving, and everything seemed to be standing still.

"If it's a good day," I said, "we might take a picnic and motor somewhere. Or if you don't want to do that, Bill and I might go and play squash at the Club in the morning."

"Squash!" Bill said. "Oh, my God, squash!" And then Kay interrupted, as though she had just been reminded of something.

"Harry," she said, and she spoke the way she did when she wanted something made perfectly clear, "Bill can't. He has to go back the first thing tomorrow morning."

"What?" I said. "Why, tomorrow's Sunday."

Then Bill spoke very quickly.

"As a matter of fact," he said, "just this evening I got called about one of those radio contracts. I've got to hop a train the first thing in the morning."

"Why, Bill," I said, "I'm awfully sorry." There were a great many things I wanted to talk to him about, and I had not really seen him at all. "Listen, it can't be as important as that, Bill."

Bill looked at Kay and Kay looked at the Inness above the mantelpiece. He seemed to be waiting for Kay to say something, but Kay only looked at the Inness.

"That's the way it goes," Bill said. "Here today and gone tomorrow, and if I'm going to hop that early train I'd better get some sleep. Good night, Kay." He seemed to hesitate about what he was going to say next. "I had a swell time. It was wonderful."

Kay moved her head impatiently.

"Don't say 'hop' a train," she said. "You catch it. You don't 'hop' it. Well, good night."

"I wish you wouldn't go, Bill," I said. "I'll see you in the morning. Have you got everything you want?"

"That's a damned silly question," Bill said, "and you know it, boy. Nobody ever has everything he wants. Well, good night."

He opened the door into the hall and smiled and waved his hand at us, and then he closed it softly. Kay sat down on one corner of the sofa.

It may have been my imagination, but I could not get it out of my head that something discordant had happened while I was gone.

"Look here, Kay," I said. "I really think you might have tried to make Bill stay over tomorrow."

"Harry," Kay said, "I wonder if you would get me a little whisky."

427

"Why, Kay," I said, "I thought you didn't believe in drinking in the evening."

The whisky and the glasses and the ice cubes and the soda were on the table near the wall where Ellen always put them when we had guests. I did not give her much whisky, because I knew she would have a headache in the morning, but I saw that she did need it. She had been doing altogether too much lately, and Bill must have been getting on her nerves, because she looked awfully tired.

"Why, Kay," I said, "your hand's shaking!"

"It's just that I'm tired," she answered. "Never mind it now. I'll be all right in a minute," and she drank her drink very quickly, in a way that was not like her at all, because Kay never did approve of drinking, particularly for women.

"Thanks," she said, "thanks very much," and she handed me the glass.

"Kay," I asked her, "did Bill get some bad news or something?"

"No," she answered.

"Well, something must have happened," I said. "Maybe I'd better go up and talk to him."

"No," she said quickly, "no, don't do that. Harry, let's stay here for a minute where it's quiet."

I sat down beside her and took her hand. It was as cold as ice.

"If you'll go up to bed, Kay, I'll get you a hot water bag," I said.

"Anything," she said, "anything but a hot water bag!"

"This is the way you always get when you do too much," I said. "If your feet are like your hands, you need one."

Kay did not answer and I thought of something else.

"Kay," I asked her, "you and Bill haven't been having a fight about anything, have you?"

"No," she answered, "no. Please don't talk, Harry. It's just everything."

"Kay," I said, "you'd better go up to bed."

"All right," she said. "It's the only thing you can really get back

428

to, isn't it? Bed, I mean. It's funny — " And then she stopped. She always did have the most annoying way of stopping.

"What's funny?" I asked.

Her eyes were closed and she did not answer for quite a while.

"How you have to keep going on," she said, "and how you can't go back." Then she opened her eyes and looked at me. She certainly did not look well at all.

"Why, Kay," I asked her, "how do you mean, you can't go back? Back where?"

"Oh, back to anything," Kay said. "You think you can, but you can't. Oh, never mind it now. I'll just go upstairs and I'll be all right in the morning. Good night, dear. Help me up, will you?"

When I took her hands and helped her up she leaned toward me and kissed me. I thought it was very generous of her.

"Kay," I said, "I shouldn't have left you here tonight. I'm sorry about the tea."

"The tea?" she answered and she looked as if she did not remember anything about it. "Oh, never mind that. It isn't anything," and then she put her hands on my shoulders and drew me toward her. "Harry — "

"What?" I asked.

"The only thing that matters is you and me."

"Why, Kay," I said, "that's awfully sweet of you to say so."

"No," she answered, "no. It isn't sweet. It's just the truth, and it's rather awful. We're all alone. There's only you and me."

"I don't think it's awful," I said, but she did not seem to have heard me, because she went right on speaking.

"Everything we've done together has made it that way — whether we've wanted it or not. Did you ever think of that?"

"Why, yes," I answered, "I have sometimes."

"So we have to be kind to each other," she said, "always, don't we?"

"Why, yes," I said, "of course."

"Don't say 'of course,'" she said, "but that's what it is — of course. Kiss me good night. Don't make me feel I'm all alone."

"Why, Kay," I said, "Kay, darling, I'm always here."

It seemed to me that she looked a little better.

"I know," she said, "but I like to hear you say it. Well, I'm going up to bed and you'd better come up too. Thank God, we're going to have a quiet week. And, Harry — "

"Yes?" I said.

"I don't think I'll get up to see Bill off. You don't mind, do you? He'll understand."

"Why, of course," I said. "I'll take Bitsey out. Just go to sleep."

It was a curious coincidence — what Kay had said, that you can't go back. I kept thinking of it as I turned on the light over my desk in the library, because it was just what Marvin Myles had said, almost the identical words, and even their voices had sounded alike. I did not know to what Kay was referring and probably she hardly knew herself, because she was so tired that she had just said whatever had come into her mind. Kay always did use up her strength when it came to entertaining. She had seen too much of Bill. He had so much vitality that he exhausted even me sometimes. But still it was a coincidence.

At any rate, she would be all right in the morning, and it was probably just my imagination that Kay and Bill had been getting on each other's nerves.

I opened the desk drawer and got out some paper. The whole house was still, but I did not feel sleepy, with all the books and pictures looking down at me. This was a fine time to write that Class life of mine and get it over with. If I had to do that work for Bo-jo, the least I could do was to get my own life in on time. I picked up the blank which I had started, and looked at it.

NAME: Henry Moulton Pulham.

BORN: Brookline, Mass., December 15th, 1892.

PARENTS: John Grove Pulham, Mary Knowles Pulham.

MARRIED: June 15th, 1921; Cornelia Motford.

CHILDREN: George, May 29th, 1924; Gladys, January 16th, 1927.

DEGREES: A.B.

OCCUPATION: Investment counsel.

It still looked a good deal like something on a tombstone, but I should have to get on with it. The main thing was not to give the impression of writing a lot in the book and of showing off. It was easy enough to think about my life, but now that I was face to face with a piece of paper it was quite a puzzle. I never did like writing. I turned on the radio for a while just to get myself in the proper mood.

The war didn't seem to be getting on any further. The French were still sitting behind the Maginot Line and seemed to have given up any idea of an offensive, but they must have had plans because Gamelin was a great general. There were no better military men in the world than the French. I thought of that single poilu marching alone under the Arc de Triomphe where the flame burned over the tomb of the Unknown Soldier. You couldn't beat the French, once they started moving. They would get organized and going in the spring, but there was no use twiddling with that radio. I had to get out my pen and write.

After graduating from Harvard [I wrote], I started by selling bonds in the firm of Smith and Wilding, where I continued until the declaration of war in 1917. During the war I was a second lieutenant of Infantry, serving with the American Expeditionary Force in France. It was a very interesting experience.

I wondered if I ought to say anything about being decorated, but I decided to let it go, because there is nothing worse than showing off.

After being honorably discharged, I worked for a year in New York in the firm of J. T. Bullard — advertising. Family affairs brought me home and I was very kindly allowed to continue with the firm of Smith and Wilding, where I remained until 1933, when I started my own investment counsel office, Maxwell and Pulham. This on the whole has been a fortunate venture. It has enabled me to make a lot of interesting contacts through the years.

On June 15th, 1921, I married Cornelia Motford, a step which I have never regretted for a moment, since our life together has always been happy and rewarding. With the children growing up it seems impossible to think that we could have been happily marrried for so long.

I thought that I had put it rather neatly and nicely and I thought that Kay would like it when I read it to her.

My life outside the usual routine of business must be the same as that of my other classmates — devoted to my family and friends and to everyday activities. Mrs. Pulham and I have had the good fortune to go abroad three times — once to England, once to France, and once to Rome, where I was deeply interested in the foundations and passages on the Palatine Hill, a puzzle which Mrs. Pulham and I were not able to work out.

In religion I am an Episcopalian; in politics, Republican. For recreation I play tennis in the summer and squash in the winter and I have been a runner-up in our local bumping tournament for the last three years.

I stopped and thought for a while, because it seemed to me that I had said almost everything, but it would have to be a little longer. It would look as if I were being disagreeable to have it as short as that.

Like all my other classmates, I look back upon my years at School and college as the happiest of my life. Among the activities the one I enjoy the most is being on the Alumni Board of St. Swithin's School. Being thus intimately thrown with the youth of today, I can not share with my classmates the discouragement and pessimism which has been engendered by the New Deal. It seems to me only a phase and that matters will be better soon in business and in national life. I do not believe that either Mr. Roosevelt or Germany can hold out much longer and I confidently look forward to seeing a sensible Republican in the White House. We spend our winters in town and our summers in North Harbor, Maine. In either place the latchstring is always out for any member of our Class.

THE END